"If you survive," Chloe hissed, "I am going to *kill* you."

"Then either way, how about one last kiss?"

"Jesus," she shouted and flung herself inboard, away from *Voyager*'s side. I shrugged as Jeeza smiled and handed down the last of the supplies to me.

"Seriously," she said in a low voice, "are you sure about this, Alvaro?"

"Who can be sure about anything, anymore?"

She swatted me lightly. "Don't be a wiseass. You know what I mean. Going there." She glanced at the stone-gray shore. "Alone."

"Well, Jeeza," I said, pushing away from *Voyager*'s hull with a gaff hook, "I couldn't really ask anyone else to do this job. But don't worry; I'll be right back."

She stared down at me. "That's what everyone says. Including the ones who never come back."

I didn't have a wisecrack ready to deflect that particularly grim truth, so I flipped the switch on the electric trawling motor and swung around before anyone could see me start to shake.

AT THE END OF THE JOURNEY

by

CHARLES E. GANNON

Set in the Black Tide Rising world
created by

JOHN RINGO

AT THE END OF THE JOURNEY

Copyright © 2021 by Charles E. Gannon

A Baen Books Original

Baen Publishing Enterprises
P.O. Box 1403
Riverdale, NY 10471
www.baen.com

ISBN: 978-1-9821-2597-4

Cover art by Kurt Miller

First printing, March 2021
First mass market printing, March 2022

Distributed by Simon & Schuster
1230 Avenue of the Americas
New York, NY 10020

Library of Congress Control Number: 2020050085

Pages by Joy Freeman (www.pagesbyjoy.com)
Printed in the United States of America
10 9 8 7 6 5 4 3 2 1

Truly excellent authors thrill and even startle us with the singular creativity and unique vision that spills from their pages. But in many cases, those same authors cannot or will not take the risk of allowing others to work within their world.

I contend, however, that among these excellent authors, the very best of them do not merely permit, but invite and encourage colleagues to expand that original edifice of imagination. This is because they have the confidence and wisdom to recognize that these enthusiastic additions only serve to enrich and adorn the world they brought into being. And in so doing, honor it.

This book is dedicated to one of those very best excellent authors:

John Ringo

Thanks for letting me play in your outstanding sandbox, John.

Part One

AT THE END OF DAYS

November 11

It's funny how getting the thing you want the most can also paralyze you—because the day after all that surprise and happiness, you suddenly find yourself asking questions you never thought you'd have any reason to ask. That's how it was the day after we heard from Willow and learned that she and Johnnie were not only still alive, but steaming toward us with new friends.

It had been so many months since we'd had to leave them behind, self-quarantined on South Georgia Island, that we'd learned to stop thinking about the two of them. So hearing their coded radio message wasn't just a surprise; it was like a miracle, a resurrection of loved ones we'd *had* to accept as dead.

So of course when we got up, it was all smiles and happiness as we looked forward to being together again. Chloe and Jeeza started the day with a hug, which they scooped Rod into: still skinny, he almost disappeared between them. Steve emerged from Prospero's cabin calling him "Percy" under his breath; I think that was his version of post-intimacy playfulness. And ex-RAF Senior Aircraftman (Technical) Percival Halethorpe didn't appear to be bothered by the teasing at all;

he seemed to like it in fact. But once we'd finished cooking and squeezing past each other in *Voyager*'s tiny galley and sat down to a community breakfast, it became obvious that we had pretty different ideas about what to do next.

Jeeza, Rod, and even Steve were all for staying put at Rocas Atoll, the weirdest little reef-ring in the world. It was easy to see why they wanted to hunker down there. For once we had enough of the right foods to eat, were on land without any infected for neighbors, and could practice necessary combat skills in complete safety and at a pace of our own choosing.

But it was Chloe who pointed out the problem with that last welcome change. "Yeah, it's good to practice," she agreed, "but it's better to get used to the real conditions we're going to be facing everywhere else in the world."

Rod and Jeeza glanced at each other. Steve frowned. "Not sure what you mean."

Prospero put a hand on Steve's shoulder. "She means that learning to move and shoot on a deserted island isn't the same as learning those skills in a—well, a slightly more realistic environment."

Steve stared at his boyfriend. "Are you saying we should go find a city full of infected to practice on? 'Cause that sounds like suicide."

"Yeah, and it sounds too much like Kourou and the ESA base," added Rod, "which I thought we just tabled *yesterday*. So yeah, I'm all for going there and saving GPS, but not if it means 'Twenty-five thousand stalkers: no waiting.'"

I folded my arms, figured I'd jump in when and if necessary.

Chloe leaned over the table toward Rod. "I'm not talking about heading to Kourou. I'm not talking about heading to any city, for that matter. Hell, I'm not even talking about going to a new place."

"Then what, or where, are you talking about?" Jeeza asked as she folded her arms.

Chloe shrugged. "We turn around and go back to Fernando de Noronha."

"And do what?" Rod's voice cracked for the first time in months. "Clear it?"

Chloe looked at Prospero. Then both of them looked at me. So I was going to have to jump in after all. I shrugged. "We're not talking going house-to-house or room-to-room." But I couldn't leave it there. "Not mostly."

Jeeza threw up her hands. "'Not mostly'?" She was on her feet with surprising speed. "Why the hell do we have to go back to killing zombies—stalkers—infected—whatever? Why not stay here? Take a break?"

Chloe's voice was a sure barometer of her rapidly diminishing patience. "Girl, we've had a break. A week's vacation. Now it's time to get back into the game. And this atoll will be right here where we left it, just a day out from Fernando de Noronha and no chance of stalkers infesting it while we're gone. Unless they've taught themselves how to sail."

"Well, I could use more than a week."

I nodded. "I hear you, Jeeza. But here's the risk: that we'll lose our edge just when we should be sharpening it even more. Getting razor sharp. And FdN is pretty much like a gift, when you come right down to it."

"A gift?" Steve repeated the words loudly. He almost never raises his voice. "That gift damn near killed some of us."

I nodded. "I know. I was there. Right next to you." *And I was the one who almost got us killed.* "But I'm saying, yeah, we have to go back. We have to train more. Figure out better tactics."

"Why?" I couldn't tell if Jeeza was going to scream or cry or both. "Because we have to get ready? Because Kourou is going to be so much more dangerous?"

"Jeeza," I said as kindly as I could, "*everyplace* we go is going to be much more dangerous than Fernando de Noronha."

Prospero nodded. "Even the smallest Caribbean islands have real towns or even a small city, with the buildings packed in tight against each other. Each one is a warren of blind corners and hidden alleys. They all started with larger populations and usually a fair amount of livestock. And most have far more square miles in which the infected can hunt, hide, and then emerge from where—and when—we least expect it." His eyes were bright with sincerity and urgency. "FdN is the toddler version. Lots of space around every building we've seen and not a single one of them over two stories. We have pretty fair pre-plague population estimates, and we can make some reasonable guesses on how many remain alive. Particularly since there was no livestock on the island and no animals larger than a housecat."

"They could still swamp us," Rod croaked through a dry throat. "They did that with less than a dozen, at the first pousada."

Chloe's fist hit the chart table. "Which is the whole damn reason for going back. If ten stalkers can almost fug us up, then we have to—*have to*—get better. We have to come up with better plans."

"Yeah? Like what?"

"Well," I said, looking fixedly at Rod, "like your Wizard's Tower."

He scoffed, which, for always-kind Rod, was on par with slapping someone in the face. "Alvaro, there's no Cat Hill on FdN. No fenced-off installation that was just one big sniper's perch."

"No," I agreed. "But we can make plans that apply the same principle. Just don't get hung up on the specifics of the Wizard's Tower. The real reason it worked boils down to this: we got the stalkers in a position where we could shoot at them and they couldn't get to us. We can do that on FdN, too."

"Yeah?" Jeeza crossed her arms. "How?"

"By finding a place near or on the shore where they can hear and see us, but from which we can retreat easily, and with plenty of time to gun them down before they can close."

Rod was suddenly frowning. "Yeah . . . well . . . yeah: I see some ways that could work."

Prospero nodded. "So do I. Which means we start by circumnavigating the island, doing a detailed survey. We know where the major clusters of buildings are from the maps we have; they're not great, but they show *that* much."

Jeeza was staring at Rod as if he'd betrayed her. "And how do any of the tweaks and precautions turn this into a *good* idea?"

Steve shrugged. "Because the stalkers don't swim. And we have boats."

I nodded. "If we can find the right kind of place, and make the right kind of noise, we can do Wizard's Tower Part Two."

If Jeeza's eyes had been scalpels, my liver would have been sagging out of my body. "Alvaro, it is beneath you trying to recruit Rod to your side by stroking his ego."

Well, I was doing that, too, but: "Jeeza, is it stroking his ego to simply tell the truth? Because Wizard's Tower is the situation we *always* want to find ourselves in; getting rid of the infected without risking ourselves. If Rod was the architect of that...well, power to him. Besides, we may need the extra food that's there. And soon."

After that, it wasn't so much a debate as it was a case of being grilled by a Congressional subcommittee of one: the right honorable and really tenacious Giselle Schofield.

Which, when the idea of returning to Fernando de Noronha started to emerge, was exactly what we'd been trying to avoid. After only one day on the island and without even talking about it, Prospero and I sensed we were leaning in the same direction: that we'd have to go back there as part of our training. As it turned out, he was thinking of it as preparation for Kourou. I saw it as preparation for the world: for whatever came next. Kourou or not Kourou, we were going to have to get a lot better at dishing out hurt quickly and effectively. We had to be able to shut the stalkers down before they could even reach us, or it was "game over, man."

After Prospero and I realized we were on the same page, I mentioned the plan to Chloe. After about two seconds, she announced that she was in full support of going back to FdN and "getting rid of those bastard skels." Bringing her in on it was the right and necessary step, of course, but it was also a fateful one. Because, for good or for bad (sometimes both), if Chloe is anything, it's passionate. Prospero and I knew that she was likely to lead with her chin if the group discussed the idea too soon, before we'd worked out the details.

Which, thanks to my darling Chloe, took all of a minute to occur, once she and Jeeza started talking about what we were going to do next. Unfortunately, when it comes to Chloe, a disagreement is an impediment, and an impediment is a full-fledged problem. And all problems are the same to her: all nails to be bashed down. With a sledgehammer. Except when she considers that too subtle an approach.

So the day after we heard from Willow was not filled with happiness and celebration, but by the predictable reaction to our prematurely revealed plans: surprise, alarm, and then Jeeza grinding away at them. Why did we think FdN was worth the risk? Why were we so sure that the risk was not as great as it seemed? What did we stand to gain versus what did we stand to lose? And what kind of circumstances or events would be grounds for backing off either temporarily or permanently?

Coño, Jeeza was worse than my mom. Her capacity for imagining disaster was off the charts. But there was a silver lining to her hyperconcern that one or more of us might get injured or killed. Because even though her smallest fears morphed into visions of B-movie death-fests, some of them grew from perfectly reasonable kernels of insight. If something *could* go wrong, Jeeza *would* find it. And that was valuable.

But there was one issue no one could answer: just how much we would actually need Fernando de Noronha's water and food supplies. And maybe other resources. Jeeza leaned away from the table, crossed her arms and shook her head. "What are you thinking, Alvaro: that we're going to have to provide for an army?"

I shrugged. "No. But a platoon—maybe."

We all know each other really well by now (sometimes I think *too* well), so Jeeza could tell by the tone of my voice that I was not joking. "A platoon? Which will come from where?"

I shrugged. "You heard Willow's closing message: 'bringing friends.'"

Jeeza held my eyes. "'Friends,' Alvaro: '*friends*.' Not 'an army.'"

I nodded. "Yeah, and what if Willow and Johnnie have found just four additional survivors? That means six new people are going to be arriving. That doubles our population, which halves how long our stores will last."

Prospero steepled his hands. "Besides, there are some items for which we lack adequate spares, Jeeza. Yes, we have enough guns to arm six more people, but we don't have enough armor or fire suits. The same is true for many of the most critical tools and electronics. We would no longer have a replacement for almost every mission critical item. Instead, we would not have enough."

Jeeza's chin lowered; she did that when she was digging in for what she secretly felt would probably turn out to be a losing fight. "And you think we're going to find the answer to all those shortages on FdN? Really?"

I spread my hands in an appeal for understanding. "Jeeza, I don't have a crystal ball. I don't know what's on FdN and what isn't. But there's an airfield, so if any planes are on the ground, there could be some excellent radios. We saw boats, particularly at the northwest end of the island. More radios. More fuel. The Fodor's book talks about tourists being able to book dives with PADI-certified operators in the only real town, Vila dos Remédios. That means facemasks and wetsuits: not as good as firefighting gear, but better than jeans and a T-shirt. There had to be police on the island, so we might find guns and ammunition." I rethought that. "Well, guns, at least. But I *am* certain of one thing; if we don't go ashore, we won't get our hands on any new supplies of any kind. And we can't live without them. So the only real question is not *if* we have to go back, but *when*."

Steve, Jeeza's primary ally now, looked up from staring at the deck. "Okay, but can't we wait for Willow and Johnnie and friends? More hands, lighter work."

I was grateful that Prospero fielded that question. He slid into the seat beside Steve, put a hand on his arm. "They could be thirty days out, yeh? Maybe more, if they hit bad weather or mechanical trouble or Bog knows what. Over those thirty days, the six of us will consume one hundred eighty person-days of rations, and, in this climate, at least three hundred sixty liters of water. You tell me, Steve; can we afford *not* to replenish?" No answer. "And so, if we have to resupply, where else should we go? Where else *can* we go?"

Steve sighed and leaned into his partner's shoulder.

Chloe had held back until that moment, and now, when she spoke, it was calm, steady, almost gentle.

"I know I sound like I'm on endless loop, guys, but this is our new reality: we survive on what we can salvage. Which means we pretty much have to fight for a living. And we're still learning how to do that.

"But Willow's friends? We can't count on them being able to fight, not even at *our* level. They might still be badly weakened by hunger. They might have no training at all. So the best way to make use of their hands is to be ready to have them help us comb the entire island for everything we can use."

Jeeza's eyes opened slightly wider. "So you *do* mean for us to clear the island."

Chloe nodded for a few seconds, ended with, "That's right, Jeeza. But gradually. We'll start by bringing the stalkers to us, like at Wizard's Tower."

Jeeza shook her head. "There will be stragglers."

"Yeah, but once we've got enough stores and can fatten up Willow's friends, we can train them to help us finish the job."

I nodded. "And as we go, we mark buildings and items for salvage. Once we've cleared it, we can search for the small spring the books mention, up in the high ground on the western side of the island. We'll walk through all the kitchen gardens, find every piece of fruit and every vegetable that we can turn into something edible." I folded my hands. "I know it sounds risky, Jeeza. But everyplace else is riskier." I glanced at Rod. "He's already done the math. He knows I'm right."

Jeeza closed her eyes without glancing at Rod, who looked as miserable as a dog caught peeing on the carpet. "I know," Jeeza said. "I just can't stand the thought, the thought..." She struggled to keep her voice steady.

"Of dying?" Prospero prompted.

Jeeza gulped out a chortle, then laughed. For a moment, I think some of us thought she'd blown a gasket. But then she said, "Christ, no. I don't wanna die, but that's not what scares me." Her eyes opened, were liquid-bright. "It's that I might lose one of you. Or more. That would be, would . . . I just don't know if I can take that." Rod leaned toward her solicitously, but she held up a rigid hand. "And don't try to reassure me. Don't tell me not to worry. Because Chloe's right; this is our life now. But that means it's our death, too."

She looked around at us all. "Don't you see? It's just a matter of time. If we have to scavenge among the infected to live, that's how we're all going to die, eventually. No matter how good we become with guns and tactics. I know some statistics, too, and with that kind of constant risk, none of us will get to die of old age, safe in our bed, surrounded by the ones we love. We're going to lose each other, one by one." She rubbed at her eyes. "And with every one that dies, a piece of us will go with them. I wonder how much will be left inside any of us when our own time comes."

Chloe looked grim and frustrated, Rod gutshot, Steve like he was on another planet, and Prospero like he had just euthanized a puppy.

I stood. "That's not how it's going to be, Jeeza." She looked up at me; I still don't know how to describe the look in her eyes at that moment. There was hope, fear, disbelief, scorn, gratitude. I don't know how it could all be there at the same time, but it was.

"That's not how it's going to be," I repeated. "Once FdN is cleared, we can use it as a base. There are a lot of boats for the taking, still plenty of fuel, although we might want to stick with sails. Yeah, we'll be salvaging for a long, long time. But here's what I think. I think we're going to continue to find more survivors. I think that safe places like Ascension Island and St. Helena aren't going to stay isolated forever: hell, they can't. And I think—I'm *sure*—there are other small islands and populations that we haven't discovered yet. And, when enough of us are working together, we're going to clear them. The infected have numbers, but they don't change or improve their game. We do. Every time we beat them, we learn better ways to do it. That's what we'll be doing on FdN. My guess is that other people are doing it in other places. And eventually, we're going to join together to take back more and more islands and eventually, the mainlands."

Prospero nodded. "These are early days. For all we know, someone, somewhere, may have already come up with a cure. But even if they don't, that will not stop us from retaking what we've lost. From making safe places where we can have children, grow old, and even die in our own beds."

Jeeza nodded. "When you guys say it that way, I almost believe it. For now, I guess I just have to get through FdN Part Two. So, when do we sail?"

"Tomorrow," Prospero and I chorused.

We stayed behind as everyone else left. When we were alone and out of earshot, he turned to me and said. "Actually, it's not the infected that worry me the most."

I nodded. "Yeah. It's others like us."

He nodded back. "Yes. The bastards who would see us as competition, targets, or both."

I shrugged. I mean, what could I say?

The guy was right.

November 14

As it turned out, we didn't leave Rocas Atoll until yesterday, November 13. Reason: weather.

We tried to leave on November 12. And technically, we did. For all of about four hours. That was when the marine weather radar started throwing back intermittent crap from directly along our course back to Fernando de Noronha. It was heavy rain or what looked like it. And it was intensifying.

So after a quick confab in the pilothouse, and a look at the darkening skies rising higher along the eastern horizon, we came about and made for the atoll, again. All the way back, it looked like the junk on the radar was moving a lot more slowly than we were but was getting steadily thicker.

Now the simple fact of the matter is that civilian marine radar made for small, personal boats is not great for analyzing weather. And that job fell to me: not because of any expertise, but because I was the one who had read—and remembered—the manual.

But still, I totally sucked at it. Translating what you see on a radar screen into reliable information is not something you really learn in a book. Just a few days out from Ascension Island (where we picked it up) I had come to the conclusion that, like most things at sea, there is simply no substitute for experience. And when it comes to weather... well, mariners have a kind of hybrid superstitious/mystical outlook on it.

The Captain's books on seafaring are full of tales about sailors who "had a knack" for predicting the weather. They also revealed that most mariners take a dim view of trying to scientifically "explain" why some people have that skill. It's almost as if they believe that asking too many questions will chase the mojo away. For them, uncanny skill at weather prediction means that person has been touched on the shoulder by fate or the sea gods or whatever.

Can't say I blame them. Science never did find any good explanations. Barometric hypersensitivity, olfactory hypersensitivity, subconscious detection (and understanding) of water pattern changes on the leading edge of a storm: all were examined, all were dead ends. The only common trait was long years before the mast. That didn't guarantee you were going to get the mojo, but it's apparently a prerequisite.

None of us could check that box: our time before the mast was measured in months. So without that sixth sense, all I had to go on was a radar screen showing what looked like a growing, oncoming storm. And once everyone else had a look at the screen and either nodded or shrugged at my interpretation, we started back.

A few hours after reaching the atoll, the wind picked up a bit, with occasional, unpredictable gusts. Hurricanes are rare in this part of the world (they all seem to get sucked north toward the Caribbean), but there was no reason to take a chance. So we guided *Voyager* deeper into the Barretinha, a small inlet between Farol and Cemiterio islands.

As the tide came in, we steered her carefully to a point where her two-point-three-meter draft would leave her beached in waist-deep water when the tide went back out. We broke out all our anchors, moored her at several points, unloaded key gear, struck and dismounted the sails, and made sure the dogs—Cujo and Daisy—were on secure leads in the stilt-legged researchers' shack to which we retreated. Then we prayed to whatever god or gods we did or did not believe in that the storm would blow over, go somewhere else, or at least not be a hurricane.

It didn't blow over, it did hit us, but it was not a hurricane. Hell, it wasn't even a real storm. It took almost a day to arrive, and when it did, it was just a series of pissy little squalls that hammered at us intermittently. It dumped a fair amount of rain but never a lot at once, and although there were a few big gusts, the risers never topped six feet. Bottom line: *Voyager* was untouched and the worst that happened to any of us was that we got wet.

The next day we reloaded her, and made sure the rising tide floated her out safely with the aid of one of the winches we'd scored on Ascension. A leisurely sail (despite constant tacking) got us to FdN at sundown. Today we cruised around the island slowly, the Zodiac towed behind in case we needed to take some soundings to double-check our crappy depth chart.

We confirmed that Baia Sueste, the place we landed just a week before, is the only place to go ashore on the south coast of the island. Everything else is

wave-beaten cliffs. The north coast is mostly approach-
able, but there's only one sheltered mooring: the
anchorage behind the L-shaped jetty at the north end
of St. Anthony's Bay. That long stone pier was also a
narrow funnel for any mob of infected we might be
able to bring to us.

There were still some boats riding at anchor there
and a few tied up to the wharf on the leeward face
of the breakwater. We weren't really worried about
the ones in the little bay; anyone who turned while
aboard one of those would have starved to death by
now. The boats lashed to the wharf were a different
story. Although it was unlikely that stalkers would
remain on them, it wasn't impossible, and we were
way past assuming anything about the infected. If
they *could* do something, we pretty much took it for
granted that one or more of them *would* do it.

So by a really obvious process of elimination, it
looked like St. Anthony's Bay was our primary site of
operations. But, being at the extreme northern tip of
FdN, it seemed unlikely that we'd be able to attract
all the infected to come visit us there. Too many
would be beyond the range of any noise we could
make. Which meant we needed to find a second landing point where we could attract most of the other
stalkers to a safe choke point.

We had seen only one other place that might answer
that need: a beach access road that led down to a juncture between two shallow bays with beaches. Lying
atop that juncture, a spine of rock from the overlooking
slopes flattened out, dipped just below the waves, and
then rose up into the stone spur the maps labeled Ilha
da Conceição. Getting there involved less than a mile

of coast-hugging to the west. We were about to come about to give it a closer look when Steve shouted *"Shit!"* so loudly that, for one instant, his voice drowned out the surf.

"What?" I yelled.

He just pointed northeast.

Over the farthest island of the FdN chain, Ilha Rata, an eye-searing pink star was slowing as it reached the apex of its ascent.

"Is that—is that a flare?" Jeeza gasped.

"Most definitely," Prospero muttered as I brought the bow around and Jeeza and Rod did some fast, efficient sail-handling to set us up for tacking narrowly across the prevailing wind out of the northeast.

Chloe had come up to the pilothouse, sat alongside me. "Can you believe it?" I asked her.

She nodded slowly. "Yeah."

"You have a bad feeling about this?"

She shrugged. "I don't have any feeling about this."

"Not even curiosity? Not even a little excitement?"

"Alvaro," she said in her flat, "wake up, cupcake" tone, "almost every surprise in my life has been a bad one."

I glanced at her. The .308 hunting rifle was cradled in her lap.

Whatever we might have been expecting when we drew into the long, shallow bay on the southern side of Ilha Rata, it certainly wasn't what greeted us.

Silence. And a deserted shoreline of water-rounded rocks.

Prospero frowned. "Well, I wasn't anticipating a brass band, but still..."

Chloe had climbed atop the pilothouse and was

lowering herself into a prone position as she dragged over the "sniper's sandbag" we had up there for just such occasions. "Not so strange if this is a draw play."

Steve frowned. "What?"

Chloe half-shrugged just before she snugged the stock back into her shoulder. "Why else would they get coy after shooting off a flare? Most likely they're counting on us to get all eager, rush on over—and right into a trap."

Jeeza turned to stare at me. "So do *you* think this is a ruse?"

"No, but I think it *could* be a ruse. Until we know which it is, we don't take chances."

"Well, that could make this kind of difficult," Jeeza pointed out.

"How?" Chloe asked.

"Mexican standoff," Rod answered. "They're waiting for us to reassure them while we wait for them to reassure us. That could go on for a long time."

"Fortunately," Prospero murmured, "time is on our side. For once."

"How do you mean?" asked Steve.

"I mean that we have at least two and a half weeks until your friends arrive. We can easily spend a day, even two, waiting for the people—or person—who fired the flare. No risk to us, and they can take as much time as they like looking us over."

"Yeah, well, if they can look us over, then they can target us through a scope," Chloe pointed out glumly.

"Agreed," Prospero said with a nod, "but that won't be of any benefit to them unless they are simply homicidal maniacs. And very, very good shots, in the bargain."

"They don't have to be very good to beat me as long as we're on a boat," Chloe groused. "Between the range and the chop, I'd be lucky to hit the side of an outhouse."

I shrugged. "On the other hand, it's long odds that someone here on FdN has a rifle capable of that kind of shot. The police on the island were standard, low-intensity types; no SWAT equipment or anything similar. Also, there was no hunting on the island; hell, there's nothing to hunt. But even if someone does have a gun with that range, one shot and we kick on the outboard. And we are gone."

Chloe's response was a subvocal grumble which meant she didn't really have a rebuttal but still wasn't comfortable with the plan.

Rod sighed. "Still, it would be really good if we could wrap this up in a day or two. At the most." He looked briefly down the companionway.

It took me a moment to understand his glance. "Oh. Daisy."

"Yup," he sighed again. "I'm no vet, but she's heavily built and even that didn't keep her from showing when we left Ascension three weeks ago. If I'm right—"

"You are," Chloe growled. "I know dogs. Well, big dogs. I think Rotties are about nine weeks, plus or minus a few days."

"And she's getting there," Rod agreed. "Decreased appetite, decreased water intake. Doesn't want to move much. So I'm thinking—" He glanced at shore.

Now his desire to get things concluded quickly made sense. "You want her on land when she whelps."

He nodded. "Dogs get fussy, nervous. Particularly if this is her first litter. Whelping them on a boat—I don't know, Alvaro. That's asking for trouble."

"It's a good point," I agreed. And I meant it. None

of us knew what long-term life in a stalker-infested world was going to be like, but dogs would make it safer. The locals, and our own experiences, on Ascension Island had proven that. So we couldn't afford to lose either Daisy or her pups.

"So what are we going to do?" Rod asked.

"It's what *I'm* going to do," I answered. "Do me a favor; prep the Zodiac."

"If you survive," Chloe hissed, "I am going to *kill* you."

"Then either way, how about one last kiss?"

"Jesus," she shouted and flung herself inboard, away from *Voyager*'s side. I shrugged as Jeeza smiled at me and handed down the last of the supplies.

"Seriously," she said in a low voice so Chloe wouldn't hear, "are you sure about this, Alvaro?"

"Who can be sure about anything, anymore?"

She swatted me lightly. "Don't be a wiseass. You know what I mean. Going there." She glanced at the stone-gray shore. "Alone."

"Well, Jeeza," I said, pushing away from *Voyager*'s hull with a gaff hook, "I couldn't really ask anyone else to do this job. But don't worry; I'll be right back."

She stared down at me. "That's what everyone says. Including the ones who never come back."

I didn't have a wisecrack ready to deflect that particularly grim truth, so I flipped the switch on the electric trawling motor and swung around before anyone could see me start to shake.

We had waited until the tide was in. That way, I didn't have to hump the supplies up above the high-water mark. I ran the Zodiac in slow until I heard the gurgle of shallow water over submerged rocks, and rolled out, kit in one hand, shotgun in the other. But rather than having my hand near the weapon's grip, I kept hold of its center of mass, just forward of the ejection port: as nonthreatening a carry as possible.

I hardly needed to go up the shore in a serpentine; the footing was treacherous enough that I couldn't have made a straight-line assault charge if I had wanted to. Besides, the sun was still strong at three p.m. and was full in the face of anyone who might be covering the slowly curving shoreline of Enseada da Ressureta, or Resurrection Cove. I hoped the name wasn't a foreshadowing of the kind of miracle I might need in the next few minutes.

Ten yards up from the surf, I settled to one knee and worked fast. Unfolded the pack, unloaded the contents: lots of canned food (mostly starchy vegetables), packets of sugar, aspirin, a K-bar, a few cans of soda, and a greeting written in English, Spanish, and what pidgin Portuguese we could put together (mostly words extracted from the "handy phrases for travelers" section we found in one of the non-Fodor guides).

I carefully picked up the shotgun again, thought about standing straight and walking back to the Zodiac— always good to send a message that you were strong and unafraid—but decided it was better to stick with smart and careful. I reversed down the surf-smoothed rocks in a crouch, face toward the trees that hemmed in the eastern half of the shore.

Once at the boat, I had to smother a surge of what would have been maniacal giggling; I have no idea where that came from. With two good shoves, I was clear of the rocks.

Swinging myself into the Zodiac was easy in the still water. I snapped on the trawling motor and turned the boat's stubby rubber bow toward *Voyager*.

As I got up on deck, the sun was starting to get orange, and Chloe's face was getting red. Not with sunburn.

She started toward me stiff-legged, each stride longer and faster than the one before.

"Behold the face of your executioner," Prospero intoned through a sly grin.

"No shit," I managed to get out just before Chloe almost rammed into me, hands grabbing my shoulders.

"Damn you!" she shouted. "I'm going to kill you!"

I just waited.

Then, suddenly, she looked like she might cry—but before she did, she kissed me really hard. Really messy. It was great.

I leaned back. "I thought you were going to kill me."

"That can wait," she growled, grabbed the front of my web-gear, and dragged me toward the nearest companionway.

November 15

Dawn revealed that our combination care package and house-warming gift was no longer on the shore. Not even the debris of having been torn apart by rats or cats. It was gone, as if it had never been there.

"I don't like that they didn't leave any sign for us," Steve said.

Jeeza nodded. "Not very neighborly."

"Well," I started, "I suppose we could—"

"—we could consider going *there*?" Prospero asked.

We all looked at him. He was pointing high up on Ilha Rata's wooded slopes. A curlicue of smoke was coming out of the green. White smoke. Dried wood.

I think we all stood at once.

"Well," Rod said, "that kinda changes things."

Chloe bent back over the telescope we kept trained on the island. "I don't see anything else that—wait! A tree just fell. Near where you left the package." She adjusted the scope, then smiled. But it wasn't a happy expression. It was more like acknowledging an opponent's clever chess move. "Oooo. Smart."

"Care to share?" I asked.

She cut her eyes at me. "I still haven't forgiven you."

"Really? Because last night, it seemed that—"

"Shut up!" Her voice was half imperious, half anxious. "Look, alongside the tree."

Most of us had our binoculars on that spot already.

"What am I missing?" Jeeza said.

"See that line draped over the rocks, leading away from the tree?"

Prospero sucked in a deep breath. "Yes. Twisted vines, I think. And yes, very smart."

I was annoyed because I could barely make out the vine-rope and even more because I didn't see what was so special about it. "Smart how?" I snapped.

"Geez, calm down, Alvaro!" Chloe said, eyes wide. "That rope was holding up the tree. Bet you five chocolate bars that the vine runs back from the tree line and up the slope."

Now I understood. "So they could drop the tree whenever they wanted, and without exposing themselves when they did it."

Prospero lowered his binoculars. "I think that's our invitation."

I nodded. "Let's not keep them waiting."

Because I'd been thinking about this situation from the moment I had turned the Zodiac away from the shore of Resurrection Cove yesterday, I had everyone's role figured out. I had also anticipated that there would be a lot of debate—if I let that happen. So I didn't.

Orders were issued and reasons were given. Chloe and Jeeza stayed on the boat. No, I'm not a sexist: they are simply the best sniper/spotter team we've got. On the other hand, while I would have liked to leave Rod as pilot for *Voyager*, I needed him on shore because he was our dog-handler.

Cujo was going to have to be up near our point man; otherwise, his senses were not going to give us the warning we needed. So if the folks on Ilha Rata were baiting us in, poor Cujo was in greater danger than if we'd been moving against infected. Stalkers aren't subtle and a dog can smell them when they're still far off. But unturned humans? They're sneaky, will leave false scents and concealed traps. So there was no way to both rely on Cujo's senses and keep him out of harm's way.

Which was why we had to have two people walking point to either flank, then Rod and Cujo just a step or two behind, and finally one more person as rear guard. So with radios on and Cujo on a short leash, we passed from the rocky shore into the humid forest.

It's not really a rainforest, but Ilha Rata's trees grow close together, so you aren't about to blaze your own trail and make any speed. Besides, our path was marked.

Just four or five yards beyond where the tree had fallen, we found a trail blaze. It took a minute or two of scouting around before we realized that we were being directed to one of several game trails. Or what looked like game trails, since there wasn't any "game" in the entire FdN archipelago.

"Why all the trails?" Rod asked.

Steve nodded at the forest around us. "So that the locals don't beat one path too often. You can't tell which one is the main one." He nodded at the blaze. "Not without that."

"Except we don't *know* it's the main one," I amended. "All we know is that it's the one they want us to follow."

Steve nodded. "Fair point. Want to take a different path?"

Rod was a second ahead of me. "They might be marking a safe trail. One without traps."

Prospero nodded. "Or they could be leading us into a kill zone." He looked up at me with a crooked grin. "Right now, I am very glad *not* to be giving the orders."

I shrugged. "We take the marked trail. This doesn't feel like someone trying to ambush us. This is someone who's trying to protect themselves by controlling our route, keeping tabs on us. Besides, I don't think we're talking about a lot of people, here."

Jeeza's voice crackled out of my radio. "Why not?"

I shrugged even though she couldn't see me. "We're not dealing with hunters; the people who left these signs are used to hiding, not attacking. Remember: to get to this island, they had to have a boat, but we didn't see one anywhere. No sign of huts, tents, or a camp when we cruised around the island yesterday. And we never saw smoke until this morning, so they must limit and conceal their fires."

Prospero nodded. "Because, after all, it's not as if the infected are about to come sailing out here." He stared up the slope. "No, they are worried about real humans. The uninfected kind."

I hitched up my web-gear. "Let's follow that trail."

A few hundred yards of winding uphill progress brought us to a concrete and stone building. Or rather, the shell of one. Prospero circled around to its other side, raised an index finger. "Look."

I did. A deadfall trap: probably about four hundred pounds of shattered masonry and rock ready to collapse on anyone who went through the doorway out of the ruin. Except the trigger had been removed and chocks put in its place.

"I think," said Rod, "that someone is trying to tell us that they could hurt us. But have chosen not to."

"Or," Steve countered, "they want us to think that so we drop our guard."

"Preach it, Steve," Chloe's voice growled out of my radio.

"Two valid possibilities," I agreed.

Prospero cocked an eyebrow. "Then which do we act upon?"

"Both. We stay alert but hope to meet new friends, not new enemies." We walked around the colonial-era ruin and angled back on to the trail.

One of the weird things about surviving after the whole world has gone to shit is that there is no "normal." I don't just mean that the old life and ways are gone forever. I'm talking about simple, mathematical odds. As in, there is no "norm," no "typical situation," no "standard distribution" that governs what you are most likely to encounter, based on statistical probability. Every situation is unique, at least when you're on these ass-end-of-nowhere islands. I guess in New York or Beijing or Berlin or London you probably can rely upon at least one probability: that *everywhere* you go will be swarming with homicidal, raging infected.

But still, as we panted our way up to the top of the hill upon which Ilha Rata's old obelisk-shaped lighthouse was perched, we were surprised by a deep contralto voice that called down to us from one of the upper windows. "Hey, you don' get it? If I want you dead, you being dead now."

Actually, the words were a lot more garbled than that. They were English—sort of—but also something else. Portuguese, I suspected, but not like any Portuguese I'd ever heard. And while Portuguese shares a bunch of the same (or at least similar) words with Spanish, knowing the one language doesn't mean you'll understand the other.

We looked up at the black-shadowed windows of the poured-concrete lighthouse; it had probably been built before World War One. "Thanks for not killing us," I said. I repeated it in Spanish.

"Yeah? Thanks your dog."

"Our dog?"

"*Sim, estúpido.* I seeing your treating him. You is *gentilmente.* Um, *amablemente*?"

"Kind," I furnished in English.

"*Sim,* yeah, 'kind.' I thinks maybe okay. You."

I put down my shotgun. "We are."

"Maybe yes. Maybe no. We talk."

I indicated the distance between the window and the ground. "This way?"

"This way or no way."

Well, that pretty much settled it. I turned to the others. "Might as well put your guns down, guys."

While Chloe screamed about it being more important to keep our guns than our balls, Steve looked at the woods that ringed the bald crest of the hill. "You sure we're okay?"

I nodded down at Cujo, who was wagging his tail and staring up at the lighthouse. He was interested, but that was all.

Rod's nod matched mine. "When we walked around the tree line, he didn't tweak to any scents." He looked up at the unshuttered, unglazed window from which the woman's voice seemed to be coming. "I think she's alone."

Steve nodded. "Yeah. Don't know why, but...yeah." He put his shotgun down.

I sat on the sparse grass, leaned back on my elbows. "So," I called up, "how do you want to do this?"

"I say questions. You make answers."

"What do you want to know?"

A pause. Then: "Ev'thing."

Even though we boiled it down to the Cliffs Notes version, it still took about twenty minutes to hit all the highpoints of our life since climbing aboard *Voyager* in the Galapagos.

At the end, she let out an exasperated hoot. "You guys sure talk lots."

"You asked lots of questions."

For the first time, she laughed. "Yeah. I do." The back-and-forth of our introduction-through-storytelling had led to the evolution of a three-language pidgin that was working pretty well.

I rolled up into a squat. "Now what?"

The door to the lighthouse opened. "Now we meet for real." A woman, probably no older than those of us who had started on *Voyager*, came out. She was dark, about five-foot-seven and as lean as Chloe was solid. As she walked into the sunlight, she seemed ready to rise up on her toes and sprint—not in flight, but just because she was ready for action. Like an athlete. Like there was a high-performance engine idling inside her body, just waiting to go into overdrive.

Rod started and jumped to his feet.

She laughed as Cujo barked, the way dogs do when they want to meet a new person. "Watch out, I maybe bite you to death! Like them over there!" She pointed at the main island and laughed loudly.

"Not really very funny," Prospero mumbled.

She shrugged. "If you don' laugh at it, it make you crazy. Le's go for walk." She shook her head when Steve reached for his shotgun. "No guns." He shrugged, then reached behind to remove the Browning Hi-Power from where it was concealed in the small of his back. He moved to lay it down next to his shotgun.

The woman started at the sight of the pistol, eyes wide, but then frowned. "Stop," she said.

Steve was confused. "But you said—"

"Juz' stop."

We stood around while she frowned, looking hard at the ground, like it had insulted her.

"Okay," she said finally, "you can bring guns."

Steve looked at me, even more confused. I nodded at the High-Power. "It's because you gave it up, even though she didn't know it was there."

She cut her eyes at me, looked like she was going to say something, but instead, launched herself toward a trail that led down the other side of the hill to the less-forested side of Ilha Rota. "Why you waitin'?" she shouted. She ran with more ease than we walked.

We followed.

"My name are Tainara Sartorio," she yelled over her shoulder as the slope leveled off into a tousled sward of grass, bushes, and low, wind-tilted trees. "This my farm."

I stopped jogging to stare around. "It is?"

Prospero did the same, panting. "Where, exactly, is this farm?"

"You standing middle of it, *Inglês*." She took two steps to the left of the path, reached down, wrenched her wrist around, came up with a small green pepper. "Local plants. Most were here. Some I...I put in as new root. I, uh..."

"Transplanted?" Rod hazarded.

Tainara smiled and frowned. "That. I think. All around. But you keep feet on trail. Traps ever'where."

I nodded. "We'll stay on the path."

"Smart." She turned in a circle, smiling brightly at her mostly invisible farm. "Lots of cassava—manioc. I give you some. As thank you for the tins."

"Tins?" Steve wondered.

"She means canned food," Prospero murmured with smile. "Clearly, she just knows the *proper* word for it."

I was shaking my head. "The tins were a gift." She frowned uncertainly. "Free?" I tried.

Tainara shook her head sharply. "No. I don' need free. I fine here."

"We know. We just—"

But she was done with that topic. "Come," she snapped and led us to a curving trail that seemed certain to bring us back to Resurrection Cove.

"You like eat *peixe*?" she shouted over her shoulder. *Damn: how do I answer that honestly?* Sure, we liked fish. And sure we'd be happy to share a meal with her. But—more fish? Really?

Prospero found the answer that eluded me. "We like all kinds of fish, yes. Which is fortunate, since we live on a boat."

Tainara chuckled. "Okay, okay. I *compreendo*. You like it, but eat too much."

"Still," I added, "we'd be happy to join you for a meal."

She nodded. "Ah. Okay. Good. We do."

We stopped in a small clearing only fifteen yards away from the shore's tree line. Through the tight clutter of skinny trunks, we could see our Zodiac.

Tainara sat on a low rock, gestured toward others around the clearing. "Ants. Bugs," she explained.

As we lifted or rolled stones into a rough circle, she unslung a satchel and produced a wide variety of fruits; I didn't recognize any of them. She saw me looking and laughed. "So now I poison you."

I smiled, gestured toward her offerings, shrugged, shook my head: "New. First time."

"Ah!" she said. She had a wide, wonderful smile when she chose to share it. "Try. All."

I nodded, selected some little fruit that looked like an undernourished pear, remembered Mom pointing out a bigger variety, once. A quince, I think. "Did you already know these foods? From home?"

She nodded. "Yes"—which sounded like *zhass*—"I come from up Amazon river. Many foods there are here, too."

"Up the Amazon?" Prospero repeated. "Where, exactly?"

She looked at him with dead, annoyed eyes. "Listen, *Inglês*, even if you are interested, you won't know it. Is a town you never heard of. On a side river—a trib'tary?—called Rio Membeca. You won't find on most maps."

Prospero nodded, looked sad. "You are right. I have never heard of that river."

That seemed to mollify Tainara. "Hated life there. But prob'ly kept me alive here."

Rod frowned. "I'm not sure I understand."

She looked at him almost pityingly. "My home, you do ev'thing for self. Something break, you do fix. Almost no cars. Bad phones. Internet mostly off. When on, it slow."

"But are the people—?"

"People were shit. Like ev'where." She spat. "TV and lots books show nice living away from cities." She sneered. "Some ways, maybe. But mostly, just diff'rent kind of bad. In small town, you only safe if your family there long years." She shook her head. "My *pai*, he from sea town. Had school until he ten. My momma was from forest. No reading. She die when I twelve, having my li'l sister. Who die next day; doctor too far."

No one said anything. Until that moment, I would never have called my childhood fortunate. I guess that was because I hadn't known how bad it could be.

Tainara hadn't stopped. She wasn't angry, or sad, or detached. It was like she was telling us a story about having a flat tire or losing a pair of socks. "*Pai* drank. After *Māe*, he drank more. I a girl. Alone." She shrugged. "I depend on me: to fix things, to be safe."

Rod shook his head. "Jeez, I'm—I'm sorry."

Tainara looked at him like a pet that had done something cute. "It that way for many where I born."

Steve had been gnawing slowly at a piece of fruit. "How did you get out?"

Tainara wiped her hands on a large frond. "Football. Er, soccer, you say it. I went to school until I sixteen, played all time. That was trouble, so *Pai* gave me money for boat to Belém. I knew jobs, made money, took night classes. That's where I learn English. Whatever you do, you make more money if you talk English."

I hadn't meant to nod vigorously, but I did, which she noticed. "My mom," I explained, "she got jobs because her English was so good."

Tainara nodded back. "So you know." She stood. "This"—she looked back at FdN, then gestured at the forest around us—"this not so bad." She noticed the glances that went back and forth between us. "I am be serious," she said emphatically. "Is less dangerous here than it was two miles away from my town. Any direction."

"Because of the animals?" Steve asked.

"Yes. Both kinds."

"'Both'?"

"Yes," she said with a hard smile. "With four legs and with two legs." She threw a hand in the direction of FdN. "Them, over there: you know what they do. No surprises." She folded her arms close against her chest. "The jungle, you never know. Always surprises."

Although it was hard to imagine two human females who looked more different, at that moment, I realized just how many similarities there were between Chloe and Tainara. I wondered if that would make them friends, enemies, or frenemies. Or if we'd ever get the chance to find out. The silence was dragging on too long. Don't know why, but I knew I had to keep Tainara talking. "So football is how you got out of the jungle, but why did you come to Fernando de Noronha?"

She shrugged. "Because football went shit. So I wanted away. Get to small, quiet place." She looked around. "Everyone else flies in. Rich *turistas* who say 'Oooo!' and 'Ahhh!' at pretty fish and beaches." She snorted. "I came fishing boat. Probably another reason I alive. Planes with people who have the virus, already infected. They dead and don' know it. Me? I come working nets and sleeping on deck. No germs; just the stars."

Her brief drift into a wistful tone snapped back into pure grimness. "But the momen' I get here, I know is all wrong. I seen disease go through li'l towns. Is like grassfire. Fast, spread in ever' direction." She shook her head. "I know the island goin' to shit. I hear the crazy talk on radio, guv'mint warning on phones. So I go to the most li'l island." She pointed to the southwest: "Sela Gineta. Nothing there. I stay two months. Hid. Ate lotta fish." She glanced at me and smiled. "Like you."

"Did you go back?" Prospero nodded toward Fernando de Noronha itself.

"Not right 'way. Firs' I watch for boats leave or arrive. Lots leave. A few go here; Ilha Rata." She shrugged. "Then fires start aroun' the town, Vila dos Remédios. A li'l later, I thin' maybe a plane crashes in sea. Then nothing. Ever'thin' stop."

She wrapped her arms around her knees. "I knowed the big islan'd be dangerous. But before boat bring me to Baia Sao Antonio, it stop here. I saw fruit, wild cassava, people fish from cliffs. So, not lot of food, but not many went here. So I—puddled? paddled?—until I reach there." She gestured behind us, where *Voyager* was anchored. "Watched, then made noise. Hoped people got here without virus." She sighed. "But only infected come down to rocks, then into water until it over their legs. They no come out more deep."

"So what did you do?" Steve asked.

Tainara shrugged. "I go back Sela Gineta. Rest. Then go to find ship I came on. Anchored in Baia Sao Antonio. Sad: captain sick. Rest dead. But a dive boat was empty. Spearguns still there. Got those. Came back Ilha Rata. Made noise until the infecteds come again." She lined up an imaginary speargun with me, made a *ssshhhhpt!* sound: "Shot three."

She paused, reflecting. "They don' die right away. First, they get angry. *Muy loco*, I thin' you say? And they hungry, too. I stay where they see me, they keep yelling, trying to reach me, but won' come out. The ones I hit with spears get weak; the others grab 'em. They forget abou' me. I paddle in. Shoot 'nother two. Same thing." She sighed. "Took two days, but all eight gone. Last one, he jus' can't go 'way, not even when he belly full. He wan' kill me so much. Took a lotta spears kill him." Then she smiled brightly. "So after, I live here. Make my farm. An' hide."

Rod was smiling and frowning at the same time. "So why didn't you send up a flare last time we were here? You must have seen us."

"Yeah, but last time, you come and go really quick. And really sneaky."

"Well," Prospero explained in his *I'm-extremely-reasonable* tone of voice, "we don't really want to announce ourselves to the stalkers."

Tainara leaned forward, frowning really hard. "Did you say walkers? Like on TV? Like Dead Walking?"

"No, no," Steve corrected, "stalkers."

She exhaled a grateful sigh. "*Graças a deus*. That show bullshit. *Total*."

Rod looked over his shoulder at FdN, then at the guns we were cradling. "You sure?"

"Yeah, sure I'm sure. Look, what about—?"

And she became animated reciting all of Hollywood's undead stupidities we knew so well. That we too had laughed and railed at. All the wildly improbable head shots, all the wasted ammunition, all the people running around without so much as a leather jacket or firecoat. It's a long list of totally moronic survival choices and tactical idiocy (if they even knew what tactics were).

We laughed, her along with us. The more she spoke, the more English she was remembering, and she was really on a roll with this topic. But best of all, it was a kind of weird bonding experience. I mean, we were all roughly the same age, had all lived through the end of the world, and so naturally started comparing our experiences with how stupid "zombie apocalypse" TV shows and movies had been. Which was a kind of back-door way to bond over how brutally different the reality had been.

"So why did you send up the flare this time?" I sighed, leaning back.

She seemed to regret the return to a serious topic, or maybe just didn't want to explain herself. "This time, when you come back, I get a better look. That told me you were prolly okay."

"What, specifically, told you that?"

"I already tell you; the dogs." Then her brow lowered. "Lemme 'splain: once it all went to shit, I see how it goes with groups people. I see how it was on the ships that left, and those that came later. Women weren't crew no more: they cargo. Cattle. You know what I mean." She shook her head. "But not you guys. Everyone working. Everyone have guns. You eat same food, laugh together, argue together. I see it through . . . bin-bokulars?"

"Binoculars," I offered with what I hoped was an encouraging smile.

"Yeah. Those. And 'nother thing; you careful. You make plans. And you clean. So this time I think chances are good that you not a bunch of filthy *filhos-da-puta*."

I wasn't certain of the exact translation, but I had a pretty good idea. I just smiled and nodded.

Steve shook his head. "Damn. How did you make it?"

"'Make it'?" Tainara repeated.

"Survive on your own."

She bristled. "You mean, 'cause I a woman?"

Steve just stared at her. "No, because you're just one *person*. In the middle of a zombie apocalypse."

His tone, so frank and even, didn't just calm her; she seemed a little embarrassed. "Oh, okay." Her smile was apologetic. "Sorry. Being woman not always easy in Brazil. Particularly if you're—what the American term?—a Tim-girl?"

"Tom-girl," he provided.

"Right. That. And it was more harder for me."

Rod cocked his head. "You mean, because of where you grew up?"

"*Merda*, no; it was because I wanted to be soccer player."

Prospero frowned. "That was a problem?"

"Brazil aren't England, *Inglês*. When my *avó* was a little, little girl, were women's team all over the country. But then, in World War Two, some government idiot made it illegal. No play sports that be 'against woman's nature.'"

Prospero blinked. "No."

"But yes, *Inglês*. They didn' let us play again until, like 1980, I thinks. And jus' changing the law didn't change the sport. Not even twenty-five percent teams were women when the virus come. And they still call us 'big shoes.'"

"Big shoes?" repeated Rod, puzzled. "Because you kick the ball a lot?"

"No. 'Cuz they thinks we all lesbians." She snorted. "When I was ten—maybe eleven?—the FIFA president say women's soccer would have more fans if we wear tighter shorts. They want 'heterosexy' girls in tight shirts. Even say national team should pose naked for a calendar."

"So you quit?"

"I don't quit nothing," she snarled. "Never. But I push back against that shit. So I miss twenty-years-old team by one spot." She spat. "Lie. I know coach's secretary. She tell me my rank for play and skill was eight. But somehow, I still don' make team of fifteen. Miss by one spot." She hugged her knees tight. "Felt like world ended. So I came here. And then the world *did* end. For real."

She had curled up around her legs even tighter. I figured it was time to change topics to something less personal. "So how often have you been back to the main island?"

"Since that first time? Just once or twice. And just to the end of the wharf. The infected don't go out there except when there no rain for a long time. Don' like being near the sea."

Prospero leaned toward her. "They go out to the wharf when it's dry?"

"Yeah. Well, not because the wharf are dry. They go because they thirsty." She looked around, realized none of us understood what she meant. "Look: is like this. When it rain, there water ev'where. On stones, in ground, in big pools and the *cisternas*.

"But when it dry for days, they move early in the day and go anwhere there are metal or flat stone. Because water in the air—uh, driplets?—uh ..."

Rod got it first: "Oh, droplets. You mean, the infected drink the dew, the condensation."

Tainara nodded vigorously. "*Condensação*. Yes, that! So I no go then. I wait until it just finish raining. The infecteds go to pools, buckets, cans in Vila dos Remédios. I paddle—yes?—over when it dark, so they don't see the boat, tie it up on far side of wharf. I come and go; they never see. Snack foods in machines and ships. But I don' like going into ships."

"Why?"

"Because infecteds get there before people knew or could leave. Those ships—some really nasty. To see and to smell."

I nodded. "Yeah, we saw. But we're going there, anyway."

"You? There?" She looked at us like we had transformed into wild beasts before her eyes. "You crazy? Why go if you no have to?"

"Because the friends we mentioned—the ones who are returning—may need more food than we have."

She frowned. "Look, I help. As much as I can. But going there is *louco. Total.*"

I smiled and nodded. "We know. But we have to be sure we can feed everyone. And we have to get ready for what comes next."

She looked suspiciously from one of us to the next. "An' what is next?"

Prospero looked like he was about to start explaining,

but this needed to be as simple as possible. "Steve," I said, "you want to do the honors?"

"Me?" he asked. "I probably understand it the least."

"Which means you'll keep it simple and direct."

He shrugged and laid out—with minimum digression and maximum brevity—the mission to the ESA facility at Kourou. With every passing sentence, Tainara's initial frown deepened.

When he got to the end, she looked around at us again. Her eyes had changed; they were less suspicious, but also more incredulous. "Well, you still crazy. More crazy, I think. But at least you have a reason." She leaned back, made to rise. "But me? I do just fine without no GPS. That world is gone, frien's. Best you learn to do without, too."

I gestured gently with one hand, encouraging her to stay seated. "There's more."

She settled back, crossed her arms. "Maybe. But what's in it for me?"

Prospero's hopeful smile was also a bit ironic. "Helping your fellow man?"

She shook her head. "No and no. People should help themselves. And why should I help men? They never help me."

"It was just a little joke," Prospero explained.

"Yeah. And not even a li'l funny." She turned to face me. "So I ask again, *pequeno chefe*, what's in it for me?"

"Well, assuming that you're not interested in the company of other human beings—"

"You right about that!" she snorted.

"—then how about a real weapon?" I put my own Browning Hi-Power on the ground between us.

Her eyes brightened for a moment, then she raised her chin and huffed. "I seen bigger ones."

"I'm sure you have. It's not a big gun. But it's very reliable and holds a lot of bullets. Question is, do you know how to use it? Or any pistol?"

Her eyes shuttered. She looked away, annoyed. At me, at herself, or both, I couldn't tell. "No," she finally muttered.

I nodded. "Then here's what's in it for you. We give you one of the bigger pistols and teach you how to use it. You help us on the main island. After that, if you decide you want to come back here, then we'll give you forty rounds and wish you good luck."

Prospero and Rod leaned forward; I stilled them with a look at the same moment I turned down the volume on my radio, just in time to muffle Chloe's roared objections.

Tainara's eyes were on the gun, but I don't think she was really seeing it. She was looking inside herself, probably weighing the safety of staying a complete hermit against the advantages of joining us, if only temporarily. She frowned. "Okay. Deal. I'll get you some cassava, to celebrate." And she was up and off into the darkening woods without any warning.

As soon as I turned the sound up on my radio again, Prospero voiced his objections. "Damn it," he hissed when Tainara was out of earshot, "don't bloody give away our guns and ammo, Alvaro!"

I shook my head. "I didn't."

"What do you mean? That's what you just offered her!"

I nodded. "Yeah. But here's the thing: she may be

tough, but she's still lonely. She doesn't want to stay here. She just doesn't want anyone to see it."

Steve arched an eyebrow. "How do you know that?"

Chloe's voice emerged from my radio; I could hear the slowly growing smile behind it. "Because, Steve, if she wanted to be alone, she wouldn't have shot the flare to begin with."

November 19

You'd think that the end of the world meant the end of being rushed, that with no businesses, no stock market, no commuting, no e-mail, that everything would slow way down.

Bullshit. When you're fending for yourself in a world without any of the amenities and conveniences all that activity enabled, you are working from dawn to dusk. Every day. And you never have a problem sleeping—except on the nights where you're going to go on salvage the next day. Like last night.

But the three days leading up to that were constant activity. When we weren't teaching Tainara how to shoot, we were getting her to go over our maps of FdN and add in anything—*anything*—that she could remember about the island. Turned out that the tourist maps were the "not to scale" kind and some things were just dead wrong, or had changed since Fodor's or Frommer's or Baedeker had last bothered to send one of their contributors to this mostly forsaken little archipelago.

It also turned out that while Tainara was only fair learning her way around a pistol, she had a natural gift for shotguns—the shorter the better. I could tell from looking at her that she wished that she had held out for one of the Rexios as her payment. I just smiled. That was all to our advantage. We gladly shifted gears and focused her training on the twelve-gauge.

In the midst of all this we fished, surveyed Tainara's well-dispersed and hidden farm, got her to tell us where she thought the best salvage targets were on FdN, and how best to approach them. Meanwhile, we brought Daisy ashore and, on the second day, she popped out seven pups. One didn't make it past the first hour; that's often the case, particularly in conditions like ours. But the others were healthy little shut-eyed balls of fluff—or were, as soon as she had licked them clean. Best of all, once Rod had made a successful approach, Daisy let the rest of us handle the new additions and accepted tidbits from us along with the slow, gentle petting that was her well-earned reward for bringing six very important—and cute— puppies into our world.

And every spare moment—when we ate, collapsed after training, or even took a piss—we were talking through the details of Wizard's Tower Two, or as Prospero optimistically relabeled it, the St. Anthony's Bay Massacre. It was a long reach from that reference to the most infamous Chicago gangland slaughter of the Roaring Twenties, but he was very pleased with himself and no one pointed out that we wouldn't have made the connection if he hadn't explained it.

But the name grew on us, because it kind of jazzed us, too. We were going to slay dozens, maybe hundreds of stalkers to take back an island for healthy human beings. The risk and brute practicality of the mission got infused with a kind of nobility, which was good for morale.

It was such a simple plan, and so safe compared to anything we'd done to date, that I really don't know why none of us slept soundly the night before. Maybe it was because it was the start of something really big—of clearing a whole island of stalkers all by ourselves. Maybe it was because we knew that although the first days would be pretty easy, we were committing ourselves to ultimately leaving our safe positions to hunt down the last stragglers. Or maybe it was a symptom of what Chloe had warned us about: that you can't afford to take too long a break from work that involves the wholesale slaughter of rabid humans, even if they are mindless and rabid. It's too easy to lose the edge—and the emotional calluses—you have to have if you're going to keep pulling the trigger.

We sailed into St. Anthony's Bay—really just a mooring—while the east was still dove-gray. On the leeward side of the jetty, there was a small floating wharf that had originally been equipped with two boarding ramps. One was nowhere to be seen; the other was still in place. We liked that it was light, steel, and sturdy yet portable. But we didn't like where it was located: halfway down the long arm of the jetty's "L," the part that connected to the shore. So the first object was to land, get the ramp, and reposition it at the end of the outer, shorter leg of the "L": a poured-concrete lading platform for boats with deep drafts. Unfortunately, we had no way of knowing whether there were any stalkers snoozing in the vicinity. Tainara told us she'd never seen them shelter there, but she wasn't offering—nor were we hearing—that as anything like a guarantee.

So we started *Voyager*'s motor and kept it low, but pulsed it. Just enough so anyone in the vicinity of the bay would hear it, but not up the road that led into Vila dos Remédios.

Wouldn't you know it; after ten minutes without a stalker showing up and with the landing team—Tainara, Prospero, Rod, Steve—newly ashore, some sleepy-ass stalker comes lurching out of the dilapidated restaurant/snack stand just landward of the floating wharf.

Chloe and Jeeza, as the sniper/spotter team on the roof of *Voyager*'s pilothouse, called the target—but I saw a problem developing: Tainara was not falling back, but racing forward to engage. "Hold your shot!" I snapped at Chloe.

"If I wait...shit; I've *lost* the shot," Chloe cursed; Tainara was blocking her line of sight. "What the hell is she—?"

Before Chloe could finish asking the question, Tainara had answered it with action. Wearing my fireman's coat and a dive mask, she leaped straight at the stalker, swinging a two-handed cleaver for whale-butchering—a flensing knife—as she did.

The heavy blade didn't catch the still-hoarse stumbler in the head—her clear intent—but it went down into, and through, the bugger's left shoulder. He fell—whether from the blow or the sudden change of balance, I couldn't tell.

And Tainara clearly didn't care. She took that moment to haul the flensing knife back over her shoulder and then struck down across the stalker's back, severing the spine with such a deep cut that the creature's torso was ready to hinge apart along the wound. Another blow took off its head.

Tainara stepped back, pushed up the mask, and, forgetting noise discipline, shouted, "Now THAT is a machete!"

"Tainara." I made the word as quiet, but also as sharp and crisp, as I could.

She looked up, surprised.

"You keep all your gear on until we can decon it. And you. And your weapon. Back away. And next time, you keep your reactions to yourself until we are done. Clear?"

She nodded, mute at first, and then hissed at Prospero, "Jeeeeez, is the *pequeno chefe* always like this?"

"He is," Chloe answered in a slow drawl from her perch atop the pilothouse. "When he's trying to save someone's stupid ass, anyway."

"Who you callin' stupid, bitch?"

"Drop it!" I shouted. I hated breaking my own rules about noise discipline, but allowing dissension and bickering was a lot worse. "You two will settle that shit later. Right now, we are mid-mission. Steve, Rod, Prospero, grab that ramp and get it down to the end of the jetty. All speed. Chloe, Jeeza, cover them. I'll do decon on Tainara."

Who stomped on board with all the maturity of a reprimanded three-year-old. "You need to get that stick out of your *bunda, chefe*."

"And you need to be a team player if you're going to work with us."

"You mean, I need to do what *you* tell me?"

"Not just me. Whoever is in charge. One day, that might be you. You want people sassing you, ignoring your orders?"

That stopped her. She clumped toward the starboard

bow, where we did most of the deconning (too crowded aft, with all the traffic that circulated around the pilothouse and the mizzenmast). "Okay, okay. I get it. But I tell you, after having nothing but little bullshit machetes made for *turistas*, it was good to swing a real one. Man, I tell you; that are the heaviest I ever swing!"

"I'm not surprised," I grunted, as I finished Tai's preliminary full-body hose-down and started sloshing her with what we called our Special Sauce. Its bleach-and-ammonia smell was suddenly thick around us. "That's not a machete. Like I told you, it's for cutting apart whales."

"No shit? I thought you were joking at me. Damn. Well, it sure do work good."

I wasn't about to debate it at that moment. The flensing tools were good if you only had to swing them once or twice. More than that and you started slowing down. And if you want to stay alive when you're being swarmed by stalkers, you *cannot* slow down. "Turn around," I ordered, then looked up toward Jeeza. "Anything?"

She kept her eyes to the binoculars as she answered. "Nope. Seems sleeping beauty was all alone out here."

"Yeah," added Chloe, "he was so slow and hoarse that I'd bet Twix to tuna that he was in torpor."

I nodded. "Looked like it." I stole a glance behind. Prospero was signaling that they had the ramp in place and ready to run out to *Voyager*.

I stared up at Tainara. "The rest of the decon protocol: you remember it?"

Her reply was part sigh, part growl. "Jus' 'cause I get excited don' mean I forget what you show me."

"Good. Now stand inboard and grab a handhold."

"Why?"

"Because we're motoring over to the lading platform. Time to set up for the dance."

Rod's response to my nod was, "Let's rock!" He jabbed an eager index finger at the sound system we had scavenged from an officer's billet at Wideawake airfield. The speakers had once been the overpowered PA system for its terminal.

Eighties head-banging rock came roaring out of them, hit the tightly packed boulders of the sixteen-foot-high breakwater, and bounced up toward Vila dos Remédios, just under a mile away.

"Think they'll hear it?" Rod asked.

I shrugged. It was the best we could do. We'd thought about various other ways of getting their attention, but all of them involved going ashore: starting a fire, setting off explosions, blowing the horns of the bigger docked boats. Problem was that if there were more torpid stalkers nearby, they could come out from places and at the moments we least expected it. Not a risk we wanted to take unless we had to.

One of the biggest problems when fighting the infected is that although their behavior is mostly predictable, their locations and lairs are not. They're like rats; they seem to be able to get into everything. And if they *can* get in somewhere, some of them always do. But there's no way of knowing where all those places might be until they come boiling out of them. Then you have to add in the further whacky variable of unpredictable timing. Not only are there always some of them in torpor on these low-meat-density islands, but they seem to show the same sleep spectrum as regular humans. Some are light sleepers, some are deep sleepers, and most are someplace in between.

So the first requirement of our plan was to reduce those uncertainties as much as we could. That's why we ditched our first version of the op plan for the St. Anthony's Bay Massacre, in which we considered putting Chloe and Jeeza at the optimum sniper overlook: the end of the long causeway—at the bend in the L—and up on the crest of its breakwater. But the stalkers were sure to clamber up the rocks after them, so we had to have an evacuation boat on the back side of the jetty. Which made us decide against that plan: way too many moving parts and we just couldn't be certain that enough of the infected would stay mobbed up for us to eliminate in large numbers.

But the real deal-breaker was the risk factor: some of the stalkers were sure to chase Chloe and Jeeza over the crest and down the other side. And if either of them twisted an ankle hopping boulder to boulder down to the evacuation boat, they'd never make it out; the infected may not be as agile and sure-footed as mountain goats, but they are at least as fearless.

But the time we spent on that plan didn't turn out to be a waste of time, because it reminded us that just because the pier looked like a natural stalker-funnel, it wouldn't necessarily prove to be so. If some of the ones at the back of the mob got impatient, they might run up the sides of the breakwater—just like a mountain goat would. At worst, they might go over its crest and then reappear someplace along its length, flanking whoever we put on shore.

So in our final plan, we put Tainara in the Zodiac

on the other side of the breakwater. From there, she could watch any stalkers who were approaching us using the ocean side of the breakwater. It wasn't likely; any infected who tried it would be slowed down big time, and you can always count on them to make a straight line for their prey. But that was our only blind side and shit happens, particularly in combat. And particularly when you're fighting stalkers.

Tainara wasn't too happy about the assignment, complaining that "Is way out away from the action!" I managed not to smile. This was coming from the same person who'd called us crazy for even thinking about landing on the big island. But now, here she was, already grumping because she wasn't in the front line...even though I'd put her on the landing team. But she couldn't argue with why I chose her for the job: she had the least experience and poorest accuracy with firearms. And guns, not machetes, were how we would win the St. Anthony's Bay Massacre. Assuming we did.

Rod was *Voyager*'s designated pilot, but at that moment, he was focused on his job as psyops overseer. Which he was working more like a deejay as he deafened us with hits from the Eighties onward. And it kept him safe and ready in the pilothouse in case we did need to haul ass for some unforeseen reason. I was the only other person on *Voyager*, which I didn't like very much, because it meant I was too far away to help if something went really wrong really fast.

Chloe and Jeeza were not in their normal sniper's roost on top of the pilothouse. Despite the calm waters, Chloe had made a convincing case that the increased accuracy of operating on land would still make the battle shorter and more decisive. So we had settled on putting her and Jeeza on top of the wharf-sheltering poured-concrete wall just five yards beyond the ramp we'd now run out to *Voyager*. That gave her a higher, stable platform from which she could still sweep the whole jetty. Prospero and Steve, FALs and shotguns at the ready, were behind a decent barricade we'd erected about ten yards away from the ramp in the other direction: the side from which the stalkers would come.

My job was command, control, and communication: I've seen it referred to as "C3" in some of the older manuals we found at Ascension (usually in the billets of career NCOs). And because it was up to me to signal a withdrawal if it looked like too many infected were getting too close, pulling the ramp back aboard *Voyager* was also my job.

I ran radio checks, made sure all the mags for my AK were both snug and easily pulled, and waited.

Forty minutes later, two shamblers came stumbling into view. From the wrong direction. Of course.

Instead of coming down the long hill from Vila dos Remédios, they staggered out of the little combination museum and restaurant just across from where the jetty's access lane met FdN's main highway. Where "main highway" is defined as the wider and longer of the island's two paved roads.

"Wow," Rod commented in a flat tone. "That's a whole two more we woke out of torpor."

I toggled the radio. "You see them, Jeeza?"

"Before you did. Chloe wants to wait until they're within one hundred twenty yards. No reason to waste ammo on anything other than a sure shot." Which meant that she'd engage them at a shallow oblique angle from across the anchorage, just as they walked beyond the floating wharf.

Okay, I look at what I just wrote and realize that, if you weren't there, it would be damn near impossible to visualize what I'm talking about. First, think of a capital "L." That's the shape of the whole jetty. The top of the vertical leg is where it connects to the land. About two hundred and twenty yards into the water, it turns ninety degrees to the left: that's the L's bottom "arm." It's seventy-five yards long and shelters the anchorage from the sea. Like I said, we put Chloe at the far end of that part, from which she could see and hit any target anywhere along the vertical leg. For those of us who do trig in our heads, that means her longest shot—to the top of the "L"—was only (only!) about two hundred sixty-five yards. (And no, it was not a perfect L, so it is not a precise trig answer. Deal with it.)

Therefore, she had lots of time to aim and shoot at every infected who charged down that vertical arm of the "L." And once they turned the corner, they were full frontal; from that angle, she didn't even have to lead them. But that corner was also only sixty yards away from the barricade being manned by Prospero and Steve. So the objective was to weed the infected out as they charged down the main causeway so only stragglers got to the bend. If they started coming at us faster than she could take them down . . . well, that's when we'd shift to Phase Two.

But the two from the restaurant-museum didn't make it three steps past the floating wharf. Chloe's

.308 barked and one of them fell like a sack of flour. A second report and the other sprawled sideways, still kicking and thrashing. She'd been hit in the hip, which, like knee shots, always causes the wildest reactions in stalkers. They keep trying to get up and run even harder, but the shattered joint won't support them for more than a step or two, at which point they once again go sprawling and shrieking in rage. And they keep trying that, again and again, until another bullet puts an end to their loud, spastic fury.

This time was no different. Chloe waited for her moment, then hit the base of the stalker's throat as she lurched upright.

There wasn't really anything to say. It was a pretty anticlimactic opening engagement. After five seconds, Jeeza murmured a thoroughly bored, "Yay. We win."

We settled in to wait some more.

What we didn't anticipate—but should have—is that the sound of the .308 was what we needed to get the dance party hopping. Rod's rock mix featured a heavy dose of drums and bass that just didn't reach out and grab attention the way high-pitched sounds do. Or maybe we just needed bigger and better speakers.

Whatever the reason, about fifteen minutes after the two museum-dwelling stalkers went facedown on the jetty's roadway, Tainara used the squelch break that signaled a request for vox-grade commo. (Because there are potentially pirates out there, we tend to keep voice commo to a minimum.) I toggled my handset. "*Voyager* here. Go."

"We have companies—eh, company. Lookit top of the hill."

I had to step out of the pilothouse to see that far behind us. Sure enough, there was a small, dispersed group of infected running toward us. Faster, it seemed, as they started hearing the music more clearly. They howled every time the lead guitar surged louder, like animals responding to the challenge calls of an enemy.

Tainara sounded very excited and a little scared. Or maybe eager. "I thin' shooting is like hook the fish, and now music reel them in, yeh?"

"Looks like it," I agreed. I leaned out the side door of the pilothouse and waved to the others, pointing back up the hill. Jeeza had eyes on them already. Chloe just smiled wolfishly and answered with a thumbs-up.

As soon as the new group got on the causeway, she started taking them on. Despite the long range, the angle was only ten degrees off a full frontal shot. Chloe's bolt-action spoke steadily, but even so, the occasional miss, and the occasional stalker who somehow survived two shots were left for Steve and Prospero. Their marksmanship had improved enough to hit more than half the time. If that sounds like miraculous improvement, remember that they didn't engage until the survivors were only sixty yards away and coming straight at them.

After almost thirty steady minutes of this, Tainara went straight to voice comms. "Hey, *chefe*, you party getting real pop'lar, now."

I turned: the road down the hill was now as crowded as an entry gate into an actual concert stadium.

Rod saw what I was looking at. He swallowed. "Alvaro, do you think—I mean, can we really—?"

I simply toggled the general channel on the handset. "Withdrawal in two minutes."

"What the hell—?" started Chloe. Then a long pause as she looked back over her shoulder. "Oh. Yeah. Two minutes. A big 'Roger that.'"

"Remember the drill. Sniper element unasses first. Barricade line thirty seconds after."

Tainara's voice came on, surf sounds behind her. "And then?" She had clearly not been listening carefully when we rolled out the final plan.

"And then," I replied, "we pull back seven yards and keep blasting the music as loud as we can. And wait."

She was silent for a moment. Then memory kicked in. "Oh," she said. "Yah. Now I remember. Phase Two."

"Yes. Remember: before you start back, toss out the chum cage as far as you can. Tow it around until you have some followers, then motor in. We need all hands for this last part."

By the time Tainara snugged the Zodiac against *Voyager*'s stern, everyone was back aboard, the ramp had been pulled in, and the party animals were lined up five deep along the poured-concrete sides of the jetty. They were typical infected; shrieking, howling, mostly naked, wild eyes, open sores; and oblivious to everything except their immediate prey: us.

Voyager's sails were reefed; that way, we couldn't be pushed back toward their snapping jaws by a sudden gust. Besides, when your sails are up, you need to man them *and* the wheel or you are tempting fate. And in this case, we couldn't spare anyone from the task at hand.

We'd kind of become deaf to the music playing on a loop, blaring over our heads at the mob of stalkers straining toward us. But they kept hearing it, reacting to it like a challenge. Which it was.

Tainara returned topside, having snagged more ammo for her Rexio.

"You ready?" I asked.

She nodded and glanced at the sharks that had followed her chum cage into the anchorage. "They looking bored. Gotta start soon."

"Right now," I agreed, and brought the M4 up to my shoulder. "Phase Two," I said loudly. "Ready on the line." I'd heard that in some movie. A Civil War flick, I think. Funny how I remember everything I read, but not everything I hear. At least not as precisely.

Everyone muttered that they were ready.

"Okay. Remember: there's no reason to rush. Look for the least stable target. If one round makes them fall into the water, so much the better. Safeties off." I heard a ragged chorus of metallic clicks. "Fire."

M4's don't sound badass. They are pint-sized, low recoil, and fire a round that a lot of people consider anemic. And when you've become used to the sound and recoil and visible effects of 7.62xAnything, you understand where that opinion comes from. But because it fires the 5.56mm round, the M4 is also very easy to control and it shoots as straight as a laser at close ranges (and well beyond).

So six of them crackling along the side of a seventy-foot cutter doesn't sound like wrathful thunder. But still, they do the job. In this case, that meant dropping targets at a crazy rate. The only imposing reports were the booms of Tainara's pump shotgun.

The tactics of engagement were basic: hit the ones closest to the edge, since the whole mass of them was behaving just as they always did; jostling, pushing, trying to get as close as they could, despite the twenty feet of water between us. As we'd suspected, one hit was usually enough to topple them. A lot of the rounds also over-penetrated: went all the way through the first stalker to hit the one right behind. These second hits were often messier; the first impact destabilized the round's orientation and spin, so it wasn't able to zip through the second body as cleanly. That meant it dumped almost all of its plentiful remaining energy into that second stalker.

Within the first five seconds, twelve of them were in the water, thrashing, roaring, swimming skills gone to whatever abyss had also swallowed their memories of civilization and love. The sharks swerved toward them like meat-seeking missiles. A few actually shied away when the stalkers met them head-on, hands raking furiously.

But the sharks swerved back almost immediately. Not only had the stalkers failed to inflict any noticeable damage, but, unable to swim or even float, they were sinking and growing weaker.

It's kind of strange watching sharks tear stalkers apart. For one split second, you're really not sure whose side you're on. I mean, the stalkers have to be exterminated. It's them or us, and we need all the help we can get. But sharks? They are ancient enemies, the stuff of nightmares and horror movies.

But then that split second is past and you're back in the present, remembering that there really aren't any sides, now. Either a critter—or person—is friendly or it's not. And if it's not, well, the cosmic butcher's bill is now collected by whoever is in the best position to do so.

It took only two seconds for more infected to shove

and elbow their way into the gaps left by those who'd become shark food. We scanned for the ones whose footing was already precarious, raised our weapons, and fired. More fell in.

After about the fourth—you really couldn't miss, given the range and the solid mass of targets—I realized that although we'd killed plenty of infected before, this time was affecting me differently. Part of it was the point-blank range; you could see details like the color of their eyes, rings, surgical scars (C-sections were always the most noticeable), teeth straightened by orthodontia, tattooed messages, and symbols that were now meaningless. All reminders that they had once been something more than mindless, rabid bipeds. They'd been people. Until now, we'd been able to forget that, more or less. But not here, not at this range.

Whether it was the blood in the water, the thrashing at the surface, or the convergence of their own kind, more sharks started arriving in St. Anthony's Bay after the first few minutes. There were close to a hundred infected in the water by then.

I don't actually remember many details after that. None of us do. Jeeza thinks it's about guilt and the repression of bad memories. I'd like to agree, but I can't. As far as I can tell, it just got kind of routine. There was a point where you stopped noticing the individual features of the infected. From there on, it became like any other repetitive job: you just did it without paying a lot of attention.

Since more and more infected kept arriving to check out the gunfire, it's hard to know how many we actually put in the water. It was somewhere over two hundred and fifty. Steve tried to keep count, claims it was someplace between two hundred eighty and two hundred ninety. Could be. All I know is that none got out. A few actually tried to jump the twenty feet between the jetty and *Voyager*. Since they were not former Olympians, that didn't work out for them.

By 0900, new arrivals had dwindled to a few every fifteen minutes. By noon, it was a few every hour. By 1400, we realized that no more were going to show. We compared our impressions and tentative tallies.

In one morning, we'd brought down at least four hundred infected.

And we'd also learned that when old books describe battles in rivers or bays by using the phrase "the waters ran red," that wasn't exaggeration. Not one bit.

November 22

We returned to try the same tactic the following day. After three hours, only five stumblers, and no real stalkers, we gave it up and re-scouted the site we'd seen at Ilha da Conceição before sailing back to Ilha Rata. We'd had no way of knowing if it would bring down a fresh wave of infected or whether we'd already reached all those that we could attract.

Much of the day was spent reviewing how much we didn't and couldn't know. Two weeks ago, we had estimated that there were probably about nine hundred infected left, of which three hundred were active—maximum. Except now we had killed almost four hundred in one day. Was that because there were more left than we had guessed? We didn't know. Was it because half or more of those who showed up had been in torpor until roused by either the sound of our guns or the activity of the other infected? Again, we didn't know. Or were our tentative assumptions about torpor fundamentally wrong? Was there some kind of periodicity at work, so that if stalkers went for more than a week without food, their impulse toward in-group predation dwindled and so they began shutting down? Of course, we didn't know that either.

Unfortunately, if we were significantly wrong about any of a dozen other variables, that made our initial estimates almost entirely worthless. Which left us with three big questions. First, how many infected were left after the St. Anthony's Bay Massacre? Second, how could we tell when we had reduced their active numbers to the point that we could safely move upon the island itself? And third, how many did we have to kill at Praia do Cachorro before we could risk pushing on at all?

After hours of useless theorizing, we kicked all those cans down the road and resolved to try yet another version of Wizard's Tower in the hope that the results would give us more insight into the actual challenge we were facing.

So today we sailed *Voyager* a mile farther west, following along the north side of FdN bearing landward as we came abreast of Forte dos Remédios. That put us in the small bay that was home to Praia do Cachorro: a beach shaped like a cutlass, bounded on the east by the high ground upon which the fort was perched and on the west by the rough, stony molar that the maps labeled Ilha da Conceição. From what we could tell, it didn't spend much time as an island. For a few hours at high tide, water did separate it from FdN. But that water was knee-high, at most.

The structure we hoped to make Wizard's Tower Number Three was located toward the end of the tapering spit of land that connected FdN to Ilha da Conceição. It was a small, one-story bar with a high foundation. It had views of not only Praia do

Cachorro but also Praia da Conceição to the west. The only avenue of access was a long, narrow road that started paralleling the beach and then descended from the steep slopes that fell away from the north side of Vila dos Remédios.

We landed with Cujo, whose nonchalant lope through and around the one-story bar proved it to be uninhabited by infected, torpid or otherwise. He stuck around with Rod, watching the road while we prepared Tower #3.

Normally, we wouldn't have taken a chance on so small and low a building, but it was made from poured concrete, and the roof was high, almost another half story. That put it beyond the jumping range of the infected. Chloe and Steve—sniper and security—went up to ready it for a long day's work while the rest of us started clearing the ground around it and filling a few small, makeshift sandbags to pass up to them.

I was shoving my third bag up toward the roof when Jeeza came up behind me. "This isn't right, Alvaro."

"Whaddya mean? The sandbags can't be any larger, but we need them on the side of the roof facing the bay. In case we have to provide flanking fire."

"That's not what I mean and you know it."

She was right; I did. But I'd hoped to be able to skip over this.

"I'm the spotter," Jeeza said, her voice low and hard. "I am going up there. You are not cutting me out."

I held in a sigh. "Look, Jeeza, I know how you feel about getting this close to the stalkers. It's not right to ask you to—"

"Alvaro, I don't like taking unnecessary chances,

but I'm part of the team. You start giving me special treatment and everyone else will resent me. Besides, if you start doing that for one person, how do you not do it for others?"

The thing about arguing with Jeeza is that you are very, very likely to lose. Because by the time she does decide to have a confrontation, she's thought out every angle and boiled it down to simple, inescapable truths.

This was one of those times. "Okay, Jeeza. Get your gear and up you go."

She nodded, looked up the one hundred thirty yards of slightly curving road to the point where it hung a sharp left and continued its ascent behind a solid wall of trees. "I'll get a double load of ammunition."

I nodded. "Better safe than sorry."

She nodded back and left. Which was a pretty terse exchange for usually expressive Jeeza, but I didn't take it amiss. If she had been angry at me, she wasn't any more: Jeeza's not that kind of person. No, she was steeling herself to being face-to-face with the infected in a way she hadn't been since she was perched, terrified, on top of the Range Rover at Ascension.

We finished our preparations by dismantling the semipermanent tin roof over the entry to the bar and pulling down the metal posts that had held it up. We didn't have any idea if the infected were good pole climbers, but we sure as hell didn't want to find out.

Tainara had finished lugging two jerricans up from the beached Zodiac. "What d'hell are dese?"

I took one, cocked my head toward the bar, and started walking. "I'll show you."

We stopped at the uphill side, where the slope hit the foundation a few feet higher than on the ocean side. I started uncapping my jerrican. She put hers down, and, hands on hips, frowned at the wall. "This wall—they gonna try an' jump up. Prolly won't make it."

I nodded. "Yeah, but no reason to take chances."

She nodded back. "So, what you gon' do? Sharp-like wire—?"

"Nope," I answered, handing her a long-handled broom. "Hold this."

She did, frowning as I tipped the jerrican so it poured out on the broom's fibers. The moment the black sludge oozed out, she smiled, eyes wide. "Yesss! That work good. Real good."

I hoped she was right. Because of its many uses, we always grabbed all the motor oil we got our hands on. But some was so old and thick and nasty that you wouldn't want to use it except to burn. Or in this case, to make the walls of the bar so slick that the stalkers couldn't get a hold of it, wouldn't somehow find some crack or crevice that would allow them to shinny up and get a hand on the roof.

When we were done, I handed another jerrican up toward Chloe. She raised one alluring eyebrow as she reached down. "To reapply," I explained, "in case so many try scrambling up that they wear the first coat away."

"An all-day slip-and-slide. Good thinking. We about ready?"

I nodded. "Weapons check?"

"Done. One of the AK mags is a little cranky. Might use some of this goop to help it along. Other than that, we're good to go."

"Okay. We'll get set in the surf and start the music as soon as we've done a comm check."

She rubbed the forestock of the .308 eagerly. "Good. I hate waiting."

I smiled. "Yes. I know that about you."

She grinned down at me, eyebrows descending into an evil vee. "Just remember that when we get back to the ship."

We started the music playing and waited. We were prepared for a longer lag time between the first chords that blasted out of the speakers and the first infected that showed up. At St. Anthony's Bay, the sound followed the smoothly rising land up to the eastern edge of Vila dos Remédios. But here, we were facing a sharp rise. The corner at the top of the slope was about sixty-five feet higher than the bar, and then rose up another forty or fifty feet beyond that. So the music was heading straight into a forested wall; the amount of sound that got over the rise and into Vila dos Remédios would be limited, at best. So every minute or so, Rod—now back on *Voyager* as the pilot—blew the ship's horns in the most annoying, ragged pattern he could.

It was over an hour before any stalkers showed up to check out our second party. Just a few, but these were fully alert. Either the walk down the switchback had awakened them or they hadn't been in torpor. Chloe, who had a full front angle on them from the moment they turned the corner, let them get to one hundred yards and brought them down with one shot apiece. We traded thumbs-ups.

Meanwhile, Prospero, Tainara, and I waited at the edge of the surf with our M4s and respective backup weapons in case of any "overflow" from the anticipated target zone. We were about one hundred twenty yards to the left of the bar, slightly offset to the rear: close enough to whittle away at any who got close, but able to get into the surf within seconds and to the bobbing Zodiac in about a minute. But it would be a bitch to get there in our protective gear, so withdrawal was really a last-ditch option. And if we did, it meant cruising back in closer with the Zodiac and accepting that we'd spend way too many rounds while on that pitching platform: first to clear the beach and then the area around the surrounded bar.

We'd also set up a drying rack with a live fish on at about the midway point. We hung a big bell on it, with the intent of being able to ping it with a round to shift the stalkers' attention to that free meal. We hadn't had much luck with that kind of distraction on Ascension Island, but we figured we'd give it one last try.

A quarter hour after Chloe dropped the first pair of stalkers, almost a dozen more showed up. Our "conops" (U.S. military shorthand for "concept of operations," which Prospero tries squeezing into every planning meeting) was to start thinning out large groups earlier. But that meant more and trickier work for Chloe. Not so much because of the engagement range—only one hundred thirty yards to the top of the slope—but because of a slight bulge in the foliage at the one-hundred-fifteen-yard mark. That could momentarily obscure targets, force her to waste time reacquiring them.

Fortunately, this bunch came down evenly distributed. So Chloe started with the unconcealed ones on the unobstructed right side of the road and worked over to the left as those came farther down and so, fully into view.

She had dropped eight by the time the rest reached

the twenty-yard mark, at which point she laid aside
the rifle and reached for her shotgun. By the time
she had trained it over the edge of the roof, though,
Steve had fired, pumped, fired, and was pumping again:
one down, one limping along on a compound fracture.
Jeeza just kept doing her job: scanning for new targets
as Steve and Chloe aimed the black muzzles of their
Rexios down into the scabrous, lesioned faces of the last
two screaming stalkers. Damn near decapitated them.

"Well, that worked well enough," Prospero muttered.

I nodded. It had. In fact, it had gone precisely according to plan. Which made me happy, relieved—and worried. Being raised Catholic has probably left me with
a superstitious side, because when anything works *too*
well—which is to say, just like you planned—I start
looking for the other shoe to drop.

After the first rush, there wasn't much excitement.
A smaller, second wave of eight; three managed to get
all the way down the hill. About two dozen more followed them over the next ten minutes. A lot of those
looked really gaunt and—no surprise—more than half
of them didn't press on to the bar; they stopped to
tear chunks out of the ones Chloe had already put
down. After she dropped the more determined ones
who kept charging down the road, she picked off the
others at an almost leisurely pace.

During this mostly uneventful process, there were
times when as many as three stalkers were active
around the base of the bar. That was the magic number we'd set as our cue to pour in some flanking fire.

To be honest, our per-round accuracy sucked. I
mean, it *really* sucked. We might have hit one time
in four. If that. But we had a lot of ammo and there

were three of us and Steve's shotgun was a lot closer and was much better at getting and holding their attention. Yeah, we were only plinking them with 5.56, but still, two or three always did the trick.

Until they came down in a single mass of at least a hundred.

We knew something was up when, despite all the shooting and the few straggling infected that swerved aside toward us, Cujo suddenly jumped up, stiff-legged. He let loose one of his long B-horror-movie howls, head so far back you'd have sworn he was trying to get a whiff of his own spine. Chloe tweaked to his Hound of the Baskervilles performance and paused; the only two remaining infected hadn't even come halfway down the slope.

That's when we heard it. For a moment, it was hard to separate the new sound from the surf—Mother Nature's version of white noise—but then it became distinct: a dim roaring.

I turned to Prospero. "You hear that?"

He swallowed, looking up the hill. "Sounds like a final game between Leeds and Manchester. Presuming the match was a mile away and they were tied one-all going into the last minute."

That was when the first of the stalkers rounded the corner at the top of the hill and the sound turned into one we were familiar with: the full-throated shrieks and yowls of a pack of infected. But we'd never heard so many screaming in such a concentrated pack. Yeah, we had heard plenty of them at the jetty, of course, but that volume had ebbed and flowed as those in front went into the water and new ones kept arriving at the back.

In this case, the sound hit our ears all at once, the volume growing as more of them came into view around the corner.

And damn, there were a lot of them. Couldn't even count them, at the time. They were packed so tightly that some were falling off either side of the raised roadbed. It was like a scene out of one of those sword-and-sandal epics or Russian Revolution docudramas where a charging mob fills the street so you can't even see the ground.

Tainara glanced up at them and then over at me. "Never heard you curse, *chefe.*"

I blinked. "I cursed?" I wasn't even aware I had spoken.

"Yeh—unless *coño* don't mean what it used to in Spanish."

Well, so much for the strong-and-silent command image. "Prospero, how many?"

"Too many," he muttered, shouldering his M4.

Tainara's fingers were tight around her own weapon's forestock. "You think mebbe it time for your guys on the roof to leave?"

It might have been, but—"No time, now. That mob will be here before they can get down and into the deep water." These stalkers were really moving, even though a lot of them were really, *really* gaunt. Like walking cadavers. *What? Reserve energy for a last-ditch attempt to get food?* I snapped the M4 off safety.

"You want we should start now?" Tainara's voice wasn't exactly shaky but had a deep buzz, like a steel wire about to break.

"No." Prospero was sighting in at the base of the bar. "If we engage now, too many of the buggers will swerve toward us too soon. The bar is flypaper; we want them to mob up there, give us an easy target. We will inflict more casualties more rapidly."

"Yah," she countered, her voice still tense, "you hope."

Chloe, meanwhile, had been keeping up a trip-hammer pace with the bolt-action. It looked like almost every shot dropped one, but that was like snatching individual raindrops out of a downpour. I saw her put the weapon aside. Jeeza started loading it, but Chloe went for her FAL and shook her head. No point to reloading. "Alvaro..." she muttered over the tactical channel.

"On it. Prospero. Shift to a FAL."

"Twenty-round magazine, Alvaro. It means reloading more freq—"

"Doesn't matter. We need one-shot kills. Tai"—I'd never used a nickname for Tainara, but right then, there was no time for all the syllables—"if I change to my AK, you take a few more shots and change to your Rexio."

"I—uh—?"

"Tai: repeat what I told you."

She sounded annoyed—and more clear-headed. "When you go to AK, I shoot a few times, then go to shotgun."

"Good." The first infected that managed to get through Chloe's semiautomatic torrent from the FAL fire leaped as high as he could, almost got his hands on the edge of the roof—but then slid off to the side, shrieking in shocked outrage.

"Slip and slide, you bastards!" Chloe yelled, ramming another magazine into her FAL while Steve fired into the bounding mob with his Rexio and Jeeza popped off a stream of 9mm from her Brazilian M9 that sounded almost as fast as autofire.

But that didn't even cause a ripple in the wave of bodies now about to hit the bar. For a split second, I had a nightmare vision of the entire structure being carried away by the sheer weight of that howling pack, then dismissed it as a panicked delusion. Which I knew it to be. *Knew* it. Almost.

Fortunately, Chloe and her team kept the rate of fire high enough, and kept it on the close approaches to the wall. Survivors were accumulating just a little faster than the rate at which the nearest ones were being killed. But the central bulge of the mob had just charged past the twenty-yard marker—

"Hit that wave!" I shouted at Prospero and Tai. "Now!"

It wasn't where we had planned to aim, wasn't like anything we had practiced. But we'd set range markers all along the road, and had a more massive target than we ever imagined.

I could barely hear my M4 over the hammering of Prospero's FAL. The need to inflict as many casualties as quickly as possible meant our "aiming" wasn't much more than recovering from the recoil, getting our weapons re-centered on the mass of stalkers, firing, recovering again. As fast as we could.

There was no time to assess the effects, watch ammunition expenditure, or consider shifting our point of fire. Maybe if we'd been The Captain, we could have done all those things simultaneously. But we were self-taught and we hadn't prepared for this eventuality.

So of course, the three of us shot ourselves dry at the same time.

Shit! So very not good. "Tai, go to your Rexio," I ordered as I backslung the M4 and wrestled the AK around on its sling. "Prospero, reload."

"The FAL?"

Really? You have to ask? "Yes. Now. Keep hitting them around the bar as soon as you're ready. We'll cover you."

At which point I saw the back half of the big wave of infected hit the bar. From a hundred-fifteen yards away, I could *still* hear a sound like fifty NFL linesmen trying to body-block a brick wall. Dust went up. So did furious and agonized yowls. I was ready to puke because I half-expected to see the bar list and collapse. Yet, when the dust cleared, it was still there.

But for some reason, these new stalkers were apparently able to jump higher than the others. Chloe, Jeeza, and Steve were backing away from the edge of the roof to stay clear of their raking, grasping fingers. So they had no way to safely apply a second coat of oil. Which meant that it was only a matter of time before these super-jumping stalkers got on the roof.

Right as the terror of that thought made my face hot and my hands cold, I also noticed that, weirdly, although the bar hadn't fallen over, it had sunk into the ground. Which made no sense...

Until I looked more closely: "Shit! The bodies!"

"What?" said Prospero.

"Huh?" screamed Chloe over the background soundtrack of their Rexios.

I didn't have time to explain, I only had time to give orders. "Prospero, shift your fire away from the bar."

"Wha—?"

"The pile of bodies: it's becoming a ramp."

"*Filho da puta!*" Tai shouted. "Li'l *chefe* is right! The bastards get running starts, now!" Head down over the Rexio, she drew a bead.

"No, Tai. You cover me."

She looked like she wanted to spit. "From what?"

"From them." I took a step forward and raised the AK.

Since Prospero was now hitting infected that had not yet reached the bar, we were finally being noticed by some that still hadn't entered the single-minded kill frenzy that comes over them when they lock in on a target. So the ones he didn't kill looked around to see why their pals were dying. And saw us. Half a dozen broke off and charged in our direction.

"We so *fodido!*" Tai shouted as she shifted her aim.

"You engage at twenty yards," I shouted at her as I brought up the AK and snapped down the huge safety. It was already set to full auto.

The first was in my sights. I grazed the trigger. Of the three or four rounds, one clipped and slowed her. Good enough; move on. The next went down. I wasted damn close to half a mag on the third, which stumbled out of my sight picture.

Three left. Seventy yards and they were fast. I hoped I had enough rounds because I had no time to swap mags.

I switched to semiautomatic and burned three rounds to hit the closest. I shifted but shot early because I was eager and anxious. Damn. Another two rounds and down went the second. Leaving one. At only twenty yards. "Tai?"

Tai had just finished off one of the first three with enough double-aught to the gut that you might have been able to see daylight. She swung her weapon slightly, pumped two rounds at the second wounded one at ten yards' range. One pattern hit, reducing its left arm to bloody tatters, but it was still coming. I shifted the AK to double-tap it.

The good news was that I hit it square in the sternum with the first round. The bad news was that the second squeeze of the trigger only produced a dry *klik*. Shit.

I dropped the AK on its sling, grabbed after my Browning, saw that the stalker was down—and was hit by a battering ram: the limper that had fallen out of my sights earlier.

I hit the sand hard and my breath whooshed out of me. I was aware of only one thing: the impact unseated my fire-mask right as the once-human monster leaped on me, clawing at my face. I got my hands up, one to block, the other to grab its neck and hold it back as long as I—

"Hands down!" Tai screamed.

I pulled my hands back; the distended gargoyle-fanged mouth pitched down—

—but disappeared before it had descended another inch. Blood sprayed, mostly to the left of me as the body fell away. Tai stood over me, one of the flensing tools in her hand. "Bes' machete *ever!*" she shouted.

I scrambled to my feet, scanning. I could hardly breathe.

Prospero had swung his FAL toward us, but had checked fire; smart, since by the time he came to bear we were clustered up. Odds were he would have hit one of us, not the stalker. He resumed firing at the stalkers up the beach, but at a faster tempo; more of them had broken away from the bar to charge at us.

The situation around the building itself was not as bad as I'd feared. Steve and Chloe had shifted their fire to those that were at least ten yards off, with Jeeza bringing her machete down on any fingers or hands that managed to get hold of the roof's edge. Chloe caught sight of me; I heard her shriek a panicked curse, saw her grab toward the bolt-action.

"No," I wheezed into the radio, "maintain local security. We're fine."

"The hell you are!" she yelled without resorting to her radio.

"Maintain local security," I repeated into my headset's mic. Right before I swayed and almost fell over.

Look: I'm not a big guy. Yeah, the stalker that tackled me was pretty gaunt, but he was also about six feet tall. Still a lot of mass. And anyone who tells you that sand is soft has obviously never been wholebody slammed down into it. So I was dazed and was barely moving air into and out of my body.

Tai had reloaded her Rexio. "*Chefe*? You okay?"

I waved off the question. I picked up the AK, pulled the mag, and grabbed at the closest pouch on my web gear. I was going as fast as I could, but I felt like I was moving at the bottom of a vat of cold syrup.

Prospero was changing mags, too. And the leading edge of the next, more dispersed gang of infected was now only forty yards off. If that.

I got the magazine in, did not switch back to auto, but took a knee. I slowly let out what little air I had in my lungs as the first charging outline rose into those really nice AK sights.

I squeezed the trigger, recovered, squeezed again.

The figure had disappeared; whether dead or incapacitated, I didn't know and I didn't stop to find out. Taking care of those was part of Tai's job: close security. Without having to fully take my eyes off the sight picture—because the AK's almost-ring-sight has a break in the top that allows you to scan around a bit—I found and swung the muzzle to the next stalker in my firing lane. Three rounds until she went down. I peeped over the sights: they were closing faster than Prospero and I were taking down the leaders.

I mentally marked the four closest, snugged my cheek down, and started in on fast semiautomatic fire. I had only dropped three when the trigger clicked dry, but this time, Tai didn't even have to rush. She took that one down with her Rexio as I changed mags again.

As I did, I saw that there were fewer infected following this bunch than I had originally estimated. In the very next moment, I learned why: I heard the distinctive bark of Chloe's bolt-action, realized it had been banging away in the background for almost half a minute. I grabbed at the radio, toggled the send—

"Don't even," Chloe growled before I could speak (well, wheeze). "If you're done wrestling with zombies for a few moments, check out our position."

I did. It was no longer surrounded by a mob. Between her team's constant hammering at the ones beyond ten yards and those we'd pulled toward us, you could actually see daylight between the bodies in that reduced crowd. I wasn't about to assume that Chloe, Steve, and Jeeza were safe, but they were no longer in immediate danger, either.

"Okay," I allowed. "Thanks for the help."

"Yeah. Remember that, too, lover." I could hear the smile in her voice. Just as the open channel *snicked* off and the bolt-action cracked again.

And again and again.

November 24

We were still pretty shaken when we got back from Wizard's Tower Three or, as Rod called it (and the name stuck) Almost the Alamo.

Part of that was because of how many things went sideways. There was the obvious stuff: the sudden, big wave of stalkers that made a mess of our plans; how they almost managed to crawl up their own dead to get to Chloe's roof team; my protective gear coming loose. But what I think really spooked us was how many of those near-disasters were the result of things we just didn't know, or guessed wrong, about the infected. From little stuff all the way up to macro-scale mysteries.

For example, when things got hairy on the beach, why the hell did the wounded stalker come after and tackle *me*? *How* he did it was mystery enough; that second, much-vented limper somehow accelerated into a double-overdrive sprint, even though infected never seem to hold *anything* in reserve.

But stranger still, he had not just been closer to Tai than to me; he came rolling in from way out on her flank. So why the hell did he totally ignore her and cross to leap on *me*? Don't know. What I do know is that if Tai hadn't been quick and accurate with her machete, I wouldn't be writing this now. I'd be dead or waiting to see if I turned, with all my adopted family pointing guns at me. As it is, when the stalker was beheaded, the spray of blood mostly arced over and past me; I got only two drops on my facemask and a thin spatter along the left sleeve of my fireman's coat. The protection had done its job, even though I screwed up at doing mine.

Then there was the large-scale mystery: how and why such a large mob of the infected came at us in that one big wave. We know they come in numbers. We know that when they start getting excited, they work each other up and start moving in packs. But how did these gaunt, recently torpid stalkers get roused and riled all at one time and in one place? Because they sure as hell didn't meet up at the town square to get organized before they came rolling down that hill.

Had the St. Anthony's Bay Massacre awakened all these stalkers too late for them to shake off the torpor and join the fun? Or did the infected share some weird hoodoo, like animals whose individual behavior changes when their group takes heavy losses—even if they are not present to see those losses occur?

Yeah, I know: all pointless wondering, since we had no way of figuring out which, if any, of our theories might be right. But it was a way to pass the time, from the moment we started scooping up whatever spent brass we could find. After that, we used what was left of the slip-n-slide motor oil sludge to start the bodies burning. And the gabbing and theorizing grew more lively as we did.

It was a mental health reflex, I think. Specifically,

people who survive a sudden life-threatening crisis will jaw about anything—*anything*—to distract themselves from aftershocks of panic and fear as their brains struggle to get distance from the incident.

By the time we sailed back to Ilha Rata, washed up, and sat down to eat, we had ridden that hyper, post-action sine wave down to inward-focused silence. I can't even tell you what we ate or what few still-born conversations sparked and faded while we were huddled around the commons' table. Only when the carbs came out—lightly sweetened tapioca—did we reanimate, mostly because we had to figure out what to do the next day.

The infected body count had been well over two hundred. So, according to everything we had ever observed about them, there should have been no more than one or two hundred remaining on FdN. Maybe three hundred, since, clearly, we still didn't have a solid understanding of how much prey had been available, how soon a shortage triggered torpor, and just how much (or little) of their reserves they lost while semi-hibernating.

In the end, we decided that we needed another look at the bar and the area around it before making any firm plans. So the next day, we rolled out of our bunks and readied our gear as Rod steered us back to Ilha da Conceição, giving Tai some basic sailing lessons while he was at it.

Once there, we dropped anchor and broke out the telescope and binoculars. The smoke from the fire—heavy, greasy, black—showed us that the core of yesterday's makeshift pyre was still flickering. The bar was intact but covered in soot, the back wall a solid mass of black. No chance that we could use it the same way today.

But it was obvious we didn't need to: dozens of new infected had come down to gorge themselves on their own dead. And I mean gorge: their bellies were distended, and their staggering progress was not the result of torpor but front-heavy guts. Chloe glanced over at Ilha da Conceição's upper reaches; it was high tide, so the steep-sided knife of rock was separated from the mainland by about thirty yards of water. "Is there a way up there?"

Rod nodded back at her. "Yeah. Spotted a few paths leading up to shelves overlooking the beaches."

"Can we get close enough?"

Prospero squinted, pointed at its flinty, northern-most skirts. "There are tidal pools around the base. More than sufficient for the Zodiac. And paths from them wind upward."

Chloe nodded. "Good. Time to go hunting."

There is no way to turn a turkey shoot into an interesting story. Particularly when the turkeys don't have enough sense to run away.

After Zodiac-ing in to where she and her team could get on Ilha da Conceição's paths, Chloe, Jeeza, and Steve ascended to a safer, more distant, version of the Wizard's Tower. From there, the range to the bar was almost exactly two hundred yards. So Chloe settled into a likely sniper's perch, Jeeza set up to spot for her, and Steve got out his shotgun, just in case the stalkers had learned how to swim. Or fly.

Chloe missed the first two shots, but after that was zeroed in; the wind speed and direction were both pretty steady. The infected began to fall over, about one every twenty seconds. Chloe wasn't in any rush.

About half of them required a second shot. Some got agitated and stormed down to the edge of the water, yowling up at the three distant figures on one of Ilha da Conceição's highest rock-shelves.

The gunfire did attract a few more of them, but by one o'clock, Chloe was out of targets. Forty-two infected had joined the corpses of the others. At three p.m., we decided that it wasn't worth waiting any longer, so we sailed back for Ilha Rata.

We brooded over all the maps of FdN as we picked at our dinners. Probably because we all knew what was coming next, and none of us liked it.

Chloe stood, her palm circling over the northern end of the biggest map we had. "We killed at least six hundred sixty or six hundred seventy in the past four days. Almost all of them must have come from around here." She drifted a finger over to the cluster of buildings that was labeled Vila dos Remédios. It was the third corner of the island's most populated triangle, the other two vertices being St. Anthony's Bay and Ilha da Conceição. "It's hard to imagine how any could be left snoozing up there."

"Unless," Prospero mused, "some are so torpid that they start out too weak to even move. They might not have been fully awake until all the noise, and killing, was over."

Jeeza shuddered. "And so could now be waiting to jump at us from any closet or back room in the whole damn town."

"Or," offered Rod calmly, "the others may be scattered throughout the outlying houses and pousadas. Or down at the airport and the housing attached to it."

"Or all of the above," I added. "And let's not forget

that we've seen that some of them avoid contact. And that there are probably other scenarios we haven't even imagined yet. But if we take what we saw on Ascension Island as a crude model, there can't be that many left. Four months ago, FdN was thirty days post-plague. The casualty rate that most communities reported at that point on their own infection timeline is pretty consistent. On FdN, that would mean about one-thousand-eight-hundred people left. For a while, the infected would have hunted. When they ran out of prey, some of them would probably turn on each other. That's probably when the first start going into torpor. But how many would be left by then?"

Prospero studied the map with narrowed eyes. "That depends upon how early most of them reach the inflection point that triggers the transition." He frowned. "If it takes even a month for them to start becoming torpid, the remaining population would have already been heavily reduced by preying on each other."

Rod nodded. "I just wish we knew if the ones that remain awake sniff out and chow down on the hibernators."

Tai frowned. "Prolly when they hung'ry 'nuff." She shrugged. "But who know when that is?"

"Not us," Steve said, staring at the maps.

I crossed my arms. "We could try playing the music again tomorrow. See if it brings down any who woke up toward the end of today's activity."

"Worth a try," agreed Jeeza eagerly. Then she sighed. "But let's put a name to the growing elephant in the room: house-to-house clearance."

I was grateful it was Jeeza, of all people, who gave a label to what we were all dreading. She's never made peace with the career that fate has forced upon us: exterminators of ex-human beings. So for her to be the one to bring up the inevitable next step—aggressively rooting out any that remained—took a lot of guts. I nodded. "Yeah. After tomorrow, I think we've got to go for it."

Chloe leaned over the map. I tried not to get distracted by what that change in position did to the outline of her body.

"Alvaro?" she asked.

"Um . . . yeah?"

"Any thoughts?"

I had plenty, none suitable for sharing in public.

She stared at my silence. "You know, on how we handle CQC?"

I had used that abbreviation for "close-quarters combat" so much that she had picked it up, too. It was also an ironic question, since Chloe knew I had been worrying/obsessing about shifting into those operations ever since we'd returned to FdN. "A few," I admitted.

Prospero grinned. "I will just bet you have." He leaned forward.

I shook my head. "For now, let's just focus on tomorrow."

After three hours, I gave Steve a break and took his role as security for the sniper team.

Two hours after that, Chloe hung her head and glanced over at me. "Can we go *now*?" She sounded like a little kid being dragged around a museum full of stuffy old paintings.

I looked back at the bar and the bodies littered around it. Today, the only visitors had been birds.

Gulls, mostly. I knew they ate carrion, but wasn't aware that included dead human. Maybe it hadn't in times past, but now I guess it was too frequent a source of protein for them to ignore.

"Alvaro. Please. Can we go now?"

Jeeza sighed. "She's right, Alvaro. They're done coming to us. Now, we have to go to them."

I sighed, too. "Okay," I said. "Let's pack it up. Time to make a new plan."

November 25

This time, when we heard the sand hiss under the semirigid hull of our Zodiac, it didn't feel like we were returning to Praia do Cachorro. It felt more like we were landing at Normandy.

No, we were not under fire, but this day, death felt much closer than it had since the first time we actually took the fight to the stalkers, back on Ascension Island. Because like that day, we were sharply aware how much we did not know about our enemy.

I jumped over the Zodiac's side, snagged the nearest grab-line and started hauling the boat higher up on the beach. I heard the others jump into the water behind me. We weren't trying to be stealthy, exactly, but we kept talk quiet and to a minimum. Today was the opposite of our typical modus operandi, where we wanted the stalkers to know where we were and come running. This was our first day playing on their turf. So, particularly during first hours, we needed to be as silent and invisible as possible.

As it was, people weren't making a lot of noise because they were just plain grumpy. Well, I guess "sullen" is the right word—although I'm not sure I've ever used it before. But yeah; they were sullen. Because they weren't happy with the plan. Which was not the same thing as thinking it was a bad plan or that they had a better one: they just weren't happy with it.

Today was going to be all about speed and endurance. Whoever was first up the road into the northern part of Vila dos Remédios had to be ready—and able—to run all the way back without stopping. And the more of us that went, the more likely we were to alert any nearby stalkers. So it was me, Tai, Steve. No one else, not for the first recon.

The bitching when I announced that roster last night was epic. It was also expected. I just folded my arms and let it run its course. Other than Tai and Steve, the only one who didn't join in the gripe-fest was Prospero. He just glanced at me, sighed, nodded, and leaned back to wait it out.

When Rod, Jeeza, and Chloe were done, I explained the selection criteria. They shut right up; none of them were anything vaguely like track stars. Frankly, neither was I, but one of my nicknames growing up was Energizer Bunny. And it wasn't because I was small (which I was) or white and pink (which I wasn't).

I filled in the rest. Tai read and spoke Portuguese: the language on every sign we were going to run into. Also, on the wildly unlikely chance that we encountered survivors, we needed her as a translator. Lastly, Tai—the lady who was supposedly on the fence about joining us—was now unwilling to stay on the bench. Fine by me; that was movement in the right direction.

Steve was fit, cool in a crisis, and an increasingly good shot, particularly with shotguns and pistols. Which we knew we might wind up using a lot: given the short sight ranges and blind corners, fast, levelheaded proficiency with close-range weapons was key.

And, in addition to being the crown idiot who had come up with a plan that put my own head in the tightest possible noose, I have a skill that could prove crucial: I know how to hot-wire cars. Yeah, that's right—even though I don't drive. And that's all I'm saying about it. Some shit you take to your grave, apocalypse notwithstanding.

There was one other reason I was going, one I didn't mention. I wasn't about to send anyone into danger that I wouldn't face myself. Which had originally scared me. A lot. But not anymore. See, once you've done it, and once you accept that being the leader means it's just part of your job, you get kind of fatalistic about it. Hell, it's not like you can chew your nails, torn between hoping you won't have to go and hating what it meant: that you would let your friends get killed in your place. Because in a small group like ours, the leader can rest assured of one thing: if anyone's going into the shit, he or she is leading the way.

Everyone was a little surprised that I had chosen Praia do Cachorro as our landing point. Frankly, I hadn't been leaning that way initially. From the first, I knew that hot-wiring a car would mean lugging around one of the charging batteries we got from Ascension. My mind's eye saw only one acceptable way of doing that: marching up the straight, well-paved road that rose from St. Anthony's Bay to the town.

Except, as it turned out, that road didn't really go straight into Vila dos Remédios. Digging into the maps revealed that the small cluster of buildings at the top of the slope wasn't really part of Vila dos Remédios. It was a kind of subtown: a dozen houses dispersed along a crooked route.

In other words, the straight road was actually less direct and, if we had to haul ass out of there, was far more dangerous. Too many buildings to check and clear, particularly since this first step was to be recon, not engagement. So, even though the road up from Praia do Cachorro was a steep switchback, it would put us right on the outskirts of town. If we could control the bend, and then the crest, we'd be able to enter the town and (hopefully) find a functional car without having to worry about getting cut off from a secure route of retreat.

Although the bitching had quieted by this morning, the "sullen" was still there, even as we beached the Zodiac and started checking gear.

Prospero was fussing over Steve's radio. "I want a radio check every five minutes."

Steve just stared at him. "Yes, mother."

Chloe looked devilish. "So, Steve, does that make you a mother-fu—?"

"Chloe!" exclaimed Jeeza.

"Jeeza!" Chloe facetiously exclaimed right back at her.

"Okay, okay," I interrupted. At least they were smiling. "Heads in the game now, guys. Prospero, you're in charge of comms."

"Yeh, and stuck back here, wanking off," he grumbled. But he knew why I put him there; although he didn't have much training at small unit ops, he had a shit-ton more than the rest of us put together. So coordinating between multiple maneuver elements while keeping the comm chatter down to a minimum was one of his specialties. And if we ran into trouble, he was the de facto XO.

Rod was with him, hand on Cujo's collar, M4 slung.

"Keep him quiet until we need him," I reminded him, nodding toward the grinning dog.

"Easier said than done," Rod groused.

"Yeah, and a lot easier down here on the beach," I countered. Cujo was with us for two reasons. First, if any stalkers had wandered down close to the shore overnight and awoke, Cujo would be the early warning system. Secondly, if anything went wrong, he was another asset. None of us wanted to put him in combat, but if our lives were on the line, it was all hands—and paws—on deck.

I nodded at Jeeza and Chloe. As soon as they had risen to follow, I started humping my load away from the surf. Lemme tell you, carrying a recharger for car batteries is no fun. Doing it through sand is worse.

We moved up the hill, the others with their weapons in an assault carry: something else Prospero had taught us. Two hundred yards up, the road turned sharply left behind low trees. We stopped while Chloe and Jeeza set up in the brush by the side of the road and radioed Prospero that waypoint one had been secured. Now, if we retreated—well, routed—back down the switchback from the northern edge of town, they'd be in a position to clip any stalkers chasing us. Presuming we remembered to stick to the far right side of the road so that they had a clear angle on the pursuit. Once they were concealed and set, Steve, Tai, and I continued upward.

Three hundred and fifty yards uphill in a fireman's coat and SCBA mask, carrying a full load of ammo and that damn recharger, is not my idea of daybreak fun. Even though we don't seal our masks, they totally mess up situational awareness. The saving grace was that the shore down to our left had been cleared, the slope to our right was more like a cliff, and we had Chloe covering us from the rear. So we could live with the limited vision through the masks so long as we kept it focused on the crest of the hill.

Which we reached safely. We drifted into the bushes where the road leveled off, and scoped out the town square. Although this was Vila dos Remédios' northernmost part, it was also the Old Town. The ancient mission-style church and governor's palace had made it tourist central. So it seemed logical that there would be a lot of cars there, but—

"So where the hell are the cars?" muttered Steve.

Even Tai was surprised at first, but then nodded. "People prolly stayed home when the sick started. Wait for it to pass." If true, that was some top-shelf irony.

Steve raised his Rexio slightly. "So whadda we do?"

I thought for a moment. "Change the order of objectives."

He nodded. "So, first the roof of the bank, then the car?"

I nodded back. "Right. We'll need that better view to spot a promising ride." I laid my finger closer to my M4's safety. "Ready?" They nodded. "Then let's go."

It was fifty yards from the lip of the hill to the bank. One story, better construction than most of the local buildings. We'd seen a picture of it in one of the guidebooks, probably because it was the only bank on the whole damn island. We sprinted toward it, Steve slightly in the lead.

He charged up its front walkway, where the edge of the roof was closest. He threw his back against the wall, crouched, braced, put his hands together as a stirrup for me.

I stopped alongside him, dropped everything except my M4 and the coiled Jacob's ladder that Tai looped around my shoulder. "Ready?" I asked. Steve nodded. I put my right foot in his linked palms and hopped up as he boosted me.

The gloves we got from Ascension saved my fingers from getting ripped to shreds; it was a metal roof and the edges had become pretty rough. But, using a fish hook in my left hand, I got a firm hold and clambered up. "Any sign of stalkers?" I asked in a very loud whisper.

Tai's voice was a little louder. "Not yet."

I got another hook under the shingles and around one of the bolts or nails or whatever held it in place, attached the Jacob's ladder, and rolled it down over the edge. They handed up my gear, the heavier parts of their own (mostly spare ammo), and climbed. I don't think any of us drew a full breath until we were all crouching on that roof.

While Steve called in our first radio check, Tai and I scanned the areas around and beyond the Old Town square for cars. She spotted one almost fifty yards up a street that led to the higher, more modern part of Vila dos Remédios. "Shit," she said. She'd adopted the English word. "Dass kinda far, *chefe*."

I gritted my teeth, made sure my voice was controlled before I continued. "Yeah, we might have to bring Chloe and Jeeza up here. To cover us from this roof when we try for it."

Steve, done with the radio check, leaned over to look at the car. "I don't know, Alvaro. Lots of places you can't see from up here."

I shrugged, trying to act like it was all in a day's work. "Yeah, but that works two ways. And having some cover on the approach is better than none." Which was true, but also not very reassuring. Which he and I both knew.

But Tai was frowning again. She rose to a squat and side-stepped farther up the slope of the roof.

"Where are you going?" I hissed.

She glanced over the peak of the roof, then laughed. It was just a low chortle, but at that moment, it seemed loud enough to wake the dead. Or the plague's equivalent.

"What's so funny?" Steve muttered.

She shook her head; suppressing laughter, she pointed behind the bank. We crept up next to her, peeked over the top of the roof...

And found ourselves looking down on about half a dozen cars parked in front of the small houses that had been built behind it.

She smiled. "Sorry. Forgot about this li'l neighborhood, *chefe*. Never walked back here much."

Steve nodded. Despite his poker face, he looked pretty relieved.

"And that," I murmured to no one in particular, "is why you always bring a local."

Even though these cars were pretty close to us, I still decided to get Chloe and Jeeza up on the roof of the bank before we got down on the ground again. So we covered their approach up the hill and then, when they'd set up, climbed down to survey the vehicles. Frankly, even if none of the cars started, some of the local dune-buggy knock-offs were light enough that we could push one an inch or two beyond the crest and keep it there with a quick haul on the hand brake. Then, if we needed a quick get-away, we'd just pop the brake and trust to gravity.

But nothing ever works the way you expect. After rejecting the first two cars (one had two flat tires, the other had been torched), we discovered a third that was not only intact, but, after a couple of tries, started responding to the charger.

But so did a stalker that had been snoozing nearby. He came out of the closest house in a rush—fast but stumbling—and Steve, who was our local overwatch, fired at him: a miss. Steve pump-fired another load of buck, which caught him in the lower leg.

The stalker stumbled but kept pushing on—but in an attempt to get *past* us.

"Down!" Chloe screamed, so loud that she drowned out her own voice coming from the radio.

We dove. The bolt-action cracked. The stalker fell headlong. We got up on the vehicle—it was a pickup truck with an empty cargo bed—and each took one hundred and twenty degrees of coverage, hunching over our sights as a dark red stain spread like wings on the back of the stalker.

We waited a full minute. No sound, no movement. Hell, not even any birds.

I toggled the radio. "Jeeza?"

"No sign of movement anywhere, Alvaro. Out to the limit of visibility."

"Then I'll call it clear," I said. "Jeeza, report the contact to Prospero."

"Already did."

I toggled off, hopped down, went toward the face-down stalker.

"*Chefe*—" Tai began.

I waved away her worry, although I was glad to hear it. She had become one of us even faster than I had suspected she might. I examined the body as best I could. "Really gaunt," I reported.

"Makes sense, if he was a passive," Steve offered with a shrug.

I nodded. "Yeah. He wouldn't have joined the ones who showed up at the Massacre or the Alamo. Maybe he was too weak to even go down to the beach and feed on the corpses."

Tai spat. "Don' matter. He dead. So he good, now."

I nodded. "We can't assume that we'll see any more like him up here. But we shouldn't be surprised by it either. And as far as I can recall, none of the passives on Ascension ever holed up together. They were always solo."

Steve nodded. "That's right." He looked at the car. "Think you can get that engine to turn over?"

I shrugged. "Let's find out."

We got the car running. Then, with Chloe and Jeeza on overwatch, we swept the buildings that faced the square. Nobody home. No one alive, that is.

What we'd seen three weeks ago, down south at the pousadas near Baia Sueste, was both more and less disturbing than this. That had been more disturbing because a lot of those corpses were still mostly intact. But here in town, it was the sheer number of bodies that was staggering. And most were so torn to pieces that it was hard to get an accurate count. Every bone had been damn near stripped clean. Limbs and even heads had been removed. In many cases, the marrow had been sucked out. And we encountered a lot of very small spines and skulls in that gruesome mix.

So with the immediate surroundings cleared, we took the risk of bringing Rod and Prospero up the hill while we got siphons going to drain the tanks of other vehicles. We left the pickup's engine running— as ragged as it was—for two reasons: to recharge the battery and to keep the truck ready for a quick extraction back down the hill.

While we were doing that, Jeeza spotted a stumbler way up on the high ground behind the governor's palace: about one hundred twenty yards away. It didn't seem to know we were there, and it moved furtively: almost surely another passive. But passive or not, it was infected and required extermination. One bark from Chloe's .308 and the stumbler collapsed. It didn't move again.

With the truck fueled and idling and Prospero at the wheel and manning the radio, Rod and Cujo joined us at the governor's palace while Jeeza and Chloe remained in overwatch. The palace is essentially a three-story structure, built on a big concrete platform that is partially dug back into the slope. Its roof was the highest point for almost two hundred yards in every direction, making it the next sniper's perch for covering our staged advance into Vila dos Remédios. We checked our gear, particularly where we had used tape to seal seams and hold crucial items in place, and then crept up the palace's long front staircase. When we got to the door, Cujo started growling—but like he was disturbed, rather than alarmed.

So when we pushed through the partially open door—Tai going high and me going low (because I do start a lot closer to the floor)—none of us were surprised to find ourselves ankle-deep in stalker spoor. Yes, I do mean shit, but not just that. Hair, old clothes, gnawed bones, bits of furniture and even plaster: the infected were pretty tough on housing.

We made sure our masks were tight and moved inside. Cujo became bored, rather than more agitated.

"I bet a lot of the ones that came to our party came from here," Rod said quietly.

"I'll bet you're right," I agreed. "Let's finish the sweep."

Physically, it was a pretty easy job. The rooms were big but few in number and the stairs wide with good visibility. We didn't like being in a plague house, so we got to the roof, let down a Jacob's ladder to the second-story veranda, and signaled the all clear.

Once Jeeza and Chloe had climbed up and Cujo joined our entry team, we were able to move more quickly. Both times that there was a live stalker in a building, Cujo tweaked to the scent at least ten yards before we got there. Maybe he smelled a fresh trail they'd left or just heard them snoring. Who knows? All I know is that we flushed each of them out with a rock through the window—which brought them right out into our field of fire.

Even so, it was a long, sweaty day, both because we were suited and sealed on an equatorial island and because—even with Cujo and our overwatch—house-to-house sweeps are more nerve-wracking than anything else I have ever done or imagined. It never becomes a routine. Sure: you eventually fall into a kind of rhythm of tactics and movement, but you never get used to the uncertainty, to the ever-present fear that the next door, the next corner, could be the one where stalkers leap out at you. And if you ever got *past* the point of fearing that every single time, then it would be time to stop. Because any time could be *that* time—and if you get complacent, you'll get dead.

At two in the afternoon, we reversed our advance, canvassing each secured building for useful salvage, spray painting it with an "X" if it had any, and sprinkling powdered chalk at each point of ingress. That was the only way to see if anything went back in after we left. Not perfect, but these days, what is?

Once we got back to *Voyager*, all of us took long showers. We really needed them. But particularly the entry team: we were rank with tropically cooked fear-sweat. I wasn't sure that any amount of washing would get the stink out of our clothes, though.

Over dinner, we discussed—with almost disturbing calmness—how we'd do the same thing the next day. And how, as we moved deeper into Vila dos Remédios, we'd move Chloe's overwatch site from one water tower/cistern to the next. We'd located enough of them that we pretty much had a route of covered advance through almost the entire downtown—such as it is. The remaining cluster of buildings is the most dense and follows along only three roads, each of which is about four hundred yards long. We figured, based on today's progress, that we could knock off one of those streets every day, assuming we didn't run into anything too crazy. The truck would follow the entry team at about one hundred yards, so we would never have far to run in case we had to get the hell out of Dodge. We congratulated each other on a job well done, expressed confidence in the new plans, and assured ourselves that tomorrow was going to be a piece of cake.

Which no one believed for one skinny second.

November 28

If there's a constant in this postapocalyptic world, it's this: the moment you think everything is going just fine, it goes to shit. And never in the way you expect.

So yesterday, the second day of clearing, went just as we planned. A few more passives, then three stalkers that Cujo smelled fifty yards away. We just let him bark. They came racing out—so emaciated that it was hard to believe they were actually alive—and straight into our guns. I think one got to within twenty yards of us; she was small and fast and took four rounds to put down. We found utility and town survey maps in the glove compartment of a public works pickup truck, and now had a precise bird's-eye assessment of every street and every building. We were feeling pretty pleased with ourselves.

Today started the same way. By noon, we'd cleared most of the more developed part of the town center. After that, it was either a branch of the main road going east or the one going west. We headed west because we were considering landing at St. Anthony's Bay tomorrow and rolling up the east branch of the main road from that side. Hell, we were already making plans for how to handle the airport, now that we had real maps.

But as we headed west, we started realizing that, as Tai put it, we were now "in Brazil for real." Which meant that we started seeing buildings that weren't on the maps, a lot of which were pretty sketchy structures. If one in three were built to code, I'd give up my carb ration for a week.

End result: things slowed *way* down. It wasn't as bad as the first day, though. With Chloe and Jeeza on water towers, we were usually able to compensate for what the maps didn't show. But not always, and that uncertainty is what eats up extra minutes and makes them extra sweaty.

So we were always a little relieved when we were going into one of the buildings that was not only on the map, but faced right on the street. That may have been what had us a little less ready for the unexpected.

Cujo didn't make any sound until the door opened. Then he yipped like he'd stepped on a tack and started growling, hair standing straight up all along his spine. That had never happened before, so we defaulted into a defensive wedge, me in the front and low, Steve and Tai behind and to either side of the doorway.

Nothing. Cujo was still growling but sniffing high in the air, from side to side, as if he was confused.

Then he lunged to the left.

As Rod hauled him back in, all of us—like dopes—aimed left.

But the rush of movement came from the right flank. We turned and fired: pure reflex.

The figure—a female—sprawled, and then scramble-crawled into the room to the left. We kept blasting rounds after her; none hit, despite the close range. Given how shaken and jittery we were, I'm just glad we didn't vent each other. (Well, vent *me*, since I was the only one out in front of anyone's muzzle.)

The radio went nuts. Prospero wanted a report. Chloe was shouting to find out if anyone was hurt. But we didn't have time to wait for that chaos to resolve. I called for a staged magazine swap. First Steve and Tai, then me. Then we swept left and entered the room into which the stalker had disappeared.

I should have known this entry would be different. Cujo's initial confusion, the stalker fleeing *across* our field of fire: looking back, it was hinky. But when the adrenaline is pumping and you're worried that you might get buried under a horde of pseudo-zombies, you're not tracking the details. You're just doing what you think will keep you alive. And that meant finishing the job we had started.

So the last thing we expected to see when we came around the door was the female on the floor, curled into a fetal position and, well, wailing. She didn't jump up or threaten us; she just stayed there, writhing from multiple leg wounds, it seemed. The only reason none of us fired was because in some part of what they call the lizard hind-brain, we knew this was a position of submission. So we were looking at a passive. But rather than flee—we had seen there was a window on the back wall, busted clear of all glass—she had charged into this side room from which there was no other exit.

Then her writhing grew wilder, and she seemed to be pawing at the floor under her—right before a kid popped out of the hole she'd been lying across.

And that kid did *not* move like a passive; he came straight at us. Reflex took over: we shifted aim and blasted away.

At a kid.

I thought I was going to throw up. Partly out of fear—he was fast and small and as ferocious and deranged as any stalker we'd yet faced—but mostly out of revulsion at what I was doing: shooting a child.

And then I was falling on my ass. The instant we started firing, the female came roaring at us, talonlike fingers raking wildly. I thought I was a goner: being the smallest and in the lead, I was the natural target. But she knocked me over in her rush to get at Tai.

Tai turned and fired, missed, and was down under the female. Steve staggered back a step, shocked (there's a first for everything) and paralyzed by indecision as the female's jaws snapped down at Tai's neck. The yellowed teeth missed Tai's makeshift gorget by an inch.

I wish I could say my actions were cool and collected and deliberate, but they weren't. I don't even remember thinking. I just rolled up to my feet, pulled my HP-35, stepped to point blank, and fired into the back of the passive's skull. Three times.

Just like that, it was over.

But panic followed. The passive had torn Tai's seals and my rounds had sprayed infected blood and brains all over the place. The truck raced in. Frenzied, Tai wanted to jump up and start wiping herself off. We had to hold her down until Prospero got there with the field decon kit, did a quick survey, and then doused her with the mix. Tai kept shrieking at him to tell her if she'd been bitten or if the blood had gotten on her; Prospero just kept asking her to stay calm, because he couldn't see well enough to answer her question.

One of our disciplines was to report any and all cuts and scratches, from whatever source. That way, we could hopefully discriminate between a wound that had been incurred in the normal course of day-to-day living (on a boat, that means a lot of scrapes) or something that had been inflicted by a stalker. But Tai wasn't much for protocols and she'd been pretty lax about this one. And now, in her panic, she couldn't remember which cuts and scratches she'd had at the start of the day. Most of them looked old, but when you sweat from dawn onward in the tropics and you're wearing abrasive makeshift armor, you rub off a lot of scabs. This day had been no exception.

Within thirty minutes, we had Tai in the truck, Chloe and Jeeza down with us as well, and were driving like mad for Praia do Cachorro and the Zodiac. There was no way to be subtle about the way we kept the Rexios trained on Tai, or that we kept Cujo close to her, figuring he might smell the onset, if she turned. We sped out to *Voyager*, fell into the roles we'd assigned and drilled for just such an occurrence, and acted calm even as we were all shivering right down to the bottom of our guts.

Tai didn't turn. Didn't get sick. So, as we'd thought, she had not been exposed. But in the same moment that we were grateful and hugged her for joy, we were also furious at her. I was composing my "get your shit together or else" speech in my head but never had the chance to deliver it. Jeeza, happy tears still on her face, switched into den-mother-from-hell mode and tore Tai a new one. Who, for a change, sat and took it like a naughty child, nodding occasionally, not daring to look the High and Imperious Giselle in the eye.

We didn't even need to discuss how this changed our plans. Everyone knew that tomorrow's op was on pause. And that it might remain that way until we had more help. Prospero made his feelings pretty plain when he looked up from under his brows and growled, "We should wait for your friends. They might as well enjoy this experience, too."

I couldn't disagree. The part of my mind that was still planning, plotting, assessing, also saw the advantage of making that change; Vila dos Remédios was three quarters cleared, now. Any increase in our numbers would make the last twenty-five percent easier. It could also become an optimally controllable "live fire" training environment for any total newbs that Willow might be bringing with her. But the deep-down reason we had to stop was because of what we—what *I*—had done: we had shot a child.

Yes, it was a ravening child who would gladly have feasted on our livers, but the fact of the matter was that we hadn't prepared ourselves for this scenario. We'd never even *seen* a child among the stalkers. We had come to believe, like everyone on Ascension, that they suffered the same fate as the wounded, the aged, and the passives: eaten as easy prey.

I tried to tell myself I wasn't to blame, that I'd taken the only possible action, under the circumstances. The others told me that I'd done the best and most important thing I could have; I'd saved Tai's life. But I keep coming back to the fact that I broke one of our culture's most basic taboos: that children are to be saved, not killed. And if that's one of the moral changes we need to make in order to survive in this post-plague hell, then I haven't yet found a way to make that leap.

Chloe tried to get me to come to bed almost an hour ago. I couldn't. I still can't. I guess I'll sit here until I can. But I don't know how I'll get to that point. I keep thinking about all that we have done and seen since we left Husvik in September. Not just the killing, but the signs of how selfish and barbaric humans became during and after the plague. But it seemed that we were better than that, that we were the good guys, the protectors and champions of what little was left of civilization.

And then I went and killed a kid. Yeah, I know the reasons why, but still: I killed a kid.

Now, for the first time, it really does feel like the end of days.

Part Two

AT THE END OF
THE JOURNEY

December 3

At dusk, four days after The Shooting (you can hear those capital letters when we refer to it), we saw smoke approaching on the darkening eastern horizon. Squelch breaks confirmed it was Willow and that she wanted to send one short message. We sent our own squelch breaks, confirming receipt and that we were standing by.

When the radio started beeping out the Morse code, Rod was ready with the pencil. He hardly needed it, the message was so short. "Request boat for meeting aboard *Voyager*, tomorrow, 0800. Only me."

We looked around at each other. Odd, but we were happy to play along. Rod sent our confirmation.

"What do you think that message was about?" Chloe asked later on.

I shrugged, tossed off the covers; it was still hot as hell. *Voyager*'s AC was just not up to the nonstop tropical heat, so we only turned it on at night in order to spare the filters. But it took the better part of an hour to really cool the cabins.

Chloe propped her head up on her palm, the sheets twisted around her. "That's all I get? A shrug?"

I resisted the urge to shrug again. "Asking what

that message was about is like one of those, 'guess the number of beans in the jar' contests. We could theorize all night long, and we'd still have no idea why she wants to come alone. So I'm going to save my energy and not think about it."

Chloe smiled. "Well, then I'll give you something else to think about."

Hearing her say that never gets old.

One of the reasons I didn't want to talk about Willow's weird message was because if I had, I'd have wound up needing to lie. Because frankly, it had me worried. And if Chloe *knew* I was worried, then she would have started a fight over me going out to meet the trawler without her. Instead, I tapped Steve for his calm and his poker face. I hoped I wouldn't need either, but better safe than sorry.

The trawler had angled into the mouth of St. Anthony's Bay by the time *Voyager* sailed in from Ilha Rata. As the others got the Zodiac down into the water, Steve and I snagged a pair of Hi-Powers and a Rexio. Wide eyes followed us as we trotted out of the pilothouse, armed, and hopped down into the boat. All except Prospero; he's even more suspicious than I am, usually. Steve gunned the outboard and we sheered away before anyone could start asking questions.

We didn't really know what to expect, but we played it cool as we approached the trawler. Willow was in plain sight on the flying bridge, waving her long skinny arms. By the time we had pulled alongside and both of us were waving back with our left hand (in case we both needed to go for a gun with our right), she was strapping into a bosun's chair and giving orders for someone named

Robbie to lower her over the side. Faces stared down at us; the only one we recognized was Johnnie's. He was grinning and waving and if he had looked like the lost son of a Norse god before, he was now a bronze-skinned, almost white-haired refugee from Muscle Beach. I don't spend a lot of time envying other people, but right about then, I'd have killed to have his genetics. Well, maybe not killed—but maimed, for sure.

The other faces were all older. Two women and two men. One of the men—whose head barely came above the gunwale—was a lot older. Forties or fifties, I guessed, and darker than either me or Tai. By a long shot. One of the women—East Asian—was barely an inch taller than he was. Only one of them—the other, sandy-haired male—seemed particularly happy to see us; he smiled faintly, waved, nodded. I had no idea why.

The moment Willow's feet hit the Zodiac, I put out an arm to steady her—and she wrapped her arms around my neck as if she would never let go. "Alvaro," she said. And then she sniffled. "Alvaro." Then she did the same to Steve, waved up at her crew, who all waved slowly back at her, and Steve opened the throttle and swung us back toward *Voyager.*

She put her face up in the sun, eyes closed. "I am going to remember this moment for as long as I live," she breathed into the rushing wind.

"Why?" asked Steve in a voice just loud enough to carry over the engine.

"Because I feel like I am living in the middle of a miracle." Her eyes got a little shiny again. "I never thought . . . I never could let myself hope . . . I—"

I put my hand gently on her shoulder. "Yeah. Us, too."

∽ ⊖ ∾

Once we were aboard *Voyager* and the hugging, exclamations of disbelief, and introductions to Prospero and Tai started winding down, I accepted that it was my duly assigned job to be the party-pooper. "Uh, Willow...that's some, uh, lively crew you've picked up."

She looked back at me with one of her knowing smiles. "Alvaro, you can come out and ask whatever is on your mind. Surely you know that."

Well, if I hadn't, now I did. "I gotta say, they look like they're a pretty sour bunch."

We had crowded into the commons and I saw her notice that Tai was watching her carefully. And maybe Tai was watching us, too. After all, our conversation was about to reveal how the original group actually felt and spoke about newcomers—like her.

"The survivors we found are not very expressive," Willow agreed carefully, "but they are good people and if it wasn't for them, Johnnie and I wouldn't be here at all."

I could believe that; neither she nor Johnnie could have run that big ship very well or very long. "Sounds like a story coming." I smiled.

"I wish," she replied, "but I don't have the time."

"Why?" Rod asked.

She sighed. "Because my crew is worried. Which they do a lot."

"Worried about what?" Chloe asked brusquely. "That we're going to kidnap you?"

Willow cocked her head. "You know, I wouldn't be surprised if one or two of them thought you might. But mostly, it's that they can't be sure it's safe to meet you without taking more, er, precautions."

"Precautions? To meet *us*?" Jeeza sounded pretty indignant.

"What kind of 'precautions'?" asked Prospero in a lower tone.

Willow spread her hands on the table. "Now you have to remember: they've never met you. And when we found them, all but two were completely alone. For months. So they do not trust quickly or easily." She frowned. "Some may never do so completely."

There was a lot of material buried in that response, but I went for the most urgent. "Tell us where you found them."

Willow smiled ruefully. "You will have to settle for the Cliffs Notes. They'll get . . . nervous if I don't come back within an hour or so."

Chloe threw up her hands. "Christ! What do they think we'll do to you?"

Willow answered with her trademark forever-stare. "They're worried that you'll infect me."

"What? On purpose?"

Willow shook her head sharply. "No. They think that you may have been exposed and don't know it because— by some miracle—you are all asymptomatic." She held up a hand against our stares. "Or that you might try to conceal it. They don't doubt that you're my friends . . . but most of them have stopped trusting people *entirely*. So being 'friends' doesn't reassure them."

"Well, they seem to trust *you*. Hell, they seem to think you're their mother."

Willow remained calm and very patient. "Chloe, Johnnie and I *saved their lives*. They all thought they were just waiting to die."

I nodded. "I think we *really* need those Cliffs Notes, now."

She laughed. "Yes, I think you do." She looked at

her steepled hands, probably trying to figure out how to deliver the most crucial information as quickly as possible. That was Willow: gentle and sweet, and yet, all about the task.

"So," she began, "almost three weeks after we stopped getting your squelch breaks, Johnnie and I heard a similar signal. But it was not on the frequency we'd arranged. It was on the frequency that Station Manager Keywood told us to use if we decided to return to King Edward Point. Since the pirates we killed would have been the only ones who could have extracted that information from his team, we decided to take a chance and break squelch in reply.

"I'll spare you the details of the cat-and-mouse radio games we played over the next twelve hours. Eventually, we shared information and location." Her small smile was ironic. "They were at the other end of South Georgia Island, the northwest tip. Just two people at a small observation post on someplace called Bird Island."

Chloe rocked back in her seat. "You have to be shitting me."

"So why didn't Keywood tell us about it? And them?" Steve asked.

Willow shook her head. "I'm not sure. The two people there—Robbie and Marian—aren't sure either. The last message they got from Mr. Keywood was before we ever showed up. He passed on Government Officer Robertson's instructions from the Falklands that everyone on South Georgia Island was to maintain radio silence except for biweekly squelch breaks."

Rod's voice cracked for the first time in months. "And they left two people way out there alone?"

"No," Willow sighed. "There were five at Bird Island,

originally. But three decided to go back to KEP by boat. That left Robbie and Marian with enough supplies to not only get through winter, but half of spring."

"And?" prompted Steve.

"A storm blew in a few hours later. The three in the boat disappeared."

We knew what that meant: it had been the onset of winter when we arrived and if they hadn't made it to Husvik—the first safe harbor on the way to KEP—then they hadn't survived. "So how did you link up with these two?"

Willow blew out a long breath and grew pale. "We had to pilot the trawler to Bird Island. In late winter. And we didn't have any idea what we were doing. Luckily, Robbie had been a machine-junky and handyman before he became a specialist in testing and testing equipment. He was able to talk us through the basic controls, helped us figure out what was what down in the engineering section." She smiled. "And to keep us from blowing ourselves up. But that was all by Morse code beforehand. So when it came time to start the engines and maneuver out of Husvik Bay, we didn't have anyone looking over our shoulder."

She closed her eyes. "Johnnie was wonderful. He is my rock. Always cheerful. Always believes in me. Even when he probably shouldn't." When she opened her eyes they were clear and very gray; I had always thought she had brown eyes. "We went very, very slowly. It didn't even feel like we were moving, most of the time. I think our average speed was about five knots, four when we were anywhere near land."

"How far was it?" Rod said, frowning as if he was trying to remember the maps. "About fifty miles?"

"It probably could have been," Willow sighed, "but we gave every point of land, every possible rock, a wide berth." She shook her head. "We started at dawn and arrived at last light. We covered sixty nautical miles in just over thirteen hours. And I never knew all the strange and worrying sounds a big ship can make. Particularly a ship that probably hasn't been overhauled in years."

I crossed my arms. "Marian looks like she's in her late twenties. What about Robbie?"

Willow smiled again. "Early thirties. Yes, I know what you're getting at. How did the eighteen-year-olds wind up in charge?"

I nodded.

She leaned forward, serious and earnest. "To be honest, the two of them made a halfhearted attempt at getting control. But, well, they are not the kind of people who naturally take action or make difficult decisions. They might be older, but we had fought pirates and infected, found our own food, faced the possibility that we'd been infected ourselves, and sailed halfway around the world with only one experienced sailor to teach us how.

"So when they suggested that they should be in charge, we asked them what they would do next, what their plan of action would be if we combined resources and joined forces. They reminded me of deer caught in headlights. Even though they were the ones with the really essential skills. Robbie is great with almost any machine, and Marian is a whiz with communications gear, computers, and data analysis. Oh, and Antarctic species of moss. We had some very interesting talks about that when we got to know each other better."

I smiled and managed not to say, *I'll bet you did.*

Bonding over cold-weather mosses? Hell, there is no one quite like Willow. I would have hugged her then and there except I didn't want to interrupt her, and I didn't want Chloe to get the wrong idea and begin plotting how to kill her. Or me. Or both of us. You never know with Chloe.

"At any rate," she was continuing, "since they couldn't think of what to do next, but weren't ready to concede the leadership role, they turned my question back on me: 'And what would *you* do if we were working together?' I pointed at the map on their wall, which was a huge nautical chart of Antarctica, showing all the bases and outposts. 'I'd go to those,' I told them. 'As many as we could.'"

Chloe laughed. "I've never met them, but still, I can see their faces!"

Willow's smile may have had the faintest shade of wickedness at the corners. "Yes, and there really weren't a lot of ways to poke holes in that plan. It was no good waiting around South Georgia once the weather started improving. We might be able to survive for a while, but the lack of adequate food is why it never had a self-sustaining colony. However, the Antarctic map was marked with dozens of stations where we would either find other survivors, or—"

"—Or," interrupted Prospero with an admiring bend of his lips, "bases filled with potential salvage. Including food. Particularly since once the infected turn, they ignore everything but fresh meat and—once they're getting desperate—carbs they can smell."

Willow touched one slender finger to her fine, narrow nose. "Right you are, English-person-whose-name-I've-forgotten. And it turned out that Marian, being a data diver and 'wireless fan,' had filled many long, lonely hours on the radio with the nearest research stations—the ones on the long, curving peninsula that stretches from the South Pole toward South America."

"Palmer Land," I added confidently. I'd read about it for a school project at some point.

Willow nodded patiently. "Yes...although the stations we wanted to visit were on its thinnest northern arm: Graham Land."

I knew from the look in her eye that she was sure she was right. I shut up.

"So," she continued with an apologetic glance in my direction, "Marian not only knew each base's complement and whether it was staffed year-round or just in the summer, but usually had a fair idea of the kind of equipment they had."

Steve nodded. "So you had a prospecting list."

"Just as important," Willow added, "we had a plan that came from Johnnie and me, but which depended upon Robbie and Marian's expertise."

I smiled. "So everyone was making a contribution, even if you and Johnnie were the leaders. I'll bet that wasn't the end of the issue, though."

Willow shrugged. "Not entirely. But it showed me how best to start out with them. I made a long list of operating decisions that we would always make communally. Then I set aside a few matters that are traditionally a captain's prerogative: marrying people and other ceremonial duties. But before long, they had become quite accustomed to my choosing destinations, plotting courses, and other command decisions. Just so long as I was polite about it and consulted with them when we had that luxury of time."

Giselle smiled. "So, what you're saying is you broke them to the saddle. Without having to use a whip."

Willow's answering grin was, again, almost but not quite wicked. "Something very like that."

Steve folded his arms. "So: the trip to the Antarctic. Did you actually go?"

Willow nodded. "We started out on September 12, after confirming radio contact with the staff at Rothera."

"Rothera?" Tai echoed.

"Rothera Research Station," Willow explained. "The largest British base in the Antarctic. It's a year-round facility, and Marian had made a 'wireless chum' there before the communications blackout. The two of them had set up squelch-break codes to let each other know they were still okay. But the chief at Rothera would not authorize even a short message. They had heard the same questionable radio traffic Marian had."

"Which is why you kept our first contact so short," I remembered with a nod.

"Yes. I'll share what we know—and don't know— about that radio traffic when we have the first complete face-to-face between our groups. But suffice it to say that Rothera's leadership was not about to take any chances sending signals that a potential enemy could triangulate upon. But at least we knew they were there, and we'd already decided that they would be our farthest stop. So we set off."

Willow blew out her cheeks as if freshly exhausted from that journey. "Over the next forty-five days, we covered almost fifteen hundred nautical miles and surveyed fourteen seasonal and eight year-round bases."

Prospero leaned forward, an eager gleam in his eyes. "And you found—?"

"Only three survivors, other than the teams at Rothera, the American base at Palmer, or the Ukrainians at Vernadsky. The plague never reached those three stations."

Rod frowned. "Any idea what was different about them, how they dodged the viral bullet?"

Willow smiled ruefully. "Bad weather. Those bases are a longer sail and usually get ice-locked sooner. In the case of Rothera, they fly all personnel in and out, so they are always reduced to winter staff by mid-May, latest."

I nodded. "So they were isolated by the time the virus hit."

"Exactly. Some of the others we visited should have been also, but, being easier to reach"—she shrugged—"various ships' crews fled there. But were already infected. And for those bases that are visited by ships and planes during the winter...well, they never had a chance. Nor did any neighboring bases. When signs of infection appeared at one facility, survivors fled to any other they could reach. The three bases that did survive were isolated enough, and big enough, to get through the winter without outside contact."

Chloe's face was one big frown. "Yeah, but how are they gonna survive *now*? Not like they grow a lot of wheat and corn down at the South Pole."

Willow smiled. "They couldn't have lasted until summer. But then, we showed up."

"Which means what, exactly?"

"Chloe, we visited fourteen year-round bases which had been supplied for three months of winter, but in which everyone died halfway through, usually earlier. The other eight bases had caches of start-up supplies for staff that never returned. Bottom line: we found *lots* of salvage. So we left the three surviving bases with huge surpluses of food and fuel."

"What? Why?"

"Because they may be the last truly safe places on Earth, Chloe. And we may want—may *need*—to return there some day."

Chloe's frown changed from annoyed to thoughtful. I could tell she wasn't fully convinced—yet—but was realizing that Willow had made a very prudent long-term investment both for us and the entire human race.

I raised my chin. "How many survivors at those three bases?"

Willow knew the numbers by heart. "Twenty-three at Rothera, sixteen at Palmer, ten at Vernadsky."

I added those to the remaining populations of Ascension and St. Helena, started doing the postapocalyptic math. "I'll bet there are a lot of scientists and doctors at those bases, aren't there?"

Willow shrugged. "More than you would find in an equal sample of the general population, but still not a lot, Alvaro."

"No," I agreed, "but enough to provide reasonable care to the populations we've seen elsewhere. And to teach the next generation. I'll bet you came across a lot of undamaged research facilities and labs, too."

Prospero leaned forward. "I would like to steer back to more immediate matters, for a moment. Exactly what salvage *did* you bring with you?"

She smiled back. "You are pragmatic. That's good. So: consumables. After all our sailing, and supplying the three bases with an extra 30,000 liters of No. Two oil—basic marine diesel, I think it's called—we still have 280,400 liters. So, full tanks plus a pair of two-hundred-liter drums."

"That don' mean nuthing to me," Tai complained.

Willow nodded. "About one hundred forty days of cruising at nine to ten knots."

Tai nodded back, satisfied. "An' *comida*—eh, food?" It almost sounded like "fudd."

Willow sat straighter. "We have slightly over twelve-hundred person-days of packaged pre-virus food."

Grins sprang up around the group. But Prospero and I looked at each other. It was my job to ask, so I did. "Willow, given the number of facilities you visited, I'm having a hard time making sense of that number. Just how much food did you leave with the three bases?"

She sat a little straighter. "Thirty-six-thousand days' worth."

The grins around the table fell off into what looked like confusion and might be shifting toward fury.

I held up my hand. "Let her explain." I was pretty sure I knew what had driven her decision.

Willow nodded her thanks. "If we, well...don't make it back, the people at those bases are going to have a lot of decisions to make. And they may well have the best scientific training and equipment left in the world."

"Yeah," Chloe snarled, "and all so far away that it's useless."

Willow stared at her. "Which is exactly why they need the time and resources to get that equipment— and themselves—to a better place, if we don't return to help them. So they have over eighteen months of food and heat and power to make that happen, if we...if we fall out of the equation."

Chloe didn't look away, but again, the look on her face was softening as the new information brushed up against her first reaction. It's not so much that Chloe refuses to change her mind; it's more like she feels that doing so in public makes her look weak.

Prospero's focus was on a different part of Willow's explanation. "Am I to understand that you promised that you would return to help them?"

Willow glanced at him, at me, then back at him. "Is there really any question that we should—that we *must*—help them?"

"None whatsoever," Prospero answered quickly. "But in what timeframe? Because there is a matter of equal importance that we *must* attend to first."

Willow looked at me again. I shrugged, nodded at Prospero.

Who, with a deep breath, launched into the Cliffs Notes version of what Project Ephemeral Reflex would accomplish.

And what it would require.

When Prospero finished, Willow glanced at her watch. "I'm overdue." She looked up at me.

I could see the question in her eyes. I nodded. "Everything he's told you about GPS is true. You can look at the documents themselves. The best and the brightest were trying to make it happen, but ran out of time."

Willow was motionless. "It sounds...very dangerous."

Jeeza stared around the group, arms folded. "As I've been saying from the start."

Willow shook her head. "I'm not saying it isn't worth the risk. I'm just worried about—about casualties."

I put my hand on her arm. "So are we. Do you think your crew will get behind it?"

She frowned. "In principle, of course. As far as fighting through infected, that depends on the individual and what the mission entails. But Robbie and Marian..." She shook her head. "Not a chance. And that's just as well. They are helpful and have excellent skills, but I think they'd freeze in a fight."

I just nodded, but my stomach had turned into a descending lead ball. If some of Willow's people were *never* going to be at risk of drawing the short straw, of facing both their fears and the stalkers, that would set a really difficult precedent. But for now—"When do we get together again?"

"Tomorrow," she answered. "Same time. But on my ship."

"Yeah," Rod allowed, "we'd never be able to fit everyone in here."

"No, we wouldn't. But that's not why I want to hold the meeting on the trawler."

"So...why?"

"Because," Willow answered, "my bunch will feel more secure. And we will want that, going into our first face-to-face meeting."

I nodded, agreed, but wondered how the hell we were going to blend two such dissimilar crews into anything like a real team.

December 4 (entry one)

The trawler, christened the *Captain's Legacy*, was a lot cleaner than I expected. I guess Willow had figured out a way to keep her crew busy on improvements without them feeling like slave labor.

The crew was sitting around a table that had clearly not started aboard the ship; it was way too nice to have spent any time around pirates. Besides Robbie and Marian, who were even more retiring and tightly wrapped than Willow had explained, the other three were a strange mix.

One was an Argentinian mechanic named Jorge who'd been the sole survivor of his nation's base on St. George Island. He made Steve look garrulous by comparison. All that he'd say about surviving at Jubary (or Carlini) base was that after he saw people getting sick, he had locked himself in the small physical plant building with enough food for a week or so. When it was clear that everyone else was either dead or had turned, he simply turned off the heat to all the other buildings.

Another sole survivor had been found on St. George Island. She, who introduced herself only as Ning, had been the senior personnel administrator at China's

Chángchéng Zhàn, or Great Wall, station. She was extremely alert, obviously well-educated, but made Jorge look like a chatterbox. However, in her case, it was unclear whether she was simply more retiring, or actively secretive.

Then again, being secretive may have been the most important qualification for her *actual* job. I mean, why does a base with a maximum complement of forty people need a separate, full-time personnel administrator? Answer: it doesn't. But Beijing likes to keep an eye on everything, especially in places where foreign contact is likely, and there were eight other bases on St. George Island, four in easy walking distance.

The third survivor was also solo, but his story was as different as his demeanor. A Czech academic, climber, and biathlete by the name of Valda (short for Valdamar) Popisil, he had been alone at the small "Eco" outpost on Nelson Island for almost four months. Separated from the Great Wall outpost by the four-hundred-yard Fildes Strait, the Eco base was apparently some kind of on-again/off-again experiment in green existence that had been perpetually understaffed and underfunded.

However, despite being fine with the isolation, Valda was also a pretty cheery guy; he was the one who had waved to me over the side of *Legacy* when they lowered Willow down. He seemed to have all the interpersonal genes that the other two lacked or suppressed, liked a joke, and was actively interested in all that we had observed.

Which was how our first face-to-face started: with us recounting our trip and experiences from Husvik to FdN. When I wasn't the one talking, I was watching Willow's five rescued survivors.

The bad news was that she was undoubtedly right about Robbie and Marian; any time we mentioned fighting or killing stalkers, they seemed to withdraw into themselves. It was like you could watch them get physically smaller.

But the others were okay with it. You could tell Valda was because he asked lots of questions—some of which were very practical and specific. Definitely a keeper.

It was harder to tell with Jorge since he doesn't seem to react to anything except his name. Ning doesn't even react to that reliably: she just sits ramrod straight, eyes moving from one speaker to the next. Maybe, behind that impassive mask, she's scared shitless—but I don't think so. I'm not even sure that she knows what fear is.

The people who had the strongest reaction to our description of our weapons and tactics, successes and failures, were Johnnie and Willow, whose eyes grew very wide. Which I suppose we should have expected; we hadn't had the chance to fill them in on the details of what happened while we were apart. After all, the only stalkers they encountered after Husvik were dead ones. Frozen solid.

Which was arguably the most important insight that they brought to the table: just how vulnerable the infected were to severe cold. Because it wasn't just that they were naked humans, but because they were naked humans without any foresight. What Jorge and Ning reported, and which was supported by what they discovered in base after base, is that the infected seemed to lack any reasonable anticipation of how cold a place might be or might become.

Ning's story of how she survived when the plague tore through the Great Wall outpost really brought that point home. Prospero had been asking questions that were ostensibly about her work at the base but were probably an attempt to discover if she could be trusted as a teammate or was still following directives set by her (presumably dead) masters in Beijing. In the course of which, he observed: "Your survival seems truly miraculous."

She stiffened a little more, if that was possible. "There was no miracle. Simply orderly observation."

"Of what?" Prospero asked.

"Of the limitations of those who had turned."

He hadn't been expecting that. "I beg your pardon?"

She looked irritated. "Were my words unclear?"

I saw one of Prospero's eyebrows lower slightly; her reply had pissed him off. "Your words were not unclear, but they do not convey any specifics regarding the actions you took to survive."

Her neck flinched forward slightly; it might have been a nod. "Very well. I capitalized upon their inability to anticipate environmental consequences." When he simply leaned further forward, she sighed and explained. "The infected no longer have foresight, not even the measure we observe in cats or dogs. Their reaction to stimuli is always, and only, immediate. So first I determined their locations. I then commenced monitoring them by sending the feed from the base's security cameras to my cell phone. Then I showed myself to them."

"Why?" Jeeza gasped.

"To induce them to chase me. Which they did. I led them toward a room with external access, its door set to lock as soon as I shut it behind me. I ensured that they remained near those doors by leaving alarm clocks cycling through snooze alerts on my side of the doors."

One cool-headed operator, I thought.

"I went outside, started our largest Sno-Cat tractor and drove it to within a yard of the main entrance. Then I reentered the room and opened the doors behind which they had gathered. They saw and chased me again. I led them to the external door, which I also slammed shut behind me, then braced it with a beam of wood."

Steve folded his arms. "That couldn't have held very long."

"It did not have to," Ning answered without even bothering to look at him. "I drove the Sno-Cat forward until it was wedged against the door. I then chained the door's external handle to the vehicle's tread. They could neither tear the door inwards, nor break it outwards."

Looks circulated among *Voyager*'s crew, all of which testified to our unanimous reaction; Ning was a serious badass.

"I ran to a smaller, maintenance door on the other side of the housing complex. From there I reentered the main working and dwelling section. Monitoring their location through my phone, I crept in behind them and locked all the doors leading into the room, where they were still trying to bash open the external access."

I nodded. "That way, they couldn't retreat back into the interior of the station."

She actually looked at me. Not friendly, though:

assessing. "Correct. Once I had trapped them adjacent to the outside access, I returned to the maintenance access point, propped it open and set it to lock upon closing. I went back to the Sno-Cat. I removed the chain, the brace, and backed the vehicle up just enough for anyone within the door to be able to climb out over it."

I saw what was coming and thought, *damn lady, you are* sharp.

"I opened the door a crack. The infected began pushing outside immediately. I ran to the limit of their vision, so they would know where to chase me. They did. I ran back to the maintenance door, made certain it locked behind me."

"D'any get close to you?" Tai asked. "Those stalkers is plen'y fast."

"They did not. As I had observed in the days before, because they strip off their clothes and are constantly expending energy, the cold not only affects them severely but swiftly. They were slowing only halfway to the maintenance door. Behind which I left another snooze-activated alarm clock. Just to keep them interested."

"I ran back into the main complex, checked the phone, discovered one infected had not gone back out with the others. I entered the room quietly through one of the doors I had locked behind them, killed him with three pistol shots, continued to the entrance, and locked that."

"Leaving all of them outside to die of hypothermia," concluded Prospero with an admiring shake of his head. "Most impressive."

But Ning had finished her story and was silent. If

she appreciated, or even noticed, his compliment, she gave no sign of it.

Willow leaned into the uncomfortable silence. "We saw evidence of this behavior again and again during our travels. The same blind ferocity that makes the infected so dangerous to us can make them almost as dangerous to themselves, under certain conditions. Extreme cold is one such."

Steve frowned. "What about fire?"

Jorge shook his head. "No. Fire looks dangerous, so they won' go near. But heat and cold don' look dangerous. So it does not stop them." He shook his head again. "Like Ning say: no foresight."

I nodded at *Voyager*'s crew. "Like at the jetty. The way some of them jumped in the water, trying to get to us."

"But some didn't," Prospero pointed out, musing. "I wonder why."

"Old memories?" Rod offered uncertainly.

"Explain that to us," I invited.

"Well," he said, "it doesn't make sense that turning destroys all a person's instincts. I mean, they all avoid fire, right? But what about people who are really good swimmers, maybe free divers? I know people who, by age ten, are almost as comfortable in water as they are on land. Particularly if their moms gave birth to them in water. So when those people turn, even though they've forgotten how to swim, they might not see water as dangerous."

Willow nodded eagerly. "Rod, I think you may be right. And besides, human babies can be taught to swim and hold their breath. And the medium in which they grow—amniotic fluid—is very like seawater

I was about to redirect the conversation, but Chloe got there first—and a lot more brusquely: "Damn, is there gonna be a quiz after class? Look: this is supposed to be a meeting about *killing* infected, not studying them."

Willow's answering smile was strained. "Know thy enemy, Chloe. But yes, we'll put aside speculation for another time. Right now, what you should know is that cold is a weapon in several ways. Not only do they fail to take precautions against exposure until they are in pain, but it saps their energy very quickly."

Chloe nodded but the accompanying gesture—folding her arms—was defiant. "Which would be great if we were fighting them in a refrigerator. But we're in the tropics, last time I looked."

Willow's smile persisted, but became slightly more brittle. "I agree; there is no immediate tactical application. But it points toward a long-range strategy."

"You mean that we should leave the tropics and hunker down in the cold and the dark?"

Prospero was shaking his head. "Chloe, I believe Willow's point is that in the months and years to come, we should think of cold environments as places where we can establish communities, safe bases, secure facilities." He stopped her attempted interruption with an upraised hand. "This means higher altitudes as well as higher latitudes."

That stopped her. "So, you mean, like using mountain ranges as operating bases. Because they won't come after us once we get up to the timberline."

"Or," I put in, "if they do, they won't be as fast, as fierce, as strong."

As Chloe frowned and started nodding to herself,

Valda jumped in eagerly. "Cold is also excellent at eliminating the virus on surfaces. It is how Willow and Johnnie cleared this trawler. If it is on a surface which freezes over, the ice seems to, eh, entomb the pathogen. If that coating of ice is then broken off and disposed of in a quarantined area, we have observed that the items so treated are no longer sources of contagion." Although Valda had a faint accent, he spoke like an enthusiastic young professor. "And *Captain's Legacy is* a long-duration trawler."

"Which means what?" Tai asked.

I nodded at Valda, couldn't help smiling. "It means that it preserved what it caught in huge refrigerators and freezers."

Valda smiled back. "Yes. Precisely. So you see the possibilities, then?"

I just couldn't believe I'd overlooked them until now. "I think I do. If there are high-value objects that have been contaminated, or we suspect they have, we can soak them in water and freeze them. Several times, if need be."

"Exactly," Valda almost exclaimed, eyes bright. "Then a precautionary rinse with your decontamination solution and we should be—eh, eh . . . ah: 'good to go,' yes?"

Valda, I decided at that moment, was probably almost as infectious as the plague. I had to work at not becoming as enthusiastic as he was. And it was important that I didn't: a captain can't afford that luxury. "We'll see, but it does sound promising."

Willow nodded. "It is. We've been unwilling to trust to the freezing process alone, but with your decon-wash, I think we might not have to abandon or avoid everything that is touched by the infected."

Jeeza cleared her throat; it was an almost dainty sound. Made me think of scenes from English movies where lace-cuffed ladies are having tea in a garden. "Willow, everything you are talking about—the survivors at the Antarctic stations, the way we can use cold to help us against the infected—is great, but without lots of other people, how does any of it matter?"

Johnnie beamed. "But that's the whole point, Jeeza! We *need* lots of other people! We want to find them as quickly as we can!"

Rod put his arm around Jeeza (was that support or a reminder to Johnnie that his fling with Giselle was long over?) and said, "Yeah, but how do we find them if you guys are so scared about using the radio? Sure would make locating survivors a lot easier, faster. And to protect ourselves against pirates, we could set up a remote repeater somewhere. With a time delay, even."

Willow sighed. "Rod, that is a very good idea. But it could still prove dangerous, given the nature of the radio traffic that we have heard. Even on our way up to meet you."

Prospero nodded. "Russian and Yank subs. I've heard them. One British, but only one time, several months before this lot arrived on Ascension."

Willow mirrored his nod. "Yes. The pirates who sailed in *Legacy* before us were deficient in many regards, but not communications gear. They understood quite well that the airwaves would be the best way to both find targets and avoid potential threats. Thanks to Marian's singular radio skills, she was able to get bearings and even approximate ranges on a variety of ships that are still signaling, sometimes in the clear."

Prospero frowned. "A *variety* of ships?"

Willow sighed. "Yes. It seems there are numerous independent factions operating in the Atlantic and the Gulf. Their signals are rarely in the clear and are often garbled by distance and atmospherics, but one that we keep detecting is a group calling themselves the Wolves or Sea Wolves or Wolf Squadron." She shrugged. "As I said, it's rare to get a clean string of even four or five words, so we can't really be sure what they call themselves. But they seem to be a flotilla or federation of ships or some other kind of cooperative that has been expanding its operational footprint dramatically since August.

"At the same time there are tense exchanges between U.S. and Russian subs. Sometimes it sounds like they may still be responding to national command authorities, sometimes not. Again, fractional reception makes it impossible to be sure. But here is the net impact upon us:

"Whatever is happening out there, we can be sure of two things. First, we are not alone. It is logical that being on a long sea voyage when the plague hit probably saved hundreds, even thousands, of people across the globe. And given submarines' capacity for extended independent cruising, it is not surprising that they are evidently the most confident, intact forces left in the world.

"But second, this means that we are very small fish in the very big pond of Earth's oceans. Beyond the subs we have heard, there are undoubtedly others which are staying off the air, and other groups nearly as large and active as the Sea Wolves or whatever they call themselves." She let her gaze travel slowly around the table. "We are only fourteen people with two ships. But we have knowledge that could be of global importance."

"How so?" Rod asked.

Willow folded her hands. "Most survivors will not be like us. They will have been exposed to the virus and proved immune—quite rare—or did not turn. Which means that we, and the sub crews and the personnel at the three Antarctic bases, may be the world's last wholly uninfected groups. That may become crucial for testing, for research that might one day lead to a cure. And—or—a vaccine."

"You mean they would turn us into lab rats?" Chloe snarled.

Willow shook her head. "No. Well, I doubt it. I am not an expert on those procedures. But I *do* know that having a baseline population—a group of uninfected individuals—would be a major asset in determining how, on the microbiological level, this virus works, spreads, and mutates. They need our blood, our DNA: samples that have never been in contact with the virus. And from firsthand experience, we have also discovered the best location for the establishment of such laboratories, and which may already have some of the best remaining staff and equipment to carry it out."

"The three polar bases," I concluded.

"Yes. Particularly Rothera. That is a top-notch facility and could easily be expanded to house over a hundred researchers and their labs."

"It's at the end of a very long supply line," Prospero observed.

"It is," Willow agreed, "but that is simply the flip side of its greatest advantages: extreme isolation in an extremely cold environment. Be assured: no pirate or raider is going to just 'stumble across' any of those bases. They would have to have a map, and decide to go looking—without any guarantee that the trip would prove profitable."

I hated to be a downer, but someone had to keep us on task: "But in the meantime..."

Willow sighed. "Yes. In the meantime, it would be best if we continued to restrict our radio use to tactical sets or short, precoded squelch breaks if we must send over any distance. If we are discovered now, and by the wrong people, we might lose the ability to do what is necessary."

"Which is what, exactly?" Steve asked tonelessly.

Valda looked around. "Surely, our tasks are clear."

"Said the Russky in the room."

I almost rolled my eyes. "Steve."

"Yeah?"

"Valda is Czech."

"So?"

"Not a Russian."

"Yeah? Well, he sounds like one. How do we know he's not taking orders from them?"

I think that was the first time I was ever annoyed at Steve. I gestured toward Valda, who seemed amused rather than insulted. "Look, Steve: if you can find a book on history, you might want to read about what Russia—then the Soviet Union—did to Czechoslovakia in 1948. And jump forward to something called the Velvet Revolution about forty years later. At which point you will realize that it's more likely that *you* are taking orders from the Russians." *And I will* not *ask you to explain how a guy stranded in the Antarctic could have been getting messages from the "Russkies."*

I turned back to Valda, whose expression was both sad and good-natured. "You were mentioning some tasks?"

"Yes. We must find a way to support the research for a cure or vaccine, either by establishing a safe connection between greater powers and the Antarctic bases, or by acting as their agents and protectors."

A pretty tall order. "There's more?"

"Of course. We must journey to Kourou and attempt to save the GPS."

I thought my jaw might drop.

Prospero's did, then he gabbled out, "And you—all of you—have discussed, agreed to, that? Already?"

It was Robbie from Bird Island who answered. "Yes. Without GPS, ocean voyages today will be almost as dangerous as they were in the 1600s."

"Isn't that a bit of an exaggeration?" Jeeza wondered softly.

It was Rod who answered. "Actually, it's probably not, Jee. Sure, the ships are stronger and bigger, but at least back then, every hull had a navigator who could steer by the stars and compass and clock." He held her hand. "How many people can do that today? Who will teach others? In time, yeah, sure, those skills will come back. Heck, *we* might wind up teaching them. But right now, every person who is still alive and looking for others needs GPS. Not just to get to places quickly, but to avoid reefs and shoals, to get back on course if we have to dodge a storm or avoid an enemy." He glanced at Robbie. "But saving it is going to be a shit job. You know that, right?"

Robbie nodded, as did several of the others.

"Frankly," Valda added, "I am still uncertain how it will be accomplished."

"Well, given that I have a captive and near-complete audience"—Prospero smiled, looked around the table—"this seems an ideal moment to explain what Ephemeral Reflex actually is and how it will work."

Chloe glared doubtfully at him. "You promise it's only going to take a *moment*?"

Prospero's smile crumpled very slightly. "I mean that more as a...as a reassuring figure of speech."

"I knew it," Chloe muttered, glancing sideways at me.

I already knew just how truly figurative Prospero's speech had been. I nodded at him. "So tell us what we'll be risking our lives for."

December 4 (entry two)

With a flourish like a stage magician, Prospero unfurled a single large sheet that covered the center of the table. It looked like a cross between a weird weather map and a sky chart.

"What's this?" Steve asked him.

"Project Ephemeral Reflex," he answered. "The basics are fairly straightforward."

"With you, nothing is straightforward," groused Chloe, who has come to like Prospero. Kind of. But she still gives him shit.

"And that is why I'm going to let a chum of mine tell you about it." He ignored our curious looks. "The best, most accessible explanation of Ephemeral Reflex was written by the Yank I was working with at Cat Hill, back on Ascension Island. Alvaro had a brief—er, encounter—with him."

I remembered the desiccated human remains chained to a pipe in the Cat Hill signaling and detection facility and nodded.

Prospero indicated the chart. "The official organizations and agencies that might have cooperated on Ephemeral Reflex did not accept the statistics on the speed with which the virus was spreading. Had we followed their timetable for full review and clearance protocols, we wouldn't have commenced work on the data analysis and coding until sometime next year."

"So, all the big shots would still have been arguing about it now." Chloe sneered. "If they had lived."

"That is correct," Prospero confirmed. "So my friend decided to say bollocks with all that and went directly to the people he and a few others had determined would have key expertise for the project, appeal to their sanity and common sense."

Rod nodded. "You mean that they had to do it without clearance. On the sly."

"Precisely. So he put together a presentation of the key parts of the concept. None of the math. Just the ideas."

I looked at the map. "And this is it?"

Prospero nodded. "Yes. And the accompanying Power Point."

Jesus Christ on a pogo stick; it's the end of the world and we're still looking at fucking Power Points? *Have I died and gone to Purgatory? Or is this the other place?* I managed to keep my external response to a nod. "Let's get to it." The sooner we started, the sooner the Power Point would be over.

Prospero nodded and opened a really big laptop.

I gotta say, as Power Points go, it wasn't half bad. And although some of the concepts had been written in a really obscure dialect of Geekspeak, I was able to follow it pretty well. I wanted to remember it, so I decided to write it out for myself here. And then I thought, hell, this could be historic. So now, with all the introductory BS left out, you get to read it, too. (Trust me; this is better than me trying to explain it.)

Project Ephemeral Reflex:

Précis: Ephemeral Reflex is an initiative to mitigate the inevitable erosion of GPS accuracy that will result from the "ephemeris drift" that is normally corrected by dedicated ground stations. Since the present plague portends the eventual loss of these ground stations, and GPS assets are inaccessible for direct reprogramming, an indirect/supplementary means of compensation must be formulated and implemented.

Assessment of Need: The possibility of restoring GPS to correct function using conventional protocols is either extremely low or nonexistent. The following SITREP of key ground-station assets invalidates any other projection.

> **Asset 1:** Ascension Island. Status: off-line and overrun. Condition: reports indicate facilities sustained significant damage to control elements.

> **Asset 2:** Diego Garcia. Status: off-line. Condition: unknown. No response to signals.

> **Asset 3:** Kwajelein. Status: unknown but presumed marginally operational, at least. Condition: unknown. No response to signals. Gradual degradation of GPS reliability suggests that some corrections are still being effected through this site, but are intermittent, unreliable, or both. Causes: unknown, but analysis suggests damage to facilities, insufficient (or absent) maintenance, or both.

Summary: Until units can be tasked to reclaim and assess these three key ground stations, it cannot be determined if they may be restored to function and, if so, when. No forces remain available for detailing to such missions.

GPS Compensatory/Support Strategy: Project Ephemeral Reflex.

Overview: Project Ephemeral Reflex will extend GPS function at reduced levels of reliability and accuracy. This is effected by a) tasking supporting orbital platforms to compensate for ephemeris drift, and b) determining predictive algorithms that form the computational basis of self-learning software that will coordinate the correctional activities of the supporting orbital platforms.

Ephemeral Reflex is executable with currently available assets.

Scientific Background:

Patterns in the ephemeris drift of dedicated GPS orbital platforms were implicit in the Heng et al. "data purification" paper of 2010. However, as the virus spread, personnel in various control sites and supporting organizations/institutes noted that GPS would cease to function when ground stations were lost and so, unable to correct the ephemerides. An unofficial collective (list attached: REDACTED) resolved to identify an alternative method for providing that correction.

After weeks of assessing dozens of proposals, the collective arrived at a wholly novel strategy for retasking other, extant orbital assets to measure the drift and 1) provide a "second channel" of correctional values, and 2) coordinate intermittent and limited "backup coverage" from non-GPS orbital assets. Both of these alternatives were dependent upon the drift patterns extrapolated from the Heng data. Heng himself, who was to have defended his related dissertation in December 2012, shifted the focus of his research to provide targeted and critical support to Project Ephemeral Reflex.

Challenges and Uncertainties:

While exhaustive modeling validates the underlying assumptions of Ephemeral Reflex, its operational design and implementation are without precedent and lack precursor, small-scale/proof-of-concept testing. Its ambitions are deemed very high: specifically, to increase the GPS system's error toleration by creating better redundancy and error-checking through a large pool of extant, international orbital assets. That asset pool is also to be used as an observational and computational distributive network for refining the "Heng algorithms" to predict and detect where ephemeris errors were most likely to occur and with what characteristics...

"Stop the ride," Steve said crisply. "I'm getting lost. Dizzy. Both."

"Just now?" Chloe asked with a sideways glance. "I gave up someplace right after 'virus.'"

"The worst of the jargon is past," Prospero said in what he no doubt meant as a soothing tone, but which made us wonder not *if* he was bullshitting us, but how much.

I just nodded. "Let's get it over with."

What makes Ephemeral Reflex particularly challenging is that all efforts to help sustain GPS by providing corrective/ancillary data to users had to be wholly external to (and without functional imposition upon) the GPS system's own operating parameters and protocols. There are two reasons for this. Firstly, the collective did not have the time, the permission, the clearance, or the access codes to effect any changes upon the GPS system itself. Secondly, there was no way to test if alterations to the GPS system would leave it operational, and if not, there was no way to be certain that it could be successfully "rebooted" under current conditions.

Success Requirements:
The three main tasks that the software package Ephemeral Reflex must accomplish are:

1) "Recruit"/retask extant satellites of at least fourteen nations to perform ancillary functions in the event that original GPS platforms are lost, damaged, or become unreliable. This is the most ambitious part of the plan, since it is not possible for one or even two satellites to fully "replace" any asset in the GPS system. At best, a matrix of different satellites can be arrayed to offer a cascade of sequential "windows of operation." In other words, groups of different satellites can briefly "stand in" for a lost (or degrading) GPS platform. The implicit challenges—of telemetry, transmission, and translation between different data formats—are considerable.

2) Many of these same international close orbital assets, in conjunction with more distant ones,

> will be tasked to assess continued functionality
> of both GPS assets and the "backup platforms"
> (from Step 1). To put this in extremely simplistic
> terms, multiple higher orbit/geosync platforms
> will use parallax measurements to assess the
> data purity and operating rectitude of all sig-
> naling assets ...

"*That's* 'extremely simplistic'?" Rod squawked. This coming from the guy who was fluent in Geekspeak.

Prospero's answering grin was crooked. "I shall translate. 'All the satellites that are working as part-time replacements for broken GPS platforms are also self-checking, with the aid of still more satellites that are in higher orbits.'"

Jeeza squinted. "That's not much better, but, okay, yeah. Go on."

> Lastly:
> 3) Without automated or human oversight to
> detect and measure the drift of the GPS plat-
> forms, this has to be accomplished by checking
> them against both a table of predicted values
> *and* highly complicated predictive algorithms
> that enable the entire "distributed computing
> network" of the non-GPS satellites to guess,
> test, and thus, conclusively identify the nature of
> the positional drift. This is how the distributed
> network can orchestrate the support assets
> (described in Step 1) to "take up the slack" of
> a degrading GPS platform or wholly replace it.

This set of dynamic and interactive algorithms grew out of the recognition of error patterns revealed in the Heng et al. 2010 document on data purification. As noted therein, different kinds of error (both in type and magnitude) were strongly correlated with different ground stations or GPS platforms. The possible variables (technological, environmental, etc.) associated with these error patterns were run through multiple regression analyses to arrive at a "correctional reference." This reference provides the distributed computing network of Ephemeral Reflex (which is anchored in the processors of the farthest geosync satellites) with the probable causes of each class of error in each GPS asset. This in turn indicates the most likely data corrections or supplantations which must be provided by the support assets enumerated in Step 1. These consequent corrections are then assessed to determine if they are effecting a return to nominal operating parameters or inducing further drift. If the latter, the result is relayed to the algorithm's driver, which initiates an adjust-and-remeasure feedback loop until best possible function is restored.

Prospero closed the laptop. "There. Now, that wasn't so bad, was it?"

Chloe was sprawled in her chair, her head so far back that I could only see her chin. "Kill me now," she groaned.

Jeeza's arms were crossed. She looked angry. Jeeza almost never looks—or gets—angry. "So: all those words—just to tell us that satellites other than those in the GPS system are going to help the system keep functioning, and will replace them where necessary, and to the limited extent that they can?"

"That is an...admirable summary," Prospero admitted with a nervous swallow.

"Then why fling all those words at us?" she almost shouted.

"Because..." Prospero began hesitantly.

"Because," Steve broke in calmly, surely, "you're going to be risking your life for all those words. So you've got to be able to ask questions. And if you don't have the details, how do you know what to ask?"

Jeeza frowned, but looked like she was considering Steve's answer carefully.

"I have a question," I said. Prospero glanced my way, raising an eyebrow by way of invitation. "How long?"

Prospero frowned, uncertain. "How long to run the Ephemeral Reflex program? Or for us to know if it has worked? Or—?"

"No. How long will GPS stay more or less fixed?" I pushed back from the table. "Since we're risking our lives for the system, how much time are we buying for it?" *And for the world?* I wanted to add. Because it was true—but it sounded way too melodramatic.

Prospero shook his head. "I wish I knew, but no one did. Too many uncertainties. How much operating life is left in the GPS birds? Or the other ones that will be re-tasked to support them? How good is Heng's algorithm? Since it won't be perfect, what is the order of magnitude of error, overall? And over time?" He sighed and leaned back in his chair. "But of this we may be certain: every day, GPS is probably slipping a little more. And the more out of alignment it is— the more drift that is in the system when Ephemeral

Reflex goes into operation—the greater the amount of permanent error that will likely persist in the system. That first moment of operation is going to be rather like a snapshot. We still have the optimal ephemerides, but those are ideal values that the system never fully possessed at any given second. There was always error creeping in with every passing microsecond. So we have no way of knowing what real-world baseline we're trying to re-attain."

"Unless Kwajelein is still sending corrections, right?" Rod asked.

Prospero's frown was one of sorrow, not uncertainty or impatience. "We can only hope so, Rod, but when we left Ascension, Kwajelein was either out of action or, unfathomably, taking a break."

"The same could be true for Ephemeral Reflex's programming team at Kourou, couldn't it?" Marian wondered. "I remember mention of three months' food supplies and a bunker?"

"Yes," Willow answered. "But those three months ended sometime in August, and there has been no communication from them since. We must presume that the ESA facility has been overrun or otherwise compromised."

I nodded. "Whatever we find there, we have to expect that Kourou will be a nasty job."

Valda nodded. "We have heard as much. Captain Willow has told us of your plans to prepare for it by using Fernando de Noronha as a proving ground. I approve. Very much."

"She . . . she's told you about that?" I gabbled.

"It is prudent to maximize readiness through live-fire training," Ning snapped. "Not only must our crew acquire adequate proficiency with weapons, but some have never encountered the infected. Except as corpses." She glanced at Marian and Robbie, and then Valda. "We are ready to help combine our arsenals and determine the optimum mix for our first training sortie on Fernando de Noronha. Assuming our captain approves." Somehow she managed not to meet anyone's eyes, not even Willow's, as she almost spat out her pronouncement.

Prospero had leaned way back in his seat, rubbing his jaw. Chloe was grinning from ear to ear. I looked at Willow and tried not to look stunned. "Okay. When do we start?"

She nodded at me. "We are ready to begin today."

December 10

As I write this, I have to admit that I still think our mission to Kourou is probably suicide. However, six days ago, at the close of the meeting on *Legacy*, I was *certain* it was suicide.

It's not that Willow's crew has, since then, revealed themselves to be commando material. Hardly. But there have been no nasty surprises, either. Valda and Ning, despite very different attitudes and approaches, were reliable (that is high praise) by the end of day two. Frankly, I'm not at all sure that Ning *really* needed the training, but for whatever reason, she certainly *acted* as though she did.

Jorge is not the kind of guy who either rises to, or shies away from, a challenge. He just did what he was told, learned when he made mistakes. And whatever else we might say about them, Marian and Robbie certainly stepped up. As best they could, that is. Despite rationing, they are still doughy, passive, codependent, and a bit passive aggressive. But even they breached their fair share of doors as *Legacy*'s crew finished combing the buildings of FdN. With three of our crew there to advise, assist, train—and save any situation about to go sideways—Willow's newbies made pretty short work of the areas that we hadn't entered.

The only real challenge was around the airfield housing. That was the area where service people stayed over during transfers and, according to documents we found on-site, that had housed a semipermanent garrison of twenty-four military police. There had also been six Brazilian Marines waiting for the next flight out when the shit hit the fan. We found them—a tangle of dry husks—in two big heaps, each inside one of the houses. Barricades had been put up, then torn down. Every magazine for every weapon was empty. It was unclear if they had all shot themselves dry or if one or two had saved a final bullet. It looked as though, by the end, there had been a pile of infected corpses around the defenders. But the remaining, ravenous stalkers didn't leave anything behind for us to identify.

Willow's crew flushed out a dozen torpid stumblers, leathery skin stretched tight across their bones, and twice that number of passives. It was easy work, perfect for trainees. The dogs gave plenty of advance warning, and in all but one case, the stalkers were loners.

I write "dogs" because Daisy is back in action, and if anything brought our two crews together quickly, it was our collective fawning over her puppies and a deep appreciation of how she and Cujo helped us all stay alive on those narrow, mostly cobbled streets.

After four days, clearing FdN was done. Well, at least it was as stalker-free as we could make it. We accepted as a given that there were some passives far out in the western jungle, probably subsisting on feral cats and any bird that was slow and unlucky enough to come near. But even with the dogs, we could have spent weeks hunting them down and still, in the end, could not have been sure that we'd gotten them *all*. So two days ago, we started the new job of gathering and storing whatever we could salvage.

No surprise that the airport was the big prize. It was apparently one of the first places that the plague hit: there was no sign of any extended struggle for control. We started by driving along its perimeter, ready for a repeat of the stalker-infested buildings at Ascension's Wideawake airfield. Instead, we discovered fully stripped skeletons in a rough ring around the terminal. Our guess, once we got inside, was that the attacks had been a complete surprise and had started near the passport and visa control offices, from which everyone ran like mad. In every direction. But most of them never got away.

The reason the trouble started at passport control became clear when we swept the terminal and discovered a 727 airliner still connected to an airbridge. It had been boarded by EMTs and, judging from the damage, several persons resisted being removed under restraint. Where "resisted" should be understood to mean "fought like scalded stalkers."

But the rest of the small airport was extremely well preserved, probably a direct result of how quickly it emptied. There had been no gun battles and no reason for the turned to stay behind in a big empty space when all the prey was running away. So the radar, comms, electronics, vending machines, employee's cafeteria, machine shop, and maintenance facilities were essentially untouched. It was a huge bonanza of carbs, decon chemicals, tools, and spare systems—for which we now had plenty of room aboard the *Legacy*.

Vila dos Remédios turned out to be a pretty good source of things like flour, dry beans, condensed milk, sugar: any foodstuffs that required longer preparation. Things like canned and prepackaged foods were pretty scarce for the opposite reason; they were convenience food in the middle of a volatile and dangerous situation.

Fuel levels weren't much reduced in either the local cars or ships. Once everything was falling apart, a few had managed to leave, but the rest bunkered in as best they could. But with the exception of a few colonial-era buildings, the stalkers ultimately tore open the lightly constructed houses with their bare (and judging from the stains, bloody) hands.

The island's desalination plant (it wasn't much more than a really big shed) was old, so there weren't any parts we could use for our own systems. Besides, it too had been torn apart. Stalkers seem pretty good at sniffing out fresher water.

And then there were the guns we found. The most common were lighter bolt-actions, but a few 5.56 x 45 millimeter assault rifles also showed up. Handguns were only legal under select circumstances, but still every fifth house had a revolver. The only downsides were the crazy mix of calibers and the shit condition in which half of them had been kept. I'm guessing that most hadn't been fired for five years and not cleaned for a decade before that. But hey, in the postapocalypse, guns were like prewar bullion. The more you had, the more you were worth. At least in the parts of the world we'd seen or heard about.

Although far fewer, the really worthwhile additions to our armory came from the site of the Marines' and Federal Police's last stand. There were two dozen

Glocks and a few older M4s, but H&K proved to be the manufacturer of choice. In addition to twenty-seven assault rifles of various marks, there were a pair of 7.62x51 millimeter HK 417 battle rifles: true stalker-killers. Still, to my mind, the pick of the litter were two MP5 submachine guns; they really changed our close-range defense equations.

At pretty much the same time, we were also inventorying the guns that Willow and Johnnie found during their Antarctic cruise. There were over fifty-five nine-millimeter handguns (mostly Argentinian USPs and Hi-Powers) and almost thirty more 7.62x51 millimeter battle rifles (again, mostly FALs). But Chloe only had eyes for the twenty-six scoped bolt-action rifles that Johnnie laid out before her. Not only were some of their scopes really high end, but some were chambered for calibers I'd never even heard of, like .375 H&H, .458 Winchester, and .300 Winchester Magnum.

But Chloe was obviously familiar with them all. She *oo*'ed and *ah*'ed over each in turn. I just shook my head. "I never knew Antarctic scientists were big-game hunters."

She turned her "you are so clueless" face on me. "Firstly, there isn't any 'big game' in Antarctica. But remember how large the walruses and leopard seals were around Husvik? And how it was really helpful to be able to hit them from *really* far away?"

"Points taken."

Glancing back over what I just wrote, I should probably clarify something for people who might one day read this, who might live in a world more like the one into which I was born.

That list of firearms may seem to border on gun-worship and obsession. I plead guilty to the latter but wholeheartedly and loudly deny the former. Do I think guns are cool? Well, sure: hardly unusual among American teenagers. In the neighborhoods where I grew up, it was kind of expected.

But it's not like I was ever counting down the days until I could buy one of my own. And then another. And then ten more. And then—well, you get the picture. I just always kind of assumed I'd have one—licensed and legit—one day (again, that's just life where I grew up). But I wasn't some kind of gun-groupie. Or junkie.

But am I *obsessed* with guns? You're damn right I am. Because these days, my old neighborhood and the whole friggin' world beyond it is populated by crazed quasi-humans whose greatest aspiration is to gnaw the last morsel of meat off my thigh bone. So until that changes, an obsession with guns is not a questionable trait: it's damn close to a litmus test of sanity. I want—I need—to know how many we have, in what calibers, in what condition, with how much ammunition, and—truth be told—which ones' actions might be cycled by black-powder reloads. Assuming we are lucky to live long enough, and well enough, to even need to know the answer to that question.

So am I obsessed with guns? Yeah. Because I am obsessed with keeping myself and my friends alive. And right now, I'm sitting next to the one that's extra special to me.

Chloe is snoring lightly in our bunk. She's pretty exhausted. We all are, because in a lot of ways, it was only after the house-to-house work was over that the less hairy but much heavier work started.

After all the uncertainty and risk and anxiety that came before, the last two days of cataloging and loading what we were taking with us felt pretty anticlimactic. We rigged the winches on *Legacy* to lift the most reliable of the local dune buggies onto the foredeck, along with a half dozen dirt bikes. While that was going on, the rest of us sealed up the houses that still had potential salvage in them: mostly supplies that were too heavy for quick removal, or which we couldn't risk using until their surfaces were decontaminated.

Robbie and Marian made a catalog of the contents of each building and cross-indexed it with a damn fine map they had built, quilt-like, out of the ones we had found in service trucks. Actually, the way the two of them were studying the streets and homes, and then stopping to appreciate the ocean views, I bet they're thinking of becoming the island's first new inhabitants.

But before they, or any of us, can take that step, we have to take one final cruise, the one we have all been dreading.

The one to Kourou.

December 13

Three days into our sail to Kourou, we started arguing over how close we should approach before trying to contact possible survivors by radio. It's not that we really expected anyone to still be alive but hey, if anyone was, that would make our job a whole lot easier.

Those of us who stayed back on *Voyager* (she was in tow) went aboard *Legacy* for the discussion. Everyone needed to be a part of it, except for whoever would man the con and watch the comms. Ning promptly volunteered and was half out the door before I could say, "Steve, would you mind—?"

He interrupted me with an agreeable wave. "I'm on it."

Ning didn't look curious, grateful, or offended. She just exited and led the way to the bridge.

Willow didn't look at me or ask any questions, which surprised her crew. But she and I had come to an agreement about Ning: she never got to perform a crucial task alone. As crappy as it felt to make that decision, it felt worse to keep it a secret. But we had to. Firstly, because we didn't really have any sound reason to suspect her of "working" for anyone else; I mean, how the hell could she, now? And secondly, if we told anyone it would be pretty much like telling Ning herself. Although frankly, I'm pretty sure she knew we were keeping an eye on her, anyhow.

I suppose I should qualify that; Willow agreed that someone on her crew would probably have let the cat out of the bag, intentionally or otherwise. But those of us from *Voyager*? Not so much. We all agreed that there was something hinky about Ning. Besides holding back her family name, information about her background, and any useful skills she might have, her total detachment from social interaction just made her seem suspect.

So after agreeing that we had to keep an eye on her, I approached Willow, who ultimately concurred. At first she had thought that Ning was traumatized, had folded into herself while being a sole survivor, waiting to die. But when she failed to come out of her shell even weeks after being rescued, and then became more cautious when we entered the picture, Willow had begun to have her own misgivings.

Ning's avoidance was particularly noticeable because of how it contrasted with the easy integration of our two crews. Valda was popular and an immediate fit. He was eager to be involved and help with everything, from the most mundane physical task to our review of tactics for fourteen, rather than seven, people. And if he ever got in a bad mood, or got out of bed on the wrong side, I never saw the faintest hint of it. The moment he came into a room, it seemed to get a little brighter.

Robbie and Marian were slower to share much about themselves, until Jeeza let it slip that she missed playing bridge. Robbie and Marian exchanged significant glances and then revealed that they, too, missed the occasional game, and would Rod be interested in being a fourth? Which was ironic because immediately afterward, game-addict Rod learned the rules in two days and by the third, was totally up to speed with the other three at the table. Robbie and Marian were "delighted" and, while chatting over the first games, revealed that both of them liked to cook (which has made mealtimes a whole lot more interesting) and were "keen on" music.

That turned out to be a huge understatement. The first time Marian showed up with a ukulele (yes, a ukulele), her fingers flew over the frets and she glanced at Robbie. Who filled the galley with the richest, purest tenor I have ever heard. Being surprised turned into being mesmerized and then into stamping our feet and clapping our hands when they finished with a flourish almost half an hour later. Blushing, Robbie and Marian smiled at each other—and I realized that they were in love. And that they had never even kissed each other. And that they might never do so. That's just who they are: complete mysteries to me, but good shipmates, nonetheless.

Even Jorge came out of his shell a bit. I think the only time I heard him start a conversation was to warn the rest of us that the fish filets we were eating for dinner still had bones in them. But he was easygoing, had a good sense of humor and was a keen observer of other people. For instance, he is still the only person from Willow's crew who has realized that we are keeping tabs on Ning. He took note when Rod jumped up to "help" Ning with a task back in engineering, saw that

I was watching the two of them leave. Once they were out of earshot, he leaned toward me and winked. "No worry. I say nothing." He nodded after Ning. "I get it."

I nodded back. "You know," I said, "when it's just me and you, you could speak Spanish."

He shrugged. "Yeah. I know. But I don't learn English so good." He went back to eating his cassava.

Jorge had a healthy appetite, particularly for cassava. He was eating it again when Ning and Steve headed toward the bridge and we started throwing out the pros and cons of trying to raise Kourou. We had just about made up our mind that it was too risky until we could send a weaker signal when Steve came running and ducked through the hatchway. "You can stop arguing."

Willow shook her head. "We're not arguing—but why?"

"Because I think Kourou just called *us*."

After the room went crazy and then settled down, Steve shared the facts. They weren't reassuring.

Kourou—if the signal was actually coming from there—hadn't "called" us. It was five seconds of a steady, pulsing tone across a considerable range of frequencies. Easy to find, if you knew when, and roughly where on the dial, to look for it.

But when we decided to take a risk and reply with our own steady tone, the only answer was empty air. So, the signal was not an invite to initiate conversation. Prospero pointed out that it could also be an automated transponder or distress beacon that just hadn't run out of power yet or was hooked up to a solar panel or windmill.

Lastly, we hadn't gotten a solid fix on the source. It seemed to be coming from the right direction, but Ning couldn't be sure. And I refer to Ning because it was she—surprise, surprise—who had the skill to get the locator on it at all.

"So now what do we do?" fumed Chloe.

"We keep a signal watch. Marian?"

"Yes, I know how!"

"That's great, but not what I was going to ask—yet. First, poll everyone to find out who has demonstrable skill in radio direction- and range-finding. Then come up with a roster for a round-the-clock watch. Try to keep it to two-hour watches. Whoever is manning that post has to be wide-awake and ready to get a bearing."

"Yes, si—Alvaro."

I smiled at her, turned to Prospero. "I need threat scenarios."

He blinked. "I beg your pardon?"

"I need you to think like the Red Team." I saw some confused frowns. "The opposing force," I added. "We assume this is bait trailed in the water. If so, what sort of assets would an enemy have to have to make it worth their while? What do we need to be watching for?"

"You realize that without confirmed range or bearing—"

"I get it: lots of guesswork. That's okay. We'll just start with the most likely scenario; that these are pirates, somewhere along the Guianas, trying to lure in ships. Maybe they're part of this alliance of Sea Wolves or whatever they are. We need recommendations on travel formations and response contingencies, which we'll refine as we get more data." Prospero started rising. "But before you start all that—"

"Yes?"

"I think it's time you told us a bit more about Kourou."

When the small number of maps we had were laid out, Prospero put his index finger on French Guiana. "The country has only two real ports. Kourou is the smaller, up here, about twenty nautical miles north of the capitol at Cayenne. And this symbol shows the location of the ESA launch facility."

Jeeza craned her neck to get a better look. "That doesn't look like it's on the coast."

Prospero nodded. "That is because it is not. To get to the launch complex, one must leave the Gulf and enter the Kourou River, which runs out along the southern edge of the city. Three miles upstream, we'd have to off-load our vehicles on the port's only major pier. From there, the base is eight miles to the northwest."

That was the moment it became obvious who among the crew had already taken the time to look at the maps and charts of Kourou and who hadn't.

Chloe's eyebrows aimed at her widow's peak. "Eight miles overland?" I had never heard her voice at that high a pitch.

Prospero nodded. He was doing his best not to look sheepish.

Chloe looked at me. "And you *knew*?"

I shrugged. "The maps were always there to look at. I did."

"And you still let us go along with this?"

I had to work at not sounding impatient. "I didn't *let* anyone do anything. The same way that I don't *order* anyone to do anything except when we're at sea or in the shit. Because that's when someone *has* to give orders. And for better or worse, you all decided that 'someone' should be me. But this?" I nodded at the map. "Agreeing to this mission is a decision each person has to make for themself. So, from the first, it was on each person to check out just what they were getting into. Because for this to be a real group decision, *everyone* has to be informed."

I paused long enough to look at each of them. "Remember what I said back at Ascension? We're all in or not at all. I still mean that. We don't split up over this. Over anything. So everybody has got to want to do this. Nothing else is fair. If one of you opts out, then so do I."

The *Legacy* crew had (in some cases, literally) taken a step back from the table.

It was Rod who spoke first. His shrug signified a settled decision, not resignation. "I'm still in."

Prospero didn't hide his surprise quite as well as I did. Steve nodded. "Me, too."

Chloe rolled her eyes. "Well, *someone* is going to have to save your sorry asses. So I guess I'm there."

I looked at Jeeza.

She looked back. "I checked out the map," she said. "At the start. Like you said, I wanted to know what we were getting into." Which put a new light on her initial fear and reluctance. "So I'm still in," she finished.

Chloe was glowering at Prospero. "Still, you could have told us about this. Before we got this far."

I shook my head. "Nope. Because if Prospero had

led with 'so we have to head eight miles up a road that probably goes through stalker country,' I'm pretty sure *I* would have told him to go to hell before I even heard what was at stake. So he did the smart thing: he started out with the stakes, not the risks. And now, well"—I turned to him—"what's that expression of yours? In for a penny, in for a pound?"

His only answer was a faint smile.

"So do you have more detailed maps? A key to the different buildings at the launch center? Floor plans, maybe?"

Prospero tilted his head. "'Yes' to the maps, but 'no' to the floor plans. And the site maps I have are mostly printouts from tourist guides. And of course we have no way of knowing how it might have changed since the virus struck."

Chloe looked at me through narrowed eyes. "So that's why we brought along the dune buggy and motorcycles from FdN. So we could drive there."

I shrugged. "That was my idea. But I suspect it's not a very good one."

Jeeza frowned. "Why not? Sounds a lot better than walking!"

"But not *much* better," Prospero added regretfully. He pointed to the most detailed map. "The pier we've identified is the only one we can use for off-loading. And the only way off that pier is along this street." He laid his finger on a northbound road. "It goes right through an industrial park: wholesale vendors, ware-houses, services, freight yards, tank farm." He tapped the road again. "Almost a full mile. And infected could be nesting throughout that entire area." He shrugged. "If we had armored cars, maybe. But Alvaro is spot on when he says the dune buggy wouldn't be much better than walking."

Valda was frowning at the map. "It might not even be possible." He looked up. "You say there are tank farms in this complex?"

I nodded. "And gas stations for commercial trucks as well as fuel lines running to the pier. So, yeah: if the infected overran the area during operating hours and there was a firefight—or just loss of control—the whole place could have burned to the ground."

"So how do we get to the flight center?" Rod was not asking us: more like the universe-at-large.

"Can't say until we take a slow cruise up the river. Scout for the best place to land."

"But if we can't use the pier—"

"Then we have to walk. Which will mean we have all sorts of problems to solve."

"Yeah," Steve agreed, "like finding a way to survive the first minute ashore."

Chloe rolled off, pushed away the bangs that had fallen down over her forehead. "Why didn't you tell me, Alvaro?"

The abrupt change in activity and context took me a moment to process. "Oh. You mean Kourou."

"Yes. Actually, I still don't understand why you didn't tell everyone. But *me*? Really?"

I sat up, discovered I was running my fingers through my hair.

She saw that—my tell—and rocked back on her knees. Now she knew I had something to say that she might not like. "Out with it."

"Look," I said. "There are actually two reasons."

"Start with the one that won't bother me."

Meaning I would start with the one likely to bother her *less*. "So let's say I died back on Ascension, not long after Prospero told us about Ephemeral Reflex—"

She was suddenly hugging, and damn near smothering, me. "I said start with the *other* reason!"

"You'll like the next reason even less," I managed to mutter around her still-sizeable shoulder.

She swayed back, looked me in the eyes. "You're serious."

"You bet. So let's say I'd died right after I'd looked at the maps of Kourou but had told you what I'd seen."

"Yeah. So?"

I shrugged. "So, what if you guys refuse to go to Kourou? Even if Prospero still agrees to travel with you, hoping that eventually he can persuade you? But when he can't, he wants to go back. And by that time, I think it's even odds whether Steve sticks with you or goes with him.

"And if Steve goes, there's no way the last three of you could even think about clearing FdN; at most it would be a quick salvage stop. And so you never hook up with Tainara, either."

Chloe frowned. "Alvaro, you're one of the sharpest people I've met, but not even you can tell the future."

I cupped a hand on her cheek. "I didn't have to, *cariña*, because I knew two things for sure. One: our group needed to grow, or this world was eventually going to kill us all. And two: when it came to deciding about Kourou, there was every reason *not* to cross that bridge until we came to it.

"All sorts of things could have happened to change any decision we might have made earlier. Me dying is just one example. Want another? Prospero dies. Then where would we be? Or GPS could have gone silent or so out of whack that there was no way for Ephemeral Reflex to bring it back. Which is still a possibility.

"So all I knew was that any decision made back near Ascension Island would have to be revisited. And also, that we had to do whatever it took to grow the group."

She frowned at me. "And the other reason for not telling us ahead of time?"

I sighed. "Because everybody needed to step up, to act like an adult."

"Huh?"

"Chloe, think about it. Going to Kourou is life-and-death stuff. People should be checking that out *themselves*—even more so, if they're scared about what they might learn."

"Yeah, well—we've been pretty busy. Not really thinking about it. Not until..." Her voice trailed off as she realized where her own line of reasoning was taking her.

I nodded. "'Not until it became important'? No argument from me, because that goes back to the first reason I gave you. The right time to make this decision was after all of you made up your own minds that it was time to dig into the information. Depending on the few of us who already had would have been wrong—and bullshit."

She put her hand over the one I had kept on her cheek. "You are so fucking serious," she sighed.

"But you love me in spite of it?"

"No," she sighed. "I love you *because* of it." She grinned. "I guess that makes me a masochist."

I smiled back. "Let's find out."

December 16

The next morning, I was standing watch when the same five-second tone came out of the radio's speakers. And again, we responded with our own.

But this time, the tone repeated almost immediately.

Everyone who did not have a must-be-manned station was on the bridge in less than two minutes. Rod finished double-checking the data and his calcs. "Same bearing. Narrower. We must be getting closer."

"Send our tone back," I said. "Any estimate on range?"

"Can't really tell."

Prospero nodded. "That's never as certain, and our equipment isn't up to that task."

Valda was scanning the numbers. "The source seems to be on the same approximate azimuth as Kourou."

I nodded. "Sure does." We stared up at the speakers for at least half a minute; it felt like half an hour. No answering tone came out of them.

"So whadwe do now?" Tai asked.

I shrugged. "We keep listening. And if they tone us again, we tone them back."

Willow nodded. Hands on hips, she shooed everyone

who wasn't needed on the bridge back to wherever they had come from. Once they were gone, she smiled at me. "This is getting interesting."

"Yeah," I muttered. "Just our luck to 'live in interesting times.'"

At five p.m., we heard the tone again. We replied. So did they. We replied again.

They sent back. We kept up that monotone ping-pong game for about five minutes. At which point, they went off the air. By the end, we were more than ready for dinner but too excited to start eating it.

"Well," Marian observed, "every range estimate indicates it's relatively near Kourou. And it's clearly not an automated signal."

"Not that it couldn't be," Robbie qualified, "but there simply wouldn't be any reason to code an automated beacon to respond the way it has to our return-sends."

Rod and Prospero nodded; the rest of us just trusted their judgment.

"So, there's someone alive in Kourou after all?" Johnnie said hopefully.

"Actually," Willow answered, "it may *not* be Kourou. It could be coming from the Salvation Islands."

"The what?" Chloe asked.

Prospero was frowning and nodding. "Several islands, a little north and east of Kourou. They were closed during launches; they monitored everything that went overhead from the ESA facility."

Jorge stared. "How they close a whole island? Where do everybody go?"

Prospero smiled. "The Salvation Islands are uninhabited. But they get plenty of visitors."

"You mean, like Ilha Rata?" Tai asked eagerly.

"Nope," I answered, finally remembering where I'd heard of the islands before. "Most of the visitors go there because of history, not wildlife."

Rod's face lit up. "Oh, yeah! Devil's Island! The French prison. I saw an old movie once about a guy trying to escape. It was called...uh..."

"*Papillon*. 1973." I nodded. "Steve McQueen in the title role."

"Who?" asked half of the room.

"Doesn't matter." It hurt to say that. I turned back to Willow. "Are the bearings closer to the islands?"

"Can't really tell; we are still too far away. It doesn't help that the signal is so brief."

Chloe sighed. "So now what do we do?" She saw my face. "Wait. Lemme guess: 'Keep listening. Reply if they send.'"

I nodded.

Tai threw her hands up. "An' when do we maybe send a real signal? Like SOS or suh'thing?"

Willow and I exchanged glances and shrugs; we'd had that convo. "We will send a real signal just as soon as they do," she answered. "And not a moment sooner."

December 17

The next day's six a.m. "breakfast tone" was considerably stronger; we were now less than one hundred miles from Kourou. "Well," I asked Valda, who'd been standing the forenoon watch, "any signal change?"

"Yes," the Czech murmured. "The sender may be moving, or—"

"Moving?" Marian gasped as she arrived on the bridge to relieve him. "Pirates? The Sea Wolves?"

"Maybe." Valda was frowning as the senders' third repetition of the tone came in. "Or maybe it *is* coming from the Salvations. From Devil's Island itself. We are closer now. But there are two possibilities. We may simply be getting a more correct bearing on a fixed transmitter, or the source started out closer to Kourou but has now moved farther out to sea."

Willow and several others had arrived. "Alvaro," she murmured, "I'll ready a Zodiac." We had half a dozen of them now; there had been plenty to choose from on *Legacy*'s Antarctic cruise.

There were a few confused looks among the crew. Clearly the decision we'd reached late the preceding night had not reached everyone. Standing as tall as I could (which isn't saying much) I explained: "Four of us are going over to crew *Voyager*." Rod, Steve, and Tai drifted closer to me.

"You gonna sail and look ahead?" Jorge asked, still rubbing sleep sand out of his eyes. "You think maybe it pirates?"

"In fact, I don't. But we're going to take point, anyhow."

"Why?" asked Marian.

"Because if it *is* pirates, *Legacy* needs to know well ahead of time."

"How far ahead will you be?" Jeeza asked.

"Ten nautical miles," Willow answered before I could.

"That's pretty far."

I shrugged. "That's the idea. We see them first. All *they* see is *Voyager*."

"Yeah, and maybe put holes in you," Chloe muttered. "*Legacy* is a bigger, tougher ship."

"Yeah," I agreed, "but it's also slower and less maneuverable. *Voyager* is *not* sticking around for a fight. We're a scout. You just watch your six."

Robbie's lips moved in silent puzzlement before he blurted, "What do you mean, 'watch your six'?"

Prospero leaned toward his countryman. "Alvaro means that if he was the captain of these possible pirates, he would *expect* we'd have a scout out in front. So he might try to send a small fast ship of his own on a long arc to get behind and hem us in."

Willow frowned at Prospero and me. "Has anyone ever told you boys that you might have *too* much natural talent at this?" Then she smiled and laughed. "Johnnie, Jorge, please see to that Zodiac."

❧ ⊖ ❧

By the time we'd run out ten miles ahead of *Legacy*, we were only eighty miles from Kourou...and staring at empty seas.

No sooner had I sent word back to Willow than she updated us on the signal's source: a new transmission confirmed that it was coming from the Salvations. Almost certainly Devil's Island. We adjusted course to take a look.

Devil's Island is a pretty forbidding chunk of rock capped with greenery. No place to put in safely. So we circled it but saw nothing. *Legacy* approached from the north, keeping the island between her and the other Salvations. If there was an ambush waiting behind any of them, she'd be long gone by the time they swung out of cover and drew near.

I piloted *Voyager* until we were standing off from the midpoint of the two-hundred-yard channel separating Devil's Island from the main island, Île Royale. That was our station, both as picket and interceptor. Meanwhile, Ning, Johnnie, and Robbie sidled up to the old prison island in a Zodiac to look for the source of the signal.

It turned out to be a remote repeater: a transmitter that received and then relayed signals sent to it at very low power levels: too low for us to have detected earlier. But where were those low power signals coming from? The mainland or one of the other islands?

We didn't have to ask that question for very long; a strong set of international radio signals came from Île Royale itself.

"'LW 1'?" Steve asked when the short string of Morse code stopped. "What's that mean?"

"It's from the International Code of Signals. It means, 'Can you take bearings from my radio signals?'"

He squinted at the more hospitable-looking island just to the south of us. "So they're asking if we can steer ourselves to the new radio source?"

I nodded. "They are. Let's get under way."

As we pulled up to the Île Royale's only dock, a man stepped out from behind a small, shadowed shed just a few yards inland. He offered one lazy wave of his left hand before putting it back into his pocket.

"He's pretty relaxed," muttered Steve.

"You expectin' he jump around to see us?" Tai countered.

"No, but—shit; it's like we're neighbors, just dropping by."

Rod shrugged. "Maybe he figures that being calm is the best way to make sure that no one gets nervous. Or, you know...makes a mistake."

Steve mumbled something under his breath. I wondered if he was vaguely unnerved to find someone more calm than he was. I also wondered if he saw the irony in that.

We were waiting for *Legacy* to cruise closer, so we weren't in a rush. Neither was the guy on shore. He waved at our trawler when it crawled into the wide anchorage, then leaned against the shed.

A Zodiac was lowered from *Legacy* and brought over the other half of the contact team: Jeeza and Johnnie. Steve and I hopped down into it. As we pulled away from *Voyager*, I asked, "Ready?"

They nodded.

Less than two minutes later, all four of us were

on the pier, strolling toward the man. I could almost see Chloe's crosshairs on his sternum, even though she was positioned well back in the dark of an open deck hatch aboard *Legacy*. Prospero was working as her spotter.

As we got closer, we could see more clearly into the shed's shadows. I was surprised to see that the guy looked like he might be white. Frankly, that was against the odds, given the general demographics of French Guiana. "*Bonjour*," he said affably, then cocked an eye toward the sun. Then in perfect, unaccented English, "Not much longer, though. Welcome to French Guiana."

I nodded, but before I could respond, a stream of French flew out of Jeeza's mouth. "*Vous êtes Canadien, n'est-ce pas?*"

The man—late twenties?—laughed, showing either perfect, or professionally corrected, teeth. "*Oh mon dieu, est-ce si évident?* No concealing the Quebecois, I guess."

"So...you're Canadian?" I excel at stating the obvious.

He nodded. "Yes. Or half, according to the locals who insisted on calling my mother Vietnamese, even though she'd been born in Montreal. You are American?"

"Some of us," I answered, "but we're getting more international every day."

He smiled ruefully, nodding. "*Oui, vraiment.* In a few years, it won't matter what country we were born or brought up in." His gaze drifted in the direction of the mainland. "It hardly matters now, I'd say." Without taking his eyes from the distant coastline, he asked,

"What brings you here? I do not find the company unwelcome, but—well, best to get the inevitable questions out of the way at the outset."

I nodded, shifted into the introduction we'd settled on for initial contacts. "We had to come here to complete a prewar mission. Pretty important for anyone who wants to keep using GPS."

His eyes turned away from the green line on the western horizon. "So, you have business in Kourou. The launch complex, I mean."

Well, he made that *connection quickly. Maybe too quickly.* "Why do you say that?"

He smiled. "There's nothing else for hundreds of miles about that could bear upon GPS. Frankly, not even the ESA facilities should matter—but I am guessing you need the satellite dishes to transmit something?"

We hadn't even considered meeting anyone who'd guess our motives and mission, so I had to go off-script. That meant going straight to the truth, which we would have had to spill in a few more sentences, anyway. I gave him a thumbnail sketch of what we intended to accomplish at Kourou.

If he was surprised, he didn't show it. He just nodded. "This will be easier if we are all discussing it together. Your people are all welcome here."

"We are grateful. But it might be easier for you to just come aboard, rather than bring our whole crew ashore."

Now the guy did smile. "And it is far more secure than setting foot in a place you do not know." He sighed. "Of course, I face the same concern if I go aboard your ships. So, perhaps this is agreeable to us both. You examine this island as you wish, and send another Zodiac to check for hidden boats along its coast and that of the other island near us." He gestured east toward St. Joseph's Island. "When you are satisfied that there are no waiting ambushes, you may bring as many ashore as you like." He turned to lead us inland toward the main buildings, less than a hundred yards away.

"You seem pretty calm about all this." Steve's statement sounded more like a challenge.

Our host shrugged. "If you wanted to kill me, you would have already done so. And it will be easier for us to talk once you have determined that I have no way to harm you." He shrugged. "This is the way of the world, now. We may assume nothing. But we still need to know what to call each other. I am Pascal Labrouse. Make yourselves at home." He began walking up the gentle slope to the buildings at the center of the small island.

I don't know why I couldn't remember Pascal's name. You'd think it would be easy, since he shared it with one of history's most famous scientists. But every time I spoke to him, even as my brain tried to utter "Pascal," my mouth said, "Papillon." The fourth time I cursed at myself.

He just laughed. "I am flattered. I think. At any rate, it doesn't bother me." He lowered his voice, even though there was no one else in hearing distance. "Frankly, I like it better than the archaic name my parents gave me. My great-grandfather's, I think."

I considered that. "I'd kind have guessed you'd want to hang on to a family name even more, now that you are the last person who can keep it going." *Wow, grim assumption there, Alvaro.* "I mean, *probably* the last person."

Papillon shook his head. "No, not probably: certainly. My father was an only child, and so was I. My mother's family in Vietnam disowned her." He shrugged. "It is beyond possibility that either of them is alive to care whether or not I keep a dusty old name in circulation. Besides, it is fitting to have a new name for a new world."

He had the same likable manner as Valda, but more laid-back. Wandering around the old buildings of the penal colony with Papillon felt more like a guided tour with a soft-spoken guide, not a site security check in a world overrun by mindless cannibal-ghouls.

As advertised, he was the only person on Île Royale. The other islands, too, so far as we could tell. He had a couple of weapons—a 9mm automatic and one of those whacky French bullpup assault rifles: a FAMAS, chambered for 5.56 like our M4s. Both looked recently cleaned and a uniform shirt (I can't bring myself to call it a "blouse") hung nearby. The color, cut, and badges looked familiar—

It was Jeeza, walking up behind us, who identified it: "French Foreign Legion!" She stared at him. "You?"

Papillon bowed. "At your service, mademoiselle."

Jeeza flushed. If Rod had been there, I think he would have reddened, too . . . but for a different reason.

I scanned Papillon again. "No offense, but you don't really look the part."

He laughed. "No, I do not. I am—well, *was*—a pilot. Helicopters. 'A gentleman's job,' as some of my comrades put it. When they were feeling charitable, that is."

"And when they weren't?"

He grinned. "I would have to repeat a long list of slurs, not suited for a young lady's ears." I swear, I thought Jeeza might start batting her eyelashes at him. "But as you no doubt guess, most questioned my toughness, my manhood, or both."

Steve nodded. "I thought the Legion was mostly in hot spots. War zones."

Papillon nodded. "Yes. Kourou was an exception. It was a permanent duty station, even though open conflict was not anticipated."

Jeeza frowned. "Why?"

"Because the launch site's security needs were constant. And their urgency grew as did the military importance of space."

"And," I guessed, "because the Legion was never subject to a nationally mandated timetable of rotations and redeployments. So the powers-that-be were able to make yours a…a dedicated unit. Always at full readiness to perform the job and to train new personnel. Which means you must know all about the launch facility."

He sat. "I knew a fair amount, but again, I was a pilot. I was either ferrying around new recruits—the Legion had its jungle training school an hour to the south—or running security sweeps. So I can tell you where we were headquartered, where we stored and maintained the helicopters, and all about the local traffic patterns—both in the air and on the ground. But I walked only a dozen foot patrols my entire time at the base."

"Still, if we showed you a map—"

He nodded. "I could tell you what every building

was—and any changes that might have been made between the time the map was drafted and the virus broke out."

I turned to Johnnie. "If Willow is ready, I think it's time for everyone to hear what Papillon has to say."

Willow and I had agreed that, if the local contact turned out to have useful intel on Kourou, we wanted the majority of our team in on the first meeting. Not the most efficient—or most secure—distribution of our people, but important for morale reasons.

Valda was left in nominal charge of *Legacy*. He was flattered when we apologized for leaving him behind and waved it off. "Just keep a channel open on a handset. I will hear well enough, and will be glad to reflect on what I hear. Sometimes that is better than adding to the discussion." He is such a cool guy.

Rod followed Valda's example, remaining in charge aboard *Voyager*, wearing one-half of a headset to keep track of the conversation. Steve volunteered for the same duty. He seemed antsy, but I couldn't tell why and didn't have the time to ask.

Robbie and Marian were curious but more than happy to remain aboard *Legacy* listening to the same handset-range transmission of the meeting. I suspect that by physically distancing themselves from our first face-to-face strategy session with Papillon, they were indulging their deepest desires not to be physically involved in the operation.

Johnnie was happy sitting out as well, which was just like him. Not that he wasn't interested, but he almost always deferred to Willow's wisdom and judgment.

The rest of us gathered in Île Royale's prisoner-built

church. It was still in pretty good condition; tough enough to endure a century or more of the local weather, six months of disuse hadn't left it much worse for wear.

The moment we were done with the introductions, my darling Chloe led with her trademark tact: "So why the hell should we trust you?"

Papillon seemed mildly amused. "Why should you not? It is the end of the world, *non*? So what do I have to gain by misleading you?"

"Yeah, well, I'd trust you a lot more if your ass was going to be on the line, too."

He shrugged. "And who says it won't be?"

That stopped her—and the rest of us—cold. None of us had even broached the topic of Papillon joining our mission. We'd given him the broad outlines of the plan, but it still had more blank spaces than not.

He shrugged again. "I shall be as frank as you, Chloe. You have not seen Kourou or the launch facility. I have. You do not know the actual difficulty of the overland routes you may be considering. I do. None of you know the internal layout of any of the key buildings, nor where there are backup generators and other systems that might prove not only useful, but essential. Again, I do. And with the exception of Percival"—Prospero almost winced—"none of you have military training. And—"

"And 'you do.' Yeah, I caught on to the pattern," Chloe almost growled. "But that doesn't answer my main concern."

"Which is?"

"Which is that somehow, although you are supposedly some badass Foreign Legion guy, only you made it out to this island. None of your buddies. No one else at all, for that matter. Why's that?"

"Ah." He smiled, nodded, as much to himself as us. "Now I understand."

"Good," pursued Chloe. "And?"

"And I commend your caution. When only one out of a group survives, it is easy to believe they did so because they ran before the rest."

"Something like that," she muttered.

He sighed. "Like most people still alive, I owe my survival to chance more than cowardice or skill." He folded his hands. "As I have told you, the launches from Kourou go directly overhead, and there are tracking and telemetry sensors here on Île Royale. The ESA was responsible for their function, but the Legion was responsible for their security. So we were routinely sent out here to check if the systems had been compromised or sabotaged in any way."

Jeeza nodded. "And you were stationed here when the virus hit."

Papillon waggled his hand. "Yes and no. I was on Île Royale, but not stationed here. A security check meant only a brief visit: a day, at most. We only remained overnight if we arrived late in the day.

"Such was the case with me. The site staff had closed up; there was a launch early the following day and they left me behind to finish my survey. I was to be picked up the next morning by a police boat." He shrugged. "The boat never came."

Tai's eyes were wider than usual. "So you never even see'd a stalker?"

Papillon straightened. "Of course I have. If I had not found a way to leave the island, I would have starved to death. Fortunately, there was a small catamaran with a motor. Not safe for crossing to Kourou in high weather, but I was not in a desperate rush. I simply waited for a calm day.

"I was not surprised by the devastation of the virus. I had listened on the radio as not just Kourou, but the whole world, began to die and go silent. So I did not land at once. I went to a drifting cabin cruiser. By the time I was ready to board it, the—stalkers, you call them?—had come on deck." He shrugged. "They knew no fear. They were easy to kill. I went aboard, found food. Tools, too, but I could not risk touching anything. So I scooped up the food with an angler's net and left everything else. Next time, I took anything that could be boiled for a long time. And so, here I am."

I gestured to the site map we'd spread out on the table. "So you actually want to join us when we go to the launch facility?"

"*Want* to?" He shrugged. "I do not want to go anyplace where the, eh, stalkers live. But I agree that your mission is important. Vital, even. And I know that without a guide, you are unlikely to survive the attempt."

Chloe bristled. "Well, thanks a lo—"

I cut my eyes in her direction. She glared back, but stopped.

"I mean no insult," Papillon explained. "But you have not seen, and cannot see in advance, how impossible it is to approach the facility in either of the ways you are considering." He gestured to both the docks south of the complex and the undeveloped shores to its east. "The roadway north from the pier is impassable."

"Fire?" Prospero guessed.

"Abandoned cars," Papillon corrected. "When the virus arrived, a freighter was docked there, off-loading materials for the launch facility. I suspect that many reasoned it was their only way to escape." He shrugged. "Those who made it on board simply left their cars behind."

"Did the freighter make it to safety?" Jeeza asked.

Papillon shrugged. "It is no longer at the dock, but it would be a miracle if the virus did not board the ship along with one of the refugees." He pointed to the shoreline to the east of the site. "This, too, is impassable. Tidal flats, which shift constantly. That is the reason there's no tourist industry along this part of the coast."

Prospero was rubbing his chin, frowning. "If we go in with two Zodiacs, leave tenders with them while we wade in the rest of the way—" He stopped when Papillon began shaking his head.

"Apologies; I should have been more specific. These are not merely tidal flats; they are *mud* flats. It means crossing at least fifty yards of sucking silt; it could mean five hundred. Either way, you will be exhausted by the time you reach the shore. And then you must go two and a half miles overland where there are no paths at all, but almost certainly stalkers."

"Well," Chloe snapped, crossing her arms, "what about the road that enters the base from the north? Uh, National Road One?"

Papillon shrugged. "I'm not sure how that would be useful. It is even more unreachable. Unless you were to land all the way up at Sinnamary, almost fifteen miles to the north. But that is a small town: no dock on which you could unload vehicles. And it is almost certainly infested with stalkers."

"Then how the hell do we get into the base?"

"I never said I *did* think you can," Papillon countered patiently. "At least, not by using your boats or wheeled vehicles."

It was my turn to cross my arms. "Sounds like you have an entirely different approach in mind."

He glanced at me. "I do. However, you may not like it."

Why do all *our plans start with that proviso?* "What I do or don't like is a lot less important than what will work. Show us."

Papillon put his finger on the road that Chloe had pointed out. "The northern road has two redeeming features. It is not much trafficked, because there is not much north of the base and any traffic through the base is tightly controlled."

"And why does that matter?"

"Because it is unlikely to be blocked by abandoned vehicles."

Prospero was frowning even harder. "But you said we had sod-all chance of off-loading our vehicles to the north in, eh, Sinnamary."

Papillon nodded. "Yes. I did. But I am not talking about your vehicles."

Ning's words were like sharp, evenly timed pistol shots. "You make no sense."

I held up a hand. "You said this road had two redeeming features. The first was a lack of obstructions. What's the other?"

Papillon let his index finger run northwest from where the road left the center of the base. "It is very straight. Particularly here where it approaches the outer gates through a mostly undeveloped area." He straightened. "There is a reasonable chance it would be clear, and so, a place we could land."

"Land?" Tai said, eyes wide. "You think maybe we will grow wings, now?"

Papillon smiled. "Something like that." In response to her stare, he added, "But I think a plane would be better."

"We don' got no planes."

"I am aware. But I know of someone who might. Or, at least, who did."

One of Prospero's eyebrows had climbed toward his hairline. "We had a good number of planes in the hangars at Ascension. I'm no aviation expert, but I'd have taken odds that none of them would have flown anymore."

Papillon shrugged. "That could be true in this case as well, but the planes I have in mind are much simpler. And the man I know of might have found a way to maintain them."

I knew I'd regret asking it, but I did: "So where do we find this guy?"

December 21

Except for my writing lamp, there are no lights on in any of *Voyager*'s cabins. Not *Legacy*'s, either. But that doesn't mean everyone is asleep. Frankly, I doubt it, since tomorrow is the first time we're landing on an unsecured island since we finished clearing Fernando de Noronha.

I shouldn't be losing any sleep over it. The island that Papillon has taken us to—Mustique—is really small: not quite three miles long and barely a mile at its widest point. And it has no town to speak of because, well, its inhabitants didn't want one.

See, Mustique is—was—privately owned. If that invites images of movie stars, rock gods, billionaires, and royalty... well, that's who lived there. No joke.

Personally, I suspected that places like Mustique were just urban legend. I mean, yeah, I knew that some celebrities and A-listers bought their own islands. But that was all about secluding themselves in isolation. Mustique was a *colony* for them, a collective refuge for the glitterati who wanted to escape the spotlight, but not be alone when they did.

From the moment we put down anchor in the wide

arc of Brittania Bay, the island's skyline grabbed your
eye. And not because it was top-heavy with mansions
that look like old colonial great houses. I'm talking
about the other, weird stuff: the turreted medieval
towers, pagodas, Balinese-style pavilions, and a few
that looked as though the designs of Salvador Dalí and
Frank Lloyd Wright had conceived a mutant love-child.

Papillon didn't know much about the place, except
that it had its own airport and several celebrities kept
their own planes there. Not luxury jets, but long-range
turboprop workhorses that were good on short runways and long on reliability. And, unlike commercial
planes, they had had probably been doted on by a
staff of highly paid mechanics retained by the island's
insanely wealthy "homeowner's association." Damn, in
contrast with how and where I grew up, all I can say
is, "same planet; different world."

What Papillon had known—or guessed rightly—was
that Mustique would be a ghost town. Just before he
was semi-stranded on Île Royale, a flurry of high-
end private jets from Rio and Sao Paolo had passed
through Kourou's own modest airport, bound for
private islands like Mustique. At the same time, a lot
of Kourou's highest-level ESA officials had decided
to jet away on unplanned vacations. In short, all the
best-informed and wealthiest rats were leaving the
ship before anyone else noticed it was sinking. But
if Mustique was any indicator, the only thing they
accomplished was to spread the plague to the places
they'd hoped would be sanctuaries. To say nothing of
probably making Kourou airport the epidemiological
equivalent of Typhoid Mary.

On the trip to Mustique, we got Papillon to tell

us everything he could about the ESA complex. Once we got all the buildings labelled (all the ones he was familiar with, anyway), we pumped him for everything he remembered about their floor plans. Unfortunately, except for his detailed drawing of the Foreign Legion station, most of that was pretty sketchy.

But our real focus was grilling him about his claim that he could fly us in by landing on that long, straight stretch of road inside the base's perimeter fence. We didn't want to get our hopes up, but I gotta say, he's been pretty convincing. Not only is it in open terrain, but the area is so undeveloped that the Foreign Legion had to patrol most of it with their tracked vehicles, mostly because the Russians were worried about infiltrators from the jungle sabotaging the Soyuz launch pad they'd been building. So if that roadway really was as clear as Papillon presumed it would be, we'd be able to land just a couple of miles from the main complex. There were even odds we might find a useful vehicle, too. Hell, even if something went wrong with the plane after we'd landed, we could escape by running for the coast and wading out into the tidal flats for pickup. Not a great alternative, but at least it involved moving *away* from stalker-central, not toward it.

That night, like the others before, Papillon was affable, soft-spoken, and patient. Still, that wasn't to everyone's liking. Steve and Prospero seemed a little unnerved by the new guy; Ning was clearly determined to avoid him. I knew I wasn't going to get an explanation out of her, and probably not much more from Steve, so I tracked down Prospero.

After trying to avoid the topic several times, he

finally replied, "I think our new friend is playing a role: the stoic, agreeable hero."

That didn't track. "Just because he's quiet doesn't mean it's an act, dude. Hell, I don't know if I could be so easygoing, having every suggestion or idea picked apart by people I'd just met." I shrugged. "It just seems like he's learned how to leave his ego off-line." *Not like* some *people I know . . . Prospero.*

"I don't disagree, Alvaro. But his humility . . . I can't put my finger on it, but it feels a bit too flawless. As though it's how he *wants* to be seen."

"What if he's just modest?"

"I think I'd be more comfortable if he wasn't."

"Why? Because you'd rather be working with someone who jumps right into the thick of every high-stakes convo and tries to control it?"

Prospero's smile was crooked. "Alvaro, are you referring to me or to yourself with that example?"

"Both."

We laughed. But I still didn't have an answer.

I guess other folks were tweaking to Prospero's vibe. That, or he was talking trash about Papillon when I wasn't around.

Later that night, Chloe propped her chin on her hands and looked up at me. "What do you think? Is the French guy—?"

"The *Canadian*—"

"Okay, you know what I mean. Do you think he's trying to impress us, or is Prospero just miffed that he's no longer our one and only guru for all things military and technical?"

I shrugged. "I've got the same questions about

what's eating Prospero. As for the new guy, I don't know him enough to draw any conclusions. Yet."

She shrugged. "Well, he's easy to get along with."

"Which tells us exactly zero about him."

"Now you sound like Prospero."

"What do you mean?"

"You know—" Chloe lifted her head, cocked it like Prospero did sometimes. "'How in bloody hell can we know Frenchy's not just play-acting?'" Prospero would never have used the term "play-acting," and Chloe's English accent was so bad that I almost laughed out loud. "That bugger is acting all honest," she continued, "because he's trying to trick us!"

I shrugged. "Well, until you know someone for a while, how can you really be sure either way? But on the other hand, *why* would Papillon want to trick us?"

Chloe flung an exasperated hand at the overhead. "Exactly! What does he stand to gain?" Chloe had given up on the British accent, which made it a lot easier to take her seriously. "But Prospero seems to think he might not be telling us everything."

"Oh? Such as?"

"Well, I don't think he buys Frenchy's story about signaling once a week for months, and that we were the first ship that pinged him back."

I shrugged, which was kind of hard with her weight pinning me down. "Hardly sounds suspicious to me. He was alone. And it made sense for him to set up the transmitter as a remote site. Anybody who meant to raid him would have gone to the wrong place, first."

"Yeah, yeah; I get all that. But Prospero's not comfortable that he never heard any of those signals while he was fiddling with boat radios on Ascension."

I pushed up on my elbows to look at her more directly. "Really? That bothers him?"

"I guess. Steve said as much, but he couldn't—or wouldn't—share why that's got Prospero's panties in a bunch. Hell, English himself stopped signaling. Didn't want to attract unwelcome attention to Ascension." Chloe ran a hand down my side. "You think maybe Prospero is kicking himself for not having the balls to keep signaling like Frenchy?"

"I dunno," I admitted. "But I do know that if I don't get out of bed right now"—I intercepted Chloe's hand—"I am not going to remember to write all this down in my journal."

"Oh, you and that journal," she muttered. "I hope it's got all sorts of filthy descriptions of our sex life."

"In fact, it does."

She snapped upright, then saw my smile. She swung and missed. "Damn it, get out of bed and write in that stupid book. Quick: I'm not gonna wait forever."

Before three minutes had passed, she was snoring lightly.

December 22

Among the many things that are gone forever, mega-bands and superstars seemed inevitable casualties. Professional musicians with high-tech setups? Global travel? Tens of thousands of screaming fans gathered in one place? I keep shaking my head and hearing the same phrase: same planet, different world.

But here's another thing that seems equally certain as the apocalypse unfolds: the moment I think I know anything, the universe shows me that I am wrong, wrong, wrong. And that's just what happened on Mustique. Well, kind of.

Mustique would have been a great island to clear slowly and carefully. Firstly, it promised to have some of the most useful, and also wildest, salvage that we had yet come across. Secondly, if we were looking for small, defensible islands to call home, this one had a lot of advantages, ranging from basic quality of the facilities and construction to a supremely handy location for reaching the Caribbean, the Gulf of Mexico, or the northern extents of South America.

But not only was the clock on GPS viability ticking down, it was also measuring the time to the next storm.

According to Papillon, the last major storm in Kourou had been back in early August. Although it is not in a hurricane zone, he expressed concern that a real storm was "overdue" and that every day we spent on Mustique was just one more opportunity for bad weather to force an even longer delay. During which GPS might wink off and be gone forever. Like rock bands. Or so I thought.

So instead of giving the turned several days during which they could attend our "dance party" at the island's one pier, we decided to reassess that strategy after the first four hours. Once we'd gone for at least two hours without any visitors, we'd secure the pier itself, land two of the motorcycles and the dune buggy, and run a few short-range recon probes.

So we started the music: a head-banging medley from the Nineties. The first half hour was just us sitting in the sun, waiting. No movement, no sound, except the music that blared up Mustique's green slopes. It was mostly bands like Golden Earring and Whitesnake and a bunch of others that were barely on my radar, but which had Valda rocking out whenever he left his rifle. (We'd decided to give Willow's less-experienced crew the opportunity to meet and greet any stalkers who came to dance.)

The first one showed up an hour after we had cranked up the tunes. She came staggering down the winding southern road that ran right down to the poured concrete of the pier. Robbie pointed at her. "A stumbler," he muttered, having adopted our term. "Engage at twenty yards, yeh?"

I nodded, somewhat distracted by the extraordinary number, diversity, and location of this infected's body piercings. The street tats made it unlikely that she had been one of the residents. Probably a human toy that one of the rich, famous, and debauched had brought to their off-the-grid playground.

At twenty-five yards, Robbie looked back at me. I nodded. He leaned over the FAL—his first time using it—and squeezed off a single round.

And missed. At slightly less than twenty yards. Robbie turned very red, hunched harder and closer over the sights—as if that would help—and fired again. Another miss, but at least it came closer: the bullet clipped the crate she was passing. She continued to yowl hoarsely, like it wasn't her making the noise, but some exhausted animal trapped inside her.

"Breathe," I coached Robbie. "Slow in. Slow out . . . and . . . squeeze."

The FAL spoke and the stumbler keeled over: a through-and-through in the diaphragm. She grunted, tried to rise up, fell back to the pier's sunbaked surface, one arm clawing the air in our direction.

Tai, who had been watching, turned her head away. "Mercy kill, *chefe*?"

I nodded.

She kneeled, brought up her M4, nodded for Robbie to watch. "I start out like you; no good with rifles. Better now. Watch. Gun can't hurt you. No get tense. Get loose. Calm at end of breath, then . . . squeeze." Her shot hit the stricken stumbler an inch above the left eye. In the silence, Tai rose, patted Robbie's shoulder. "Takes time. Remember: no tense." She nodded to me and scanned the surreal collection of mansions dotting the green slope in front of us. "All th' stalkers dead, you thin'?"

I shook my head. "Naw. No way we'd ever get *that* lucky."

She smiled one of her spotlight-bright smiles, then squinted and pointed. "Comp'ny coming."

Sure enough, two more were coming down from the other direction. If anything, they were even more emaciated than the first one. "Marian," I murmured to Robbie's invariable companion, "your turn."

By the end of the second hour, we'd had a total of five infected show up, shuffle to the end of the pier, and flail until our less experienced shooters dropped them. Three fell in the water. The other two bled out on the sunbaked concrete, which meant we had to decon it before the security team clambered up on it. So, while they waited for the Special Sauce to do its work, they walked the length of the beach that stretched north along the bay.

When the security team returned from that uneventful sweep, they settled in behind some empty oil drums at the head of the pier, dogs in tow. We had Daisy and one of her puppies on the job: best teach them when they're young, because this is going to be their daily existence, too. But everything remained silent, except for the shouted instruction and rattling of the winches as we off-loaded the vehicles and coaxed them into life. It was as if even the birds had deserted this place.

With the security team—Johnnie, Jorge, Robbie—in a prepared position on the pier, and covered from *Legacy* by Chloe and Prospero, those of us on the recon team set out. That meant me, Tai (who was good on a motorcycle), Valda (who was even better), Ning (as competent with a car as everything else, or so it seemed), and Papillon, who was officially along to assess the planes at the airfield. But we also wanted to see if he was as badass as his Legionnaire pedigree suggested.

We drove up out of the bay using the right-hand road. It started out heading south before connecting to the northern route, which made it the longer way to the airport, but it skirted the small village of Lovell. It was the only cluster of buildings on the island and so exactly the place you wanted to avoid if you didn't want to be jumped, even by stumblers. The lanes and alleys were tight enough that you might not take all of them down before at least one of them got to you.

If Mustique looked surreal from Britannia Bay, it was positively bizarre up close. It wasn't just the mad opulence and a lingering sense that every architect who'd ever had a gig here tried to outdo all those who came before. What made it unnerving was seeing it in various states of wrack and ruin. Kind of like what you'd imagine when the barbarians came and sacked Rome in its final years. Except that on Mustique, it was like every culture on Earth had been here to die all at once. Polynesian pavilions; lancet-windowed Moroccan palaces; Mediterranean villas; Shinto-influenced great halls: all were as desolate and dead as the wealth and egos that had built them.

We came around one corner and discovered three bleached horse skeletons; all were stripped clean, the saddles and tack laid neatly to one side. Just a bit beyond, four dog carcasses were strung up on a decorative yardarm; they'd been hung there while still alive. Three neat piles of lizard skeletons led up the driveway of a large house which had been burned to the ground—except that a bedroom set had been brought outside, as if waiting for its owner to sleep under the stars. To get the full picture, add in a wide assortment of crashed golf carts, a few burned-out cars, and a generous scattering of corpses—some naked, some still in rags. It was like driving through some nightmare collage designed to creep out any sane human. Because before you could make any sense of each new morsel of weirdness, you turned the next corner and found another freakshow scene.

But wherever we were, whatever we saw, there was always the same, suffocating silence.

Just after 1300, we arrived at the airport and experienced a perverse sense of relief: nothing more than the typical postapocalyptic ruin we'd come to expect. The small passenger terminal (which had handled customs, immigration, and security) was a single wood-frame building with a now-wrecked facade of fake "primitive" woodwork. About a dozen bodies littered the stretch between the main doors and the landing strip. The single small fuel storage tank had burned and taken a plane with it. Seen from the corner of one's eye, its charred airframe looked like the blackened skeleton of a mechanical dragon.

Papillon pointed out signs that other planes had made hasty departures: chocks tossed aside, convenience ladders thrown over, luggage abandoned at the flight line. We looked for hangars, were worried not to see any, then discovered three aircraft that had been rolled to the far side of the de-planing apron. They had been stored under large, ground-moored tarps, but Papillon warned us not to get our hopes up. Planes that just sit around usually require lots of maintenance before they can be flown, even when they've been stored in the equivalent of shrink-wrap.

But we couldn't stop to assess them until we finished our recon of the island. After that, we planned on splitting into two groups. One team would be the folks who had skills that might prove useful for repairing planes. The other was a general salvage team. So we started back south to check out the parts of Mustique south of the pier.

Except, before we got there, Ning motioned for us to stop the car as we were passing the Berber citadel-house that topped the highest of several ridges overlooking Britannia Bay.

Tai killed her dirt bike's motor as she pulled up alongside and asked, "Wazzup?"

Ning made an impatient motion for silence, cocked her head. "There. You hear it?"

I listened. And heard what might have been—a buzzing?

Tai stood up from the seat of her bike. "Yeah," she muttered. "Like a . . . a . . ."

"A drone," said Papillon, who vaulted out of the back of the car, head on a swivel.

Ning stood on the seat of the buggy, turned slowly, eyes half closed, stopped when she was facing directly behind us. She opened her eyes, smiled—not a heart-warming expression—and pointed: "There."

About forty yards behind us, just drifting to a stop, was one of those quad-rotor drones that people use to take aerial movies. And its lens was aimed at us.

Tai brought her weapon up; I gestured it down.

"Mebbe has a li'l bomb," she muttered.

I nodded, glanced at Ning. She returned a "why are you looking at me?" stare, eyebrows raised. I jerked my head at the drone. "What do you think? Armed?"

She frowned, but also kind of smiled. I think that was the moment she realized that we knew she had "professional training" but decided not to be jerks about it. She shook her head. "Not armed."

"Too small?"

"Not the right model to carry a payload; it would lose too much agility."

Those few words were the most I had heard her speak in a single sentence since we met. I nodded, slung my weapon, glanced at the bushes and the ruined mansions to either flank. "Cover me," I said, got out, and walked toward the drone.

Which backed up and ascended slightly.

I stopped. "Can you hear us as well as see us?"

No reaction. I scanned around. Although the operator did not have to be in line of sight, it was unlikely that he or she was too far out of it, either. Not a single intact house in sight—except, I realized, the one with the small medieval tower. Because the, the—damn it; what are they called?—the *merlons*, were studded with spikes and strung with what looked like barbed wire, I had written it off as the sad remainder of a failed last stand. Except, what if it wasn't? What if it had held out?

I pointed at the house. "That your place?"

The drone boosted straight up.

The moment after it did, I was hit by a blast... of wild sound. At first I couldn't make it out, but then a few bars survived the static of the overloaded speakers: "Gimme Shelter." But not from the intro: it started right at the chorus, the guitars wailing away.

Tai was pointing at the tower. "There!"

I nodded. I glanced up at the drone, gestured at the house.

The drone bobbed a few feet up and down before whirring off toward the tower.

I turned back toward the others. "I'm pretty sure that's an invitation."

The house with the tower shared a driveway with another one: the Berber castle that really wasn't. They both overlooked the bay, but the one we were heading toward was built a little below the crest of the ridge and was a third the footprint of the other.

The front walkway was pretty overgrown, but we could still make out the sign—Grayrock Manor—and the reason for its name: the house was quite literally built out of gray rock. Obviously really old, despite all the modern features. Looking through the ruined front door, you could see through to the empty infinity pool.

The music stopped. "Well," drawled a loud voice with a midwestern twang, "you comin' on in, or whut?"

I looked at the others. We exchanged shrugs. We pushed the remains of the door out of the way, walked in.

Actually, we entered a covered walkway joining two separate buildings: a solid, squat house on the left and the tower on the right. And leaning over the tower's parapet was a tall, lanky man: in his fifties, I guessed. He had long stringy hair, a Cubs baseball cap, a gun sling around his neck, and a week's growth of beard. I was impressed that anyone in his situation was still shaving at all.

"Hi," I said.

He stared, then threw back his head and laughed; either his parents hadn't been able to afford an orthodontist or hadn't cared. "Dude!" he said still chuckling. "I like you; I like that: 'hi.'" He chortled some more. "End of the world and the dude just waves and says, 'hi.'"

I could feel more than hear Tai and Ning moving their hands closer to their weapons.

He was still chuckling, but his eyes narrowed, grew sharp and bright. "Now don't you all start thinking of doing something stupid. Not when we're just having fun getting acquainted."

I nodded, sent a palms-down gesture back at them; I sensed the guns lowering, saw it in the survivor's eyes. "Sorry," I explained. "Just like you're not used to new people saying 'hi,' we're not used to new people laughing."

He nodded. "Fair enough. But I gotta tell you, I'm not used to new people at all. So you gotta fergive me my manners. Which will get a lot better once you all put your guns down. Sling 'em, would be best."

"I could send a couple of my friends to wait outside, with all the guns, if that would—"

"Shit, boy! No guns? Here? Or *any*where, these days? Look: I don't think you're here to kill me. But these days, it seems like all kinds of misunderstandings could occur, so just—well, keep 'em handy, but keep 'em stowed, okay?"

I had been worried that his laughter meant he was halfway to insane. And I supposed he still might be, but if so, he was a very reasonable and practical madman. We did as he asked.

He came down from the tower, toting—I will never forget this—an M60 machine gun. I figured the strap around his neck meant he was carrying a pretty heavy weapon, but this? It took me a moment to realize it might also be a great conversation starter: "You know, we have ammunition for that gun. A lot, actually."

His eyes grew bright. "You don't say? You thinking of trading it?"

I shrugged. "Maybe. Why don't we talk first?"

He smiled. "I like you, son. You're calm. Rare quality, these days." He cackled. "Never had it, myself." He collapsed into a weather-worn sofa, put down the machine gun, started picking at a callus on the side of one of his toes. He stopped, looked up at us. "Well, you gonna sit or what? I can offer you a drink. Water. Guaranteed uncontaminated by the virus."

I think several of us started at that. "You can get the virus from water?"

"Sure, son. Where have you all been?" He considered. "Well, probably someplace without community water mains. Yeah, all it takes is one of the damn infected to find their way into a water tank, or cistern, or pumping plant, and die there. Or paddle around in it for a while. That's how the plague got the people crashing at Mick's house. I told 'em to stick with bottled water. Hell, I offered them mine. But they were too scared to come and get it. Not that I blame them; everything was starting to go to shit right about then."

"Mick?" Valda asked. He didn't sound perplexed so much as . . . hopeful? Expectant?

Our host stared at him. "Yeah." Stared some more when there was no change in our expressions. "Mick? The guy who cut the record I played to get your attention?"

I thought Valda might cry or wet himself or both. Thanks to YouTube, I'd seen saved souls at revival meetings look less transported than him. "You mean—?"

Our host scratched the side of his neck. "Damn it, don't you people know where you are? This is Mustique, folks: home to rockers, movie stars, fat cats, and everyone else who made a lot of money doing shit that doesn't matter anymore. Like me." He smiled.

"But I did pick up a few skills along the way. Now, who the hell are all of *you*?"

We gave him the very short version. It still took close to half an hour, during which our comms kept buzzing and we kept signaling that all was okay.

He craned his neck to look at *Legacy*. "You got some nervous friends. But at least they care about you. That's good." He said that as if it was unusual, rather than commonplace.

"And who are *you*?" I asked.

Another display of teeth just uneven enough to make you look twice. "I'm no one, now. But I used to be somebody. Shit, I used to be *every*body!"

I found myself worrying about his sanity again and measuring the distance between his hand and the M60.

He rolled his eyes. "Damn, you people got no poetry in you. Or maybe all this apocalyptic shit ran it right out of you. Well, I am here to put it back!"

He jumped up; some of us flinched for our handguns as he reached behind the couch.

But what he pulled up was a guitar: acoustic, and a really, really pretty one. He slammed through a few driving chords before I caught the tune: "Cat Scratch Fever." I think even Ning recognized it.

Valda jumped up: "Wait! Are you—are you—?"

"I am"—our host clawed out a harsh, ending chord—"Ozzie Nugent: wildman, impresario, and imitator of the great and near-great! At your service!"

He slung the guitar behind him on the couch, plopped down next to it. We all stared at him.

Valda looked like he'd awakened from a coma. "Wait. You . . . you're *who*?"

"Ozzie Nugent," our host said, a little more slowly.

Valda shook his head. "I don't understand."

"Ozzie" frowned, then laughed. "Oh. I get it. You thought I was the Madman himself, straight from the Motor City! Sorry to disappoint, but no. I am—well, was—the frontman for his A-list tribute band."

Papillon frowned. "An A-list tribute band?"

"Sure!" Ozzie frowned. "Never heard of that? Yeah, well, it was a thing. A big thing. Lots and lots of money. I was the frontman for a whole bunch of bands, along the way. Nugent, Black Sabbath, Pink Floyd—"

"That!" shouted Valda. "That is where I saw you! In Brno! You sang lead for the Pink Floyd tribute band. You were almost as good as they were!"

Ozzie smiled. "That's the idea. And do you know how we made so much money? By playing cities too small to be world-tour venues, and just far enough away that the locals hadn't travelled to hear the real band." He sighed. "Damn, that was good money, and great puss—" his eyes shot toward Tai and Ning—". . . parties. Great *parties.*" He picked at his toe again. "At least, that's how I started in the business. But unlike most *real* rock stars, I had a good head for business, too. Started managing, putting together mega-tours of tribute bands. That was even better money and better, uh—times. Much, *much* better times." He stared out to sea wistfully. Then he looked straight at me. "So, what's the gig?"

I think I blinked. "I beg your pardon?"

He smiled. "You are so polite. You had one helluva momma, am I right?"

That caught me off guard. "I—I—"

He put up a hand. "Hey, I'm sorry, man. I got a big mouth. Can jam both feet in there, sometimes. Like just now."

His regret was so clear, and the image of him with both feet jammed between his crooked teeth was so funny, that I smiled. "No worries. And actually, yeah: she was." And suddenly, I wasn't angry he'd said what he had; I was grateful. It was like some little bit of my mom was still alive in the world. "Not sure what you mean by a 'gig,' though."

"I mean, what comes next?"

"Well, we didn't expect to find anyone alive here, actually. So that makes it a little more complicated. We were planning on salvaging whatever we could, seeing if we could get one of those planes to work—"

"Yeah, yeah: I get all that. I mean, where do *I* fit in?"

Where does he *fit in?* "Um, er, well . . . do you want to? Fit in, I mean?"

He snorted. "You think I wanna stay here? To do what? Play my old records and starve to death alone? I mean, yeah, I got one hell of a stash—food, weapons, ammo, you name it—but that's not a forever solution. And I'm a people person. So, unless you have something against ex-kinda-rockers of a certain age, I'm with you guys. Besides"—his face slipped on a sly grin—"your pal Papillon here isn't the only one who knows his way around a plane."

"Really?" I just said it to cover how stupefied I was.

"Really," he asserted. "De Havilland Twin Otter 300s. The STOL plane-of-choice for the islands, and *mine* has wingtip tanks. She'll get you wherever you need to go. Although, I gotta say: Kourou is *pret-*ty far." He leaned back; I think he was enjoying watching us goggle at his revelations. "Too far to get there in one go. No mid-size commercial turboprop can do that. And there aren't a whole lot of airfields between here and French Guiana."

He smiled. "But I just happen to know where they are. Damn near all of them, I reckon." He stretched. "It's odd, the things you pick up when you are managing bands and cutting costs to ferry them around."

Papillon's left eyebrow had climbed toward his hairline. "What made you decide to learn to fly?"

Ozzie dusted off his toe-picking fingers. "Same thing that got me familiar with airstrips all over the world: shuttling bands across its entire surface. And besides liking the parties, I also liked doing things—real things—with my money. So I figured: hey, I'll learn to fly. Which turned out to be real useful later, when I was a manager. As long as I could book a plane, we were good to go." His eyes slid northward significantly. "Just like now."

Papillon's eyebrow remained raised: "And you are familiar with the maintenance of such planes?"

"Listen, friend; anyone who has the skill to maintain his own plane but trusts his airborne ass to some day-wage mechanic is either suicidal or stupid. I'm neither."

I nodded. "That's very clear. But it also makes me wonder if you'll be, um, happy travelling with us."

He frowned. "Oh? Why's that?"

I shrugged. "You're probably twice as old as any of us. You've done and seen a lot. But we've got our own way of doing things, and our own—"

He held up his hand. "I get it. You guys are in charge . . . you, particularly," he added, looking at me. He leaned forward. "You know why I'm still here? Why I wasn't taken down by drugs, or drinking, or delusions of grandeur?"

I shook my head.

"Because I control my ego, not the other way

around." He shook his head. "Probably why I wasn't a rock star myself. Getting out center stage with your lyrics, your music, your voice, your guitar: Christ, you *have* to be damn near insane with arrogance." He shrugged and smiled. "Or maybe I just wasn't good enough. But that doesn't change the fact that I always made decisions with my head, not my pric—pride." He sighed. "I succeeded because in a business where almost no one was a team player, I was. So I was the guy that kept things working. And now? Well, you all seem a whole lot nicer and more levelheaded than the people I worked with most of my life." He leaned back. "So, do you have a space for me?"

I looked around, saw wide eyes, the kind that told me they all thought I'd be nuts if I said "no." I agreed with them. "Seems like you might. We just need to talk to the rest of the group. But..."

"Yeah?"

"I gotta ask one thing."

"Yeah?"

"Where the hell did you get that machine gun?"

"What? Old Betsy?" He smiled. "There's almost nothing you can't score when you manage a rock band."

"Okay... but *why*?"

He chuckled. "Well, I'd like to be able to say it was foresight, that I was some kind of guru prepper." He smiled. "But that would be pure bullshit. Fact of the matter is I got it for the Madman himself."

Valda's jaw dropped. "You mean... for—?"

"Lemme tell you; the videos of him—actually, *us*—shooting feral pigs in Texas? Well, the big fun we had wasn't safe for YouTube." He patted the M60. "Potential litigation and all that." He frowned, put his hands in his lap. "Actually, before this gig starts, there is one favor I'd ask of you guys."

I was hesitant, but Valda, still a bit star-struck, nodded eagerly. "Name it!"

Ozzie looked away, out over the bay. Then his gaze slid to the Berber castle just to the south of his own, humbler property. "My neighbor."

"Yes? Is he a *real* rock st—?" Valda bit off the end of the sentence, tried again. "Eh, is your neighbor *also* a rock star?"

"No. But I need help with him."

"What kind of help?"

"I need someone to ... well, see to him."

"What do you mean?"

I managed not to roll my eyes. Hell, we all have our weak spots and if Valda's was being a rock-and-roll fanboy, no big deal. Not much of an Achilles' heel in a world where it's all but gone. Except, possibly, in that very room. But it was time for me to intercede. "So Ozzie, this friend of yours: is he alone?"

Ozzie looked up at me, hangdog. "Yeah. I'm pretty sure."

Valda's mouth opened into an "O" of horrified realization.

I followed Ozzie's eyes. "Next door?"

"Yeah."

"What can you tell us?"

Ozzie shrugged. "Not much." He slapped at a fly with far more force than was necessary. "I told him, y'know? *Told* him." He shook his head. "Don't get me wrong; I understand why he did what he did. I might have done it myself if I had any kids. I mean, any that I know about."

I nodded. "And he let in one of his children who was infected?"

"Yeah. I mean, I think so. She flew in on the last plane. With family friends. Didn't seem sick...or at least didn't let anyone see it." He ground a fist into his palm. "They were all fine before then, buttoned up like I was."

He looked at the place. "I keep trying to tell myself it was going to happen anyway. I mean, look at his house, man. It's got doors and windows like a castle, but it's all spread out. Three separate wings, none much taller than the others. How was he gonna defend that?"

"He probably was not thinking of that when he bought it," Papillon offered mildly.

"Yeah. Prolly not. But he should have, y'know? I mean, I did. That's why I got a place with a tower on the highest ground. Put in a generator, a well, basement storage, steel doors, and shipped in enough belted 7.62 NATO for World War Three. Just in case, well"—he waved around him—"something like this happened. 'Cause man, some of the places I've been...Shit: I started figuring this maybe *had* to happen. All the hunger, all the disease, all the have-nots hating the haves. It was gonna be this or something else." He looked up at us, miserable, heartbroken. "Am I right?"

I nodded. "Sure. Tell me: what's the safest way to approach your friend's house?"

December 23 (dawn)

I had wanted to finish yesterday's entry last night, but I was too damned tired and there was too much to do. Besides, Ozzie started jamming with Robbie and Marian and we all stayed up way too late and drank way too much.

But mostly, I just didn't want to write about what happened after we left Ozzie's house.

So Ozzie had told us that he had seen movement in his pal's mini-Alhambra only a week ago. The kind of manic chasing about that was typical of the turned when they were in the midst of, or getting revved up for, a feeding frenzy. That struck me as odd. Any infected that active within the past week should have come down to our dance party on the pier. But I figured maybe it had chowed down so heavily that it was catatonic with overfeeding. Not that I have ever seen any get to that state of satiation, but hey: there's a whole lot about the infected that we don't know and probably never will.

We made our way through the forty yards of steeply sloped brush and forest between the estates, constantly

216

worried about stalkers that might jump out of the shadows. But Ozzie had noticed that, as the turned became weaker, they started staying away from steep hillsides and thick undergrowth. Logical: as predators already low on food, most will try to conserve their strength. On Mustique that meant staying on roads and cleared properties.

Ozzie had only seen three stalkers in as many weeks. More and more of them were either slipping into torpor or becoming prey for the few remaining active ones. So despite being terrified, we got to the neighbor's house without incident.

It was laid out as three parts of a broad-based vee: a central open pavilion and two flanking buildings. The one closest of those side structures was low and fairly conventional. The farther one looked like a mix between an ultra-modern house and a two-story nightclub. It was almost half glass, backed by steel-shutter blinds that Ozzie hadn't seen open since August.

We kept to our standard entry drill. First we crept around the building: the grounds were secure, no sign of recent movement. Which was kind of weird; if the turned neighbor was still active, how was he getting out to feed? But given how many secret passages and hidden basements Mustique's residents had added at God knows what cost and for what perverse reasons, maybe Neighbor Guy had remembered some of those details and now had a hidden lair. Maybe lots of others had, too, since the weirdest thing about the local spoor was what we *didn't* see: evidence that stalkers had ever gathered in packs. While that was reassuring on one hand—maybe fewer had survived long enough to turn—it was worrisome on the other:

if the infected had lived and died in big bunches, we might now run into stray, half-active stumblers almost anywhere we went.

But since this area had no active infected, we turned our attention to the building closest to Ozzie's house. Again, we followed standard entry tactics: breach the door with a firefighter's hammer, wait for a reaction, then toss in a noisy wind-up toy. If none of that got a response, one of us went in low (Ning, Tai, or me) and one of us went in high (Papillon or Valda). Whoever wasn't on the entry team was either covering them or watching our six.

There were no stalkers inside, torpid or otherwise, but it was creepy, even by postapocalypse standards. Dried blood all over the place—and I mean all over. Almost every square inch of floor, a lot of the walls, and even the ceilings had gotten their fair share of arterial sprays.

But no bodies. Or any parts thereof. Another mystery without any apparent answer other than, "some seriously weird shit must have gone down here."

Next on our line of advance was the central pavilion. This presented a more typical jumble of trashed furniture, scat, gnawed bones—but again, no actual bodies. Of course, in the open, that's not too unusual. Roving stalkers grab up any remains when prey gets scarce.

It also looked like Neighbor Man had been a dog owner; there was a free-run line strung beneath the up-curving roof, from one peaked end to the other. It looked like a late addition—the work and materials were pretty crude—so maybe they got the dog for protection. If so, it hadn't done much to change their outcome.

That left the shiny, two-story Palace of Chic. It was flanked by a constant-flow lap pool on the side and an infinity pool facing the bay. Both were filled with green algae sludge. The door—glass—had been shattered, but the steel shutters were fixed in place, locked into the frame. They had taken a real beating—lots of blood and scratches—but were intact. Still, the shutters just didn't look solid enough to keep out a whole pack of infected.

We ran the same opening drill as at the first side building—but here, what was left of the door swung wide the moment we hit it with the breaching tool. We listened: nothing. Threw in the toy: a Tommy-knockers monkey that bashed its cymbals together. Still nothing. So Ning led crouched low and Valda followed high.

Or that was supposed to be what happened. Instead, the moment Ning put her left foot inside, the floor fell away: it was hinged. She yelped, but, with reflexes that would have shamed a leopard, managed to turn as she was falling, reach across and grab Valda's pants leg.

Valda had just barely managed to sway back away from the sudden pit under his feet, but with Ning grabbing on, he started tipping forward—but Papillon got him by the rear straps of his web-gear and hauled him back from the ledge. I let my own weapon loose on its sling to grab for Ning's other arm and haul her up.

Tai had just turned to ask what the hell was happening when a metallic grinding noise came out of the darkness. A moment later, it was drowned out by a rapidly rising howl—as if a feral sound was being released from an opening vault door.

The sound became a solid mass rushing out of the darkness: a ravenous stalker leaped into the dim light, talon-fingers stretched toward Ning.

Ning twisted to face the noise as Valda strained to yank her out of the pit and Papillon kept trying to haul him backward. Not an easy job, since Valda was about thirty pounds and four inches bigger. Tai saw that and grabbed Papillon to steady him. I kept pulling up on Ning, saw the stalker's hand grab at her arm, realized that the yellowed teeth would be next, pawed at the holster of my HP-35.

Everything happened at once. I got the pistol clear. Valda heaved hard on Ning's belt, breaking the stalker's grip on her arm. The monster's teeth darted toward her neck. Ning got her other arm up to block. I raised the pistol as the stalker's teeth slid off Ning's elbow protector but snagged on her sleeve, in her flesh, or both. And as Ning screamed—and she, Valda, and Papillon, all went backward and cleared the hole—I unloaded half the mag into the stalker's face.

Ning did not scream again, but was cursing—I guess—in Chinese: her voice was low, ferocious. Tai was gasping about amputating Ning's arm at the elbow, or maybe the shoulder. Papillon was scrambling to his feet. Valda, still flat on his ass, was trying to get his gun aimed through the doorway. Which I was covering with the last half of the Hi-Power's thirteen-round mag, hoping it would be enough.

Nothing else emerged. There was no further sound.

"Sitrep," I said. Actually, what came out of my mouth sounded like a dog's bark. I was shaken, angry, and horrified at the thought of putting Ning down if she couldn't—or wouldn't—do it herself.

Valda, God love him, uttered two calm words: "Covering front." Papillon did not reply: he was examining Ning's arm. Who turned toward Tai and snapped, "Shut up, idiot." Which silenced all of us. She sounded more annoyed than terrified. I mean, yeah, we knew she was tough, but—

"Stop staring," she ordered. "I shall be well."

"Ning," I started.

"You shut up, too. Do you not understand? I am immune."

We all sat there, mute, for—well, I don't know for how long. I guess it couldn't have been more than a few seconds. But despite the open door and the possible threats beyond, we just stared. Because although we had heard statistics that some people—maybe ten percent—are immune, we'd never encountered it before.

Okay, maybe we had, particularly if the odds really are really one in ten. Hell, for all we know, maybe that's why Johnnie never got sick after going aboard the trawler back at Husvik, before it was (maybe) freeze-sanitized. But Ning was the first person who ever said that she *knew* she was.

Which made a lot of sense, in retrospect. I mean, badass or not, it was beyond crazy that she could have won out over a whole Antarctic base full of infected. She only had to miss one, make a single mistake, and it was all over. Because the stalkers didn't have to live to finish the job; their teeth, claws, and spittle were all more lethal than cobra venom.

Unless she was immune.

Ning rose in one smooth motion, gestured angrily at the med kit we'd given Papillon. "Just because I cannot contract the virus does not mean this bite will not infect. Have you seen their teeth? Quick! Antiseptic!"

But I wasn't thinking about medical treatment. Not yet. I backed away from the door and let the HP-35 fall on its lanyard as I brought up the M4. I snapped on the underslung flashlight.

The room beyond was like a scene from a snuff film (okay; I'm just guessing about that). Bodies everywhere. Partially eaten arms and feet scattered across the blood-brown floor. A thick carrion stink. But also, lots of foil and plastic wrappers, some gnawed on. None of it made any sense. I raised the rifle higher, angling the light deeper into the room.

The stalker, who had once been a tall and very shapely brunette, was very dead. She was also wearing a collar fastened to a chain which disappeared into a small room that faced the entry from across the room. Judging from its thick door and acoustic-tiled walls, it was soundproof. That's when I realized the chain and its fittings were a match for what I had seen under the roof of the central pavilion. So, not a dog run, after all.

My stomach had tightened and grown cold; a fresh wash of sweat ran down from my armpits. "Guys . . ." I started.

"*Mãe de Deus*," I heard Tai mutter over my shoulder.

"*Vraiment*," breathed Papillon.

Ning leaned around. "She was someone's idea of a mastiff?" Her tone was equal parts amazed and scornful.

"What deranged monster would do such a thing?" Valda wondered, his accent unusually thick.

"That would be me," came a hoarse answer from high in the darkness beyond.

More out of reflex than alarm, I snapped the M4's muzzle up toward the source of the voice.

The second floor had a small, all-glass balcony, probably created so that partiers could sip their drinks while watching the crowd below. Standing with both hands on its Lucite railing was a guy who was probably in his early sixties but looked a lot older. Hell, he looked like he was dead. Like some B-movie crypt-creature. His eyes were that sunken, and his face was that pale.

His voice was dry, creaky. "Is she dead?"

"Yes. What—what the hell is all . . . all this?"

"This was how she—we—lived."

"What do you mean, how you lived?" I glanced at the floor; the trapdoor was almost flush with the door frame. I stepped around the jamb sideways, kicked a skull out of the way so I could get my feet on the floor. "Are you fucking insane?"

"Yes, very probably." He straightened his shirt, which was apparently a high-end casual button-down. Louis Vuitton, or something like it. Very classy. Before it got covered with chunks of dried flesh, that is.

"You would *have* to be insane," Ning shouted over my shoulder, "to keep a stalker as a guard dog. Or a pet."

"She was neither. She was my daughter."

Suddenly, everything looked different. The collar, the chain, the small room, the trap. "This was all to—to feed her."

"Yes."

"You are a . . . a monster!" Tai screamed from the doorway.

"Yes, that too." He looked down at the kill-room he

had created. "Very much so." He shifted, as though he were taking his hands out of his pockets.

I sighted down the barrel of the M4. "But...why? Why not, well...?"

"Kill her?" He nodded. "I intended to. I wanted to. But then, you see your baby. You see her in diapers, taking her first steps. In her Communion dress. With flowers in her hair at the beach." He closed his eyes. "So I would tell myself, 'I shall kill her tomorrow.' And again, the next." He opened his eyes. "So here we are."

"You did not just delay killing her," Valda choked out. "You kept her alive. You helped *her* kill."

The man shrugged. "It was not difficult. The kitchen in this section of the house was designed so we could cater large parties. It had a commercial walk-in freezer. And there were always enough bodies. Lots and lots of bodies."

"You mean, stalkers that fell into your trap?"

"Those, too." It sounded like he was trying to say something else, but his voice—suddenly a sob and a groan together—strangled the words.

I may have let the M4 slip a millimeter. "What do you mean, 'those too'? Where did most of the bodies come from?" I snapped the weapon back up. "Did you bait healthy people into this trap?"

He started, as if he'd been hit with a cattle prod. "God, no. I just...I mean...There were many bodies already here. In the house."

His sudden silence suggested a scenario far more horrific than baiting in strangers. "Wait a minute, are you saying—?"

"Yes. My wife. My sons. My friends." He shrugged.

"All dead from the virus or killed when they turned. Until only she and I were left. And I couldn't lose her. Not her, too. Not my baby. Not my—"

He straightened up, as if trying to push away the misery in his voice and in his hunched shoulders. At least for a second. "Thank you."

"For what?"

"For doing what I could not." He raised his shadow-hidden forearm, up toward his chin.

I did not see the gun until it went off. A dark patch splattered—thick, mudlike—on the wall behind him. He toppled forward, over the railing. He landed across the body of his daughter.

That's when I puked.

I wasn't the only one.

There comes a certain point in the postapocalypse where you reassure, even comfort, yourself by saying, "Well, I've seen it all now. There are no new shocks, no new horrors, to send me into another spiral of suppressed anger, lost appetite, and sweat-soaked nightmares."

But then something like this happens. And so like I said at the outset of this two-part journal entry, you may assume that rock music is dead, or that you've seen all the horrors to be seen, but the reality is that you just can't be sure of anything. Not anymore.

As we went through the neighbor's house, we found all the clever ways he'd managed to keep his daughter fed while also remaining at a safe distance. Her collar was on a kind of windlass, so that he could reel her back into the soundproofed room when he went out to gather bodies, get water, repair the solar cells, or supplement her diet with raw "meat" from the freezer. His own room—it had been a servant's, once—was as foul-smelling and lightless as hers. I doubted he had bathed or eaten anything other than packaged food in months. Everything about that room screamed what he could not: that he was living in a hell beyond anything he had ever imagined, and that he deserved to be there. It was tempting to burn the whole place to the ground.

We returned to Ozzie's and drove Ning back to the pier for treatment aboard *Legacy*. There, we added Johnnie and Steve to our team for better security and kept Ozzie with us as a guide. He'd been in about half of the homes on Mustique and had heard tales of most of the others.

We made a lot of progress. Those of us who had been at the Berber House of Horrors were all more talkative and more animated than usual—because that's how we kept going, kept focused on the job. If the others noticed it, they didn't say anything.

Mustique did not disappoint. The stuff we found just lying around, undamaged, was mind-boggling. It was no surprise that almost everybody on the island had sneaked in a gun or two. Some sneaked in a *lot* more. Two were major preppers with very deep pockets. Thing is, most of the firearms were custom jobs or rich-man toys: long on bells and whistles, short on down-and-dirty reliability and standardization. For instance, we found dozens of perfectly good weapons that had been fitted with crazy-fancy scopes—but had been stripped of their iron sights in order to mount them. And only a few of the owners kept an actual armory, or gun room, or safe, where you could lay your hands on the original parts.

When we got to the sixth palace, Ozzie scooted inside ahead of us, knew right where the gun safe was, and even knew the combination to the lock. He fished around a minute, pulled out a gun that looked like a hybrid M4 with a heavier barrel. Or was that a—?

"Integral suppressor," he breathed. "This is one sweet gun." He looked at it longingly for a second, then held it out to me. "Here. Take it."

I might have blinked before I shook my head. "Wha—? No. We've got all the guns we need."

"You got one like this? *Exactly* like this?"

"No. Why? Is it, uh, special or something?"

He started to roll his eyes but stopped. "Look, little boss-man. You want this gun. You have *no idea* how much you want this gun." He shook it slightly, as if to emphasize its importance. "This, my friend, is called the Honeybadger. Chambered for .300 Blackout. More quiet than the MP5 SD that SinoSpy Sally is carrying and a shitload more powerful than the plastic poodle-shooter you've got pointed at the floor." He waved it around. "Floats like a butterfly, stings like a battering ram. Well, like an AK, but you get the idea."

I did. "And I bet it also bucks like a mule."

He shook his head, still grinning. "You'd think so, being this small a package. But it doesn't." For one second, all his showmanship and palaver dropped away. "Trust me, Alvaro. You want this gun. You, specifically."

"Why me?"

"I've watched you. You haven't assigned yourself a long gun. Prob'ly 'cause you ain't a great hand with it. And also, in a posse this small, you gotta lead from the front. So I say one more time: You. Want. This. Gun."

I stared at it. "Probably shoot it dry in an afternoon."

Ozzie Nugent the showman was suddenly back. He stood aside with a bow, introducing the contents of the walk-in safe with a wide sweep of his arm. "Meet twelve hundred rounds of .300 Blackout. My late friend knew what she was about when it came to guns." He was reflective. "Pity the same couldn't be said about her choice in men."

"Okay," I said, as much to move the op along as anything else, "if you tote it out of here, I'll take it to the range and...well, we'll see." We got back to our salvage survey.

As we guessed, almost every house had an individual generator. And a lot had saferooms, which was one of the reasons why the infected hadn't surged as large packs: a lot who turned early had been shut up in those soundproofed cells, or hidden basement hidey holes, and died there. In almost as many cases, it looked like the turned had become impossible to control, so the families hid out in those rooms until they believed the danger was past. But, in every case, they had evidently become sloppy, distracted, or just plain deranged and let down their guard. Bottom line: not one of those refuges saved the people who initially sheltered in them.

And if gold and jewels ever became valuable again, we were set. Hell, we found almost twenty gold bars and hundreds of Krugerrands and other coins. Now, they were only useful as ballast or really heavy paperweights.

When we got back to *Legacy*, we learned that Ning was not mistaken and had not exaggerated; she seemed totally immune. Before sitting down to dinner, we assigned a team to assess the planes and another team to guard them while they did it. With the exception of a small anchor watch, the rest of us were responsible for scavenging what we could from the mansions of Mustique.

None of us who had been at the Berber House of Horrors were hungry, but we sure were ready for a drink. Or three.

By the time we had finished knocking those back, the faces of our friends and the sound of their laughter had chased off the horror-show scenes—at least long enough that we could eat a meal and enjoy listening to Ozzie rock out with Robbie and Marian. And then go back to our bunks and fight against the lurking memories. With immediate, sweaty sex, if we had a steady partner. And maybe even if not.

Anything to make sure we were all totally exhausted. That way, maybe, just maybe, we'd sleep deeper than nightmares' tentacles could reach. Anything to put that day behind us.

Hey, it was worth a try. But now it's time to start the next one.

December 25

We hit the next day running. The nonstop work kept us from thinking back on what we'd seen, rather than looking forward at what needed to be done. And that was a long task list, which probably helped morale. Also, it wasn't just that there was more work, but the jobs were changing and we were busy adapting to new roles.

Including Ozzie, there were now sixteen of us, splitting up to handle very different tasks. Ozzie and Papillon recruited Robbie to help them check out and hopefully ready the planes. Rod and Jeeza were handling the air and sea transport logistics. Also, given Rod's computer skills, Prospero was drilling him on the upload and activation procedures for the Ephemeral Reflex software. The mission was too important to succeed or fail based on any one person's survival. Marian was at least as good with computers—better, probably—but of everyone aboard, she was the most likely to freeze up and go catatonic on what was sure to be the most unpredictable mission we'd ever undertaken. Besides, now that we were coordinating two ships, various comm links and channels,

Jeeza ran her finger between Mustique and Totness again. "Five hundred twenty nautical miles. You see the problem."

"Yes." Papillon rested his chin in his hand. "If our maximum flight range is nine hundred nautical miles, we still do not have enough fuel to fly directly to Totness and return. Even though it is closer than Kourou."

"Correct."

Willow frowned. "But, you could carry fuel drums inside the plane. Land and refuel before you return."

Ozzie shook his head. "Yeah, but the first time you fly to Totness, how will you know you can *land* there? Runway could be jammed with dead planes, abandoned cars. Trees could have fallen across it from ___ of ___ that runs here, just along its ___ wildlife."

and maintaining status on all of them, Marian was the natural person to run the nerve center for what Prospero calls our "C3I": computing, communications, control, and intelligence.

With two ships, a bunch of Zodiacs, and several land vehicles, Jorge quickly became a full-time grease monkey. Both Willow and I needed relief captains for our two ships, since putting together the ground-side plan for Kourou with Prospero was consuming more of our time every day. So I tapped Chloe to captain *Voyager* and Willow chose Jeeza for *Legacy* (who was using the bridge-adjacent chartroom full time, anyway).

That left Tai, Johnnie, Ning, Steve, and Valda as the salvage team. But before their first run, I slipped away long enough to field-test the gun that Ozzie had almost forced into my hands. More out of courtesy than anything else; I was perfectly happy with my M4 and knew I was going to keep it.

I was a convert to the Honeybadger after the first half magazine. The recoil was barely more noticeable than the M4's. Even better, it was hardly any louder than the MP5 SD. And judging from the mess it made of everything I used as a target, the .300 Blackout cartridge clearly had much better first-round lethality (although "double-tap to be double-sure" is always going to be my mantra). Its layout and function were like the other guns of the AR-15 family, with one exception: this one was supersmooth. Maybe it's just me. Guns are like people; no two get along in just the same way. Me and the Honeybadger? We just clicked.

By Christmas Eve, the plane team confirmed that Ozzie's Twin Otter 300 was in the best shape, and that a second could also be restored. Eventually. But

Ozzie's bird was the key, because without her wing-tip tanks, we'd lose a lot of range. That would really complicate an operation that was already looking way too complex. Kourou was just under 675 nautical miles from Mustique, so a round trip was about 1350 miles. But what if we had to dodge weather? And what about loiter time to actually get a good look at the ESA facility? Best guess: plan for an aerial mission of 1600 nautical miles.

Problem: even with its wing-tip tanks, and a custom reserve that Ozzie had installed shortly after buying the plane, its maximum range was 900 nautical miles. And that was with eight passengers and light luggage, whereas our mission called for putting eleven people on the ground with moderate combat loads. So, working with initial input from Ozzie and Papillon, Rod and Jeeza had been crunching the numbers on the best way for us to get an advance look at Kourou from the air.

That meant computing a lot of ranges, speeds at various ladings, and how to stage a round trip to Kourou using several airfields, all of which had to be assessed in advance for runway and perimeter safety. By the end of our fourth day at Mustique—Christmas, no less—our two brain-trusters had arrived at what they called "a tangly bitch" of a travel plan. Unfortunately, as Jeeza said when we gathered to hear the details, "it is our only feasible option."

She glanced around the gathered faces—Willow, Prospero, Papillon, Ozzie, and me—as she called the waypoints. "The actual mission flight is pretty simple. We take off from Mustique and fly here"—she jabbed a cleaning-rod pointer at the map—"to Totness. Five hundred and twenty nautical miles."

"Wait: we fly to *where*?" asked Willow, leaning forward; there was no Totness on the map.

"Totness," Prospero explained with a frown, "is an airstrip on the coast of Suriname. And it is so small there isn't even a dot on the map."

Papillon folded his arms. "I know this airfield. Although it is being generous to call it that." He leaned over the map, put his finger on the coastline. "It has no facilities."

"Have you flown into it?"

He shook his head. "No, but I knew people who did. It has no fuel storage tanks. So if you mean to refuel there, you will be disappointed."

Jeeza nodded. "We'll get to how we refuel later. But yeah, that's why we have to land there. Kourou still anot⸺

and maintaining status on all of them, Marian was the natural person to run the nerve center for what Prospero calls our "C3I": computing, communications, control, and intelligence.

With two ships, a bunch of Zodiacs, and several land vehicles, Jorge quickly became a full-time grease monkey. Both Willow and I needed relief captains for our two ships, since putting together the ground-side plan for Kourou with Prospero was consuming more of our time every day. So I tapped Chloe to captain *Voyager* and Willow chose Jeeza for *Legacy* (who was using the bridge-adjacent chartroom full time, anyway).

That left Tai, Johnnie, Ning, Steve, and Valda as the salvage team. But before their first run, I slipped away long enough to field-test the gun that Ozzie had almost forced into my hands. More out of courtesy than anything else; I was perfectly happy with my M4 and knew I was going to keep it.

I was a convert to the Honeybadger after the first half magazine. The recoil was barely more noticeable than the M4's. Even better, it was hardly any louder than the MP5 SD. And judging from the mess it made of everything I used as a target, the .300 Blackout cartridge clearly had much better first-round lethality (although "double-tap to be double-sure" is always going to be my mantra). Its layout and function were like the other guns of the AR-15 family, with one exception: this one was supersmooth. Maybe it's just me. Guns are like people; no two get along in just the same way. Me and the Honeybadger? We just clicked.

By Christmas Eve, the plane team confirmed that Ozzie's Twin Otter 300 was in the best shape, and that a second could also be restored. Eventually. But

Ozzie's bird was the key, because without her wing-tip tanks, we'd lose a lot of range. That would really complicate an operation that was already looking way too complex. Kourou was just under 675 nautical miles from Mustique, so a round trip was about 1350 miles. But what if we had to dodge weather? And what about loiter time to actually get a good look at the ESA facility? Best guess: plan for an aerial mission of 1600 nautical miles.

Problem: even with its wing-tip tanks, and a custom reserve that Ozzie had installed shortly after buying the plane, its maximum range was 900 nautical miles. And that was with eight passengers and light luggage, whereas our mission called for putting eleven people on the ground with moderate combat loads. So, working with initial input from Ozzie and Papillon, Rod and Jeeza had been crunching the numbers on the best way for us to get an advance look at Kourou from the air.

That meant computing a lot of ranges, speeds at various ladings, and how to stage a round trip to Kourou using several airfields, all of which had to be assessed in advance for runway and perimeter safety. By the end of our fourth day at Mustique—Christmas, no less—our two brain-trusters had arrived at what they called "a tangly bitch" of a travel plan. Unfortunately, as Jeeza said when we gathered to hear the details, "it is our only feasible option."

She glanced around the gathered faces—Willow, Prospero, Papillon, Ozzie, and me—as she called the waypoints. "The actual mission flight is pretty simple. We take off from Mustique and fly here"—she jabbed a cleaning-rod pointer at the map—"to Totness. Five hundred and twenty nautical miles."

"Wait: we fly to *where*?" asked Willow, leaning forward; there was no Totness on the map.

"Totness," Prospero explained with a frown, "is an airstrip on the coast of Suriname. And it is so small there isn't even a dot on the map."

Papillon folded his arms. "I know this airfield. Although it is being generous to call it that." He leaned over the map, put his finger on the coastline. "It has no facilities."

"Have you flown into it?"

He shook his head. "No, but I knew people who did. It has no fuel storage tanks. So if you mean to refuel there, you will be disappointed."

Jeeza nodded. "We'll get to how we refuel later. But yeah, that's why we have to land there. Kourou is still another two hundred and twenty nautical miles, so if we don't top off our tank at Totness, we'll arrive at the ESA site with less than five percent fuel." She smiled. "And I don't want to *stay* at Kourou."

"Agreed," Willow said with a slight shudder.

Ozzie was scanning the map. "Ya got a lotta lines drawn all over the place, sweeti—eh, Jeeza," he corrected, seeing her look. Ozzie had come aboard calling the various female crewmembers "sweetie," "honey," and "babe." But after the first two hours and a couple of blunt corrections he had learned to check himself. If he wasn't careful, though, his groupie labels still bled through.

Jeeza answered him with a small but approving nod. "We drew the other lines looking at all the routes that might put us in position to complete this preliminary step."

Ozzie nodded. The rest of us just looked at each other. "Preliminary step?" I asked.

Jeeza ran her finger between Mustique and Totness again. "Five hundred twenty nautical miles. You see the problem."

"Yes." Papillon rested his chin in his hand. "If our maximum flight range is nine hundred nautical miles, we still do not have enough fuel to fly directly to Totness and return. Even though it is closer than Kourou."

"Correct."

Willow frowned. "But, you could carry fuel drums inside the plane. Land and refuel before you return."

Ozzie shook his head. "Yeah, but the first time you fly to Totness, how will you know you can *land* there? Runway could be jammed with dead planes, abandoned cars. Trees could have fallen across it from the margin of jungle that runs here, just along its southern edge. Or there could be dangerous wildlife."

Papillon frowned. "Dangerous wildlife?"

Ozzie turned toward him, face stretching as he champed his teeth, mouth and eyes wide. Maybe, if his teeth had been better, he wouldn't have looked so much like a stalker when he did that.

Jeeza nodded. "So we can't fly from here to Totness until we know it's safe for us to land and refuel."

"I don't like where this is going," Prospero muttered.

"I didn't either," Jeeza agreed. "But there's no choice. Our first flight has to be to a closer airport. We've gotta be able to check out Totness from the air and get back if we can't land. And then—"

"—and then, if Totness *is* safe, you can return and preposition fuel for the eventual flight to Kourou."

"Okay," I agreed. "I see why no one likes this plan. I also see why there's no way around it." I spread my hands toward the map. "There have to be a dozen airfields that we could use for staging the recon flight to Totness. How do we choose which one to check first, so that we don't just fly around and waste aviation fuel visiting every damn airstrip?"

"Well," Jeeza started, "Rod and I have been giving that a lot of thought, and—"

"Tobago," Ozzie said flatly.

Everyone stared at him, silent. We waited.

He looked up, started and stared back, surprised. "What? There some reason not to go to Tobago?"

"No, Ozzie. We just want to know why you're so sure it's the *right* airfield."

"Oh. That. Yeah, well, it's actually your only real choice."

Prospero folded his arms, frowning. "Explain. Please."

Ozzie shrugged. "Sure." He put his finger on Mustique, swept it southwest over the wandering trail of small islands known as the Grenadines. "Buncha airports and airstrips all the way from us down to Grenada. But that's still only seventy-five miles from here and not even in the right direction. Flying to Totness from these other islands will take just as much fuel as it would from here."

He slipped his finger across a wide gap of water farther south, stopped it on a big island. "Now Trinidad has two airports. They're nice ones, but there's a problem."

"Which is?"

"Which is that, when the plague started, Trinidad was home for about 1,300,000 people. And both airports are in densely populated areas. So, even if the runways aren't cluttered with vehicles and aren't burned to shit, I don't like our odds of getting in and out before the infected find us." He ran his finger farther south, until it touched South America itself. "We don't even have to talk about the mainland, do we?"

We all shook our heads. We'd found fighting to secure little towns on little islands hard enough. Caracas airport and others like it weren't even in the realm of possibility.

"Okay, then," Ozzie resumed, sliding his finger back up to a small island to the east of Trinidad, "so that leaves Tobago. The airport is seven miles from Scarborough, the capitol. Ocean on three sides. Big runway: one hundred fifty feet wide and almost nine thousand long. I can land a Twin Otter on a tenth of that length and a third of the width. So unless everyone in Scarborough drove out there to abandon their car, we should find enough usable airstrip."

"And what about the 'wildlife'?" Papillon asked with a small smile.

Ozzie smiled back. "Well, no guarantees. But Scarborough, including the areas around it, had a population of only about fifteen thousand. Shit: the whole island had maybe, what?" He glanced at Jeeza with a shrug. "Sixty thousand? Sixty-five? Maybe?"

Jeeza was clearly trying very hard to accept that the hours that she and Rod had spent honing their carefully calculated plans were being trumped by a rock-refugee's casual, but hands-on, knowledge of the region.

Willow glanced at Jeeza. "Still, I'm certain that *your* choice for an airfield would be a good backup plan. Which one did you and Rod decide was most promising?"

Jeeza turned pink. "Tobago."

Willow darkened, fought to find words. "Well . . . well,

that certainly makes me quite sure—*quite* sure—that we have found the right airport from which to fly on to Totness."

Prospero, arms crossed, was staring at the map as if it was a disobedient dog. "So just to work it through. We fly to Tobago, land if we can, off-load cans of fuel to use for a return flight. Unload more fuel to fill up the Twin Otter's tank for flying on to Totness. We see if we can use it. If we can, we return to Tobago, fill up again. Return to Mustique."

Jeeza nodded.

"The next flight goes directly to Totness and drops off as many fuel drums as the plane can carry. Refuel from some of those and fly to Kourou to suss it out. Return. Assuming we can land somewhere inside the ESA site, we start ferrying more fuel to Totness in preparation for the mission flight."

Papillon nodded slowly. "Which takes off from here, lands and refuels at Totness, and then lands at Kourou."

"And reverses that process to return here," Jeeza concluded. She looked at me. "Alvaro, you have been very quiet."

I nodded. "Yeah."

"Why?"

I shrugged. "Well, first, this is a discussion for the experts, not me."

"And second?"

I sighed. "Second is that it looks like this plan might work. And it damn near scares the piss out of me."

Rod smiled crookedly. "Consider it our Christmas gift." He looked around the table. "Season's greetings, everyone."

∽ ⊖ ⟋

We wandered into the galley after we'd settled on a timetable for getting the right fuel into drums and hauling them up to Mustique's airfield. Tomorrow and the day after would be all about deciding who would go on each flight, what support equipment that might be needed, and all the rest of the bullets, beans, and buttons crap. We were more than ready for dinner.

Everyone else was already there, Ozzie and Tai telling stories about the day's salvage haul, which almost always included some pretty funny discoveries. Granted, you needed a pretty dark sense of humor to laugh at some of them. Today they had come across a mansion with a pretty wild collection of sex toys, some built right into the walls. The less-than-funny part was that one of the, ah, restraint frames had evidently had someone in it when the stalkers barged in.

But that would be one of the last stories. The salvage team had cleared the northern half of the island, which translated into roughly eighty percent of the properties.

It had also translated into a lot of cool new stuff. The biggest, and best, surprise was all the drones they found. These were almost always in perfectly good shape, left in a drawer or on a garage shelf. Batteries were still a problem; rechargeables were scarce and ours drained faster and faster. But hell, even five minutes of bird's-eye recon from a drone could be invaluable, maybe decisive when we landed in Kourou. Three houses had night vision gear; not as good as our milspec NODs, but in better condition and hey, more is always better. Lots of shotguns for skeet shooting, good handheld radios with headsets, and even unused medical supplies: the beautiful people had been overcome too quickly to use much of it. Same for canned and dried goods; even the locals who got through the first week or two had such well-stocked larders that there had still been plenty left when the grim reaper finally caught up with them.

In the entire course of their salvage ops, the team had only come across five live infected, two just out of torpor. But the other three had been surprisingly active. They had also been atypically large and travelling solo. That led Willow to wonder if stalkers became loners when their numbers started thinning out as severely as they had on Mustique.

She made a pretty convincing case for it. She pointed out that one of the reasons that there aren't many "social apex predators" is because the advantage of hunting together is always offset by the need to share each kill. But when the kills become too scarce to feed all the members of the group, then what? It often caused tensions among naturally evolved pack predators, but their behavior was also constrained by breeding imperatives. So they still tended to stick together even if some marginal members, like the sick and the old, were chased off.

But stalkers aren't naturally evolved creatures, not anymore. The virus had short-circuited every behavioral imperative except the desire to kill and eat. Even self-preservation had been undercut and, so far as we could tell, the young and the pregnant were just handy snacks.

But Mustique was now so hunted out that even their "pack hunting" impulse had apparently been overridden by the two remaining imperatives: kill and eat. Which meant that the remaining stalkers would consider others as potential food sources. But if they weren't careful when hunting their own kind, they were about as likely to become dinner as to get it.

I expressed doubt that this would apply any place other than the small islands that we'd visited. On a big island or the mainland, there'd always be another town, another forest, another stretch of land where they could find fresh prey. But on islands like Mustique, FdN, and Ascension, the stalkers could literally hunt themselves into extinction.

Willow smiled and leaned over the table. "And if you are right about that, Alvaro, we may want to reconsider the strategy of 'clearing' islands."

"Our clearing tactics are just fine," Chloe grumbled. She didn't like constant revisions to plans and protocols. Besides, tonight, like every odd-numbered night, was fish night, and no one was happy about yet another seafood dinner.

I shook my head. "Willow really does mean *strategy*, babe."

Chloe stopped chewing. "Strategy. Tactics. Same thing. *Babe*."

"Actually," began Willow, "they are not really the same. Strategy is—"

Chloe got up, slung her plate into the sink. "Funny how thin the air gets when the big brains start working overtime. And I hate eating at such high altitudes; makes me wanna puke."

I stopped in mid-chew, wondered: *Whoa! Where is that coming from?*

Chloe headed for the hatch. "Have fun theorizing about your theories. I'm going topside for some fresh air." She stomped up the companionway.

No one said anything. I mean, what do you say to that? None of us like being wrong, but Chloe *really* doesn't like it. Still, my gut was telling me her attitude had deeper roots. Ever since we'd joined forces with Willow's crew, planning had become more complicated. Before, it had been really straightforward stuff. Like, how much food do we need? How do we get it? How do we make it last? How do we tackle the next objective?

But now it was more about how we juggled people, tasks, assets, and longer-term objectives, not the nitty gritty of how we would attack this house, or clear that street. And Chloe hadn't been enjoying the change much.

It was about five full seconds before Valda broke the silence. "I take your point about changing our strategy, Willow. What you suggest is very, very wise."

Jorge stopped chewing on his third slab of sea bass. "She suggest su'thin?"

Tai crossed her arms. "Kind of. See, if deh stalkers kill each other when they got no more to eat, maybe the best idea is to wait. Instead of us going in, let dem get rid of each other."

I nodded. "Yeah. If stalker populations actually consume themselves on smaller islands, we should let that happen. Because bigger islands aren't going to be like that. We will have to actively clear them out. And a larger landmass means there will always be enough prey that repopulates itself. So, at some point, the number of stalkers will stabilize in balance with that food source."

"Or maybe not, if dey eating own babies," Tai pointed out. "If there no new stalkers, then one day, there's no stalkers at all."

I shrugged, smiled. "You've got a point. But that could take years. Or decades. I don't think we can wait that long before taking back islands. Or even the mainland."

Prospero frowned. "Even if we could wait, it still might not work." He met our glances. "You are all assuming that the turned follow the same aging curve as regular humans."

Steve stared at him. "You mean, the virus could also be the fountain of youth?"

Jeeza blew her bangs high up on her forehead. "Well, it could be. I mean, they seem really tough, don't they? It's like they're on meth *and* PCP."

Willow nodded. "If they had only the usual reserves of endorphins, they should collapse after each of their attack frenzies. They would also be more sensitive to pain."

Papillon frowned. "So you are saying that they are no longer truly human? That they have—eh, mutated?"

She shook her head. "No. Mutation—the kind that is passed to subsequent generations—is generally not the result of a single viral epidemic. But something *has* changed in them, chemically. We've seen them eat carrion that we would immediately vomit up. They drink fouled water. They ignore pain which would render most humans unconscious. So if their biochemistry has become both more robust and more supercharged, it is possible that their entire immune and cellular replacement systems have been similarly altered."

"You mean, they might live forever?" Jorge put his fork down, pushed his plate aside. It was the first time I'd ever seen him willingly move food *away* from him.

Willow shrugged. "Well, I don't know about that, but as Prospero points out, we should not assume that they have the same aging and disease mortality curves that normal humans have. Which means we have to remain very cautious when projecting how many we will have to deal with, as time goes on."

When I sat down to dinner, I had been looking forward to dessert. Now, I had zero appetite for it.

Nobody else had any, either.

January 4, 2013

Been too busy to write at night. Hitting my rack later, up earlier, and always exhausted.

Prepping planes for flight and accelerating the clearance of Mustique became top priorities. Completing our sweep of Mustique quickly required more vehicles in good running condition. We discovered a couple and cut Jorge loose on them. He worked his mechanical magic and now we have two (insanely high-end) Land Rovers with which we not only finished surveying the island, but put to service moving loads to and from the airstrip.

Clearing Mustique meant getting a look at its less developed parts. So we ran two night recons from inside the vehicles, using NODs to watch for any stalkers in the modest undergrowth. We didn't find anything, but we did learn which NODS are reliable, which aren't, and how long the batteries would actually last.

After that, the flight tests began. Ozzie was in his Twin Otter's pilot seat as it took all the necessary baby steps: taxiing, short hops, takeoff with immediate circle back for landing. There were a lot of delays at first: every time he landed, he reported some disturbing rattle or hum. Which sent him, Jorge, Papillon, and Robbie diving into the plane's guts to sort it out.

Meanwhile, the rest of us started basic maintenance on both ships, and, after the plane was cleared for flight, Jorge returned to *Legacy* to begin the task he'd been dreading: rehabilitating her engine. With Robbie as his assistant and the rest of us as a rotating team of grease-stained gophers, he did what he could. There was neither the time nor the facilities for a full rebuild, but *Legacy*'s plant ultimately did run faster and smoother.

By the time we were done, Ozzie had trained Papillon on the Twin Otter—not a long learning curve—and the rest of us started moving fuel barrels up to the runway. We're not talking half a dozen drums; we needed over thirty, mostly at Totness, to be sure we were ready to handle any of the most likely failure contingencies.

The day after we finished moving all that fuel was also the day of the first flight: the recon of Tobago. Ozzie was in the pilot's seat (of course), Prospero was aboard to handle any photography or other dedicated ground observation. Ning went along to get basic lessons in both. Our official explanation for that was our belief that she was a good candidate as emergency backup for either of their roles, but most of us suspected that her recon skills might prove better than Prospero's and that she might have some flying experience, as well.

Most of us stopped working to watch them take off. Ozzie saw and acknowledged our waves, banked south—and I suddenly realized I had never expected to see that again. A plane taking off over the water, tilting its wings to wave back at watchers on the ground. I hadn't even thought about missing it until that moment.

I just assumed it was gone for good. And yet, here we are, doing it again. It wasn't just the early morning sun that made the sky seem a little bit brighter.

We hovered around Marian as she monitored their progress through short, coded signal exchanges. After thirty minutes of uneventful flying, the rest of us went from anxious, to relieved, and ultimately, bored. So we rolled out to take a last detailed look through the nearby mansions, just to see if we'd missed anything.

At least, that's what we told ourselves. I think all of us were actually checking out where on Mustique we might want to live. Because, frankly, it was damned close to perfect. Almost the entire island had roads, and so little was undeveloped that we'd be able to comb it thoroughly—aided by Cujo, Daisy, and pups—for any passives or active solos. So the most important criteria—safety from the infected—was the work of just another day or two.

Almost every home was equipped with a stand-alone generator, solar panels, or both. About half had protected cisterns with sustainable filtration systems (one was nothing but layers of sandstone). So now that we had the time to just look around, we all came to the same conclusion: it just won't get any better than this. Not in *our* lifetimes.

Even the little hamlet of Lovell had turned out to be safe. Half the small houses—the "servants' quarters"—were tidied up, shuttered, and locked. Not a surprise: they were essentially efficiencies for the "domestics" who worked there on extended contracts. So as fears of the plague grew, they had returned home to St. Vincent or other nearby islands. Whether to help their families or simply die with them we'd never know.

That drive was the first easy day we'd had in weeks. Yeah, we were still carrying guns, but it was almost like being on a holiday. I made sure that, tactical optimization be damned, Chloe and I rode in the same Land Rover. I figured she'd like that. We hadn't been together during the day for . . . well, I wasn't even sure how long it had been.

But if she did enjoy sitting beside me as we cruised the palm-lined lanes, I saw no sign of it. She mostly just looked out the window, distracted and unsmiling. I couldn't tell if she was sad, frustrated, angry, or all three at the same time.

Which was kind of what had happened to our sex life, too. There was still plenty of activity, but not a lot of words exchanged before, during, or after. It was like makeup sex right after an argument. Except the closest thing we'd had to an argument was when she had stormed out of the galley, so I couldn't figure out what needed "making up." But there was definitely a rift between us, and it had definitely started that night.

I'm not great at starting "relationship conversations," but my gut told me we *had* to talk. So I promised myself I'd do just that as soon as the car ride was over.

Of course, as we pulled up to the pier, Jeeza and Rod were already there, waiting. Which meant there was important news from Tobago. Part of me regretted having to put off another attempt to talk to Chloe, but part of me was secretly relieved. I'm pretty much a wuss when it comes to warm-and-fuzzy stuff. I gave Chloe's hand a quick squeeze and opened the Land Rover's door.

Jeeza didn't even wait for my second foot to touch the ground. "Tobago is out of the loop."

"You mean—?"

"We don't need to use it after today," Rod almost hyperventilated. "They put down at Tobago, refueled without seeing a single stalker, and flew straight on to Totness. We just got their recon report: the airstrip there is clear. They're already headed back for final refueling at Tobago and then home."

Papillon came up behind them. The small, pleased smile on his face made it clear he'd already heard the news.

"So it looks like we've got a green light for Kourou!" Rod finished breathlessly.

Papillon's smile faded. "Let us hope so."

Rod looked at him. "What do you mean?"

"I mean that just because the airfield at Totness is clear does not mean that we can use it."

Jeeza nodded. "The 'wildlife.'"

Papillon nodded. "I know something of that part of the Wild Coast. It is aptly named. Infected could have been hidden within ten yards of that airfield and they would never have seen them."

Chloe's voice startled me. "I've been doing some reading in the pre-virus guidebooks. Totness is the capitol of the Coronie district, right?"

All three of them nodded at her as she slid out of the Land Rover to stand beside me.

"Okay. So that district had a total population of about three thousand. Two-thirds of them were in Totness."

"True," agreed Papillon, "but the important question is: how many are left there?"

Rod shrugged. "If what we've seen on the islands is any indication, maybe a third."

"And most of those have been in torpor," Jeeza added.

"So," Papillon said, "A third of two thousand . . .

say, about six hundred fifty left, no? Still quite a lot of stalkers."

Chloe shook her head. "Guys: you're basing those numbers on *islands*."

Papillon frowned more deeply this time. "I fail to see—"

"Look, you need to remember that stalkers are predators now, not omnivores. So, on an island, when they hunted out the prey, they had to turn on each other. Or go into torpor. They had no choice."

Jeeza started nodding. "But, on a large landmass, they could move on."

Chloe nodded back. "Yeah. That's what predators do. So, when they hunted out Totness itself, they'd increase their range, look for more prey. They'd go to farms, then after herds, then into the jungle itself."

Papillon's frown had become thoughtful. "So you believe there may be *more* than six hundred and fifty stalkers from Totness still alive and active?"

"Yeah, but a lot fewer near the town. I'd be kinda surprised if any except passives remained there."

Now Rod was nodding. "Yeah. Yeah, they'll want to avoid actives, and buildings are good places to hide. Particularly since there's nothing left in the area that could feed a whole pack of hungry stalkers."

Jeeza developed the theory. "But there will always be rats breeding in the buildings, probably even some stray dogs. And small animals like rabbits. Enough for passives to live on, at least."

Chloe nodded. "That's what I was saying." She turned and walked toward *Voyager*'s gangplank.

Papillon stared after her while I smiled. "So, if Chloe is right, then—?"

"Then Totness is probably a go," Rod said, enthusiastically.

I nodded. "I guess we'll find out as soon as the Twin Otter returns there to land and check it out."

"Can't happen too soon!" Rod whooped.

I wondered if he'd be so stoked when we finally boarded it in combat gear, bound for Kourou.

January 10

As Chloe predicted, landing at Totness was a nonevent. With Papillon manning the stick, they orbited the area a few times, saw fields of overgrown crops and stripped bones: mostly from cattle, but more than a few human ones. No stalkers, though. Papillon landed and kept the engines idling, while the ground crew got to work.

Johnnie and Steve got the Twin Otter refueled while Tai kept an eye on the perimeter. But no one saw anything bigger than a few of the local rodents, which ran like they were on fire when they detected human movement. That gave everyone a pretty good idea of what—or who—had hunted them most recently.

The fuel drums for staging farther flights were off-loaded in fifteen minutes and then they were airborne for home. Another two runs and we'd have all the gas we needed prepositioned at Totness.

Over the next three days, those runs were completed, along with the first recon of Kourou itself. It was about what we expected. The ESA facility base had been breached but suffered only scattered damage. The city, however, was a horror show.

251

We watched Prospero's videos and pictures in total silence. The streets were thick with bodies, most of which were reduced to skeletons. Stalkers prowled restlessly, but not in packs. Only groups of ten or twenty: never more.

Willow nodded somberly. "They could be transitioning into smaller groups as the prey becomes more scarce."

"Yeah," muttered Chloe, "but even if they are, I wonder how long that lasts if they hear a dinner bell. Like a siren, or a car horn—or a plane about to land."

Willow glanced curiously at her, but simply nodded.

As expected, the airport was a mess; a couple of planes had burnt, two on the tarmac. The industrial and commercial zone around the pier was only half-incinerated, but a single glance at the images made it clear we couldn't use it as a landing point, even without vehicles. All things considered, it was good that we had decided to look at the images *after* dinner.

Bottom line: we had no way to get to the ESA complex other than the stretch of roadway that Papillon had suggested the day we'd met him. So our remaining recon flights would be dedicated to assessing its safety and the route to our primary objective: the combined mission control and headquarters building. And I could tell that Willow, Prospero, and Papillon were already planning to stay after dinner to start evolving those plans. But this time, I figured I'd better catch up with Chloe.

Except, when I turned around, she was already gone. I looked at the only hatchway she could have left through. I told myself I needed to go after her. Right now.

"Alvaro?" It was Willow.

I kept looking at the hatchway. I knew I should go, but damn it, not only did I absolutely suck at starting a heart-to-heart talk, but Chloe wasn't much better. Truth is, she's even worse at it than I am. But shit: if I was able to think about landing in a derelict space center populated by an unknown number of stalkers—

Prospero's voice was careful. "A minute of your time, mate?"

I closed my eyes . . . and the moment I stopped seeing the empty hatchway, I lost my nerve.

I turned back to the others. "Let's get out the ops map and label everything you saw."

But what I heard in my head was:

Wuss.

Two days later, just after breakfast, we were all gathered on the pier. All except Jeeza, Marian, and Robbie. They were staring at us over *Legacy*'s side, *Voyager* riding in tow behind her.

I don't know what I expected that farewell would be like, but I hadn't foreseen complete silence. No one made a sound as the three of them mounted the stairs to the bridge to get under way.

Jorge sidled up to me. "So, how long it take dem?"

"If the weather's good, they'll be at the Totness anchorage sometime on the fourteenth."

"So long?"

I shrugged. "Maximum caution while towing another ship. After *Legacy* is secure, Robbie and Jeeza will sail . . . well, probably motor . . . *Voyager* down to Île Royale. That way, if we have trouble at the end of the mission, either on the flight back to Totness, or if we have to exfil overland to the mudflats, we've got help waiting where we need it."

"Yeah, but: Marian. She gonna be okay, you think?"

I nodded firmly, but I wondered the same thing. Marian didn't have a problem being alone, but being the only person on an intercontinental trawler without a friend inside of two hundred and thirty miles is not merely "alone." That is *isolated*, and none of us really knew how she would handle that. But if *Voyager* developed engine trouble, there had to be two aboard to really handle her sails. So we didn't have a lot of choice; we just had to hope that Marian could hack it.

That left fourteen of us for the landing team. That might sound like a lot, but the ESA facility was big: two hundred seventy square miles. The facilities themselves only took up ten percent of the footprint, but we had no way to be sure just how much of that ground we might have to cover if we simply couldn't follow the road to our objective.

Smoke jetted out of *Legacy's* stack—Robbie had juiced the idling engines—and she started angling slowly out of Britannia Bay, *Voyager* following smoothly behind. No toot of the horn, no last waves once under way. Rod was standing with his toes over the end of the pier, his whole body straining toward Jeeza and the departing ships. Seeing that, I glanced at Chloe . . . just in time to see her face hardening into a mask as she turned and strode stiff-legged toward the motor pool.

"Chloe—" I called after her.

But before her name was fully out of my mouth, she had thrown her leg over one of the dirt bikes and was gunning it up the slope away from the pier.

I hung my head, started following up the hill in the gray, hanging wake of its exhaust.

"Hey, mate."

I turned toward Prospero. He held out keys for one of the Rovers. "Go on. Catch up to her."

I shook my head. "You know I drive like shit."

From over his shoulder, Willow nodded and said, "Yes, Alvaro. That's true. We can afford a scratched bumper. Just don't wreck it. Now go."

I wanted to race right up the hill after her, but I knew better. It was a blind curve, so if Chloe had stopped or come off the dirt bike, I might have gone over her before I could stop. But also, I was really, really scared I *would* wreck the Rover.

So it took me almost two minutes to reach Ozzie's house, where we had started camping out a few days before the ships left. No sign of her or the bike.

I listened, heard a faint motor sound to the north. I sighed, swung the Rover around—slowly, carefully, like some friggin' ole granny—and headed toward the airport.

There's a spot about a hundred yards from the head of the runway where the land bumps up and then falls away toward the sea. Not a sudden Wuthering Heights kind of plummet, but smooth and steady. All the mansions with ocean views march away beneath you, dotting the slope until the carpet of trees ended, their morning shadows drooping over the white beaches.

That overlook was where I found Chloe. As I'd expected.

I pulled the Rover off the road, let it roll slowly

over the grass until I was about fifty feet behind her. She was sitting to one side of the dirt bike, her arms around her knees, staring after *Legacy* and *Voyager*.

I sat beside her. I stayed quiet for a long time. I didn't realize at first that I was being chickenshit, waiting and hoping that she'd say something first. When I figured that out, I drew in my breath and started: "Chloe—"

"You don't even feel it! You don't even *see* it, do you?"

I remember some gabbling sounds coming out of my mouth; I had no idea what she was talking about. But whatever it was, it was serious. "S-see what?" I finally stuttered.

She flung her hand and outstretched fingers in the direction of the two departing ships. "That! Right there!"

"You mean—*Legacy*? And *Voyager*?"

She groaned. "Alvaro, that's our *whole life* leaving, right there. Everything we've done and been and shared for the past half year: all sailing away."

Still baffled, I looked straight at her—and realized she'd been crying. Hard. Her cheeks were streaked and her eyes were still shiny. I reached toward her.

She shied away. "No! Don't you get it? Jeeza's gone. So is *Voyager*; she was our home. And the rest of us are all running around, hardly seeing each other anymore." She frowned. "Although maybe that's just as well. The whole group has been changing."

"Changing how?"

She turned, stared at me, her eyes getting liquid-bright. "How can you not see? We're changing away from the way we used to be. From what we used to do."

"But, *cariña*, isn't it better this way? Not having to risk our lives every day?"

"Not when we're running around like suits, heads down over calculators, and no one knowing what anyone else is doing." She glanced away. "Or why."

I frowned. That didn't make sense. "But we go over all the plans every night. We—"

"Yeah. The Big We." I think I blinked. "Alvaro, we used to plan everything together. *All* of us."

"Chloe, that was back when there were only five of us. Adding Prospero and Tai took it to the limit. But when the number doubled after Willow arrived—"

"Yeah: then it was time for the big brains to drive the bus. 'Cause really: who needed *any*one else's advice once *Willow* showed up?"

Huh? "But I thought you liked Willow."

"Well, I do, but . . . Damn it: so why didn't *I* become one of the decision makers, too? Or why wasn't I put in charge of something? Because I didn't do that well in school? Because I'm just stupid Chloe?"

"But you *were* put in charge of something. We needed you as captain of *Voyager.* No one else could have—"

"—Could have what? Sat around like a lump of lard just beyond the edge of the pier, waiting to respond to emergencies that never happened? My big thrill was being sent out to go fishing. Yeah: real life of adventure and purpose."

Actually, we had made Chloe captain of *Voyager* because she was the best solo sail-handler. By a huge margin. And because even if she was usually a beat behind on the navigation numbers, she had a natural feel for piloting in every kind of weather. But I knew that wouldn't matter now. "So, you wanted to be a part of the planning group?" Which I also doubted.

She started to answer, stopped, looked away, then turned back. "No. That shit bores me to tears." Her eyes became wet. "See?"

I saw the tears, but I knew they were about something else. "*Cariña*, what's bothering you . . . really?"

She drew in a big breath, released it as an even bigger sigh. "Alvaro, what I'm going to say won't be logical. But I have never claimed to be. Hell, if I need logic—as in a metric *shit*-ton of it—I can always go to you."

"So then—?"

"Hear me out." She looked down, took my hands; oddly, they were almost as big as hers. "I don't like all this planning. I like *doing*. I liked it when I was the sniper that everyone depended on. I liked being the strongest person on the boat, because damn it, I was. Until Johnnie came back, I guess. And I liked being the sergeant to your lieutenant. I liked being right up in the face of anyone or anything that gave us shit."

She looked out after the boats. "But that's all gone now. It's like you said; we're seventeen people, now. A lot of bodies, a lot of options, a lot of decisions to make. A lot of management and planning." She shrugged. "So, no place for me. And now with Jeeza gone—"

As she sighed over the top of a sob, I remembered her sarcastically nicknaming Jeeza "Gazelle" because she had been overweight. And here she was, half a year later, crying because Jeeza was leaving. "What can I do?" I asked.

"I don't know, Alvaro. If I knew, I'd tell you. I feel—I dunno: like I'm a dinosaur, now. But instead of being king of the hill for half a billion years, I only got six months." She smiled through more tears; each felt like a stab in my heart. "I was the baddest ass and best stalker-killer in the group. But now, I'm—well, I'm kind of like my bolt-action: only needed if the shit hits the fan."

I've actually gained muscle mass, and Chloe has dropped a bunch of weight, but it is still awkward for me to put an arm around her. But I did, and she leaned into me with a long sigh. "You're wrong," I whispered.

"About what?"

"Pretty much everything," I muttered.

She looked up sharply, saw my eyes, smiled and shoved her shoulder into me. "You prick," she said softly.

"Yeah," I said, "I am. But I mean it. Look: some of us make plans. But they'd all be pointless if we didn't have *you*."

"Bullshit."

"No: *fact*. And the only reason you can't see it is because you're too close to it. Way too close."

"What do you mean?"

"I mean you can't see it because it's not just inside of you: it *is* you. Look: every group has to have at least one person who will not freeze up or flip out. Because the group knows that when the shit hits the fan, that person will hit right back, yelling 'bring it!'" I hugged her close against my side. "That's who you are, Chloe, and that's a big part of why we can make the plans we do, and why there's actually a decent chance that they'll work. Because everyone knows that you'll be there, kicking ass. And giving zero fucks while you do."

She turned toward me slowly, like she was seeing

me for the first time. But in a good way. "You . . . you actually love me, don't you?"

"Well, sure I do. You didn't know?"

Her brows climbed. "You didn't say!"

"Well, uh, neither did you!"

"Well . . . well, I love you *too*, Alvaro Casillas!" She hugged me hard, then whispered: "Even if you *are* a prick."

January 16

Tomorrow is game day. Finally.

It's two days later than we planned. The first time, the "game" was called on account of rain. A lot of rain. So much that we could have lost *Voyager*. And the worst part was that we hadn't prepared a single contingency. It reminds me of a Yiddish joke Marian repeats way too often: if you want to make God laugh, just tell Her your plans.

About four hours after shearing away from *Legacy's* anchorage just off Totness, *Voyager's* radar picked up signs of a storm rolling in from the east. She wasn't going to make the Salvations before the weather got to her, no matter how hard she ran her motors, and sails wouldn't help. They'd have been fighting head-winds all the way.

So Jeeza and Robbie checked their charts and made a run for Paramaribo, which was both smart and risky. Smart because Paramaribo has a west-facing bay, so the weather would mostly roll past, rather than into, it. But like most of the Wild Coast's river mouths, it is silty as hell.

Fortunately, they kept *Voyager* out of the muck,

watched the squall blow past, and made it to the Salvations by noon the next day. So with our backup extraction teams right where they should be, the rest of us gathered for a final review of our plans and information.

I had learned enough to realize that a lot (maybe most?) COs have their XO or senior NCO give the mission brief. Besides, it made Prospero feel "chuffed" and, more importantly, he was better at it. So I leaned back, arms crossed, and tried not to notice that if it wasn't for Ning, I would still be the shortest person in the room.

"Right, then," Prospero started, using a cleaning rod as a pointer (kind of a tradition with us, now). "Day start is 0330. Light breakfast, gear up, drive to airfield, last check of personal load. Wheels up at 0500. Assuming moderate weather and slight headwind, wheels down at Totness at 0800. Set security, full refuel, comm check, maintenance walkaround on aircraft. Wheels up at 0900."

He paused, made sure everyone was paying attention. "Enter Kourou airspace 1050. Low-altitude recon to confirm there have been no substantive changes in the ESA site. Then we assess stalker activity at the base perimeter and finally, downtown. Assuming all observations match prior conditions, we commence landing from the north on National Road One.

"Wheels down anticipated at 1120. That sets the clock running on our five-hour ops window. We set perimeter security and unload. Refueling is effected while the vehicle assessment team and dedicated security element moves to the two patrol tracks we spotted on a side road near the end of our projected landing. Pending assessment of their functionality, final movement plans and waypoints will be determined for advance to primary target:"—Prospero's pointer moved to the approximate center of the site—"Launch Control Center Three. In the event you lose comms, this is our default rally point until and unless you see an ops clock reset flare, or the mission has been completed.

"Lastly, you must memorize the location and appearance of two other facilities that could become mission-critical.

"First: the ESA satellite tracking dish Diane. Note again that it is located close to our final rally point: the plane.

"Second, the headquarters and operations compound for Third Regiment, French Foreign Legion. Besides the launch control center's bunker, it is the only facility in which survivors might have been able to shelter this long.

"You must be able to navigate to the target, and to these other two facilities, from anywhere in the anticipated area of operations. Questions?"

Chloe leaned over to inspect the collage of aerial photographs littering the screen of one of our largest, best-resolution laptops. "There are some new images here. Wanna explain those?"

Papillon inclined his head. "These were taken on the last reconnaissance flight, two days ago. A predawn start and fewer clouds helped us get sharper pictures of the Legion compound." He pointed to the squat building complex to the west of Launch Control Center Three.

Rod crowded in for a look. "So, did you guys finally figure out what that white thing is on the west side of the Legion garage?"

Papillon drew the outline of the bright rectangle with his index finger. "That's an awning. I only saw it deployed once."

"For what?"

"Storing a helicopter outside, at least partially. The garage is too low to serve as a hangar."

"You mean"—Willow sounded like she was suppressing excitement and maybe a bit of squee—"there might actually be a working helicopter there?"

Papillon shrugged. "Just because the awning is out doesn't mean there is a helicopter under it. It could be there as cover for additional vehicles brought to the HQ. Or it could have been put up as a . . . a medical shelter."

Tai frowned. "Whadyoo mean, a 'medical shelter'? Why you say it like that?"

Rod's face had become grim. "He means a quarantine tent." Tai shook her head at the word "quarantine." "A place to put people who are sick with the virus to keep them away from everyone else. 'Medical shelter' is just a euphem—a nice word for it."

Willow was now frowning, too. She glanced at Papillon. "So you think the awning *isn't* for a helicopter?"

Papillon squinted, made a doubtful *tch*ing sound he might have picked up from his mom's side of the family; I'd noticed something similar in the Vietnamese communities near the barrio. "I cannot tell, but it *is* one of several indicators that the Legion didn't get overrun right away."

Steve uncrossed his arms. "What are the other signs?"

Papillon shrugged. "I left base only a day ahead of the virus." He touched a zoomed-in image of the stretch of road where we were going to land. "So what are these two abandoned patrol tracks doing here?" He switched to a split-screen display to show a close-up of each. "It's a bad angle, but take a close look at their windows."

"Busted," Johnnie said with a casual shrug. "Isn't that kind of what we'd expect if they were mobbed by stalkers?"

"No," Chloe muttered, her nose almost against the screen. "Those windows weren't just busted. Look closer." She glanced at the faces that leaned in to squint over her considerable shoulder. "They've been caged, barred. For protection. Like on the Land Rovers we used on Ascension Island."

Papillon nodded. "Exactly. And those bars are welded."

Willow was staring intently. "Meaning the Legionnaires had time to adapt to the situation. Enough time to modify their patrol vehicles to deal with stalkers." She frowned. "So these two vehicles were *not* overrun while out on patrol. That would also explain the lack of bodies around them."

Papillon nodded again. "It seems more likely that they were trying to make a run for the north gate. Together. If they had been on routine patrol, they would never have been at the same part of the perimeter, let alone just a few meters apart."

Prospero was nodding in sync with Papillon. "And if they were trying to break out to the north, that may have only been one part of their escape plan."

"Explain that," I said.

Prospero gestured toward our intended "airstrip" and the vehicles. "Where were they going? All the way north to Sinnamary? What good would that do? They would just be running from one bin of bollocks to another."

Ning's eyes seemed to light up. "They were trying to leave the mainland."

Jorge's face crinkled slightly; for him, that was a full-blown scowl. "Leave the mainland? In those?" He pointed at the vehicles. "Like I say before, I know dem. Dey are 206 Bandwagons—"

"Hagglund BV 206 *Bandvagns*," Prospero corrected.

Jorge checked his eye-roll. "Yah. Whatever. Ting is, like I tol' you, I work on them. I know what dey can do. Yeah, dey can swim." He pointed at the coast. "But dey can't swim out to sea, not dat far. And yeah, dey good in mud...but not *dat* good."

But Prospero was smiling. "They wouldn't have to be: not if there was also a working helicopter."

Chloe rolled her eyes. "And if they have a working helicopter, then why are they bothering with these overgrown ATVs?"

"Too many survivors to evacuate," Willow breathed, realizing. "And they couldn't leave any behind, waiting for a second flight. There might not have been enough to hold off the stalkers."

Ning nodded. "Yes. The tracks were driving here." She pointed to a stretch of clear ground that started just north of the Soyuz launch complex and then meandered east through two miles of marshland before reaching the coast. "Once at the shore, they drive out on the flats and wait for the helicopter to come back for them. Or if it can't fly again, they are rescued by boat."

Willow nodded. "Of course. Because by then the

helicopter would have already flown one group—probably civilians—to safety."

Jorge actually did scowl now. "Yah, but *where*?"

Papillon sighed, ran his finger over to the Salvation Islands. "To Île Royale's helipad."

Ning looked at him. "But it never landed there. Probably crashed. Either way, there is no helicopter in the compound."

Prospero was frowning. "Hang on. What if the Bandvagns left the compound *first*?"

Ning frowned back. "Why would they?"

"To draw off the infected. Engines roaring, Legionnaires' guns firing in all directions."

Papillon's eyes widened. "*Merde*! Of course: rolling a helicopter just part of the way out of the garage would take a fair amount of time." He glanced at the aerial photographs. "If they had ever come that close to taking off, they would have pushed the awning over to move as quickly as possible."

I tried not to sound hopeful. "So you think the chopper is still in the garage?"

Papillon shrugged. "I cannot even guess. We have so few facts and far too many conjectures. All we know is that their plan did not succeed. The compound may have been overrun before the helicopter could take off. Or there may have been a mechanical failure."

Rod's comment was barely a whisper. "So, even now . . . there could still be survivors holed up in the compound."

Papillon frowned. "Stranger things have happened. But this is all profitless conjecture. Our focus must remain on what we can see: two patrol vehicles that could be extremely useful—even crucial—to our mission."

Prospero nodded curtly. "Agreed. The vehicles must be sorted out straight away. On the hope that one or more will prove to be operational, we are bringing fuel. Jorge has put together the best toolkit he can for those vehicles, in the event we must attempt repairs."

Tai was eyeing the distance between the vehicles and the launch control center. "And if none of them can be started for running?"

Prospero glanced at me. *Sure—because this is the part no one will want to hear.* I cleared my throat. "Too early to decide, because there are too many things we don't know yet. We might even try major repairs to the most promising vehicle, if Jorge thinks the odds are good that we can get it working again. Or, if stalker activity and density on the base seems low, then we might go forward by foot."

Before anyone could draw a worried breath, I doubled down: "Look. We've known from the beginning that was a possibility. Just because we may have other, easier options doesn't mean we automatically back away from the mission. But if we can get one of those vehicles running, it makes our job a lot safer, so it's worth some additional risk."

Chloe was looking at the pictures of the stubby, tracked Bandvagns. "They're not very big." She glanced at Papillon. "So if one of those tracks runs into stalkers— *literally* runs into them—can it just grind through a whole pack? I mean, like dozens?"

Papillon shrugged. "Probably. But we won't need to find out."

"Why?"

Ozzie grinned his disconcerting grin. "Because, Chloe, we have Ole Betsy."

"Your M60?"

"Right. No ring to mount it on, but there's a hand-bar that runs around the front hatch. And besides, we have something even better than her!"

"Which is?"

"You, sweetheart!" He said "sweetheart" in a "fond uncle" tone. That's probably why she didn't cut off his nuts right then and there.

Besides, she was too busy being really surprised and a little worried. "Me?"

"Of course, *you*! C'mon, look at all the pictures of the base. Not enough bodies for there to have ever been big packs of infected inside the fence. Which means a crack shot like you should be able to keep any we see way the hell away from us."

She goggled at him, then at the pictures of the Bandvagn. "Ozzie, you are my favorite crazy old coot, but there is no way we're all going to fit in one of those. I've read the specs; five passengers and one driver. Maybe seven passengers if everyone gets way too cozy. So how in hell—?"

It was Prospero who answered. "We put two more standing in each hatch, feet in stirrups on the back of the seats beneath them."

"Okay, so ten. But—"

"Not finished, yet. Three more on the roof; two prone with scoped rifles, one spotter kneeling between them."

She studied the Bandvagn wide-eyed, and then her mouth sagged open. "So you want me perched on the roof of this metal box when stalkers are swarming us, jumping up to take a bite?"

"Not perched," Prospero corrected. "Lashed securely in place."

"Now you're going to put a *leash*—?"

"—a lanyard—"

"—on me? No. By which I mean, *hell* no." Her head swiveled toward me. "And you are okay with this?"

"I was the one who suggested it."

She goggled, then her eyebrows cut downward; to call that look a frown would be like calling a monsoon a sunshower.

"Look," I explained. "Valda is good with a scoped rifle. You are a wizard with one. Between the two of you, you'll push back anything short of a full-on charge. If any stalkers get too close, we've got Ozzie in the front hatch with the M60, and Prospero in the rear, shooting over the two of you."

"And if that doesn't work?" She leaned toward me aggressively.

I leaned in sweetly. "We just drive away, get some distance while they get exhausted chasing us, and then we just—"

"'Lather, rinse, repeat.'" It was a poor imitation of my voice, worse of my accent. "Yeah, I know; I've heard that often enough." She glanced at the Bandvagns, the map of the complex, and her frown started fading. "Could be fun," she admitted finally. "But no one is lashing me down. I won't be hogtied just so some stalker can—"

Prospero shook his head. "You will be able to slip the knot with a single tug. But since there may be abrupt turns or reverses, no one can safely lie on the roof, unsecured."

She looked at me. I nodded. "Bet you wouldn't be so quick to agree if it was *you* up there."

I smiled. "And just who do you think is going to be spotting for you?"

"What? Wait: you're small! You've got to be in the cabin of the—"

I shook my head. "Not enough room left on the roof of the vehicle for anyone else. But look: this only matters if we can get one of the Bandvagns running. And we've beaten that to death. So let's go back to where we were: any new questions or concerns?"

Valda put up an index finger. I nodded at him.

"I am wondering why we are bringing almost all the NODs and several pounds of batteries for them."

Chloe shrugged. "So, let's say we're done with our mission. We get back to the plane—and it doesn't work."

Valda's slow nod marked the beginning of understanding. "We will have to leave by going to the shore. Either with the vehicles or on foot."

I nodded. "Right. Now, if we've got one of the Bandvagns, we can try—*try*—to go overland like the Legionnaires. But they knew how to stay on the one dry path through the marshland. And I bet they were doing it in daylight. So if newbs like us have to try in the dark, we'll sure as hell need the goggles. Whether we're in vehicles or on foot."

Steve looked around. "Is everyone drinking this Kool-Aid? That we have a chance in hell of making it to the coast on foot? In the dark? With stalkers nearby?"

Prospero should have been the one to respond, but he hesitated—because it was Steve. So I jumped in. "Steve," I said, "I can't tell you the odds. But here's what I *can* tell you: if there's the slightest chance we might make it, we're going to need people who can see at least as well as they can run. And if stalkers do get our scent and come after us—well, I'd rather see the stalkers before they see us." I looked around the group. "Any more questions about the plans, the new images?"

For the very first time, Rod did not put his hand up before speaking. "I understand why we're so focused on reaching the control center. But what if the dish we're counting on for the uplink—Diane—doesn't respond to commands? I mean, why are we expecting the control links to be operational? And what if the problem is, well, mechanical?"

"Eh?" said Tai.

But Jorge was nodding. "*Si*. That means no plan will work."

Johnnie frowned. "Wait: what kind of mechanical problem are you guys talking about?"

Rod gestured toward the picture of Diane. "Johnnie, look at that dish. It's *huge*. Must be some big motors in there to move it. But how do we know they still work? And if they don't, then what's the point of all this? It's not like the dish is going to be pointed in the right direction."

"Not all the time, no," Prospero commented, "but like a clock's arms, it's likely to be in the right position twice every day."

Johnnie said "Huh?" as Rod frowned and then started nodding.

Prospero leaned toward Johnnie. "It might not be necessary to move the dish at all. Given the transmission instructions, it sounds as though the team here 'parked' Diane in the correct orientation. But that still presents us with a problem."

Rod nodded vigorously. "Sure. GPS birds aren't geostationary or geosynchronous; they rise and set twice a day. So even if the transmission instructions for Ephemeral Reflex will work with Diane's current orientation, we still have to be on hand to send during one of those windows of opportunity."

Johnnie worked through the implications. "So, if we come just a little bit after that time, we might have to hang around for—damn: as much as twelve hours."

Prospero nodded. "It could be that bad, yes. But the most recent images of the dish made it possible to establish its transmission vector. It *is* aiming at the approximate part of the sky where the uplink target is located at 1500 hours."

"*Approximate* part of the sky?" Ning echoed, her eyebrows arching. "Is the precise position not embedded in the code?"

Prospero flapped a hand at the main map of the launch site. "The code of Ephemeral Reflex is thick with self-correction contingencies, based on what it encounters when it comes into contact with the computers in Kourou. But those contingencies—what triggers them and what the responses mean—are not explained; they are just strings of commands."

"So," Willow said, "Ephemeral Reflex has an automated troubleshooting function, but no user's guide."

Prospero nodded. "The team here was racing just to complete the code. They hadn't the time to create documentation."

Chloe leaned heavily on her elbows. "So there are all sorts of ways this could fail."

"We always knew that," Rod murmured. "If there's no way to power up the systems, if the computers have been compromised or destroyed, if the transmitter is damaged: then, all we can do is turn around and leave.

But if Prospero's right—if Diane is aimed where the GPS bird is located at 1500 hours—I think he's right to be optimistic about things working when we get to the base. Because if someone *did* purposely park Diane to aim at those coordinates, then they probably realized they wouldn't be the ones to throw the switch."

Willow crossed her arms. "Explain."

Rod hunched forward. "Look: if the coding team at Kourou was losing control of the site—things breaking down, experts dead or turned—then the position of Diane suggests they realized that, by the time they finished the code, they wouldn't have enough time or control left to execute. So they made sure it's all ready to go, that whoever might come along after them could transmit the program as easily and quickly as possible. That's why they didn't just pre-aim the dish; they aimed it at coordinates for later in the day."

Chloe looked up. "Because, for anyone fighting their way in, that gives them the greatest amount of time to reach the controls, send the signal, and get the hell out again before nightfall."

Rod nodded eagerly. "Yeah. And if they were thinking that far ahead, there may be other, uh, system elements they might have prepared. Or protected. Like dedicated computers. A backup generator. That kind of thing."

Willow was nodding slowly. "So time becomes even more crucial. If we are not on the ground until 1120, we will have only three hours and forty minutes. And we conceived of this as a five-hour mission, with an emergency contingency to expand to six."

Chloe shrugged. "So we start the party three hours earlier. O-dark-thirty for real."

Willow glanced at me.

I smiled, tilted my head toward Chloe. "What she said."

"But that's only six hours from now."

I shook my head. "Nope: thirty hours. Radio *Legacy* and *Voyager*. We're setting the op clock back by twenty-four hours. We are going into this fully rested."

"Yeah," Chloe drawled, "because if neither of those Bandwagons work, we're gonna be taking a long walk through zombieland."

Prospero was about to answer, but I gestured for him to wait: this had to come from me. "Maybe, but only if we've encountered minimal presence of infected. And no, I don't have a calculus to define 'minimal' yet. But if the probability of success gets too low and the probability of major casualties gets too high, we *will* scrub the whole mission." I looked around at all the faces; on most of them, I saw a weird mix of regret and relief.

"Like we said from the start, this is not a suicide mission. No one can force anyone to go. But there's no point in debate until we get on the ground, find out what works, what doesn't, and how many of our assumptions about the site are accurate versus dead wrong."

Steve folded his arms. "Yeah. With special emphasis on 'dead.'"

That's how the mission to Kourou got pushed back a second day. Twenty-four hours later, we all headed to our cabins to try to get as much sleep as we could, despite the fact that the sun wasn't even touching the western horizon yet. But I wasn't sure that darkness would help that much; I wondered just how many of us were going to do anything other than stare at the ceiling tonight.

I sat down and wrote what I thought would be a short entry (good luck, trying to synopsize six days of events). But just as I was closing the cover of this journal and finally feeling drowsy, I heard a soft knock on the doorjamb. I tiptoed over, opened the door a crack: Willow.

"Alvaro," she whispered, "we need to talk. Now."

Willow doesn't do drama: she never pushes, never demands, never says that things have to happen "right now." So when she showed up at my door with an ultimatum after everyone was asleep—or trying to be—I was suddenly wide-awake again.

I slipped out the door. She was already moving toward the bay-view side of Ozzie's infinity pool. The sky was now very dark and the stars were very clear. Probably good weather for tomorrow's mission. "Is this about the recorders?" I whispered after her. "Look: I know it's just one more thing to carry, but—"

She shook her head. "No, the recorders are fine. Actually, they're a really good idea."

Which was a relief. Having kept this journal, I know first-hand how much you forget about what happens during an operation. And if we have to withdraw tomorrow, we'll need every observation, every detail, to figure out how to adjust our plan for a second try.

Willow stopped at the windiest part of the walkway: nonstop natural white noise. "I am worried about Ning."

Her tone alarmed me. "What happened?"

Willow sighed. "I wish I knew."

"Huh?"

She wrung her hands. "Just after dinner, I noticed Tai sitting well down the slope. By herself. And pensive."

Those three details—that Tai had gone outside the perimeter, alone, and in a state of anxiety—are the direct opposites of her usual behavior. "And Ning is involved . . . how?"

Willow shrugged. "Earlier in the day, Tai had seen Ning in almost the same place, staring out at the bay, brooding."

"Over what?"

"Over our imminent demise." Willow glanced at me. "According to Tai, Ning is worried that one or more of our team may be . . . unreliable."

"In what way?"

Willow shook her head. "Tai was so surprised and upset she started asking 'many, many questions.'"

Which, given Tai, meant she'd launched into a wide-eyed, full-blown, and very loud interrogation. "So Ning shut up?"

Willow nodded. "Except to tell Tai to 'watch her back.'"

I cursed. "So why didn't Tai come to me with this? Hell, why didn't *Ning* come to me?"

Willow shrugged. "Tai wanted to but also didn't want to betray Ning's trust. That's what she was fretting over: when and how to tell you. And as far as Ning sharing her suspicions . . ." Willow's eyes met mine. "Alvaro, don't you find it dubious that she was assigned to the Great Wall station as a 'human resources director'?"

"Doesn't everyone?" I frowned. "Except you, I thought."

"That has become less true over time," Willow murmured.

I heard a dark tone in Willow's answer, one that I had never heard before. "Wait: do you think she's trying to sabotage the mission? To ruin our trust in each other, to divide us? Really?"

Willow's gaze and tone both became more chilling. "I think it is a possibility, yes."

Damn. "But . . . why? What would make her think that's still a good idea, even if she is—was—some kind of Chinese agent?"

Willow nodded slowly. "Because if Ephemeral Reflex works, it will confer a strong advantage upon the U.S. and its allies for the foreseeable future."

"Willow, as best as anyone can tell, there is no U.S. anymore, let alone any of its allies."

She shook her head. "Alvaro, my maternal grandmother was from Shanghai. She had a saying: China's government may change, but China itself never does. Its very name—the 'Middle Kingdom'—means that it sees itself as the center of all things. And whereas we in the West typically think about the months or years ahead, China thinks in terms of decades or even centuries. And its agents' directives are structured accordingly."

I could hardly believe Willow was serious. "So you're saying Ning is still following some kind of contingency plan? Like, 'In the event that the world ends, try to cripple the West'?"

Willow shrugged. "From what my grandmother told me, that would not be inconsistent with Beijing's thinking."

"Damn, Willow: your grandma sounds almost as scary as Ning."

Willow sent a brief, sad smile up at the stars. "Alvaro,

I'm sorry to worry you. Particularly now. But...we need to be ready. Just in case."

I shrugged as we turned back toward Ozzie's tower. "Yeah. I get it." We started up the stairs. "You know, there *is* a third explanation."

"Which is?" she asked as we stopped at her door.

"That Ning is just wound way too tight. That she's seeing and worrying about things that just aren't there."

Willow smiled. "I hope you're right." She started to slip into her room, then turned back. "Oh! And happy birthday."

"Thank you," I said as she closed the door.

I wasn't sure how she knew it was my birthday, since I had completely forgotten about it. We don't celebrate them anymore, probably because it just makes you remember all the people who aren't there—and makes you wonder if you deserve to be. So today sure didn't feel like my birthday.

Hell, I just hope I'm still alive after my first twenty-four hours as a nineteen-year-old.

January 17 (Alvaro's recorder; transcript one)

I'm making this recording while crouching on perimeter security at Totness. It was weird this morning. No one slept much but you'd never have known it. Everyone was wide-awake, their hands moving constantly, checking their gear. A lot of leg-jiggling, too.

But no one spoke. Only the orders and ops checks. Then, after shoehorning ourselves into the Twin Otter, we took off with a rush and climbed into the higher, silent air. Mustique fell away into the rushing darkness below.

Landing in Totness was creepy. An abandoned town next to the sea, hemmed in on all sides by rainforest. And again, almost no sounds. Maybe that's because of us. Maybe it's because passives lurk nearby, eager to grab birds and small game. Or maybe stalker packs roam back here too often for other species to settle down. I sure didn't want to find out about the latter.

We've topped off the tanks, and Jorge and Ozzie have done their flightline check. I'm getting the thumbs-up. Time to go.

The landing strip was everything we could have asked for: a 1.75 kilometer stretch of arrow-straight double-lane highway in great condition. Ozzie was flying this leg of the journey because it was the only place we hadn't landed yet. If something went wrong, he was the guy who knew every quirk and shimmy that the plane might produce.

Which turned out to be a really good choice.

We had reached Kourou early. It was the first time I'd ever seen it. I guess it might have been okay before the plague, but now it was just a half-burned-out shithole, particularly its waterfront. We stayed pretty high and Ozzie let the engine's RPMs decrease: all to keep the noise down. There weren't many infected in sight, but the last thing we wanted to do was see how many more might pour out of the buildings if we did the audio equivalent of kicking their anthill.

Next we turned a slow orbit around the launch facility. It must have been really cool at one time; three major launch pads, others that were smaller or retired, big assembly buildings. But now it was deserted, which in one way was sad—spaceflight was deader than rock bands—but in another way was excellent: anything moving down there would have been something we'd have to kill. So I was glad to see that the ESA Kourou was just what Ozzie and Papillon had described: a ghost town.

"Ozzie," I shouted over the engine.

"Yeah, wazzit?"

"Your last pass here: did you see any infected near the jungle?" Which was a lot of terrain to look at, since the facility was bordered on the north and west by rainforest.

He shook his head. "If they're in there, they don't come out. Then again, why would they? There ain't much game that stands around in the open."

I leaned back, discovered Chloe looking at me with a smile that was pure sass. "Even *I* coulda told you that."

I just nodded.

Ozzie reached up, did some pilot stuff. "Okay, kids; here's the best part of the ride." Then he turned one last grin back at us and flipped a switch. The plane's sound system crackled to life: Guns N' Roses' "Welcome to the Jungle" blared around us.

Ozzie eased the Twin Otter into a wide, smooth, one-hundred-eighty-degree turn that ended with us right over the northern stretch of National Road One: the approach to our "airstrip." He leaned toward Papillon, who was in the copilot's seat. "Like what you're seein'?" he shouted.

"Everything looks good," Papillon shouted back. "But the music: too loud!"

Ozzie shrugged, killed the audio. "Down we go!"

The nose lowered toward the green beneath us. Which grew bigger. Really quickly. Then the nose came up and I had that stomach-floating feeling when you are leveling out from a dive. I craned my neck to get a window view.

Mixed savannah and marshland went ripping past in a blur of greens, browns, tans, yellows—and we bumped into contact with the ground. We came up a bit, then settled into three-point contact and Ozzie juiced the engines into reverse.

"Damn," said Tai, looking around at all the faces within a few inches of her own (we were packed that tight), "that wasn't so bad, hey? I could get used to—"

There was a pop like when you step on bubble wrap and the Twin Otter lurched and started skidding to the left—

Ozzie was already yanking the stick over, standing on the pedals, and either trying to idle the left-side engine, or maybe re-reverse it. Or something like that. It all happened so fast. I remember thinking, "we're going to die" and then thinking, "Or, we may not" just before the plane started slewing sideways to the right and then came to a stop.

"And what the *fuck* was *that*?" Chloe roared.

"That, my bodacious darlin', was a blowout," Ozzie shouted with enthusiasm that sounded like it was layered on top of a bad case of the shakes.

Willow looked gray. "A blowout? How?"

Papillon sounded weirdly calm. "We didn't see all of the debris, apparently." He checked the instruments. "Props are still. Systems secure. Deplane." We did.

Jorge stuck close, expecting me to lead the security detail that was going to cover him as he assessed the three vehicles. I glanced at Ozzie, then at the listing Twin Otter. "You want Jorge here?"

Nugent thought. "Yeah. Another set of eyes, and maybe hands, would be good right now."

Prospero came over. "That will eat into our operations window."

I shrugged. "First, we're almost fifteen minutes ahead of schedule. Second, and more important, the condition of the plane dictates what we do next."

Chloe had overheard. "How?"

"If it can take off safely, and land again safely, then we proceed as planned. But if it can't, then the condition of the Bandvagns becomes the fulcrum point. If one of them works, we go forward."

"And if neither do?"

"Then the rest of our day is about one thing: getting

safely to the extraction point on the shore. In the meantime, get one drone airborne. Keep it high, in overwatch. No swooping or buzzing."

They nodded, moved off, passed the word.

As Ozzie, Papillon, and Jorge assessed and confabbed about the Twin Otter, we saw one stumbler. Through binoculars. Heading the other direction.

After ten minutes, the three leaned away from the plane and approached as a group. We could tell from their faces that the news was not good. I crossed my arms. "Tell me, Ozzie."

"Sorry, but my beast won't be safe for flying—well, actually, for *landing*—without a new tire."

I nodded, but was already thinking about the fastest way we could get a spare to Kourou. It would mean scrubbing the day's mission, exfilling from the mudflats, sailing back to Mustique, readying the other Twin Otter, and—

Ozzie must have seen the wheels starting to spin behind my eyes. He shook his head. "Hold on, tiger. There's more."

Jorge nodded. "One of the struts in the landing gear looks bent. I'd need to get it off to tell. No way to do that here. No tools to remove. And none to fix it if it's bent."

Papillon squinted into the distance. "Which is why we cannot land safely. Or even safely retract the landing gear."

I'm no aircraft genius, but I knew what that meant. "So even if we got airborne, we'd have reduced range because of the drag."

Papillon nodded. "So: what shall we do?"

Prospero had drifted over. So had Chloe. The rest

of the security perimeter started collapsing slowly upon our huddle.

"Man your posts!" I shouted. "We'll tell you when there's something to tell you." I turned to Ozzie. "The other Twin Otter: she can make it to Kourou via Totness, right?"

He sucked his unfortunate teeth. "Yeah, but we didn't get her ready for it. Every minute was dedicated to getting this bird flawless."

"So how long to get the other one ready?"

Ozzie shrugged. "Half a month. Minimum." The other two nodded. "And if we find that a major part needs replacing, maybe never."

Which meant: "Jorge, it's all on you."

"Wha-what you mean, on me?"

"I mean you need to tell me if you can get one of these Bandvagns to run. And soon."

"Uh, how soon is soon, *jefe*?"

I spun the hands of the mental mission clock. "Ninety minutes."

He nodded. "I can do that."

"Vehicle security team," I said just loud enough to be heard (no shouting in stalker country), "we are escorting Jorge to the Bandvagns. HQ security stays with the plane. Snipers, keep an eye on the perimeter and the approaches to the Bandvagns."

Chloe was already unlimbering her rifle. "You got it."

I nodded to the vehicle assessment security team. "Okay. To the nearest Bandvagn, at the trot."

The first Bandvagn was pretty good mechanically, but there was something wrong with its wiring. Possibly from overheating, Jorge speculated, with a grim look at the dried, raw meat caked tightly between its rubber treads. The vehicle had clearly been used as a weapon. To considerable effect.

Even so, he tried jumping the battery, but after one attempt, he pulled the clamps. "Alternator," he explained. And coolant had leaked out; apparently, some impact had jarred a line loose.

There were no remains of occupants, but there was plenty of spent 5.56x45mm brass on the floor of the cabin, along with other odds and ends of military gear. Along with the vehicle's interior, it was all coated in blood.

"How'd deh stalkers get in, you think?" Tai asked over my shoulder.

I tapped the broken handle on the rear driver-side door. "Either this was already broken or they pulled it to pieces."

I stared farther out, sweeping through a hundred-yard perimeter. Not many more bodies visible, even here on the ground. A few were Legionnaires, which we only knew from the bits of uniform still stuck to dried-out remains. The others were either civilian or infected: hard to tell the difference, at this point. If there had been more, they'd been dragged off into the grass, which had long since grown over any signs of struggle.

By the time Jorge was ready to move to the second Bandvagn, I suspect we were all thinking the same thing: did we want it to work or not? On the one hand, going home to Mustique was getting more attractive every second. But on the other hand, if both Bandvagns were inoperable, that pretty much meant the end of the mission. Hell, it would be a major undertaking just to get back here to repair and retrieve the Twin Otter.

And then what? We'd have to return several times to tinker with the Bandvagns, trying to get one to work? No: if the second Bandvagn was a write-off, then so was the mission. Which in turn meant "goodbye, GPS" and "hello" to a longer, harder climb back to the top of Earth's food chain. Assuming we even managed to stay a part of it.

The second Bandvagn had an articulated rear, or "passenger," half attached and told a very different story than the first track. The only open door was the front passenger's side, but its latch was not broken. On the other hand, its inside surface looked like it had been used for point-blank target practice. The driver's seat had a half-devoured corpse in it and the floor and dashboard were littered with spent 9mm parabellum casings. The driver's weapon—a Euro-made Beretta 92—was glued into its one remaining hand by a mix of dried blood and tissue.

Steve glanced into the back seat. "Looks like someone left their Playstation behind."

I craned my neck: it was a handheld remote-control device. But for what?

Jorge called from the rear of the vehicle. "Hey!"

"Yeah?"

"Alvaro, you pray?"

What? "Uh…"

A clatter of resisting circuits, then a cough, and the Bandvagn's engine growled into life.

"I guess God like you, even if you don' pray! We in bizness, *jefe!*"

∽ ⊖ ⊶

This Bandvagn was a whole lot uglier than the first one, but was in pretty good working order. Jorge immediately started griping about how it had been left out in the elements and all the maintenance mistakes its prior owners had made. But always with a smile on his face...which meant we had a solid set of wheels. (Okay, tracks.)

Unfortunately, the rear section—which pulled its power from the cab's engine—wasn't going anywhere. Something was fouled up with the transfer, something so bad that Jorge just threw up his hands and said, "No way. Not dis lifetime."

So as he uncoupled the passenger section, the rest of us checked the compartment. That's when we discovered why there had been a remote-control unit in the cab.

The only passenger left in there was a four-wheeled robot. It wasn't big—not more than two feet per side—but it had a pair of manipulator arms and a pretty large sensor blister. Best of all, it was equipped with "hot swap" batteries, with a recharger built into its trunk-sized carrying case.

I toggled my comms. "Rod?"

"Yeah, Alvaro?"

"You need to see this."

Rod trotted over and promptly had what, during earlier incidents, he freely called a "nerdgasm." Jorge announced that the Bandvagn was ready to go and that he had already called back to the plane to unload enough fuel to top off its half-full tank of diesel.

"Then drive us back to the plane."

"You bet!" he said. I had never seen him that animated about anything before.

Rod appeared out of the passenger section. "You are not going to believe this."

"Try me."

"They never deployed that ROV."

"So it's still brand new."

"Not just that, Alvaro; they never even put in the batteries. So they haven't been cooking in this heat for months. They're still in the factory packaging. Hell, there's some juice in one of them, and the recharger still works!"

"And the handset: is that still—?"

Rod was nodding like the bobble-head doll in a car one of my L.A. buds had, uh, borrowed late one night. "Totally fine. Same story with its batteries. And we can juice both rechargers with this adapter"—he waved it emphatically—"that plugs into the Bandvagn's outlet."

I smiled. "Load our newest team member in the back."

Rod ran to get help with moving the robot.

Jorge leaned out the door of our new ride. "Hey, you guys comin' or what?" He stared at the ROV that Rod was already lifting into the back seat with Steve's help. "That thing work?"

I smiled and shrugged. "Believe it or not, yeah, it does. We sure got lucky."

Jorge shook his head. "Not luck, frien'."

"No?"

Jorge smiled and closed the door. He glanced at the plane. "The Lor' takes"—then he glanced at the robot—"but He give back, too. Let's go."

January 17 (Alvaro's recorder; transcript two)

We've got a minute or two now that we've stopped. Everyone is slugging down some water. Ning and Prospero are trying to raise Jeeza and Robbie by radio, who are just fifteen miles away. Not everyone was on board with prepositioning them in the Salvations. But if we hadn't, they wouldn't be close enough to save our sorry, grounded asses. And yeah, I do feel a little smug about being right. So sue me.

After twenty minutes, we had the plane unloaded and all of us were in or tethered on top of the Bandvagn. By that time, the robot's best battery was finished charging and Rod sent it down the road just ahead of us. Yeah, that meant one less gun on the line, but he's not one of our better shots, and he'd have been distracted by controlling the aerial drone, anyway. Bottom line: two remote platforms were a lot more important than a little more firepower as we headed into zombieland.

Jorge put the Bandvagn in gear and it lurched forward. I grabbed for the edge of the hatch so I didn't go over the side of the roof and started watching the trees to either side of the road. Damn engine is not just loud; it sounds like a dinosaur with indigestion.

In stopping my fall, I had half-sprawled across Chloe. She glanced back. Her flash of annoyance changed the instant she saw my face right behind her left shoulder; it became a sly grin. "Save that for later; I'm busy now." She chuckled—no, she *giggled*—and went back to scanning her sector. Pure Chloe.

The Bandvagn is not a smooth ride, even on a level, paved road like National Road One. But the jostling wasn't so bad that I couldn't spot key landmarks. I pointed to the southwest. "Look. Eight o'clock." A bright white rim poked over the trees before a brief gap in the foliage fully revealed ground station Diane's fifteen-yard dish. It looked intact, but looks had often been deceiving in our postapocalyptic experience.

"It's just over a kilometer down that road," Rod shouted up through the rear hatch. "I could scout it with the drone." He wanted a look at it. A lot of us did.

But we had to keep to the opord and the timetable. "Have the drone orbit it once, look for structural damage, then bring it right back. We're getting close to the built-up part of the complex." Not the time to sacrifice our ability to see trouble before it saw us.

Rod nodded; the drone veered sharply to the right, following the road that led to the dish and its few associated buildings. I went back to watching the horizon. I wished there had been room for Tai on the roof. She had the eyes of a hawk.

Which was probably why she saw the stumblers even before I did. "You gettin' slow, *chefe*!" she yelled. "Two 'clock!"

About a hundred-fifty yards ahead, rising up from underneath an abandoned work truck, one stumbler, and then another rose into the noonday sun, blinking.

"Chloe," I said, "call it."

"Really?" She sounded irritated. "Okay: stop the 'wagon.'"

"Already?"

"Yes, 'already.' Look: since this place is so deserted, it doesn't make any sense to keep rolling. If we stop, I can gun down the lead of those two, and I'll bet the other stops to make a meal of him. Or we can keep on rolling and, thanks to the supersmooth ride, I won't hit a damn thing. So which is it?"

Ozzie, standing tall out of the top hatch, looked back from his M60. "They'll be here in about half a minute." He slid the weapon's cocking handle forward.

It's hard to express all the things that can go through your mind in a single second when you make a battlefield decision. In this case:

—no plane means no margin for error;
—the site is quieter than we expected;
—maybe most of the stalkers are in torpor;
—the M60 could wake them up;
—the Bandvagn could, too, particularly if it's starting from a full stop;
—and we need to get to the objective ASAP;
—but we're going to have to drive back through here;
—probably with stalkers chasing us;

so—

"Jorge," I shouted down through the open hatch, "full stop! Chloe, single shots whenever possible."

She snapped off the safety. "Not like we need to worry about ammo."

"No," I agreed as the stumblers came within fifty yards, "but we need to worry about sound."

She squeezed the trigger and the rifle cracked like a small lightning bolt.

The first stumbler staggered to the side, bleeding heavily from a chest wound. The second one glanced at it . . . but kept coming.

"Shit," Chloe muttered as she slapped the bolt down on the second round. She breathed out slowly—

That second shot couldn't have been any louder than the first, but still, it *seemed* louder. The second stumbler went backward, sprawling her length in the dust. It did not move. The other crawled in her direction but collapsed before he got there.

"Jorge," I called down into the cab, "just in case we're in the middle of a thousand sleeping stalkers, try to keep the engine steady. Don't gun it when we start moving again. Let it build up speed slowly."

"You got it," he said and did an admirable job of letting out the clutch so gradually that we sort of drifted into forward motion. It took about five seconds for us to get back to our prior speed.

Chloe was staring back at me. "There's no way to keep quiet on this op, Alvaro. You know that, right?"

I nodded. "Yeah, but the more we can limit noise— particularly loud, sharp sounds—the fewer we wake up, and then have to fight, at any one time. And that means getting the job done faster and getting out of here sooner."

She nodded. "Amen to that."

"'Amen'?" I echoed. "I thought you were an atheist."

"And I will be again," she muttered, "as soon as we get out of here."

~⊙⊙⊙~

It was kind of eerie from that point on. We'd cruise for a few tenths of a mile, then catch sight of a few infected, drift to a stop, and Chloe would go for a head shot. She might miss once, rarely twice, but when she hit, the closest stumbler always dropped like a slab of beef—which the others treated like an all-meat buffet. They were so ravenous they didn't even notice as Chloe picked the others off, one by one.

Meanwhile, the rest of us watched the trees, fingers hovering just outside our weapons' trigger guards. No infected ever emerged, but that didn't make us feel any safer. We kept expecting hordes to come howling out of those shadows. That's the problem with an enemy that you can't see or count; they might not even be there, but if you ever assume they're not, that's the moment that they could roll over you like a wave.

So by the time we caught sight of the gate into the main complex, we were all soaked in sweat: partly from the unremitting fear, partly from being crammed into the Bandvagn's tight cab or baking on its metal roof.

"Slow to a crawl," I called down to Jorge. I got out my binoculars; Prospero was already scanning the entry with his own.

He was narrating what I saw just a second before it came into focus. "Gate's buggered. Truck crashed through: tires are flat, suspension broken. Someone propped up the gate, though: rolled the truck back to pin it in place. Also, the perimeter wire is down in several places."

"Cause?"

"Bog only knows. Could be the sheer weight of bodies that charged it. Lot of dried-out corpses hanging on the remaining strands."

I adjusted the focus on my binoculars. "The gate is crooked, like people pushed past since it was put upright again. Question is, were they going in or out?"

"Could be both," answered Valda, eye level with his rifle's scope. "First, people force their way inside for safety. Then, when the virus breaks out at the site, they push out to escape."

"That is probably exactly what happened," Prospero murmured, lowering his binoculars. "At any rate, the truck's only pinning one side of the gate; we can push it down by rolling through the other side."

Jorge nodded as he approached and slowed the Band-vagn until its nose came to rest against the unsupported side. He coaxed the track back into a slow-motion crawl. The gate leaned, tipped and fell with a dull clatter; we drove over it into the guts of ESA Kourou.

Up until that point, we had only passed a few build-ings and never very close to them. The only reason we even knew we were in a spaceflight center was what loomed above the trees to the east: empty launch tow-ers and gantries, pointing like lonely fingers toward a destination humanity wouldn't return to for decades, maybe centuries. Maybe never.

But half a minute after driving between the buildings at the heart of the complex, there wasn't any time for melancholy. Stumblers started emerging from buildings, from weed-choked culverts, from among vehicles parked under flimsy carports. And these infected were more alert, showed fewer signs of shaking off torpor.

Jorge knew the drill; I didn't even have to call for the stop. "Rod," I said as the Bandvagn drifted to a halt, "time to deploy the robot. Tai, you're with him."

Rod opened the rear driver-side door, hopped out

cradling the ROV. Tai was right behind him, shotgun up and ready.

When the stumblers saw the activity, it was like they'd chugged a triple shot of espresso with an energy-drink chaser. They straightened up and started running: stiff-legged and like they might fall over any second, but running.

"Chloe, Valda, you're up." Their two bolt-action rifles started cracking. I turned to Prospero, who was cradling his FAL. "You can join them, you know."

He nodded. "Watching for bunches, Alvaro." He patted the weapon's twenty-round magazine. "Just in case." He leaned toward Nugent, who was poised over the M60. "Ozzie, down in front, if you please."

Ozzie said something about jackasses in the cheap seats behind him, but complied—just in time for Prospero to pour a steady stream of semiautomatic fire into almost a dozen infected who emerged from a squat concrete building. The first few fell; half of the others stopped to feed. The others kept coming.

Rod called up to me: "Ready!" Waving a thumbs-up behind him, he leaped back into the Bandvagn, Tai right behind him.

"Stand by with that robot," I called down to him.

"Wall-E is standing by."

I rolled my eyes. Did everything have to get a nickname *immediately*?

Chloe's and Valda's rate of fire was dropping off; there weren't that many targets left. Prospero scanned through three hundred sixty degrees, nodded to himself, and swapped magazines. Ozzie leaned back from the M60 with a sigh. "I never get to have *any* fun," he muttered.

Frankly, I hoped he didn't. Because if I called for the M60, it meant we were fighting so many stalkers that I was willing to risk its roar waking up hundreds more.

"Okay, Jorge; take us to the primary objective. You know the way."

"I do!" he confirmed and let the clutch out slowly. With a cheery whirring, Wall-E rolled right after us.

We'd fought in built-up areas before. Fernando de Noronha had sections that were mad jumbles of cottages, stores, garages, shacks. But this was our first time between buildings that were so big they went on for half a football field—or more—and were too tall for us to see over. The drone helped at first, but its recharged batteries crapped out so fast that it faltered and fell before Rod could get it back to us. So, until we had enough time to let Rod unpack another one and activate it, the only thing we could do was keep the Bandvagn in the middle of the wide roads (rocket parts and stages are *not* small) and hope that gave us enough time to react.

I'm not sure it would have, if it hadn't been for Wall-E.

The infected started coming out more frequently and in bigger bunches. Not so big that I was willing to unleash Ozzie's M60 yet, but too many to risk bringing the track to a full stop. So Chloe and Valda switched to their own FALs and the folks inside the cab started shooting at any stalker that got within ten yards. So far there weren't many of those.

But the more we fired, the more that showed up. They were all thin—most had probably been in light torpor, at least—but they arrived fully active. Which we hadn't seen since FdN. However, in Kourou, the pre-plague population had been so large that you couldn't really estimate the maximum number that might show up. Because stalkers could have wandered in from any-where . . . and, well, South America is a *big* continent.

We were getting close to one of our final waypoints—a left-hand turn—when two packs of at least twenty each emerged, one from either side of the intersection to which we were heading. Ozzie looked back. I nodded, pointed to the group coming from the right, and shouted down through the hatch: "Jorge: slow roll! Rod: target left. Foxes and hounds!"

"Engaging!" Rod screamed up at me, his voice crack-ing into a falsetto.

Quick as lightning, Wall-E swerved out from behind the slowing Bandvagn, manipulator arms waving—and playing *music*?

The left-hand group of stalkers and stumblers paused, almost in the same step. The little robot swerved and swirled in time to its own tune—a hyperactive mariachi version of "La Cucaracha"—and then shot away toward a bunch of parked cars, farther down the road. All but a handful of that pack of stalkers charged after it with frenzied yowls.

I leaned over the hatch to find out: a) how Rod had discovered that Wall-E had a built-in speaker, b) why he had music with him, and c) what made him choose such a shitty tune? But I never got the chance.

Ozzie cut loose with the M60. You couldn't hear anything else over that high-speed hammering. A knot of bigger stalkers leading the right-hand group melted away under that fire, maroon puffs marking exit wounds, the next rank thinned by over-penetrations. Only three got so close that they went beneath the weapon's maximum angle of depression—but that put them right next to Tai's shotgun and Johnnie's M4. As those two opened up at point-blank range, Willow linked belts of ammo to replace those that had been feeding upward into Ozzie's "Old Betsy."

I could barely hear Rod through the hoarse ocean-roar that the machine gun had left in my ears, but I could still tell that he was shouting: "Fox is bringing back the hounds!"

I half-spun front and shouted, "Ozzie!"

"What?" he shouted back. It sounded like he was whisper-yelling across a mile of Malibu surf.

I pointed down the street.

He turned to look.

Wall-E had eluded the stalker pack by scooting under a parked vehicle. The first rank of infuriated pursuers had come up short against the rear quarter panel; the ones immediately following had crashed into them. As they did, the robot shot out the opposite side, sped through a tight arc and headed back toward us, playing a new song: "Werewolves of London." The stalkers spun, leaped after the robot. They were faster, would probably catch him right about as he reached the Bandvagn.

Willow shouted something up at Ozzie, holding up three fingers; she'd managed to link three new belts.

Ozzie grinned, leaned over his gun, and started the music.

He had to cheat his aim a little high to avoid hitting the robot, but the closer Wall-E got, the more leeway Ozzie had. As spent brass cascaded over the right side of the roof, I had to resist the reflex to put my hands over my ears. But I needed to keep my gun ready and my head on a swivel; another pack could materialize from the corners or buildings behind us at any moment.

Somehow you can be functionally deaf and still hear when a machine gun stops firing. I turned toward the front. The road was littered with infected.

My own voice was faint in my head when I told Jorge to "drive on." But he clearly heard me; the Bandvagn picked up speed.

Only three hundred yards to our objective.

Two more times in those last three hundred yards, we had to pull the same trick. The last time, one of the most angry, active stalkers took a huge leap after Wall-E and caught hold of his left manipulator arm.

That didn't end well for either of them. The sudden yank sent Wall-E tumbling onto its (his?) side. The stalker hit the ground awkwardly, and Ning put two in his head before he could get up. Wall-E looked like a goner as the rest of the pack bore down on him, but between its built-in balance-recovery system and Rod's wizardry with dual joysticks, the robot spun itself until it started to wobble. It tipped itself toward the ground, bounced down onto its wheels, and sped back to us, its dead robot-arm dragging uselessly behind. The rest of the stalkers chased it and ran straight into a wall of machine-gun, battle-rifle, and shotgun fire.

Two minutes later, we pulled up in front of the launch control center: a three-story building with two wings of offices angling out from either side of a broad central section with a long, roofed stairway. Had we

been able to drive right up to the doorway, we probably would have. It was fortunate that we couldn't.

We were all grabbing a quick drink of water—
canteen levels were already lower than they should
have been but there was no fixing that—when Tai
cocked her head, looked up high through the hatch,
and asked, "Hey, you hear tha'?"

Frankly, I don't know how she heard anything after
all that gunfire, but that didn't matter: when Tai thinks
she hears or sees something, that's good enough for
me. I rose into a crouch—just in time to see a flood
of stalkers come out the front door.

But as I shouted, "Engage front!" I kept looking
higher, because that's where Tai's attention had gone.

Stalkers on the third story were jumping down to
the roof of the stairway, following it toward us like
a ramp—from which they'd be able to leap across to
the roof of the Bandvagn. Hoping he could hear better than I could, I screamed, "OZZIE! Target front
and *high*!"

He flinched, stared at me, looked confused, then
saw where I had my own weapon pointed—directly
over his head—and turned. In a moment, he was down
over the M60 and burning through belts.

It was the first time since landing that I had even
shouldered a weapon. I guess that's why the handbooks
for officers don't even mention shooting at the enemy.
It's not job one or job two; hell, they don't even assign
it a priority. It's like what you're supposed to do if
you *don't* have something else to do.

As Ozzie's M60 roared and deafened me all over
again, I started putting rounds down the length of
the roof/ramp, tapping any stalker that appeared in

the Honeybadger's holographic sight. And for a split second, I was afraid I had gone fully and finally deaf. Until I realized that, no: the Honeybadger is just that quiet and just that smooth. And what I saw down the sights told me that Ozzie had not exaggerated the power of .300 Blackout.

It was like hitting those hyperactive stick figures with an AK; a quick dark red puff and they disappeared. Off the roof, sprawled on top of it: I didn't have the time or inclination to give a damn. More like: *That one's gone? Okay, next customer.*

When there were no more left on the stairway roof, Ozzie kept a watch on it while the rest of us lashed atop the cab leaned over the side and sent fast semiautomatic into the ones that had swamped around the Bandvagn's tracks. Between the fire from inside, and from us overhead, they were all dead or dying in about twenty seconds.

That was about ten minutes ago. Since then, we've reloaded, had a snack, sipped some water, taken a lot of deep breaths and gone over the objective's floor plan once more. Because now it's time to do what we came to do.

Time to finish the long journey that has been Ephemeral Reflex and, maybe, help buy humanity a little more time to take back the world.

January 17 (Willow's recorder; transcript one)

Things have changed again, so while I have a few spare minutes I should record an entry.

Just before entering the launch control center, we got an update from Jeeza. She and Robbie have already moved *Voyager* to a position just two miles off the shore, due east of the ESA complex. They've already reefed the sails because, until we are on board, they will rely on the motors alone. No one wants to sail along the edge of mudflats which have almost certainly changed since they were last charted.

Robbie has already prepped the Zodiac and the smaller inflatable that it will tow. Once we are loaded on them, we'll have to go more slowly than if it was the Zodiac alone, but that hardly matters. The key objective is to get everyone off the stalker-infested shore ASAP, and all in one trip.

It was reassuring to hear that our ride home is ready. And there is a sense of accomplishment as we respond to new problems by activating well-honed contingency plans. But still, it is unsettling how many failures have occurred already. On the one hand, all our preparation has clearly paid off, but on the other, we have been reduced to almost minute-to-minute improvisation. Maybe it does not bother the others as much as it bothers me. Maybe they are just better at concealing their irritation. I only know that I do not like it. At all.

Once *Voyager* signed off, we exited the Bandvagn. That was also when the adrenaline surge began wearing off and we all became very aware of just how impossibly hot it was in the leather jackets and fire coats that we have adopted as armor. We have modified them where possible to improve ventilation without sacrificing protection, but in the heat and humidity of midday French Guiana nothing helps much.

We formed up and moved into the stifling darkness of the Launch Control building. Jorge and my Johnnie stayed behind, quiet in the shadows of the Bandvagn. They would reveal themselves only to eliminate any stalkers that tried moving into the building behind us.

Once inside, we put on our night vision gear—NODs—and Rod removed the broken arm from the robot before sending it ahead of us. It too, had a light intensification system.

It was very fortunate that it did. As Papillon helped keep Rod and Wall-E on the fastest path to the control room, we turned many dark corners and approached many open rooms and offices. Because we advanced carefully, the robot found four infected emerging from torpor. I was surprised that they were still sluggish after all the gunfire at the entrance of the facility, but they *were* extremely thin. In each case, Rod used the robot to guide Ning to the creatures. As silent as a ghost, she slipped into their hiding spots and dispatched them with two silenced bullets from her machine pistol.

This was when I became aware that "silenced" weapons really aren't (which is probably why the soldiers among us prefer the term "suppressed"). In the case of the last one Ning eliminated, the noise elicited a grunt from farther down the hall. As she exited that office, two far more active stalkers appeared at the end of the corridor. They couldn't see us—at least, not very well—but their next actions revealed just how thoroughly they had changed into a true predator species; they put their noses high in the air and sniffed in a half circle. They ended up facing us directly.

There really wasn't time for orders, and Ning's position made it impossible for us to fire safely—except for Alvaro. He pushed himself against the opposite wall, his new weapon raised and his eye close to its sight. The gun spat, or coughed, five times. The stalker on the right, the one partially blocked by Ning, was hit once; the other, twice. Ning turned on her heel as if it were a dance step, bringing her machine pistol to bear upon the one directly behind her. The gun made two thinner spitting sounds: that stalker, already staggered, went down and did not get up.

It happened so quickly that there really wasn't time to be scared. Rather, what made me the most fearful was that Papillon insisted, and Prospero agreed, we had come to a point where we had to leave a rear guard. Although Johnnie and Jorge were watching the entrance, we were now so far into the building that stalkers from other floors, or from sections we had bypassed, might hear our movement and converge upon us. So Tainara and Chloe remained behind, taking cover behind already-overturned desks, their radios open so we could hear whatever they said or did. Alvaro seemed to feel the way I did about leaving people behind (isn't splitting up in a dark, dangerous building always a prelude to mayhem in horror movies?), but he nodded for Rod to continue forward, Ning a few steps ahead.

We slowed as we drew near the control room, which was laid out like a theater: rows of fixed seats arrayed to watch the technical staff as they performed their jobs behind a glass wall. At least, that was how it had looked in pre-plague photos. Now, the double doors were thrown back, one hanging from a single hinge. We could see bodies slumped across the seats, in the aisles. Beyond them, the glass wall had been cracked in several places, although it had not shattered. We crept up to the doorway; Rod sent the robot in. He stared intently at the screen, gulped hard two times, then nodded. "It's clear," he said, "and no windows or doors, so flashlights are okay."

It is a sad fact that we had little time or interest in the various bodies, except insofar as they were clues as to what had happened. Many had been armed, several had carried backpacks that were now torn to ribbons. Most were dressed practically: no dresses or suits. They had died ill-shaven and poorly groomed. "They must have held out here for a while. For several days, at least."

Papillon had already led the others to a side door that accessed the control room. "Same here," he called. I went to join them.

Total wreckage. Most of the computer screens were broken. Paper and DVDs and ring-bound manuals were strewn everywhere. There were a few bullet holes, mostly in the wall and several consoles flanking the doorway. But no bodies.

Prospero was frowning. "This . . . is not right. The dates on these sheets"—he was scanning the top pages of a clipboard—"are from well before this facility stopped communicating."

Alvaro nodded, scanned the floor—for bodies, I presumed—looked at Papillon. "Where are the survivors?"

Papillon was staring back out into the small hallway that connected the door into the control room with the theater/VIP seats. He glanced at a dry erase board cluttered with Post-it notes, saw a security key hanging in front of it, its tether looped over the receptacle that should have held a marker. Papillon smiled sadly, took the key, said, "Follow me." He exited the control room. We filed out after him as he turned right, heading toward the small hallway's dead end.

Or at least that's what we had presumed it to be. He leaned close and found a small slot in the wood paneling. He inserted the key, turned, and shoved. The panel swung inward, revealing a narrow descending staircase, faintly lit by the amber flicker of failing emergency lights. Weapon held before him in one hand, he started down. Rod stepped aside and sent the robot back toward the theater's entry to keep watch behind us.

I slipped past him. As I started down, I glanced at the construction of the door; it was set to swing closed on its own. That made it impossible to know if the corpses in the viewing gallery were people who had fought against the initial attack of the infected, or who had reemerged from this shelter but never made it past the first room.

The subterranean area was cramped and putrid

with a rotting vinegar smell: long-dead flesh, almost dried out.

There were only three chambers: a small barracks with floor-to-ceiling triple bunks and a partitioned fresher; a kitchenette and freezer-pantry not much bigger than a walk-in closet; and another control room. That was where all the bodies were.

Papillon was in the lead, but he stopped short. He had grown pale, looked like he might become nauseated. Alvaro drew up beside him, asked, "You okay?"

"Yes, but I . . . I knew people here." His Adam's apple pumped sharply. "It is different if you might see someone from . . . before."

Prospero, a step behind, looked away and nodded. "It is."

Alvaro glanced at him, saw me watching. His eyes were mournful. He had told me about how Prospero had found what was left of his friend in a different control building on Ascension.

Papillon blew his breath out in a rush, snugged his weapon up to his cheek, advanced in a crouch.

No one alive. Not that we had expected anyone to be.

"Clear," Papillon announced, and started to move from one body to the next. He paused several times, winced once, but kept looking for—what? Or who?

Prospero went to the cluster of computer terminals that dominated the center of the room.

Meanwhile, Alvaro sent Steve up to stand watch at the top of the stairs, Ning to comb the barracks more closely, and Valda to do the same with the kitchenette. He kept Ozzie with him near the doorway, positioned so they could see into the other two rooms and up the staircase as well. Which was all part of the plan:

leave me and Rod and Prospero to look at the computers, and Papillon with us to translate any documents.

At about the same time that Valda returned from the kitchenette, Prospero and Rod and I were exchanging worried looks. None of us had found anything that was still operating, or any live power sources.

Alvaro sounded worried as he asked, "Valda, what did you find?"

"Well, a lot of food was eaten. And they obviously brought the virus down here with them."

"Why do you say?"

"Because there are two turned corpses stuffed in the freezer."

"Bagged?"

Valda nodded. "Triple-bagged. Trying to contain the infection."

"Well, that didn't seem to work very well," Prospero muttered. "Most of the damage to the computers was caused by someone laying about with a chair leg. And a boot, I think. There are some bullet holes, as well."

"Yeah," muttered Rod. "This naked guy under the map table: he turned for sure. And then someone gut-shot him."

Papillon grunted, toed an empty pump shotgun out from behind a printer stand. "People's exhibit A."

"They tied down the first cases," Ning called out from the barracks. "Three bunks have medical restraints." She appeared in the doorway, holding torn pieces of a wide brown belt. "One chewed through his wrist strap."

Alvaro glanced at the scattered papers, then at Papillon. "Can you put together a timeline on what we're seeing here?"

The Legionnaire shrugged, but it was a strange, rigid

motion: almost a flinch. "It appears they were all right for the first two weeks, maybe three, but then . . ." He gestured at the chaos around us. "I think they turned in waves. Each one caused the new infections that led to the later waves. At some point, they lost Internet connection and internal communications."

"In that order?"

"Yes, I think so."

"Why?"

"Because they stopped making notes about compiling Ephemeral Reflex about the same time they stopped logging new e-mail traffic."

"Wait," snapped Prospero. "Show me those records."

Papillon held them out absently. Prospero snatched them. Papillon remained focused on Alvaro. "It was some time after that—weeks, I think—before the survivors finally split up."

"Split up? You mean, some left?"

"Yes. There are many missing."

"You're sure of that?"

"Yes, of course. I know this place. There are not enough bodies to account for the complete staff."

"I am sure that is accurate," Valda agreed, "but is it not possible that some did not survive to reach this bunker? They might have—"

"No." Papillon's interruption was as sharp and clipped as his voice. "You do not understand. Look around this room. Count the personal data slates. Many more than there are bodies. There are also not enough guns." He stared at Ning. "Tell me; are there spare clothes or toiletries in the lockers built into the foot of each bunk?"

Ning stared back at him. "No. A third of them are empty. Mostly."

Papillon nodded vigorously. "Mostly empty," he repeated. "I shall guess what was left behind in them: money, books, house and car keys, dress shoes, and dress belts..." He waved to indicate her sharp nod and hard-eyed silence, before turning toward Valda. "And you: when you searched the pantry, did you find any portable food remaining?"

Valda frowned. "You mean such as, eh—?"

"Power bars, candy, granola, energy drinks?"

"Erm, no."

Papillon turned back toward Alvaro. "Which is why there are not enough bodies, either down here or up there. They left."

Alvaro shrugged. "Okay, maybe so. But where would they go? And why?"

Prospero slammed his palm down atop a shattered computer monitor. "We need to focus on a different question: *what now*?" He pitched the monitor off the table; its screen splintered as it crashed to the floor. "Everything in here is rubbish. Not a single working computer. But, hold on: no matter, that. Because there is no electricity." He pushed away from the computers. "Brilliant. Just fucking brilliant. And they were so damned close."

"What do you mean?" I asked.

He waved at a folder. "Status reports on Ephemeral Reflex: the version we have *is* complete. And they *did* finish programming the interfaces between—" He stopped, his hands waving in the air as if he was trying to catch words that the rest of us would understand. "All the preliminary work—all the hand-offs from one system to another: they were all done and dusted. The bird has been ready and waiting for the code for months—months! Christ, they even *did* manage to park Diane in the right position for an optimal transmission window—"

"Prospero." Rod was leaning forward, studying the map table more closely.

"—but no, some wanker had to turn stalker and wreck every bloody—"

"PERCIVAL!" Rod shouted.

Prospero stopped, mouth still open.

"Percival," Rod repeated quietly. "Is that the term the launch controllers would use: 'optimal transmission window'?"

Prospero shook his head. "Eh . . . yes, maybe. Probably."

"And it would be defined by a time code and two long coordinate strings, right?"

Prospero's voice became slow and suspicious. "Yes. It would. Why?"

Rod pointed to the map. "Because I think I know where Papillon's missing experts went."

I don't remember rushing over to that table, but in three seconds, we were all crowding to get a look.

On the stylized map of the ESA Flight Center, several different notes and routes had been sketched and crossed out (a few very vigorously). But one remained. It went from the building in which we were located to a point far north, just west of the Soyuz launch pad.

"Bloody hell," Prospero breathed, "really?" He laughed. "They went to Diane? To do it manually?" He squinted. "I don't read much French but—"

"*Non, non*, you are right," Papillon interrupted, reading what was scribbled in the margins. "That is where they went. Well, where *one group* of them went."

Alvaro did not sound surprised or enthusiastic. "And where did the second group go?"

Papillon was his calm self again . . . mostly. "I am not sure there *was* a second group." He leaned very close to the map. "These notes were very rushed. Shorthand. But I think . . . yes: this seems to indicate there was another team. Here are some of its orders: 'Security/extract. Transponder handshake EZMROV-526-Z3—'"

"Wait," said Rod. "Read that string of numbers again. Slowly."

Papillon did. The rest of us watched Rod, who looked like he was in a trance. At the end of the string, his eyes were fully closed.

"I know what happened." He nodded to himself.

Alvaro used that same calm voice. "Rod, if you don't explain what you're talking about, and right now, someone—maybe me—is going to choke it out of you."

Rod opened his eyes. "That string of numbers is the communications code for Wall-E. It's his—well, actually, it's the *controller's* handshake."

Steve frowned. "And what the hell does that have to do with anything?"

Rod was nodding again. "Okay: so, whoever had Wall-E was going to activate him. Which meant they would be using the handset controller. Which meant that whatever group was labelled as 'security/extract' could 'ping' the handset if it was in range. That way, even if they lost radio contact, they could use the handset's transponder to locate the group that was going up to Diane." He grew quiet. "Which means that we now know why those two Bandvagns were up there. I just wonder why they had Wall-E."

Papillon was frowning as he studied the rest of the scribbles. "I think I can answer that." He put his finger on a phrase scrawled in red ink, right under dish-symbol designating Diane. "They wrote '*Station compromise?*' They feared that the compound—Diane's immediate facilities—had been compromised."

Prospero nodded, chin between his thumb and index finger. "So that's why they had the robot: to run a recce inside the wire. Maybe inside the buildings."

"Except the virus broke out among them before they uncrated little Wall-E," Ozzie sighed.

"So who or what does 'Security/extract' refer to?" I asked the room. Alvaro and Ning looked at Papillon.

He held up his hands. "I am—was—only a pilot. There were many contingency plans for site security about which I was never informed."

One of Ning's eyebrows raised. "You were not entrusted with that information?"

He shrugged. "No. It simply didn't *concern* me. The Third Regiment's Kourou security duties did not include air assault. I was mostly a chauffeur. But..."

"Yes?" Alvaro prompted.

"Our helicopter, an Aerospatiale Puma, is equipped with a radio direction finder."

Prospero nodded eagerly. "And the only reason a bunch of lads in two patrol tracks would need to be 'extracted' is if their final destination wasn't someplace they could *drive* to."

The room was very silent—until Ozzie Nugent laughed like a hyena and shouted, "Really? Ain't none o' you gonna say it? We're going to be leaving this damn place in a helicopter!"

"No," Alvaro stressed, "we *may* be leaving in a

helicopter." He glanced at Papillon. "You don't look too optimistic, either."

The Canadian almost smiled. "One learns not to hope too quickly, for too much, or very often, once the world has ended. It may be that the helicopter did get airborne, planned to extract them from Diane. But, like the Bandvagns, they may have had infected passengers who turned during the trip." He kept reading notes scrawled on different parts of the map. "But, I think—" He looked up, scanned the walls, pointed: "There."

Our eyes followed his finger. It was a grid of security lockboxes for items such as cell phones, thumb drives, other personal electronics. One had a small red ribbon tied on it.

Papillon nodded at it. "That one. Check it. This note calls it a 'final update.'"

I was closest to the lockboxes and went to the one with the ribbon. "It is secured by a five-dial combination lock."

Papillon looked more closely around the same part of the map. "Some of this was written very quickly. Hardly legible. It seems as though they were interrupted by one or more people turning." He almost put his nose to the table. "Try combination 11446. If that doesn't work, try 11445."

The latter worked. I removed the contents—a small documents folder, a key, and a Post-it—and brought them to Papillon. "My French is not what it used to be." Which, in fact, was never very good.

He nodded. He scanned the Post-it. "Yes. They went to Diane. But they had more people turning, even as they were closing up here." He opened the document folder, read the important parts aloud. "It is a journal, of sorts. They had to get to the facility by 1430 to ensure power up and handshake before the transmission window closed at 1521. A new person writes that too many people are turning; this may be their only chance. So they are leaving this bunker to rendezvous with the 'security element' that will take them to Diane. But only once the ground station is secured."

He flipped through several sheets, then: "This seems to be meant for, well, for us. 'If GPS is not functioning, we did not succeed.'" Papillon's lower lip quivered. "'You must try where we failed.'" He scanned down. "There were copies of the Ephemeral Reflex code on their laptops. But if those were lost, then we are to...er..." He skimmed the paper quickly. "Willow: is there a thumb drive in that lockbox?"

I leaned over, checked again, and extracted a black fob from the back of the box. "They might have chosen a more readily visible color." I held it out to him.

He shook his head, nodded it toward Prospero. Who pulled our smallest notebook PC out of a foam-lined pouch as he took the thumb drive.

Papillon continued to read. "More notes for us. Before the line to the Diane site went dead, the original team there confirmed that they had prepared a secure transmission asset in a locked maintenance closet." Papillon held up the key, scanned down further. "There is a stand-alone generator. The dish is confirmed as parked in correct position. A long string of coordinates." He looked up. "That's all they wrote."

"You might say the same about this," Prospero sighed as he removed the black thumb drive from his notebook computer. "'Data corrupted.' Not a surprise in this heat and humidity. At least we're all carrying a copy of the software."

I nodded. "I just wish we knew what happened to the people who left the bunker, and what became of their mission."

Rod tilted his head from side to side slightly. "Well, according to what Papillon read off the map, they were apparently going to rendezvous with the security/exfil team heading to Diane, with Wall-E's handset locator as backup in case comms went down. But since the Bandvagns never got there—"

"—The experts had no way to complete their mission," Papillon interrupted, "even if there was a working helicopter." He nodded, thinking it through. "But none of that was known before they left this bunker. In fact—" Papillon stopped suddenly; his lip quivered again.

Alvaro stepped closer. "Tell us what you're thinking."

"It is madness, you understand, but—it is possible there may be survivors in the Legion headquarters."

"What? How?"

Papillon was still looking at Alvaro, but his eyes seemed very far away. "Firstly, this bunker was abandoned in a rush, in total chaos. If the Legion had removed them, there would be more order. And they would certainly have left a more coherent record and instructions for us."

Valda objected, "Although if there were hordes of infected still in the building..."

"Then we would have seen signs of an engagement upstairs."

Ning frowned. "But how would the survivors have gotten past those infected?"

Papillon smiled. "They wouldn't have to...if the stalkers had been drawn away."

Prospero frowned. "A diversion?"

Papillon smiled. "Exactly. Just as you conjectured earlier. The two Bandvagns drove north, shooting, revving their engines, honking their horns."

Valda's frown rivalled Prospero's. "But even so, it is four hundred yards to the Legion HQ."

Papillon nodded. "Yes, but there is a tunnel that links this building's basement with several others. If the survivors knew the right path, they could have remained underground until they were within sixty yards of the compound."

Alvaro was frowning. "So the Bandvagns roll past this building making all the noise they can. The stalkers run outside to join the party, and the survivors in this bunker sneak out and get to the basement." He shrugged. "I suppose your CO might have even sent a team through the tunnel to work as guides for the survivors."

"Yes, and if the helicopter was unable to take off, or was damaged and had to abort the mission, those people might still be alive in the compound."

Steve raised an eyebrow. "So you guys had a bunker, too?"

Ning waved away his surprise. "This is a strategically significant launch facility. The security compound will have a shelter."

Alvaro shrugged. "Either way, we need to get a look at the Legion HQ."

"Alvaro," I said, "it is even more important that we complete the mission."

"No argument. That's why we're splitting into two groups."

That was not the reply I had expected. "Alvaro, that may not be wise."

He nodded. "You're right. But here's the way I see it. Right now, we need a better way out of Kourou. Like a helicopter. And even if it needs some work, spending half a day doing that is less risky than trying to exfil overland to the shore.

"But even if there is no helicopter, there might still be survivors. Getting them is not just a good deed, it's a smart play. The survivors are going to be—literally—rocket scientists and highly trained soldiers. Both could help us make sure we get this mission done right, whether we finish it today or have to come back. And they would be invaluable afterward.

"So a small team is going to go through the tunnels and get to the HQ; that's me, Steve, Ozzie, Valda, and Papillon. The rest of you are going to take the Bandvagn and Wall-E to Diane. You've got the software you need, and the experts have apparently prepared a stand-alone system to transmit it.

"Along the way, we'll update each other on our status and what we've found. We'll adapt and overcome. Or we'll rendezvous and run like hell for the coast."

Alvaro has a way of sounding so matter-of-fact and confident that people start nodding, as if things were going to turn out exactly the way he says. But I am not one of those people. "And if the helicopter isn't there or won't work, how do we rendezvous? What if the stalkers in this complex continue to come out of torpor? What if we're both surrounded?"

He looked a little annoyed. "You've got a vehicle that can mash them. So you break out and head to the coast."

"And your team?"

"Well, if we can repair the helicopter at all, we'll follow. If not, Papillon briefed us about the vehicles that might be in the garage. Maybe we can use one of them. If not, we'll bunker up until you can come back for us."

"And how will we come back for you, since you're taking both of the pilots in your team?"

Alvaro's jaw worked from side to side, like a small, disgruntled bull chewing his cud. "Look, if we take only one pilot with us and we lose him along the way, then it won't matter if there is a working helicopter at the compound. So we need a second pilot as insurance. Besides, if you have to fly back in here to fetch us, Ning took some lessons. And I understand that she's, ah, a 'natural.'" He glanced at her with a small grin.

She waved an annoyed hand at Alvaro but did not contradict him.

I looked at Ozzie. "Mr. Nugent, are you comfortable with the idea of flying a helicopter?"

His eyes were a bit wider. "Um, uh, I'll take a crack at it."

"Okay, then," Alvaro said a bit more loudly than he had to. "Let's get what we need and get moving."

That was about thirty minutes ago. We are approaching Diane. Soon it will be time to have Rod reactivate Wall-E. The Bandvagn is much less crowded, but I liked it better before, when we were all together. I do not like splitting up. That doesn't mean that I disagree with Alvaro; I just don't like it.

I understood why Alvaro assigned the groups he did. Just as he put all the pilots in his team, he put all the computer people in mine. Prospero and Rod have both familiarized themselves as much as possible with the Ephemeral Reflex program, particularly its error codes. Ning and I have also been briefed on getting it loaded and transmitted, since we too are quite comfortable with computers.

Chloe is with us because her long-range marksmanship would be wasted in dark tunnels or among close-set buildings. For the same reason, the cumbersome M60 remained attached to the Bandvagn. Prospero had learned the basic operation of belt-fed weapons during basic training, and Chloe had been tutored in its use by Ozzie in the week leading up to this day. But Ning surprised all of us by waving both of them away and manning the weapon, loading it with almost lazy familiarity. Johnnie and Tai watch the terrain around us, which remains much calmer than the buildings at the heart of the launch complex.

But still, the grounds are less quiescent than when we landed. Stumblers, and even an occasional stalker, are visible as distant silhouettes loping between the empty launchpads. When they hear the noise of our passing, they always change their direction toward us.

We only encountered three on the roadway, but rather than stop, I instructed Jorge to run straight over them. Which he did, almost gleefully.

We are turning left onto the small road that runs past Diane. I see the white rim of the dish rise above the trees. There are no infected ahead of us.

So why am I filled with a growing sense of dread?

January 17 (Alvaro's recorder; transcript three)

If it wasn't for the NODs, I might have had ten heart attacks since we went down into these tunnels. I would have *surely* pissed myself that often.

They didn't turn out to be that bad, but you have no way of knowing that going in. All you know is that if you run into more than a few stalkers, you're probably screwed.

Most of what we found was scat and remains from a kill that some stalker wanted to devour in private. The tunnels are great places to do that because they are really narrow. I'm not big, two of me couldn't walk abreast.

Hiding was the other reason solo stalkers seemed to use the tunnels and basements. We only ran into four, all in deep torpor, and wouldn't have spotted them except for the NODs. Since I had the only suppressed weapon, I always got to do the honors. Miserable job, but better than running into them when they're trying to bite out your throat.

Still, it's hot and damp and thick down there, and on your first time through you have no way of know-ing what you're going to find when you turn the next corner. But even with noise discipline at max, you've only got the voice in your head for company, and it starts talking to itself about other things. And mine had started talking about Papillon and how anxious and on edge he was from the time we entered the launch control center.

I guess I feel a little guilty about that. I mean, the rest of our group came to know everyone else over days and weeks. So there was enough time, and few enough people, for each person's sad story to emerge naturally, bit by bit.

But it had been different with Papillon. Our original group of five had grown to fourteen and the moment we met him, it was all business: get to Mustique, salvage and repair and plan, and hit Kourou as soon as possible. It wasn't like he had been an unwilling participant; he was one of the most determined, in fact. But that didn't change the fact that we hadn't really spent much time getting to know him.

I guess the same could/should be said of Ozzie, but he's so out there, so on-stage all the time, that you kind of get to know him whether you want to or not.

But here in the dank, breathe-through-a-straw tunnels and basements of Kourou spaceport, I was realizing that for Papillon—no: Pascal Labrouse—returning here would be like me returning to my neighborhood in L.A. Every second, you might run into a corpse, or a stalker, who had been your friend, neighbor, colleague, even lover.

So after we cleared the last basement and decided to hydrate before going back aboveground, we split into two groups to cover both of the entries into the small room where we stopped. Wouldn't do to be ambushed while taking a water break. I teamed up with Papillon, and after sipping in silence for a few seconds, I said, "That must have been tough, back there at the control center."

He started. "What do you mean?"

"I mean, going into a place where you might have known people. I mean, you knew right away that there weren't enough bodies. It seemed like you'd been there before."

He stared at me. "Many times, actually. Not down in the bunker, of course, but a lot of them talked about it."

"Them?"

"Yes. The ESA big shots." He replaced the cap on his canteen. "That was part of my job. Shuttling the movers and shakers to and from the airport."

I was a little surprised. "That's only a few miles. I figured that they'd just get back and forth by car."

He nodded. "Yes, usually. But if there was political unrest, or if there was a security concern, or if the bosses at my base wanted to impress an incoming VIP, there I was at the airport, holding up a name placard."

I almost laughed. "Damn. You think of all the missions that a Legionnaire gets . . . that's just not one of the ones you imagine."

He smiled. "It certainly doesn't leave one with many thrilling war stories."

"But I guess it did allow you to see places you might not have, otherwise."

"You mean the inside of the Launch Control Center?" He shrugged. "Other than the gallery and the control room, it is like any other building: one small office after another. I had been briefed about the bunker, of course.

Its safety and, if necessary, seizure or evacuation, were part of the Legion's mandate regarding site security." He smiled. "But as I was just a pilot, I had never even seen its floor plan."

I nodded, then angled toward the real topic that needed to be addressed. "So, if we do find survivors in your headquarters bunker—"

"An exaggeration. The shelter is more like an out-sized saferoom."

"Ah. Well, if we do find survivors there, do you think it likely that you'll know some of them?"

He shrugged. "If they are Legionnaires, of course. If they are the Kourou ESA staff, very probably." He looked at me out of the corner of his eye. "But that is not really what you want to know, is it?"

I shook my head. "No. Well, not all of it."

He nodded at me. "You want to know how tractable they will be, particularly in response to what is mostly a group of teenagers."

I nodded back. "Something like that. Frankly, we don't have time for debates. They've gotta toe the line, or we're going to have trouble. And if we have trouble, they'll get left behind."

Papillon frowned. "That is very foresightful. I wish I could assure you that they will be as cooperative as you need. On the other hand, the saferoom does not have supplies for months; it is, at most, equipped to provide for a few weeks. And for a dozen people at most. If there are survivors, either civilians or Legionnaires, my greatest fear is whether they will still be ambulatory. If they organized soon enough, they might have been able to empty the various commissaries and vending machines in the complex. Still, they will be very weak. Evacuating them could prove very difficult. And so, very dangerous." He stowed his canteen. "But rest assured of this, Alvaro: if there is a difference of opinion, or a test of wills, I shall back you."

"Thanks," I said.

"You are welcome, but understand: my resolve is not because I am willing to choose you over my old comrades. It is because we are in the middle of a mission. As you say, we do not have time for debates. We must follow the plan as well as we may. Anything else invites failure and disaster. And I am not willing to allow survivors, even old friends, to jeopardize our success or survival."

I nodded. "Good. Then let's get going."

January 17 (Alvaro's recorder; transcript four)

Papillon looked at me patiently. "Even if they are there, they will not answer."

Steve, who had been slowly tuning through the frequencies, looked from him to me. I signalled for him to stop. "Why not?"

Papillon looked across the wide road at the squat HQ complex of the Third Foreign Legion. "Because they cannot have any power or batteries left. If any are still alive, they are trapped. Otherwise, they would not leave the complex unsecured."

Two of the four smaller garage doors, those on the side of the building facing us, were open: one fully, one partially. Bone-stripped remains of infected littered the approaches. One lay athwart the threshold of the fully open door. A few equally desiccated corpses with shreds of clothing were in a rough hemicircle around it.

Steve stowed the radio. "It doesn't look good."

"No," Papillon agreed, "it does not. Of course, even if survivors in the saferoom still had a working radio, they wouldn't know we are out here. And they probably stopped hearing any signals long ago."

Frankly, I had already concluded that both batteries

and any survivors that might use them were long gone. Within a minute of emerging back into the blinding sunlight, I'd called for an area survey and tasked Steve to do a quick radio check with Willow (her team had unloaded Wall-E without incident), and then scan for any activity on the radio. He'd finished his second profitless sweep of the dial just as Ozzie and Valda finished assessing more distant structures.

I checked the mag in my Honeybadger: full. "South report."

Valda was still peering through his binoculars. "Two stalkers. Approximately sixty yards down the road. They keep wandering near the end of the resurfacing building."

I nodded. We had come back up in the administration wing of a large, interconnected clump of structures that housed, prepared, and managed the readiness of rocket fuselages. The actual assembly took place in a cavernous, rail-served warehouse to the south. Before planning for this operation, I hadn't known how many separate steps, technologies, and substances go into preparing a spacecraft for launch. No wonder the term "rocket scientist" became synonymous with "big brain."

But now our only concern was how many stalkers were around who might see us if we sprinted across the sixty yards of extra-wide roadway—with broad sidings, and wide grassy margins—that separated us from the HQ. Or how many more would be likely to hear us if we got into a firefight on the way across.

I turned to Ozzie. "North?"

"Just one," he mumbled, squinting into the binoculars. "A way the hell out there. Three hundred yards or thereabout. Near that light blue prefab whatever-it-is. He's slow. Prolly just out of torpor."

I started considering the options. A second passed. Then another. That's when I learned what is really meant by a "deafening silence." But I was probably the only one who "heard" it because I'm the one who was causing it.

I can usually make decisions pretty quickly when I have to, but this one required some extra thought. I had to remind myself—again—that the old, conventional tactics for this situation were not just useless; they'd get us killed.

See, this was the moment when, if you were fighting humans, standard tactics would be to form into two elements. The first, or movement, element would run across the road while the support element provided a base of fire to cover them. But that only works when you're fighting an enemy that uses and fears guns.

Stalkers, on the other hand, just attack everything in sight. So if they hit us while we were using conventional tactics, they'd catch us with our force and firepower split in two. And with neither half in a defensible position. That would violate the two principles that had kept us alive: concentrate maximum firepower for maximum effect, and never face the infected in the open. Because if you do, and if there are enough of them, you *will* be swarmed and die.

Before another second of deafening silence passed, I gave orders: "I'm leading us across." I raised the Honeybadger. "I'll try to keep it quiet. Everyone else switches back to CQC weapons until the interior is clear. Except you, Valda. You stick with your FAL. Once we're inside, you turn and cover our six."

Valda's eyes roved from one vanishing point-end of the road to the next before he nodded. It was a lot to cover. "I shall make every shot count."

I nodded back and fixed my eyes on the fully open garage door. I don't know how other people lead charges. In the army, I'll bet they teach you how to time them and mentally prepare yourself. But I'm just a kid who learned on the job, fighting stalkers. So I always do what I did the first time I went off the high-diving board: once you decide you gotta, you just jump. Right away.

"Now!" Starting from a crouch, wearing a fireman's coat in tropical heat, I ran as hard as I could. There were lots of nasty sensations—forehead burning, body soaked in sweat, throat dry as paper—but when it's your life at stake, you're not really paying attention to what you feel. You're aware of it, you remember it, but you don't really have time to pay attention to it. Because it's just a distraction that could get you killed.

I slipped around the left side of the garage door and kept low. Thanks to Papillon's floor plan, I knew to cross-step farther left into a corner. The wall that met my shoulder was the one separating the vehicle bays from the HQ.

As the other guys came in, I kept the Honeybadger's muzzle aimed out into the garage. I was laser-focused on the edges of the shadows. So, other than a recon car perched over a mechanic's pit to the left of the half-open garage door, all I could make out were dark objects, every one of which might be hiding stalkers. I wasn't aware of anything else until Ozzie and Steve shouted, "Clear!" and Papillon trailed to a stop in the middle of the wide concrete floor. "*Merde*," he breathed.

He was staring across to the far side of the garage, the spot where we expected to see awning. Some kind of prefab expanded out beyond an open garage door, creating a boxy alcove. And with light streaming in through the gaps in the prefab, the shrouded, dragon-shaped relic at its center could only be one thing: the helicopter we'd hoped to find here.

And, just like a lot of other legendary holy artifacts, it was surrounded by the bodies of martyrs and monsters. Papillon walked into their midst, his movements short, abrupt, tightly controlled as he studied one face after the next.

Like the bodies we'd found in the Launch Control Center's bunker, these were more recently dead than the ones we'd encountered elsewhere. Eight still wore the shredded remains of Foreign legion field uniforms. There were six civilians, too: almost certainly the experts who had come here through the same tunnels we had. Their laptops, notebooks, cellphones, even two headsets, marked them as the team that had hoped to upload Ephemeral Reflex. Killed within a few steps of the helicopter.

"Pascal," I said. This was not the moment for nicknames.

He turned, eyes wide, haunted.

"Check the HQ. I know you said it looked secure from the air, but let's be sure."

He glanced back at the bodies, swallowed, blinked, and strode quickly toward the door that connected the garage and the Legion command center.

I stepped closer to his dead comrades and colleagues. Their last stand—an outward-curving arc—was a tragic testimony to the wisdom of the same tactical axiom we'd applied just moments earlier: never get caught in the open. There were about fifty infected corpses around and among them; the center was an undifferentiated heap. I saw five FAMAS assault rifles, but there could have been more under the core of the melee death-scrum. There was no way to tell if they had all been shot dry—the FAMAS's bolt runs home after the last round—but most of the Legionnaires and a few of the civilians had gone down using handguns. The probable reasons were no time to reload, point-blank targets, or both.

The helicopter itself looked untouched. The shroud had been smeared by a few arterial sprays, but the stalkers hadn't shown any interest in it. The same could not be said about the infected who had tried to get through the prefab panels around the Puma. The scratch marks where they'd tried to slip between them were as deep and ragged as if they'd been at them with chain saws.

The alcove itself was pure genius. Whoever built it realized the Legionnaires could hold off the stalkers long enough to roll the bird outside and get airborne. So they'd used rocket test-blast baffling as the prefab sections, which they kept upright using pulley-mounted wires. Release the pulleys' locks and the whole structure would fall outward in a radial pattern. Probably achievable in thirty seconds, start to finish. Less, maybe.

I just about jumped out of my skin when a FAL barked twice, the echoes ringing up against the high roof. "Alvaro!"

I was already charging back to the open garage door as I shouted, "Valda, report."

"The two I saw at the south end of the assembly complex: they must have seen movement."

"Are they—?"

"Dead. They must have smelled us; they started rushing the garage."

"See any more?"

"No, not yet—Wait! Three, no four, more. Coming from the south."

As Papillon returned, Steve muttered, "And a bunch coming from the north. Can't get a count." He was surveying that end of the road from under the rim of the half-open garage door.

I glanced at Papillon. "Report."

He shrugged. "No sign of a mass break-in on the ground floor. Didn't get to the second floor, but there's no way stalkers could have gotten up there."

"So we can get out the front door?"

"What? Uh, yes, there's nothing blocki—"

I ran to the open garage door, looked for a handle, a crank. "How do we get these things down?" Steve had already started checking the other door. Ozzie joined Valda, unslung his own FAL.

Papillon shook his head. "Power doors."

"There's got to be a release."

He pointed halfway to the ceiling; the door's chains passed through a box. "Uncoupling lever on the side. It's red."

But there wasn't a way up and not a ladder in sight. Could have been one tucked away in a dozen places; it was a big garage. But in ten seconds the stalkers would be through the door.

Barricading ourselves in the HQ? The door from the garage didn't look sturdy and there was no way to be sure the main entrance could be made stalker-proof. Besides, losing control of the garage meant losing control of the helicopter.

I jumped into the recon car that was parked just beyond the half-open garage door. As Valda's and Ozzie's FALs started cracking, I scanned the layout and controls.

"Alvaro," Steve yelled, "we can't run—"

"Not running. Get over here and help me push." I hit the clutch, put the vehicle in neutral, and released the hand brake.

Steve jumped over, got the other door open and leaned into it. I braced myself against the door frame, kept one hand close to the steering wheel, and counted down: "Three, two one: push!"

We weren't big guys, but once it started to roll, it was quick work. Flush with the wall, the patrol car rolled past the half-open door right toward the fully open one. The only problem was me versus the steering wheel. Little guy, heavy vehicle, no power: not your best combination.

Papillon called out to Valda and Ozzie, who stepped back from the garage door just two seconds before the car rolled into place across the opening. I wanted to let the front bumper run a foot past the far edge of door, but the steering wheel fought me again; the front left quarter panel crunched into the wall just before I hauled back on the hand brake.

As we were pushing it, I'd spotted a tire rack. I had intended to tell Steve to shove some of them under the car, but judging from the off-road monster tire he was already pushing into place under the partially open door, he had the same idea and had found his own supply.

Which was really lucky, because there's no way he would have heard me. Ozzie and Valda were braced on top of the hood and rear of the recon car, their slow, sustained semiautomatic fire a pretty much constant roar. A few seconds of intermittent quiet—as first one and then the other swapped in fresh mags—gave me the opportunity to yell: "Steve; cover the gaps with your shotgun. Papillon: help him." They weren't the clearest orders, but they were the only ones we had time for, and the only gaps that mattered were pretty obvious: the ones between the tires Steve had jammed under the partially open garage door and recon car.

I closed the driver's door, slid across and out the passenger side, turned and stood, my feet on the rim of the step-up into the cab. The first stalkers were within twenty yards. I brought up the Honeybadger, rested my elbows on the vehicle's roof, looked in the holographic sight, found the closest, and squeezed the trigger.

It had taken half a year, but I had become a halfway decent shot. And thanks to Ozzie, I had also found a weapon which felt like it had been made for me. And that extra confidence may have increased my accuracy a bit more.

I don't know how many I hit. I don't know how many got back up and had to be tapped again. I don't even know if I was the guy who put in that second tap. All I know is that any that came closer than thirty yards, I hit. Sometimes it took a third shot. Sometimes I got them right away (you have to *love* holographic sights!), but the important thing was that none of them got close enough to leap over the car at us.

I'd heard Steve's shotgun and Papillon's FAMAS roaring and popping to the left every once in a while and when we finally got a break—no stalkers left, and no stumblers within eighty yards—I shouted, "How's it going over there?"

"Fine," Steve replied in a very loud voice. Pure Steve.

Papillon gave a more useful sitrep. "Only about half a dozen tried to get under the door. Killed them there. That has plugged most of the holes."

"Good. Get over here, binox out. Hop up on the roof. Okay, now lean out. Don't worry; I've got your belt. What do you see?"

"To the south, there's just the one stumbler. He's about fifty yards awa—"

Valda's FAL spoke. Then did so again.

Papillon resumed. "There are now no infected in sight." He turned to look back at me. "Although for all we know, a new wave of them could be about to boil up out of the tunnels we used."

I nodded. "Yeah. You—and Steve, you too—find a ladder or big boxes or something and get up there and pull the garage chains' release levers. We've got to get these doors closed and see if we can use that chopper before any more show up. I'll watch your door while you're working that problem. Valda, Ozzie: you keep doing what you're doing."

"And if more stalkers attack before we are finished?" Papillon asked.

"Then you'll drop what you're doing and come help. But right now, you're wasting time just by asking that question. *Get those doors closed!*"

It took a few minutes to find a ladder. It took a few more to clear the stalker bodies out of the gap under the half-open door and then pull the tires back inside. And then, after a few more minutes, the rusty levers released (I don't think those doors had *ever* been shifted over to manual operation). Gears squeaked as the chains took the full weight of the doors. Just before we started cranking them down, another stumbler wandered into view, far to the north. Valda settled in to watch him, just over his FAL's sights. He was still two hundred yards away when, cranking as hard as we could, we got the second garage door down.

We were all sweating, but until we heard those doors clank into contact with the concrete, I was not aware of how thirsty I was, how rank I smelled, or how much I had to take a piss. And I was not the only one having those sudden realizations.

We took turns, and when I came back from mine, I asked Valda and Ozzie, "About how many did we take down out there?"

"'Bout sixty," Ozzie said with a waggle of his hand that meant "more or less."

"Actually," said Valda, a hint of apology in his tone, "sixty-three." Knowing Valda, he wouldn't have said it if he wasn't sure.

Ozzie glanced at me with a smile and shrugged. Then he was loping after Papillon, who was about to slip under the shroud and assess the helicopter. "Hey," I called after the Legionnaire.

He turned, still looking a little haunted. "Yes?"

"What about the saferoom?"

He stiffened. "We should check that last."

"What? Why? If there are survivors, they could tell us the last time that the chopper was—"

"Alvaro." His eyes were grave, dark.

"Yeah?"

"There's no sign that anyone went back inside after

the battle around the helicopter. But if they did"—he inhaled deeply—"and if some of the survivors there were still turning, they might have used the saferoom as a quarantine chamber. And since we do not know how long the infected can stay in torpor..."

I nodded. "You don't want to open the door and have to kill a friend. Sure. Some of us can—"

He shook his head. "No. It is my job, *particularly* if it is a friend. I owe them no less. But first things first; we must assess the condition of the helicopter and hopefully, ready it for flight. Then, before we leave, I will...will go to the saferoom."

Which made perfect sense. And which gave me enough time to make this recording.

This is kind of strange. After almost fifty minutes ducking in and out of the shroud with Ozzie, moving around containers and cables, and using some of the other vehicles in the garage to help the process, Papillon comes out alone and reports that the chopper is ready. I thought I'd misunderstood what he'd said, at first. He used a lot of fancy terms that I can't remember hearing before, but it boils down to this: whoever was in charge at the Legion complex understood that they had to store this chopper so that it remained in near-complete readiness. But they had also realized that it might have to be in storage for a long time. So they disconnected a number of systems and drained or lowered the levels of fuel and some other fluids. That's what he and Ozzie had been doing: checking, reattaching, refilling, recharging.

I thanked him, asked when we'd be leaving.

"Soon," he says. "I shall go check the saferoom, now."

I unslung my Honeybadger.

He shook his head. "No. I will do this alone."

"Look," I said, "no offense, but that bird is our only ticket out of here, and you are the only guy who can fly it."

"Yes, but I found a roster of survivors in the cockpit. Some of my friends on that list are not here." He gestured toward the corpses. "So this . . . this is a personal matter." He stood straighter. "I have not once questioned your orders, Alvaro. I have worked and fought as hard and as well as I know how. Hopefully, that loyalty and performance has earned this much trust, *non*?"

I'd like to say I'm a super-empathetic guy who was moved by his speech, but I'm not. The only reason I didn't object was because if I refused, he could cross his arms and refuse to fly us anywhere. So, my choice was between being gracious (and maybe increase his loyalty) or being pigheaded and make a potential enemy *and* get everyone else killed. And we both knew who would win in that pissing contest.

So I nodded him inside.

Just after, Ozzie comes out of the chopper. I ask him about it. He says it's a sweet machine. "An Aéro-spatiale SA 330 Puma. Damn good condition, all things considered. Where's Papillon?"

I jerked a thumb at the door into the HQ.

Ozzie frowned, shook his head once, then started stalking around the base of the Puma.

"You looking for something?"

"Not really. But—well, Papillon's been acting mighty weird."

I nodded. "It's tough for him, here. These guys were his buddies, comrades in arms."

He glanced at me narrowly. "Yeah, but, I dunno: it's not like he's upset in general. It's more like he's hoping but also fearing he's going to find something specific."

I shrugged. "Like what?"

Ozzie's frowned deepened. "Wish I knew." He continued to pick his way through the pile of bodies clustered just fifteen feet beyond the draped tail rotor. Then he stopped, as if startled.

"What is it?"

He shook his head. "Nothing. I'm just getting ticked at how much time we're spending here. Particularly since our comms to Will started going to shit. Old, much-recharged batteries and this roof aren't helping us. I'll be right back up with our boy."

He stalked away on the same path that Papillon had followed to the HQ.

So now I'm wondering: what *is* eating Papillon? Could there be something here that—?

Wait: Steve's got news . . .

So Steve finally got through to Willow, but only for twenty seconds. Seems like the gate into Diane's perimeter was down, and no sooner did they send out Wall-E than some stalkers came out of the surrounding forest in threes and fours. More active, more aggressive. They took them down—Chloe continues as our star sniper—but it took a lot of time. Sounds to me like Willow is being too cautious, but since I'm not there, it's not my call. Besides, about three seconds after learning that much, the connection was devoured by static. Again.

But before I forget, I've got to go back to where

Ozzie looked at the corpses and seemed to flinch. As if he'd seen something that surprised, or worried, him.

It was right about here, at the center of all the bodies. Not a place where I want to spend a lot of time. Was he looking at this stalker? Or was it this guy that died with his pistol's slide back?

Yes, probably him, because this guy's wearing a pilot's pin. So Papillon would certainly have known him pretty well, might have mentioned him to Ozzie, even. There's just enough of his flight suit left that you can still make out the name tag:

"P. Labrouse—"

January 17 (Willow's recorder; transcript two)

Alvaro was right. If I did not have this recorder with me I would not remember a fraction of all the decisions and crises we have faced, just in the process of making our way from the Launch Control Center to here, the ground control complex of the Diane site.

Ironically, I got so distracted that I forgot to turn it off for almost half an hour. But what it recorded has given me all I need to remember, reconstruct, and recount what has happened.

We reached the perimeter of the Diane complex without incident. But the front gate was down, rammed by some vehicle, apparently. Chloe's scan through her rifle's scope revealed multiple gaps in the perimeter fence.

Fortunately, entering the Diane complex was one of the contingency plans we had developed in some detail. And now we had Wall-E, which was a great advantage. However, there were rival opinions about how best to use that advantage. Most wanted to stick with the plan we had formulated: conduct general reconnaissance of the site's control building. A few wanted to scout the tree line. I understood the concerns of the people advocating for the latter; the forests could conceal an army. But building entries were especially risky and we had to make sure that there was minimal collateral damage; it would be particularly ironic if a stray bullet destroyed the one control system upon which our mission now depended. So, assuming Wall-E survived that top-priority assignment, I was agreeable to dispatching him immediately to conduct the other.

However, less than a minute after Rod and I exited the vehicle to ready the robot, the needs for tree line reconnaissance became moot. Stalkers—well-fleshed, energetic, ferocious—started emerging from an isolated stretch of woods that ran from the east to the south. Chloe's rifle started cracking, but not as sharply as usual: possibly a damping effect of the soaring humidity.

We finished readying the robot and scrambled back into the Bandvagn. Rod remote-steered Wall-E along the two-hundred-yard stretch of ruler-straight road to the control building. Just beyond the gate were a few single-story utility buildings, looking much worse for wear. After Chloe's fifth shot, a few stumblers came out of them, rail-thin and blinking. Johnnie and Tai shot them before they started to charge.

Wall-E performed a slow orbit of the control building, which was actually three buildings kludged together into a rough L shape. Two were the site controls and the much smaller third one was a large garage. Probably for a fire truck or vehicles of similar dimensions. The windows were closely boarded and there were only a few shriveled, naked corpses scattered around the walls. If there were any stalkers inside, there was no sign of them.

We brought the Bandvagn so close alongside the main entrance that, if any stalkers rushed us from outside, they'd have a difficult time slipping between the flank of the vehicle and the wall of the building. Meanwhile, Rod sent Wall-E back out the gate and set him following the perimeter track, sensors turned outward to scan the edge of the trees that hemmed us in.

The rest of us spent a few moments getting sips of water from hot canteens, wiping sweat off our faces, and checking our gear one more time.

A pair of stalkers broke from the tree line, chasing after Wall-E. Tainara, who was temporarily spotting for Chloe, raised her voice, "Hey, eleven o'clo—"

"Got it," Chloe interrupted. Her gun barked. She worked the bolt, fired again. She squinted in the scope, cursed, took the last stalker with a third shot. Shortly after, truly active stalkers started coming out of the forest in twos and threes, but fewer from the east.

"Wonder why that is?" Jorge muttered.

Through the hatch, Chloe called down: "Probably less to feed on there. It's not connected to the main jungle."

Johnnie peered around, watching as the stalkers emerged in pairs, sometimes singly, continued watching as they fell before Chloe's steady fire. "Not as though we'd be a good meal for even ten percent of them."

Tai shrugged. "Yah, but they don' care 'bout that."

Prospero nodded. "Bloody stimulus and response, it is."

"Yes, and about as discriminating as amoebas," I added. "Rod, how's Wall-E doing?"

"Just fi—oh, shit!"

"What?"

"Battery level just tanked. At least, that's what the controls say, but given how long it was in that case—"

"Does it have enough power to get back to us?"

"Power isn't the worst problem; it's speed. Fading along with the charge."

Even as we watched, three stalkers broke from the tree line, less than two hundred yards from Wall-E. Moments later, another pair did the same.

"Coordinated attacks?" I wondered aloud just before Chloe's rifle barked and one of the stalkers staggered.

"I don't think so," she answered as she worked the bolt. "To me, looks like they are different groups brought here by all the noise." She fired again. Another infected fell face-first, did not rise.

Even though she killed another, the remaining two caught up with Wall-E. They dove, one grabbing his remaining arm. Dust arose. More of the stalkers emerging from that part of the tree line swerved in that direction. The screen on the controller went blank; Rod put it aside with a sigh.

I stood. "Well, it was a stroke of good fortune to have had Wall-E at all. Time for us to complete this mission. Chloe, keep them off our back."

"Yeah," she muttered, "about that." She paused to fire. "Look, I'm as happy as the next gurrll to play whack-a-mole for keeps, but if the pace at which they come out keeps increasing, they'll get in behind us."

Johnnie glanced at the wall against which we were parked. "How?"

Chloe fired, smiled down. "Not right behind us. I mean the building we're up against creates a blind spot. I can rise up a little higher, but once the ones

from the southwest get so close that they're under
the line of the roof, I can't hit them. Which means
a lot of them will make it to these buildings. They'll
either come at us around corners"—she gestured both
in front of and behind our side-parked vehicle—"or
they might find a way into the complex itself. Which
you definitely don't want."

I agreed. "Then it sounds like you need to reposition yourself."

She bit her lower lip. "We need to move the whole
vehicle if I'm going to get the ones coming up out of
the southwest. Gotta get far enough from the building
so it isn't in the way."

"Where?" I asked sharply. I was very conscious of
the seconds slipping away.

"Northwest corner of the building." She pointed
behind the Bandvagn. "About ten yards beyond the
west wall of the garage. I can see all the way down
the western tree line from there, and all the way
along the north."

"And the east and south?"

"South is open ground for almost a mile. Not a lot
of activity, there. This bunch seems to like staying in
the shadows."

"More careful?" Jorge guessed.

I shook my head. "No, they are behaving more like
hunters than killers." I waved at the trees. "In the
jungle, if they can't creep up on prey, they will not
eat. Even predators that are much faster and better
climbers than they are—jaguars, for instance—have
to use stealth to get close enough to strike. They are
simply adapting to their environment. To the extent
they can."

Chloe fired again and called down. "Yup; what she said. And that's why there aren't a lot coming out of the east anymore. That patch of trees won't feed many of them. Odds are that most of the stalkers in there have already come out."

I looked up through the hatch. "I agree with your assessment, Chloe. But I do not like you being so far from the building."

She smiled. "Hell, neither do I, but they can't get inside the track, and they can't leap up far enough to get me. Besides, we've got the M60."

"Which we do *not* want to use."

She looked away, tracking a new target. "Yeah, I know: the noise. But if it's die or make more noise, I vote for the noise."

"So do I." I nodded at her. "Do what you must."

She nodded back with a small smile. "I'm right on it, Cucumber."

"'Cucumber'? W-why that?"

Her smile became a wide grin. "Because: you are . . . Just. That. Cool."

I did what no leader ever should: I giggled.

Jorge drove the Bandvagn to the new position after we checked our gear and "deployed" from the vehicle, as Prospero put it. As he is my XO, he lined us up outside the control building in entry order. We had hoped to get a glimpse inside, but the windows were tightly boarded-up and the door was locked.

Prospero moved us along quickly, and he was right to: the less time we spent outside the building, the better. He positioned Tai to the side of the door, with Johnnie and Ning ready to enter. Ning would go in first and stay low. Johnnie would be second, tucking close against the opening door. They secured their face shields, checked to make sure that each others' armor—well, fire coats—were properly seated, and turned toward the door, faces tilted slightly downward. Rod stepped in between them, the lighter of our handheld rams at the ready. Tai snapped her shotgun off safety, aligned its muzzle with the top hinge, and nodded.

It is always hard to watch when my Johnnie is in a fight, but it is hardest when he is part of what Alvaro and others call the breaching team. I shouldn't worry— Johnnie is actually at his best when he has to react quickly—but because he can be so, well, unfocused at other times, I become nervous. Besides, since we rejoined Alvaro, I have learned—firsthand—the utter unpredictability of what can be in each new room, behind every unopened door.

My anxiety undermined my readiness. I was startled when Prospero shouted, "Go!" Tai discharged the shotgun, then pumped the action, snapped it down, paused an instant to be sure it was in alignment with the lower hinge, and fired again.

Rod brought the breaching tool back slightly, then stepped sharply toward the sagging door, adding his strength to the ram's forward swing. The door tumbled away into the darkness; Ning and Johnnie were already darting into the shadows as he stepped back.

I heard rapid movement inside the control center, then a sputter of automatic gunfire. Another, longer stream. Then silence.

A long moment passed, during which I noticed that the pace of the reports from Chloe's rifle had increased.

And then Johnnie came out of the door, smiling the way he always does. I was elated, grateful—and then, suddenly, I was angry, bitter. I hated this world. All over again. It's a feeling that catches me by surprise, usually when we breach a new door. Because when we do, the rest of us hold our breaths and clench our fists so hard that our nails bite into our palms. And in that moment, I hate hate hate whatever person or persons killed Earth's billions and condemned the thousands who remain to this existence. I do not hate much—it is not healthy—but I do hate the people who did *this*.

But at that moment, all I could do was nod and enter the control station, with Tai and Prospero to either side, guns out and eyes narrow.

The interior of the control building was mostly one room, dominated by cubicles and two map tables. There was also a row of linked workstations: telemetry monitoring, which Prospero expected to find. Flanking the central work area on the south and the west were a few small offices, two locked restrooms, and—in a slight alcove between them—a single door with a red thread and green ribbon tied around its handle.

Prospero had already seen it. He moved in that direction, but Ning put up a pausing hand, then extended it toward him, palm held ready.

As Prospero gave her the key from the bunker's lockbox, she waved Tai closer with the other hand. When Prospero moved to follow them toward the door, Ning shook her head, then approached it slowly. Tai, following, glanced at me over her shoulder. "You stay." She smiled and half-rolled her eyes. "Aft' all, you gotta be alive to save the worl'."

I am a good ship captain and team leader, but when guns come out, my focus tends to narrow down, not widen out. So while this was happening, and the other team members were checking the remainder of the control room, I was only dimly aware of their actions. Because I was too focused on the door with the ribbon affixed to its handle. Because everything we had planned and practiced and travelled and fought for would be determined by what we found behind it.

Ning listened, pulled out one of her several knives, then slipped the key into the lock, tested if it would turn. It did. On cue, Rod readied a high-intensity flashlight and Tai moved to stand beside Ning. Who turned the key until it made a small *snick*.

Rod turned on the light, aimed it at the door; Tai unsheathed her machete and met Ning's eyes. Ning nodded, and together, they mimed counting *one, two, three*—

Tai kicked the door open; Ning was inside before it had swung all the way against the wall. The beam of light sliced into the darkness.

In what had once been either a large janitor's closet or a very small maintenance room, were a gas-powered generator, a set of power cables running into the wall and one into the ceiling, a desk, a computer and a backup, and two screens. It looked like the seams of the room, walls and floor alike, had been sprayed with some kind of insulating foam.

Tai and Ning looked around and behind and even under everything in the room, and only then did they announce what we already knew:

"Clear."

∽ ⊖ ∾

The electronics even had dust covers. Once they were off and the generator kicked to life (on Johnnie's third pull of its cord), Prospero and Rod studied the data connections and found several thin, hastily printed manuals (in four languages, no less).

Somewhere, water gurgled. The lights in the main control room flickered, and about half stayed lit. About two seconds later, what sounded like a second generator clunked and thumped to life on the other side of the cinder-block wall.

Rod nodded. "Must be in the garage. Maybe to power heavy gear, charge vehicle batteries."

Prospero held up a dusty sheet that had been paper-clipped to the front of one of the equally dusty manuals. "Inventory," he announced. "And instructions. But before we start—"

I picked up on his cue. "Assume defense perimeter for the interior," I called out. "As we drilled it." As Rod, Prospero and I emerged from the maintenance room, we discovered the others already at their assigned posts. They were distributed around the room so we could respond to a surprise from any direction and so that several people could bring their weapons to bear on any point of attack. I also became aware of the pace of Chloe's fire; it was almost constant.

"Structure check?" I asked.

"The boards are solid," Johnnie answered with a smile. "All doors are sealed. The door to the garage is reinforced; deadbolted and barred. This part of the building is all cinder block. No roof access. Well, none that I can find."

I nodded. "Spoor?"

"Almost none," Tai answered. "Look like some

stalkers may have got in, or people turned in here. But they were controlled quick."

"Right, then. We're facing out, but preparing to react in any direction. Prospero, as you've asked, we've stationed Rod closest to the maintenance room, so that you can bring him in as—"

My personal comm toned: Chloe. "Go," I said.

"Cukes, I'm losing at whack-a-mole. And they are not stopping to eat their dead."

"Expected." The jungle-stalkers were better fed. "Recommendations?"

"You know what I'm going to tell you, Cucumber. We either rock and roll with the M60 or we leave the party."

"Question."

"Make it quick."

"Are you confident using the machine gun?" Ozzie had never had much opportunity to teach her, and if Prospero's military training had prepared him to use the weapon, he'd never said so. Besides, he had to remain with us to upload Ephemeral Reflex.

Chloe's answer was gruff, annoyed. "I can use it better than anyone else, I guess."

A new voice joined the comm channel: Jorge's. "I can use the M60."

"You can?" Chloe and I chorused.

"Sure. I was in the army. Never a soldier, though. Mechanic. Fixed guns, too."

"Why didn't you ever mention that?"

I could almost hear his shrug. "You never ask. And before we come north, we never need guns."

I didn't know whether to be annoyed or relieved. I was also distracted by a sound from the garage: not the

kind a portable generator would make. I caught Johnnie's eye, waved him toward the door into the garage.

Chloe's tone was now exasperated: "Well, Jorge,
we really need you and the M60." She paused, then
pressed me: "And Willow, we need them right *now*."

"Yes. Jorge, use the M60." More noise in the garage.
"Willow out." I looked around the room. Rod and
Johnnie were already moving toward the door to the
garage. Ning was coming away from the wall directly
across from the restrooms. "Those sounds—" I started.

"We're on it," Rod muttered.

But Ning was no longer just walking toward me. In
a single second she went from striding to sprinting.
At me. And her expression was that of an executioner.

I gasped—thought *No! It can't be! Not her!*—at the
same moment that I heard shrieking and a metallic
crack, right behind me.

Ning's eyes flicked, looking past my face. They
widened—and she leaped forward with a move that
was half ballet and half kung fu.

I'm not sure what happened. I think she grabbed
and then yanked me forward—and so, past her—while
using me as a launch platform to go in the direction
of the noise.

I fell, rolled—and chaos erupted all around me.
Gunfire so close that it should have been deafening.
Shouting mixed with the wild, ecstatic shrieking of
frenzied stalkers. They were pouring out through the
right-hand restroom door—now shattered—and flood-
ing into the main control room.

But Ning stood before them, her submachine gun
in one hand, a knife suddenly out in the other. Two
were already dead, but she was also bleeding from one

arm. A death sentence for the rest of us, but only a stitch-worthy wound for her.

I remember getting up, Prospero yelling something about flanking fire, Tai rushing past me toward Ning. Who emptied her submachine gun at the stalkers: several fell. She clubbed the next one with the empty weapon, slashed another as she drew her pistol and started firing.

But despite the growing pile of infected at her feet, they came out of the bathroom in such a rush that, even as the ones closest to her were dying, they fell into her.

And the live ones behind bore her down.

Tai let her shotgun hang on its sling as she tore her flensing tool from its makeshift sheath and started hacking at the ones atop Ning. Rod, Prospero, and Johnnie fanned out, were firing rapidly into the restroom doorway; it was stemming the tide. I tried helping, but Tai was in my way. Then she slipped, and one of the half-dead stalkers hopped in her direction.

I fired at it five times. I think I hit it twice.

The important thing was that it fell over and did not move.

But neither did Ning. A stalker had its fangs locked on her neck even though its femoral artery was severed and gushing.

I jumped forward. I was not thinking when I slid my rifle's sling off my shoulder. I swung the gun up so that it was butt-first when I brought it down on the stalker's head. I think the first blow killed, or at least stunned, it; I hit the occiput squarely and there was a sudden spray of blood. But I did not stop hitting it.

Not until Johnnie caught my arm and said, "Hey," softly. In that way he has.

I have not asked, but I think I must have been

crushing the head of that stalker for at least five seconds.

I looked down at Ning and cried. I made no sound, but I could not stop.

I had been too late. Her jugular was not merely severed, but torn from the surrounding tissue. Her eyes were already blank, dulling in death. I had seen that once before at a car crash. Eyes relax almost immediately upon expiration, and they seem to become less reflective. I was trying to think about that when I was crying, to focus on something else, to help me stop, but it did not do any good. Nothing did.

Not until Prospero walked up to me and, with great pain in his own eyes, asked, "Orders...ma'am?"

Something about his tone, his calling me "ma'am," seemed to shut off the tears. My grief became anger. Ugly, cold anger. And I used it. "How could all those stalkers fit in the bathroom?"

"They didn't," Rod replied. "They came through the garage. Water pipes go through the walls to sinks, in both directions. They must've pulled them out, tore out the wall around where the sinks used to be."

"And are they all dead?"

"We think so, but—"

"Then why are you all standing here? Guard the hole!"

Johnnie's voice was soothing. "Tai's there. But Prospero and Rod need to talk to you, Willow. They've got to find out what to do next."

I started. "To do next? Send the damn code!"

Prospero's eyes had never left mine. "But that means pulling at least one of us off the security detachment."

"Yes. You. Go."

"Are you sure you—?"

"I will be fine." I raised my gun. "And I will be more focused, now." I looked at the stock of the M4; it was cracked in several places and coated in gore. "But with a different weapon, I think."

Prospero nodded and ran for the maintenance room. Johnnie patted my arm, went toward the shattered bathroom, half-turned. "Oh, and Tai's got something to tell you."

"Send her back to me. Rod, support Johnnie."

Tai slipped out around Rod as he ran over the dead stalkers and into the restroom. She came straight up to me. "You come and look." She said it as she passed me and went to a set of printed forms posted on a stretch of wall between the boarded windows. She pointed at a row of them.

I frowned. "They're—they're just launch schedules."

Tai smiled. "Maybe not *just* launch schedules."

"Tai, we have to—"

"You have to look. Right now. Ning and I swept this room together, called it clear. We still walking side by side when she sees these. She walks another step, then stop, goes back, leans closer, reads careful." Tai mimicked a sudden, surprised start. "Then she jerk back, like a pin stuck in her. And she say to me, 'Read this.'"

Tainara shrugged. "I don' read English so good yet, but I know numbers. So I knew why she point out this paper." She frowned. "An' since some you didn' trust her, I tell you special: she never touch the schedules."

I felt a flash of shame, of anger at myself, for ever having doubted Ning and thinking that she might have been coming to kill me. Still, the clock was ticking . . . "Can't the schedules wait?"

Tai put her hand on my arm: gentle, but firm. "No,

too important." She led me to the first schedule in the sequence. "Look you'self."

It was ESA Kourou's integrated 2012 launch schedule. The lines were crossed out through the middle of May. "I'm sorry, but—"

Tai put her finger on the last of the crossed-out entries. "Look dis one real, real close."

I did. It read:

Mission	Launch Time/Date	Vehicle	Facility	Payload ID	Payload M/T
VA-206	15 May 2012 22:13	Ariane 5 ECA 562	Kourou ELA-3	JCSAT-13 Vinasat-2	8,381 kg

I stared at it. I felt precious seconds slipping past. "I'm sorry, I don't—"

"Look da date. Now look da date *this* one."

Mission	Launch Time/Date	Vehicle	Facility	Payload ID	Payload M/T
VA-207	5 July 2012 21:36	Ariane 5 ECA 563	Kourou ELA-3	EchoStar XVII MSG-3	9,647 kg

I frowned. Something felt wrong about the two dates, yes—but I was so distracted I wasn't seeing it.

Tainara helped me. "Look. First one is da last launch, yeah? Crossed out. Makes sense: the virus isn't here yet."

I nodded. "Exactly. That was before we left San Diego for the Galapagos. Almost two weeks before we were on *Voyager*." What was Tai getting at?

She moved her finger to the next launch date. "Not crossed out, so didn't launch. Makes sense: July 5. Virus is all over. Kourou and world go to shit."

I agreed, frowning—and then I saw it. And in my mind's eye, I saw the empty launch towers over the eastern forest, blocked from view by the planks over the windows. "The ESA wasn't even preparing for the next launch when the virus hit."

Tai nodded.

"But if their last launch was on May 15, then—"

"Then why did Papillon leave Kourou—just before plague—to check machines on Île Royale if that *wasn't* the day before a launch? And so how he see a rocket fly over that islan' when next launch isn't 'til July 5?"

"So Papillon . . ."

"Is a liar. Was from deh minute we met him."

My head hurt, and it was hard to think through the long, sustained rippling blast of the M60 out on the Bandvagn. "But why?"

Tai flipped that question aside with her hand. "Don' matter why. What matters is letting our friends know what we learn here."

It was probably close to one hundred five degrees Fahrenheit in the control building, but a wave of cold ran through me and I shivered. I stuck out my hand: Tai was our "RTO." "Radio! Now!"

Her face was fierce, but her tone was wry: "'Bout time." She raised the handset into my field of vision.

It was only then that I realized she'd had it at the ready for almost a minute.

January 17 (Alvaro's recorder; transcript five)

I was still staring at the "P. Labrouse" name tape on the corpse's fatigues when all hell broke loose. *Inside* the Foreign Legion garage.

The door to the CP slammed back on its hinges. Ozzie was running toward me, shouting a warning.

Behind him, pistol shots—three—and he sprawled.

Before I could get my weapon up, Papillon strode out, Taurus M-9 up and steady, tracking across me, Steve, and Valda. There was no sign of unsurety in his eyes or posture; if we tried to raise our weapons in his direction, we'd be dead where we stood.

That one moment of silence was drowned out by eager and angry howls from beyond every wall of the building. Ozzie couldn't hold back a groan.

The man we'd known as Pascal Labrouse smiled faintly and moved into a position that gave him an optimal shot at all of us. He unslung his FAMAS, brought it down to join the pistol, then shifted the smaller weapon to aim in Ozzie's general direction. A *real* Mexican standoff. Suddenly I couldn't get images of *The Good, The Bad, and the Ugly* out of my head.

Papillon nodded at us. "Put your guns down."

"You first," I suggested.

He sighed. "If you don't disarm, I will shoot your only pilot." He wiggled the pistol meaningfully toward Ozzie. "Other than me, that is." His smile returned, faintly condescending.

Steve spat, muttered, "I can take him."

"And if you miss," I hissed, "or if he fires that pistol first, we are totally screwed."

"You see?" Papillon's comment was aimed at Steve. "Alvaro understands. Now, put down your weapons: all of you."

My radio paged. Command channel: Willow.

Papillon's pistol was poised at the back of Ozzie's head. "If you answer, I will shoot Mr. Nugent."

I nodded. "I understand. Well, all except for one thing: why the hell are you doing this? And who the hell are you, since I'm looking at the body of the real Pascal Labrouse over here."

"Papillon is no one," Ozzie muttered through a grimace. "That's why he was trying to kill me."

Valda frowned. "What do you mean, 'he's no one'?"

"Mr. Nugent means that I am no more a Legion-naire than I am Pascal Labrouse."

"Okay—but then who are you?"

Ozzie's answer was grunted through mostly clenched teeth. "Civilian chopper pilot. Judging from the pictures in the office, flight trainer for the local *gendarmerie*. Probably had a similar gig with the Third Foreign Legion. A contractor. Looks like they mostly used him for shuttling big shots back and forth from the airport. Which is why he's not better with a gun: no training."

"Not entirely true," Papillon corrected. "I had many friends in the Legion. They took me shooting. Which proved to have been a fortunate pastime, once the virus struck." The stalkers were still emitting howls of frustration, just beyond the two garage doors.

"But still—why lie to us? And why shoot Ozzie?"

Ozzie clutched his leg, grunting. "Because he came out of the saferoom and saw me looking at the pictures." Ozzie grunted. "I saw his face off to the side of photos of what I guess were missing Legionnaires. Except he wasn't in uniform and the name under the photo is Michael Gaulmin." He looked sideways at Gaulmin. "And there was a girl. In a second picture, with a rocket in the background. He had his arm around her."

Papillon nodded; his lower lip trembled. "And I will find her."

"You mean . . . alive?"

"Of course." I tried to keep the doubt off my face, but he saw it all the same. "I *know* she is alive."

Valda was nodding. "So she was from here. A scientist?"

Gaulmin shook his head. "Her job is unimportant. All that matters is that she and I were—*are*—meant for each other. Our love is perfect; it was preordained."

And now I understood why he had done what he had. Like some of the folks back on South Georgia Island's King Edward Point station, Michael Gaulmin had gone calmly and completely mad. "So all this—all the planning and pretending to be a Legionnaire—was so that we'd bring you here. To find her."

"And so you did."

Valda shook his head. "But Papill—Michael: she was not among those in the bunker, and you obviously did not find her in the headquarters' saferoom."

He shrugged. "That was always a possibility. The search continues."

"But where? Surely you must see that she is—"

"Pamela is not dead!" Gaulmin shrieked. That elicited new howls from beyond the garage door.

But there were fewer than before. Much fewer. Which worried me: stalkers don't wander away from prey just because they can't get to it.

Gaulmin had not stopped talking. "I know she is alive. I can *feel* it. I can feel *her*, even now. I knew she was alive, even before she finally reached me through the satellite phone in the control center. Then by the Internet connection to Île Royale, while it lasted. That's how she told me about the helicopter, that they were making plans to escape. Even when her messages stopped, even when it seemed that their plans must have failed, I knew—I could still *feel*—that she was alive. I *always* feel it. Even now."

"Then why didn't you tell us?"

"Because if you don't experience this kind of love, this kind of feeling, it sounds like madness."

You think? I was careful to keep my reaction off my face.

Valda was shaking his head, palm raised in an appeal to reason. "But Michael, surely you must realize—"

Gaulmin snapped the FAMAS up so it was aimed straight at Valda. Who had the good sense to shut up. But Gaulmin kept pointing the gun at him, hand shaking slightly.

"Listen," I said calmly, "you can't find Pamela all by yourself." Gaulmin turned his head toward me. "Yeah, you've been a jerk. But you haven't killed anyone—yet. Now let us tend to Ozzie's wound, and afterwards, wherever we go, you can look for her. We'll help you—"

Suddenly, the gun was pointed at me. "You are lying. You do not believe me. Because you do not know this feeling."

Yeah, because I'm not delusional. "I give you my word, Michael—"

"Your word to me means nothing. You only care for the others in your group. You would kill me the moment I lower this gun."

Okay, so you're not totally *delusional.* "I would not do that," I semi-lied.

"Oh, I suppose you might be merciful and strand me somewhere, instead. But that is just as bad. As you will do anything for those you lead, I will do anything for the woman I love. And that means finding Pamela, taking her someplace safe."

"You mean, like Mustique?" *Killed two birds with one stone, didn't you, Michael? Helped us launch our mission here while we cleared a whole island for you.*

Gaulmin was shaking his head. "I would not go to Mustique. I know you will return there."

Now you're the one lying, because you have no intention of letting any of us live that long. But if I didn't keep him talking, he might start shooting, so: "Okay. Then what's the plan?"

He almost managed to keep the hint of a satisfied smile off his face. "All of you will kick your weapons into the mechanics pit." He jutted his chin at the trench atop which the recon car had been parked. "Your radios as well. Then Mr. Nugent boards the helicopter with me. The rest of you will release the prefab sections; I will be watching and will shoot Mr.

Nugent if you attempt to reclaim your weapons or disobey my instructions. Once the prefab sections are down, you will board and I will fly you to Île Royale. Once safely away, I will radio your position to Giselle. And so we will go our separate ways."

Ozzie shook his head vigorously.

I ignored him, nodded at Gaulmin. "We can live with that."

But I knew we couldn't, because Gaulmin wouldn't let us live at all. He wouldn't risk having three other people in the helicopter, even if he did have a gun trained on Ozzie the whole time. Besides, choppers are fuel pigs, and he wouldn't want us coming after all the barrels we had positioned in Totness; without those, he had no way to continue his insane search or make it to Mustique. Or any of the other places we had left all sorts of useful supplies just waiting for him and his "preordained" love Pamela. Nope; the moment the prefab was down, he was going to fly off—and let the stalkers come streaming in through the gap left behind.

Gaulmin moved so that Ozzie was between us, pistol aimed at the back of his head. "Very well. We begin. The three of you: move next to the mechanic's trench. Keep your hands where I can see them."

My radio paged again. I moved my hand toward it by reflex—

"If you answer," Gaulmin reminded me loudly, "I will shoot you where you stand."

I had already stopped my hand in mid-grab.

"Very good. Now, as I call your name, you will step to the trench, remove your weapons with your off-hand, and drop them into the trench, followed by your radio. When you are done, I will allow one of you to bind Nugent's leg." He shifted the pistol to his left hand, unslung the FAMAS and cradled it in his right. "Steven: go to the edge of the pit."

I was thinking how satanic that sounded as Steve, toeing his shotgun ahead of him, approached the trench—and recoiled: "Fuck!"

As Gaulmin jammed his pistol against the back of Ozzie's head, shouting threats, I saw why Steve had jumped back: a stalker was scrabbling up out of the trench. Which made less than no sense, but there wasn't any time to think about that: I just dove for my Honeybadger and drew a bead.

Or tried to. Steve bent over for the shotgun, blocking my shot. The next second, the stalker was on top of him. I dropped the Honeybadger and grabbed for my knife.

Gaulmin was yelling something. Ozzie was shouting for him to shut up. Steve kept trying to pull a weapon from his webgear. The stalker kept biting at his protected neck as I leaped toward them.

A shot—but it was from a FAL, not a FAMAS. Gaulmin and Ozzie were suddenly silent. Steve pitched to the side to get his weapon clear. Doing so, the chin-rim of his face shield slammed against the stalker's oil-covered shoulder and the latch popped.

I stabbed down at the monster's back. It turned toward Steve's unintended blow. My knife went into its back the same instant that, smelling or seeing exposed neck flesh, its head snapped forward, jaws wide.

Steve's pistol went off. I cut deep into the stalker again. Steve screamed, fired two more shots. The stalker went limp.

All in less than five seconds.

I pulled the stalker off Steve, saw the blood well-ing up from the ragged bite where his neck met his shoulder—and heard a scrabbling sound in the trench.

I pulled my HP-35 as a shape rose up from the pit. I knew I wouldn't get the pistol raised in time—and flinched at a sudden hail of gunfire from my immediate right: Steve had unloaded into it.

I got the HP up and braced just as another stalker appeared, moving forward from the rear of the trench. I fired five rounds, hit her three times. She fell.

I listened. More scrabbling, but distant.

"Where the hell are they coming from?" I shouted.

Gaulmin's only reply was a moan.

Valda shouted: "Alvaro! Re-arm!"

Valda never overreacted or shouted; I leaped back toward my Honeybadger, was scooping it up as another stalker almost vaulted straight out of the pit. It was greeted by two thunder-cracks and fell right back down.

Valda was in a flanking position, head still low over his FAL's sights. "Gaulmin's down," he muttered.

I nodded, spared a moment to look at Steve. "Are you okay?"

"Yeah," Steve sobbed. "But I'm dead."

"Alvaro," Valda said, "flank them."

Nodding, I stepped wide, out of Valda's line of fire, but able to look down into the trench. Two more were emerging from a hole at the far end of it. "There's some kind of access in the floor. Tires scattered all around. Gaulmin, what is it?"

Gaulmin groaned. "Not sure."

It was Ozzie, now holding a gun on Gaulmin, who answered. "In this part of the world, there are mechanic's pits so large that they've got big drains for all the crap that leaks down. The Legion probably stacked those tires on top of the drain, all the way up to the belly of the recon car."

The two new stalkers were starting to scramble up at me. I double-tapped each of them. "And so they'd plugged that hole . . . until I rolled the recon car away."

I looked at Steve. He saw the apology coming, shook his head. "It was the only solution. Even if you'd known. And you didn't. So shut up; there's no time."

The irony of that final phrase gutted me. "Okay. Steve, Valda, hold the trench with CQC weapons. We're getting out of here." I started toward Gaulmin.

Who managed to smile through the pain: it looked like Valda's shot had hit his femur. "We are not 'getting out of here' until we come to an agreement."

I drew and cocked my HP-35. "We're leaving," I told him. I aimed the pistol at his forehead. "I take it you agree."

He maintained his smile. "You will not leave if you kill your only pilot."

Ozzie tilted his head. "Now, about that—"

I stared at him. "You're *sure* you can fly a helo?"

Ozzie abruptly beamed his full-voltage Motor City Madman smile and almost shouted: "What part of 'I managed rock bands' do you not understand, Alvaro?"

"I have miscalculated," Gaulmin observed, calm again—just before he punched the half-forgotten HP-35 out of my hands and grabbed his own gun. He swung it toward Ozzie. I dove after my pistol, knew I would be too late.

A single coarse roar erupted over my shoulder.

Gaulmin went back, his head and upper torso shredded by single aught buckshot.

Steve walked up, cycled the action, fired again into the man's already ruined face. "One less monster to worry about." He looked at Ozzie and then me. "You're welcome," he said. Then he trotted back toward the trench, where Valda was now using his own shotgun.

"Sitrep?" I shouted over my shoulder as I got to work on Ozzie's leg.

"They keep coming," Valda shouted back. He fired, finished with, "But we are barely holding them. When we have to reload—"

"Understood." I lowered my voice as I made sure the wrapping was tight. "Ozzie, I don't think this needs a tourniquet, but—"

"No, it doesn't," Ozzie interrupted. "This will do for now."

"Can you really fly this thing?"

He grinned. "Guess we're gonna find out." He saw the look on my face. "Like I told you, I've flown some, smaller than this. Not qualified, though. Just kinda—ah, picked it up. From friends. Near the border."

I reflected that the less I knew about those particular "friends," the better. "Okay, but if you go into shock—"

"Nope," he interrupted, "not happening."

"You sound pretty confident." The steady pace of shotgun fire increased, became ceaseless.

Ozzie tested the bindings with one hand, fished in a pocket with the other, looked around for something crutch like. "This isn't my first rodeo, Alvaro. I'm not heading toward shock. And these are going to keep it that much further away." The hand in his pocket went to his mouth; he swallowed several pills at a single gulp.

"What the hell are tho—?"

He silenced me with a wagging finger. "If you don't ask, then I won't lie."

I figured it was probably better not to know, anyway. I helped him up. "Now what?"

"You tell me; you're the boss"

I started toward the helicopter. "Now we get out of here. But I don't know helos and you do. So tell me what you need."

Ozzie pulled away the last of the shroud. "You get me to the cockpit. I'll get the bird ready, engines warm. But I can't spin the rotors until the rest of the shroud is off and the pre-fab is down. Once they're clear, I can spin up and we can be gone in thirty seconds. Probably less." As we reached the pilot's hatch, my radio paged. Willow again. I opened the channel: an ocean's worth of static. I shook the radio: "What the—?"

"Could be this building," Ozzie grunted as he maneuvered himself into the pilot's seat. "Could be on her end. Could be this damn humidity. Could be the batteries want changing. Could be all of that, and we don't have the time or ability to even fix one." On the other side of the pre-fab, we could hear stalkers yowling and scratching. "Get going, Alvaro."

I ran back into the garage, tearing the remains of the shroud off the Puma. The awning—stretched across the pre-fab verticals—would be pulled outward and down with them, so no worries there.

I ran over to the trench. Steve was hammering bullets downward with his M4 while Valda was feverishly reloading his shotgun. "Guys!" I yelled, "we hit them with a final wave of fire and then run for the chopper." I felt like I was living a scene right out of that old sci-fi flick, *Predator.*

"What about the pre-fab?" Valda muttered as he slid the last shell into his gun's magazine.

"We bring it down while the next wave of them climb out over the bodies piling up in the trench."

"Good luck with that," Steve muttered, firing the M4 until the bolt flew back and stayed there. "They're using them like a ramp."

"Well," I said, putting the Honeybadger up to my shoulder, "at least this should break the tide for a while." And I started firing down into the trench as Steve slapped a new magazine into his weapon.

With the three of us blasting away at the same time, the trend reversed for about twenty seconds: more of them were dying than were emerging. That also meant that a new corpse pile was accumulating toward the rear of the mechanic's pit.

Valda emptied his mag first: no surprise, with a pump shotgun. "Go!" I yelled.

Steve ran dry next; it often took three, even four rounds of 5.56 to stop stalkers. I nodded him back toward the Puma.

The stalkers had such a hard time getting around the bodies near the drain that I had three or four seconds between each shot, and plenty of time to line them up. And at this range, a hit with the .300 Blackout almost always meant either a kill or incapacitation.

But after five shots, the slide stayed back. I turned and ran.

I don't know when the Puma's engines had started—that much shooting that close meant I was almost completely deaf again—and Valda and Steve were already waiting, flanking the side door, weapons at the ready. There was also a door gun to one side, belted into the single biggest hopper of 7.62 NATO that I had ever seen or imagined. "Time to go!" I said. "I'll yank the pulleys, and—"

Steve stepped forward. "There are two pulleys. Gotta do them at the same time. Otherwise, half of the infected outside will get in before the panels fall and the helo can get airborne."

"Where are the pulleys?"

He pointed ten feet to either side of the tail rotor. "We go on three?"

"On three," I agreed.

Just as Valda raised his FAL and muttered, "More from the trench." He tipped his head down toward the sights.

By the time he had fired—once, then again—Steve and I were ready at the pulleys. I nodded. "One, two...three!"

I pulled the restraining pin and stepped back as the line started whining up out of the pulley. Once I was sure it was running clean, I turned and ran to the helicopter, Steve right behind me.

Valda was in, swung around to provide cover from the doorway: the machine gun was tempting, but too imprecise. I hopped up, turned to offer a helping hand to Steve.

But he had stopped five yards away.

My stomach went into free-fall. "Steve?"

He shook his head. "I'm not going."

"But—"

"Alvaro. Shut up. I'm dead. And if I get on that bird, you might be, too. And maybe everyone else depending on this ride." He started stepping backward, reloading his shotgun. The pre-fab baffling started to groan, the sound rising in pitch as the panels swung outward.

"Steve, you might be like Ning. Or we might—"

"—Find a cure? Alvaro, this is out of our hands. Even yours. Except for one thing."

"What?" I croaked; my throat felt like it was not merely cramped, but crushed.

Steve spoke more quickly, glancing to either side of the Puma. "I don't want to die...not that way." Then he looked me straight in the eyes. "I want it to be you, Alvaro."

I wanted to puke. But there was only one thing left that I could give to Steve, and that was peace. The peace of knowing that I would not fail him. So I swallowed the bile. "I understand."

To the sides and behind me, the panels toppled with a crash. The eager screaming of the stalkers on the other side of them transformed into squeals of agony.

Steve looked at the machine gun. "You've got to make sure."

Since I wasn't letting myself puke, the wuss part of me tried to send up a sob. I choked that down too. "I'll make sure. I won't leave until you're...until I've done what I've promised."

He smiled and started jogging backward. "That's all I needed to hear. You're a good guy, Alvaro."

Outside, the screeches of agony were now being drowned out by those of rage. In the now-sunlit garage, blood-soaked figures were struggling up out of the mechanic's trench. The Puma's engines roared; the rotors started turning. More quickly than you see in the movies.

Steve checked that the flaps on his holsters and mag pouches were all loose. "Tell Percy that I think... I mean, I might have actually..." He shook his head. "Just say that. I gotta do this. Now."

He turned and sprinted into the garage, blasting the stalkers at the trench back down into its darkness.

"Time to go!" yelled Ozzie from the cockpit as the rotors became a blur.

"We're clear," I forced out. "But hold at thirty yards."

We lifted, just in time to watch claws stretching, even leaping, up for us. We wobbled a bit.

"Sorry," Ozzie shouted back. "Puma's a bigger beast. Different feel." He paused. "The MAG works almost exactly like the M60. At this range, you don't have to move it to get the beaten zone you want. Just trying to keep it on target will do that."

I blew all the air out of my lungs as I got behind the weapon and watched the horde beneath us lose interest in the biggest, liveliest, noisiest object in the area and discover the one human still in reach, firing down into the trench. As if possessed of a single mind, they shrieked in chorus and charged Steve.

Who emptied his shotgun. Then his M4.

"Alvaro," Valda whispered in my ear.

"I know." I leaned over the sights.

Steve had pistols in both hands. He could not miss; they were closing in from all sides.

Right before I pressed the firing studs, I think—or maybe I just want to believe—that he smiled up at us. At me.

As the rounds hammered out of the gun, I watched for the tracers, tried to keep them centered where Steve was. Or at least, had been. Even though it was in a firm mount, the MAG sent vibrations through me like a lowrider burning rubber over speed bumps.

I felt something on my shoulder: Valda's hand. "You're done, Alvaro."

"You saw him—?"

"Yes."

"Did any of them—?"

"Not one touched him. And there have to be a few dozen fallen around him." Valda's eyes were wet. "If he were a warrior of old, they would sing songs of how he left this world: ringed by the heaps of his enemies."

I discovered that my face was wet, too. "Let's get to Diane," I croaked toward the cockpit.

I expected that as we banked away, I would continue to see Steve's face in my mind, but I didn't. I only saw Gaulmin's, because I wanted—I *needed*—him to be alive. So *I* could kill him all over again. And then again.

And again, and again, and again.

January 17 (Willow's recorder; transcript three)

It is easier to breathe now that Alvaro has radioed. The connection was poor but I heard him say, quite clearly, that they had "handled" Papillon. I am not sure exactly what "handled" means, but there isn't enough time to wonder about that or whatever else might remain unspoken. What matters is that the helicopter is flying and inbound. Their flight time to Diane is two minutes, maybe less.

I leaned through the doorway of the maintenance room. "How much longer, Prospero?"

His eyes never left the screen. Neither did Rod's, who was simultaneously watching a progress bar creep toward completion on his laptop.

"Prospero?"

"Just a few minutes more."

From outside, I could hear the machine gun on the Bandvagn firing almost nonstop. "I suspect we have two minutes. Possibly less."

"And in order to be sure of complete reception, we should send the Ephemeral Reflex code no less than three times."

"Yes, I remember the briefing. But unfortunately, the whole jungle is waking up. Two minutes. At most."

"Willow!" It was Johnnie.

I turned. He was peering between the boards on the windows. "Yes?"

"They're getting real close to the Bandvagn. *Real* close."

I thought. "Tai, any more movement in the garage?"

Her voice came around the corner from her post near the breached wall in the bathroom. "No, but it ain' safe."

"Why?"

"Garage windows: they broken. When that swarm outside get close, and if any wanna see what inside, they might be able to leap up, get in."

Which would give them a direct pathway to us inside the control center. "Tai, Johnnie: change posts. Johnnie, stand some desks upright to block off the wall breach. Then keep jamming things behind them until you can't fit anymore in. Then seal the door."

"Willow, that door swings *in*."

"Do what you can. Prospero; you have one more minute."

"I need two. At least."

"Then we may not leave here alive."

Rod looked up. "There's another way."

Prospero glanced over at him. "Yes?"

Rod shrugged. "The system could be set to repeat automatically. It's slower, but it would finish in about ten minutes."

I may have frowned. "And ten minutes is better than two minutes—how?"

"Because *we* don't have to be here," Rod explained, his voice getting higher. "As long as there's power in the system, we can just let it run when we leave. It could upload dozens of times before the transmission window closes."

I looked at Prospero. He was frowning, but in the way he does when he checks a good plan for weaknesses. "Only one wrinkle," he said.

Rod nodded. "Yeah. Unwanted visitors." He tilted his head in the direction of the breached bathroom on the other side of the wall. "But if the stalkers never hear us inside the building, why would they try to leap up to get in the broken garage windows? And even if they did, if we close and lock the door to this room, why would they try to break it down? There won't be any noise or movement."

I nodded. "And the generators?"

Prospero shrugged. "Stalkers haven't shown any particular interest in cars left idling."

A new line on the comm channel crackled; the sound of intermittent machine-gun fire almost drowned out Chloe's shout: "Whatever you guys are going to do, do it fast. Jorge's down to three belts and they are getting within fifty yards. We've gotta move."

"We will be leaving the building in a moment."

"How?"

"Excellent question," I replied, glancing at Rod and Prospero, who both shrugged.

"Uh . . . Cukes, the stalkers will swarm you. And I won't be able to stop it."

"Not if we are on the roof of the building."

"And how will you get up there? You said there's no access from inside."

"I know. Is the Bandvagn's engine running?"

"With stalkers this close? You bet your sweet, skinny ass the motor's running!"

"Then prepare to return to your prior position outside the door. I have a plan."

A long pause. "I'm not going to like this plan of yours, am I?"

"I doubt it. I'm going to get Alvaro in the loop as I explain the basics..."

January 17 (Alvaro's recorder; transcript six)

"We will support as requested, Willow. Out."

Ozzie Nugent looked over at me from the pilot's seat. "That's some crazy plan."

I nodded. "It's also the only one any of us can think of."

Ozzie nodded, banked the chopper sharply . . . but the movement was incredibly smooth, graceful almost.

I glanced at him. "What are you doing?"

He nodded over toward the white disk of Diane. We'd been heading straight for it, but the dish was now disappearing to our three o'clock. "If we want to attract their attention"—he nodded down at the hordes of stalkers—"we want to come in from behind them. Nothing gets an animal's attention like a loud, threatening noise coming in on its six. Particularly when that animal presumes itself to be the apex predator."

I nodded. "So, a threat and a challenge, all in one."

"There you go," Ozzie affirmed with his unfortunate smile. He banked again, turning a butter-smooth loop while also backing off the rpms. The Puma was now merely growling rather than roaring.

As we levelled out into a course that would bring us

in directly behind the stalkers approaching Diane from the west, I grinned at him. "Seems like you may have piloted a helicopter more than once or twice before."

His smile widened. "Yeah."

"Then why so cagey about it?"

"At first, I just didn't want to steal Papillon's thunder. Then—I dunno: the whole gig started feeling hinky."

"Those are some pretty keen instincts, right there."

"More like well trained. Courtesy of life lessons learned from scheister agents and lying promoters in the hard-knocks school of rock-n-roll." He was bringing the Puma lower, both in altitude and rpms.

"So where and when did you learn to fly a helicopter like this?"

He stared. "Do you really need to ask?"

I just shook my head; I had no idea what he was talking about.

"Alvaro, whose name did I adopt? Who have I been imitating for weeks, now?"

"Uh, you mean, uh, Ted—?"

"JC on a pogo stick: who do you think was flying the bird in half of those pig-shooting videos on You-Tube? He pissed off the original pilot, who'd been teaching me. I took over."

"Didn't he think that was...risky?"

"They didn't call him the Motor City Madman for nuthin', Alvaro. And he wasn't going to let anything stop his pig hunts. Particularly the ones he did with machine guns. Which never made it to YouTube. And which reminds me: time to man the MAG."

I shook my head. "If I'm going to call the ball on this next play, I've got to sit in a CO's seat. Besides, Valda's got that MAG in hand. Right?"

Valda shouted "RIGHT!" over the headset. It was pretty loud back near the open door.

Ozzie Nugent shrugged. "Your call." We were skimming near the treetops, Diane and its clearing racing toward us.

He put his hand on the throttle. "Here goes."

January 17 (Willow's recorder; transcript four)

As the Bandvagn pulled up alongside the control center's entrance, the helicopter howled overhead.

The converging horde howled back. Many broke their headlong charge to do so.

"Go!" I shouted.

As the great mass of stalkers charged toward the descending helicopter, Rod and Prospero yanked the control center's doors open, spun right and left respectively, their weapons covering the narrow gaps between the wall and the vehicle.

The Puma was now hovering at an altitude of about four meters, a solid mass of infected racing toward it, their combined shrieks and yells louder than its engines.

Tai and Johnnie leaped into the Bandvagn's cab through the driver-side back door, dragging Ning's body between them.

The helicopter pivoted its nose to the left; Valda and the doorgun rotated to face the horde. The machine gun started stuttering; the howling got louder. All that noise and activity pulled almost all the stalkers in that direction.

However, the rest of them charged the Bandvagn.

Chloe shot at them from the front hatch. Jorge did so from the cab. As I ran from the interior of the control complex to the interior of the vehicle, I flinched, flanked by twin shotgun blasts. Rod and Prospero were engaging the stalkers that tried squeezing toward us between the vehicle and the wall. As soon as I was in, the two of them backed in hastily and shut the door. Within seconds, infected were clawing at the windows from that side, too.

Johnnie had come up with Ning's silenced machine pistol, Chloe the other. They methodically fired into the small pack that hemmed us in. With the exception of Jorge, I got everyone else lined up beneath the rear hatch.

A few of the new stalkers that appeared around either side of the building noticed the Bandvagn and the thinning ring of infected around it. At least half of them swerved toward us, but those replacements were far fewer than the number we were killing—quietly—with our suppressed weapons.

Meanwhile, the helicopter rose, flew about two hundred meters, and started descending again, the machine gun firing into the packed stalkers. Like a swarm of enraged hornets, they rushed toward the spot where it seemed to be landing. If the Puma had possessed infinite fuel and ammunition, it could have probably done that all day long and piled the ground high with their corpses.

I checked the stalkers around us. There were fewer than half a dozen left, and the helicopter was drawing the new infected directly from the jungle; they were not passing the control complex. "Alvaro, this is Willow. Over."

"What is your status? Over."

I looked up; the last of the stalkers around the Bandvagn went down with three bullets just below the neck; Johnnie had become quite proficient with short arms. "We are clear. Over."

"Evacuate the track. We will be there in sixty seconds. Out."

I reached up, opened the Bandvagn's rear roof hatch and yelled, "Go!"

Johnnie went first; he is so agile and strong. As soon as he was out, he spun and lay flat, reaching down a helping hand. Prospero and Rod were up and out in a moment. I heard their boots thumping on the Bandvagn's roof, then saw a sliver of shadow as each leaped the small gap to the roof of the control complex. As Tai went up past me, I turned to look at Ning's now fully unequipped body. It bothered me that we had to leave it behind, but—

"Hey! Willow! We're not safe yet!" I think that was the closest tone to impatience that I ever heard Johnnie use. And he was right: we were far from safe.

I turned, half jumped up out of the hatch, his strong hand helping me make it in one smooth motion. Then I jumped over the gap, to where Prospero, Rod, and Tai were covering the approaches to the Bandvagn. I ran past them, heading to the center of the roof.

Behind, the helicopter's engines roared again. I glanced back. It lifted to ten meters' altitude and headed straight toward us. The rotors kicked up a following lane of dust, obscuring most of the horde.

But only for a few seconds. Their homicidal screaming grew and peaked as a tidal wave of the biggest among them broke through the flying grit and sand the same moment the Puma slowed into a thunderous

hover right overhead. The bosun's chair they'd rigged—
Jorge's part of the plan—was lowering quickly toward
the roof. We were almost safe—

Prospero's voice came in on the general channel.
"Trouble. They are mobbing up"—he paused to fire his
FAL several times—"all around the track. Too quickly."

"Chloe?" I called into my headset, over the hammering rotors.

"You gotta go. In a few seconds, I'm gonna have
to button up. At least for a while."

That made no sense. If she had to seal the roof
hatch, then we would have no way to get her, or Jorge,
out. "No, Chloe. We will cover you while—"

"Negative, Cukes. We are"—she must have leaned
away from the pickup; the rotors now drowned her out
completely—"so get up into the chopper. I've got a plan."

Ozzie cut in. "Willow, get someone into that damn
chair. I can't stay here all day."

Chloe clearly understood that the sudden wave
of stalkers meant that they'd ultimately follow us by
scaling the Bandvagn itself. "Cukes, I am now buttoned up. Really loud in here. Jorge and I are going
to stay with the track for now. Get our people out of
there! Go. Go. GO!"

I gave the order. Johnnie and the other three backed
away from the edge of the roof and sprinted over
toward me. I waved the first of them—Tai—into the
bosun's chair. As soon as she was secure, I looked up
into the hurricane of the rotor downdraft and waved
for Valda to pull her up. As she went, I kneeled,
motioned the other three to do the same. "Each of
you hold the chair for the next to go up. I'll be last."

"Willow..." started Johnnie.

"No argument. Those are my orders." Then I was running at a crouch back toward the edge of the roof. "Chloe? Can you hear me?"

It was Alvaro who answered. "Probably not." He sounded far too calm. "She's pretty busy." I reached the edge of the roof, peered over.

There were, quite literally, hundreds of stalkers surrounding the Bandvagn. There were hundreds more trying to leap up the side of the control complex and catch hold of the roof's edge. They weren't reaching it so far, but the more shot by Chloe and Jorge from the caged windows of the Bandvagn, the higher the piles of their own dead became. Soon, they would get up on the roof of the vehicle. And that meant a short easy leap to the roof...

The Bandvagn's motor roared and the vehicle leaped forward—before swinging directly away from the building. After it rode over—well, pulped—the first two or three ranks of stalkers, it picked up speed. Then its orange warning lights began flashing and it emitted the warning tone common to vehicles of its class. A few of the stalkers still ran straight at it. When they went under the treads, I knew that they were screaming—I saw their wide mouths and desperate, rolling eyes—but couldn't hear anything over the engine, the rotors, and mob of infuriated stalkers that now loped alongside and behind the vehicle.

"Chloe?" I waited. "Chloe! What is your plan?"

Silence. Then Johnnie was on the general channel. "I'm not going up until you get to the rope, Willow."

I wiped away tears and ran back from the edge of the roof.

I cursed all the way.

January 17 (Alvaro's recorder; transcript seven)

Once Valda signalled that he had Willow on board, we swung sharply away from the roof. The move was a little wobbly. I looked over at Ozzie; he was gray. "You going to make it?"

He nodded tightly. "Just pain. Bleeding stopped. That was a good field dressing."

"Helped that it was a through-and-through. But your color...you going into shock?"

"Nope," he said with great determination.

That made me more worried. "What can I do?"

He smiled. "Learn to fly a chopper? Seriously, hand me that little bag right beneath your feet. I put it down there thinking it would be easy to reach. That was before the leg got so stiff."

I complied, removed and opened his canteen. He nodded his thanks, bolted back a handful of pills. "That should keep me going for as long as this lasts. What now?"

"I'm going to figure that out. Don't crowd the Bandvagn. Bring us down away from it, draw some of them away." As Ozzie complied, I toggled the comms. "*Cariña*, talk to me."

"On the condition you don't get mushy, Alvaro."

"Okay. So: how much belted ammunition do you have left?"

"Plenty."

I knew she was lying, but there wasn't time to argue. "You said you had a plan. Fill me in."

"You're executing part of it right now by baiting away about half of the skels chasing us."

Behind me, the MAG cut into the packed crowd of stalkers with a sound like a vindictive, high-pitched jackhammer. "Okay. Next part?"

"Pick a spot that draws some far away from us, but puts you in a flanking position to turn your bullet hose on the ones still tailing me."

"Got it."

"Jorge will keep moving while you grind away at them. Once you've whittled them down and we've tired out the survivors, we'll pick a spot far away from the pursuit."

"And?"

"And isn't it obvious? Jorge and I will stop the vehicle, get on the roof, and you pick us up."

I glanced at Ozzie; his eyes were wide. He chinned into the channel. "Chloe, darlin', that's some very precise flying you're talking about."

"And you're just the guy to do it."

Ozzie sucked at his teeth. "What about fetching you from the roofs on the buildings back by the gate?"

"Already thought of that. Looked at them recently?"

I did. There were about half a dozen stalker silhouettes ranging back and forth across those roofs: impatient, furious, eager. Ozzie boosted the Puma up, headed toward a new spot.

I kept my voice firm and steady. "Chloe, you could drive farther. Outrun the ones chasing you. Leave Diane entirely, head back to the main road, then down toward the open spaces near the launch pads."

Valda's voice was the one that answered. "Alvaro, look back. At your four o'clock."

Near the closest of the launch pads, the once open fields were now speckled by moving dots. Stalkers, thousands, converging on Diane like army ants. As if their anthill had been kicked. Which is pretty much what we'd done by driving into, and shooting our way through, the heart of the launch facility. "Christ," I muttered.

"He ain't on call today," drawled Chloe. "Besides, Jorge is telling me this track's motor is getting hotter than it should. Might be low on coolant, might be a slow oil leak, might be both. Either way, we may not be moving much longer."

Which meant that the diminished and winded horde of stalkers from the Diane complex was far less worrisome than the new ones approaching. So: "I guess we're going to let you wear them out while we grind them down. But we've got the best view for choosing an exfil point."

"So you call the ball, Alvaro. You tell us when it's time to break off and where to head, and we'll do it. Out."

Ozzie's color was a little better. "Let's go hunting!" He whooped, and banked toward yet another spot that flanked the Bandvagn's current direction.

We did that three or four times, left each spot marked by clumps of bodies. But Valda reported we had burned through about seventy percent of the ammo, and Ozzie was less than confident in the helicopter's and his own endurance.

I scanned the open grounds around the control complex. The one place the Bandvagn had not driven was south, away from the dish and its infrastructure. Far away from the tree lines and the new stalkers that kept trickling out of them. A long run for the ones already there, and still numbering at least five hundred. "Chloe, Jorge. Roll southeast. Best speed."

Jorge sounded skeptical. "You seen the recon photos of that ground. Marshy."

"Yeah, a little," I agreed, "but not so bad for a tracked vehicle. Awful for the stalkers. And there aren't any moving through there."

"Yet," Chloe added.

"Do it," I ordered loudly, and turned to get people manning the winch for the bosun's chair.

We dipped one more time, all the way at the north of the clearing, pulling the majority of the horde in that direction, then, once they were almost a whole mile from the planned extraction point, we roared back along the path Jorge was driving.

We arrived at the exfil point about twenty seconds ahead of the Bandvagn and about forty seconds ahead of the leading edge of the pursuing stalkers. I had hoped they'd get stuck in the boggy ground but clear skies that had helped us fly in so uneventfully had also helped the ground dry out.

"Ready?" I shouted into the headset's pickup; it would be hard to hear anything in the track now, with the Puma less than thirty feet overhead.

"Yeah," said Chloe, "but can you burn down some of our devoted followers?"

Ozzie spun the bird ninety degrees. A moment later, Valda reported. "If I am firing, it may be hard to use the winch. Noise. Flying cartridge cases. Almost no experience."

"Okay," Chloe answered before I could. "I'm on it."

"What the hell is she doing?" Ozzie asked.

I knew it a second before I saw it. "She's popping the front roof hatch. To man the M60."

Jorge was half out the back hatch by the time she had checked the gun and trained it down at the leading stalkers as they stumble-ran through the sloppy, uneven ground. The weapon started spewing brass. Half a dozen tumbled aside. Twice as many replaced them.

"A little help here?" Chloe muttered as the bosun's chair landed on the roof.

As Jorge started lashing himself into it, I heard small-arms fire in the main compartment. Stalkers fell, more flinched or howled as rounds hit, but did not stop, them.

"Rod, take my place!" I shouted over the headset, and ran back.

Prospero and Johnnie were pounding out rounds at the stalkers, but couldn't cover the area right around the Bandvagn; they were too likely to hit Chloe or Jorge.

Who finished cinching himself into the bosun's chair and gave us a thumbs-up. Valda and Tai—the only ones among us who had any prior experience with winches—started reeling him in. They struggled with the unfamiliar equipment and controls, but he was coming up.

Not as fast as needed, however. Chloe had burned through the last belt for the M60. She climbed up on the roof, began firing at the closest stalkers with her FAL. More were closing in. She wasn't going to make it; she'd never get into the bosun's chair before one or more of the infected clambered up on the roof and got to her.

Unless . . . "Valda, you get Jorge aboard. Tai, you worked boats: can you rig me a line with a toe-loop?

"Uh—what? Why you nee—?"

"No questions. Can you do it?"

"Yes."

"Get on it." I started checking my ammo, waved to Johnnie. "I need your MP5. And all the mags."

"Alvaro, I've only got a few loaded. You—"

"Start reloading."

Prospero leaned in as Jorge got pulled on board. "Alvaro, what do you think you're—?"

"I've done the thinking. Now I'm giving orders. I need supporting fire in a ring around the Bandvagn. I'm going back down with the bosun's chair, and I'm taking a toe-looped line with me. Take up any slack on that line, once you see me on the roof of the Bandvagn."

"But—"

"Just do it. Johnnie! Mags?"

"I only—"

"Whatever you have." I looped the bandolier over my shoulder. "That loose line with the toe-loop?"

"Here!" Tai fixed it to my web-gear. "Good to go!"

"Valda?" I screamed over the rotors as Prospero clipped me to the line for the bosun's chair.

"Yes?"

"Get me down there: fast!"

Like I said: if you are going to do something you've never done before, either plan it carefully ahead of time and rehearse it as much as you can—or don't think. Just go.

That's what I did. It seemed like I fell half the distance to the Bandvagn. Stalkers were already swarming up its sides. So much of the razor wire had come off that they were able to use the window grates as handholds.

At the halfway mark, the line jerked; they had cut the reel-out rate so sharply that I almost lost my lunch. Instead, I shouted into my comms link. "Chloe?"

"Yeah."

"I'm right behind you."

"You are WHAT?" She spun, looked as pissed as I had ever seen her. "I am going to *kill* you when—"

I raised the MP5 in one hand.

She shut up, her mouth frozen in the open position. I fired.

I missed the skel who was just pulling himself up toward the roof behind her. But then I landed and got my other hand on the submachine gun as he climbed higher, exposing half his torso.

I fired three fast rounds. Didn't know how many hit. Didn't care, since he went backward.

She spun back, yelled over her shoulder as she fired into the next infected trying to pull itself up on the track's roof. "Don't need you! I can—" She stopped; the stalker fell away but the FAL's bolt stayed back.

"Yes," I said as she grabbed for another magazine, "you do need me. Now get in the chair."

"What? I'm not—" Which was the moment she realized she had no mags left. She yanked out her nine millimeter.

"The chair," I said. I walked the perimeter of that tiny roof, emptied the MP5 three or four rounds at a time, dropped it, unslung the Honeybadger, saw that she had almost finished strapping in.

"Alvaro—!" she shouted angrily as she snapped the last clip into place.

I shook my head. "Go."

"I'm not going anywh—!"

"I wasn't talking to you."

She yelped as the line yanked her off the roof. I had about one second to get the toe-loop line unhooked . . . and discovered I couldn't do it with my gloves on. *Balls*, I thought, *it's always the little bullshit things that get you*. I bit down on a fingertip of my left glove, pulled it off with my teeth while I kept the Honeybadger up.

The moment the glove came free, I unhooked the line . . . and heard a foot thump down on the roof behind me.

I spun, firing as I did.

Good thing: the stalker's claws were only six inches away when two rounds hit him. I danced aside so he didn't knock me off the roof. He fell past me—and, still grabbing for me as he fell, got his hand tangled in the toe-loop line. He went over the side of the Bandvagn. The rope dragged across the window grating and jammed on a rough weld point. As quick as thought, one of the stalkers grabbed it and so, had another handhold.

No time to do anything about that: I felt a different hand grab at the back of my boot. Evading the stalker, I'd stepped too close to the far edge.

I spun, fired three rounds down into the boot-grabber's face. Two more came up over the rear, just as the one on the line pulled himself level with the roof.

I had to blast them all without much aiming; there wasn't time for anything else. By the time I was done, I'd emptied the mag.

More hands were appearing on the edge of the roof. *Damn.* I pulled my Browning Hi-Power. No way I'd have time to reload.

I heard some shouting over the headset; not at me. An argument. Pretty heated. *Really guys? Now?* "Do you have Chloe aboard?" I yelled. I don't know if anyone heard me. I was too busy double- or triple-tapping stalkers as fast as I could turn in a circle. Because I had foreseen how this trip down to the track might end, I knew that when I pulled my pistol, I should start counting rounds.

I had two left.

There were four snarling faces pulling themselves level with the roof. Too many.

I backed to the center of the roof, pistol ready, tilted my head back to look up toward Chloe one last time...

Right as she plummeted straight into my face.

January 17 (Alvaro's recorder; transcript eight)

I don't think I lost consciousness, but I don't really remember anything other than noise. Chloe screaming. One of the fully automatic AKs ripping out rounds. The MAG raining bullets down all around us.

And then rushing upward. Not toward some spiritual light, but the windmilling rotors of the Puma. And Chloe's eyes. Wet, joyous, furious. I think I smiled; I wanted to say something.

But then I got dumped down on the deck. So hard the air went out of me in a rush. The world tilted— Ozzie was banking—and then it was like being in the middle of one long roll of thunder as the engines spun up to max rpms. Or so I guessed.

"That was awesome!" Rod was shouting.

"Never seen anything like it," Prospero commented quietly.

"You rock!" Johnnie yelled happily.

I tried raising my head. "Hell, guys, I just did what any self-respecting—"

Willow kept my head down. "Yes, yes, Alvaro. What you did was wonderful, too."

The air did not rush out of me again, but I felt

every bit as deflated. "Oh." Then I remembered the image of having Chloe fall out of the sky on me. "What . . . what exactly did she do?"

Willow shook her head, smiling. "She wouldn't come into the Puma. Braced her legs. Insisted we send her back down. Had a pistol and threatened to shoot us if we didn't."

"Yeah," Rod gushed, taking up the story. "So Prospero gave her the milspec AK and down she went. Almost knocked you off the roof. But got you around the chest with her left arm just before the next stalker was about to bite you. Shot him at point-blank range, and then the other infected that got on the roof a second later. Then we were reeling you both out of there. It was epic, man!"

I smiled. "Yes. It most certainly was." Saved from on high by a black-haired Valkyrie of truly goddess-grade proportions: it doesn't get any more epic than that.

Ozzie was making for the water. Île Royale, I guessed.

I rose to my elbows. I'd been pulled, or maybe thrown, to the center of the compartment. Everyone was congratulating each other, but Willow had moved close to Prospero, who was just realizing that Steve was not in the cockpit with Ozzie. His face grew pale as I watched.

I looked around for Chloe.

She was sitting in the Puma's still open waist-door, her feet dangling over the jungle a hundred feet below.

I slid over to her. She saw me, smiled. No yelling, no threats, but also no big hug or big kiss. "What's up?" I asked.

She looked out the door, shrugging. "Nothing."

That's when I noticed that she was cradling her left arm. I saw teeth marks on the armguard. Some of them had pierced it. She saw that I was staring at it, flinched it away.

I looked back out the door, down at the treetops speeding past far below us. *No.* "Chloe."

No answer.

"Chloe?"

Her chin may have quivered.

"You are not jumping."

"And *you* are not going to tell me what to do."

I nodded slowly. "Okay. But I will not let you die." I turned, got one foot under me and leaped forward onto her. Because she was completely surprised, I actually got her down on the deck. My one intent? To hang on and not let go.

For a moment, she, and everyone else, was speechless. Then:

"You idiot!" Chloe shouted. "Are you trying to kill yourself? You'll die, doing that!"

"Only if you jump."

"You—you son of a bitch!"

"Don't you ever talk about my mom that way. Willow, check her left arm."

Willow pushed Johnnie and Jorge and Tai toward us; they grabbed Chloe. With all that weight on her, you'd think she would have been motionless, but she came damn close to bucking us off.

Willow calmly positioned her torso so that Chloe couldn't see her remove the mauled armguard. Chloe was too busy struggling to notice.

However, when Willow started rolling up her sleeve, Chloe lost it. "What the hell? What do you see? Tell me! Damn it, you are *all* assholes! I will kill every one of you, if you don't tell me what's going on with my—"

Willow turned to stare at her. Gravely.

That hit Chloe's off-switch. "What?" she said in a very small voice.

Willow's voice was thick with regret. "I am sorry to say...well, this may be the worst of all outcomes."

"Tell me; I can take it."

"You can, but *we* can't—not easily." She moved aside; Chloe's arm was unharmed. "It seems as if we will have to continue putting up with your insane outbursts. At least for the foreseeable future."

When I went to sit next to Chloe again, she was staring sheepishly at the two rising welts where the stalker's upper and lower jaws had clamped on her arm. Instead of mine. "Thanks for saving me," I said.

She nodded, glanced at the Salvation Islands; we were coming in slightly to their north and Ozzie was banking toward them.

"I'm sorry I can be, such a...such a—"

"Such a pain in the ass?"

"Hey!" She turned, but she was smiling. "Takes one to love one."

"Well, I guess that's true enough." She was leaning toward me, her lips parting. I leaned toward her—

Just as Rod jumped at us, startling us apart. "Alvaro, you've got a—well, a call!"

"A 'call'?" For a moment, I thought it was a prank by the others, but then I remembered Steve. Remembered Prospero's face as he went up front to sit in the copilot's seat. No; there wouldn't be any pranks today. "A call from whom?" I asked, slipping my headset back on.

Apparently, the mic had been hot. "My name is not important," said a woman's voice. "You only need to know that I am effectively in command of all U.S. units still responding to comms and instructions. Am I now speaking to, eh, 'Alvaro'?" She sounded a little confused, a little annoyed, and very convinced that my name was an alias.

"Yes, this is Alvaro, and yes, that's my real name. But who are you?" I gave the "eyes around" signal to everyone in the compartment; they started checking the horizon.

"I am General Shelley Brice. I am in command of...let's call it interservice field operations."

"And what kind of operations would those be?"

"That is 'need to know,' 'Mr. Casillas.' Furthermore, it is not a topic I would ever discuss over this channel, no matter who you might be."

Sure. "And where are you located, General Brice?"

"That's classified, Alvaro."

Sure it is. "And I'm actually from Mars. Look: don't give me that 'classified' bullshit. If you're legit, come clean. Tell me who you are and why I should be talking to you. If you don't, I'll presume you're just part of the, uh, Sea Wolves that seem to be making a habit of raiding the entirety of the northern Caribbean."

General Brice suddenly sounded like someone had over-starched her panties. While she was wearing them. "Wolf Squadron is not a pirate organization. In fact, they may be one of the last functional forces working to preserve both U.S. interests and civilization. Which may be very close to synonymous, these days."

Well, if she was a pirate, she had learned to lay down a pretty convincing military tone, frosty formality and all. Which is to say: I can't imagine a pirate doing a good imitation of someone with permanent "broomstick-in-butt" syndrome.

She hadn't stopped. "Right now, they—and we—are breaking comms protocol to confirm your location and your suspected activities."

I tried very hard not to sneer. "Good luck with that."

She answered without pause. "We have you approximately six miles west-northwest of the Salvations, approaching same. And your activities—why don't you tell me about them?"

I was pretty impressed with them getting such a close lock on us. But still, if General Brice was really who she said she was... "Actually, General, why don't *you* tell *us* about our recent activities?"

There was a pause, the kind that usually indicates that people are conferring off-line. "I will meet you halfway," she said when she returned. "I will tell you what we have observed, and how. You will tell us if we are right, and if so, how you achieved it."

I stared around the Puma's compartment. Prospero had stuck his head back in, listening on his own headset. He looked like he was as dead as Steve... or like he wanted to be. I made a mental note to keep a collective eye on him at the very moment I caught his eye, pointed at the headset, and shrugged.

He nodded gravely.

I nodded back. "Okay, Generalissima-in-Charge-of-Everything Brice; you're on. What have we been up to?"

"Fiddling with GPS. Or rather, assets that seem to be, well, augmenting it. But we can't be sure. We've dug up a few old proposals for something like this—a white paper about some harebrained scheme called Ephemeral Reflex—which looks like it might be related. And our backtrack on the signal that initiated the altered posture of those assets shows it to have come from your immediate regional footprint. Send-codes indicate the source was via the Diane satellite dish at Kourou." A silence before she resumed, a bit smug now. "So tell me, 'Alvaro,' am I warm?"

"Firstly, General, my name really *is* Alvaro Casillas. I sailed out of San Diego on May 29 of this year, on a transport ship bound for the Galapagos, where I boarded the Sail To Discovery ship *Voyager.* If you want to check."

There was a longer pause, but when she came back, I couldn't tell if it had been to confab with her staff or because she wasn't sure how to proceed. "Alvaro, I believe you, but I have no way to check those records. We have . . . have lost a great deal of data."

Well, that was certainly logical. "As for what we've been up to since then . . ." I laid out the short version of our story, ending with what we had just accomplished at Kourou. "Frankly," I finished, "we had no way of being sure that it would work. And the only way we would have been able to tell was if our GPS remained operational."

"Well," she mused, "it is early to assert that, but it certainly seems to be heading that way." She paused. "Am I to understand that some of you have established contact with three Antarctic bases that have never had contact with anyone or anything connected with the virus, other than yourselves?"

Because the convo was now on the Puma's intercom, Willow was able to jump in. "General Brice, my name is Willow Lassiter. Actually, my group avoided face-to-face contact with those three groups. And as I understand it, Alvaro's group observed the same protocols with the population of St. Helena."

This pause was shorter. Brice's tone was very serious when she answered. "Young lady, it sounds to me that you understand the significance of what you are saying."

"Yes, ma'am. That we have identified pre-infection baseline populations in environments that have not been subjected to any possibility of contamination. Their future research value is crucial. And, in a worst-case scenario, they might collectively be large enough for species propagation. Although, I suspect that is not a primary concern for you."

"Oh? And why do you say that?"

"Because, we have heard Wolf Squadron in various positions. We suspected it had elements on both sides of the Atlantic at the same time. Your description of its significance suggests something about its probable size. And given the authority and rank you claim, I further conjecture that you are also controlling the actions of the American submarines that we believe avoided infection. In which case . . ." Willow stopped; she seemed to be on the verge of hyperventilating.

"Yes, young lady," said Brice, almost coaxing. "Follow that deduction to its logical conclusion."

"In which case, given the extensive and stable forces under your control, and your surprise at and interest in the nonexposed populations, you must have formulated a cure."

"You," murmured General Brice, "are indeed a very, very clever young lady."

"You bet she is," Chloe almost shouted. "That's my girl Cukes!"

"Yes," Brice resumed after a moment, "and we very much want to meet you. All of you. Several of you have skill sets that have now become very rare. And you clearly are able to apply them with a high degree of . . . er, versatility. And innovation. And the rest of you? Well, we have an even more urgent and immediate need for *your* skills."

"As what?" I asked. I gotta confess: I was suspicious. It sounded like we were about to get separated into Team Genius and Team Grunt.

"At first, as local guides and liaisons."

Well, once again: logical. "You mean, for the islands and populations we've had contact with?"

"Exactly. I wonder if you fully appreciate just how important your activities have been."

But now it was my turn to do a little deduction. "Well, let's see: by visiting Mustique, the Salvations, Rocas Atoll, Fernando de Noronha, Ascension Island, and St. Helena, we've pretty much trail-blazed a path of stepping-stones right across the equator to the South Atlantic. Three of them have airfields. One has an actual GPS monitoring site and ground antenna, which is not just a major asset, it's one you can't afford *not* to invest in, not if you want to keep GPS going even longer than the patchwork fix we just made. All those are things that are already on your 'to do' list, I'm betting, but for which you don't have enough resources. You are stretched way too thin. But now, all the first steps have been completed, and you've got the closest things to native guides to help you capitalize upon it." I paused. "Is that a reasonable, first-pass summation, General?"

"Don't be smug," Brice muttered, but there was some

kind of amusement under it. Or grudging appreciation.
Maybe both. "But yes. Now, a couple of guidelines
for any forward steps.

"Firstly, do not attempt to contact Wolf Squadron.
They have other jobs to do: bigger jobs. Also, they are
a much more—er, diverse group. Extremely capable
professionals with high levels of classification at the
top, but some of the next tiers down . . . Well, let's just
say we are still assessing their reliability. Therefore,
it would not do—neither for our success nor your
safety—for any 'questionable elements' among them
to become aware of your existence. Or of what you
have accomplished."

"The Russian subs?" I guessed.

"I am outlining protocols. I am not responding
to speculations," Brice countered. "Next, there will
be no further communications until such time as we
contact you directly. That shall take place at your
northernmost destination to date."

Which meant Mustique. Which also meant they had
probably heard enough of our commo to know that it
was our home base.

"At that time," the general continued, "we will
establish secure codes, provide you with encrypted
comms, and exchange information that should be
valuable to your operations and security."

I knew better than to ask what I really wanted:
"information such as . . . ?" Instead, I affirmed, "Received
and understood. At that time, I assume we will negotiate a mutually agreeable set of objectives, actions, and
remunerations."

"Negotiate?" Brice said after a moment. It sounded
like she was unfamiliar with the word.

"Negotiate," I repeated. "We are civilians, General Brice, with one exception. But he is not a member of the U.S. armed services. So unless forced induction has become the postapocalyptic standard—"

"—It is still on the table," she growled.

"—then we are still free individuals. And since we are no longer in the U.S. or its territories, I am going to presume that, for all intents and purposes, you are not going to try to invoke martial law."

"That seems reasonable," Brice said in a tone that suggested her response just barely conformed with her actual opinion. "We would certainly like you to continue and even expand your contacts with all these communities. We would also like you to survey the islands you believe cleared or almost-cleared for investment by our security forces and reconstruction teams."

"That sounds agreeable," I replied, seeing nothing but nodding heads in the Puma's compartment. "However, I am afraid there is one item that will be nonnegotiable."

"Oh? And that is?"

"That we stay together as a group. We may operate in smaller teams, of course, as necessitated by the missions we agree upon. But we are—well, we're the closest thing any of us have to a family. That is what's kept us alive. Maybe what's kept us sane. And surely a person in your position must find a lot of value in the axiom 'if it works, don't fix it.'"

"In fact," Brice said more pleasantly, "I do. And I like it when a young person will say as much to someone like me. Speaking truth to power is also going to be a rare commodity in this new world we are building."

She downshifted into a brusque "wrapping it up" tone. "You know where we will contact you. We will signal by lamp. You may ask anything you wish to confirm that it is us. Until then, travel safely and take a well-earned vacation. It may be the last one you get for a long while. A very long while. Godspeed to you all."

The comm channel snicked off.

We looked at each other. I tried to think of something to say—

"Well, hell, everyone," Ozzie shouted over the rotors as we angled in toward Île Royale, "unless I am very much mistaken, you guys just got offered the last, best gig in the whole damn world. Or what's left of it."

Willow nodded. "I was thinking exactly that."

"Me, too," Prospero said. "I just wish Steve was here to see . . . to hear . . . all this."

I nodded and met his gaze. It seemed like he wanted to look away, but he didn't. Instead, he sighed, nodded back, and peered out the door at the blue-on-blue horizon. I released the breath I'd been holding. He'd just given himself, and me, a solid reason to believe he wouldn't try following his lover into the Great Beyond: his resolve to work in, and for, Steve's memory. To create the new world they had hoped to share.

"And Ning," Willow added. "I wonder—" She let the thought trail off.

But I knew what she was thinking: that Ning had tried to warn us about Papillon. But because she herself was such a thorny mystery, from a potential rival state, we hadn't trusted her.

And who was she, actually? What had her role, or even her mission, been? We'd never know, because the real world isn't like movies or novels. There's no guarantee that you ever get an explanation or resolution. You just accept the unknowns and move on.

I turned to Chloe. "And how about you?"

"'How about me' what, Mr. Big Shot?"

I rolled my eyes. "How do you feel about the deals we may be making?"

She shrugged. "Don't really care."

"What?"

"Hey, calm down. As far as I'm concerned, you already got us the only deal that really matters." She put her palm against my cheek. "That we stay together. All of us. Like a family."

Tell you something about my Chloe: when she's right, she's right.

And she was right.